Enter at Your Own Risk

Ford Brothers Series

Sandra Alex

Keep in touch with the author by subscribing. Please visit www.sandraalexbooks.com for details.

ISBN 978-1-989427-09-5
ISBN 978-1-989427-10-1

Chapter 1

Booksie

Live the life or die trying

Just as I begin to think I've got a leg up for my team, a bullet hits me in the back of the head. My helmet shudders and I can't help but laugh when the paint drips down the back of my neck. It'll be a gooey load in the washing machine tonight. I hear Jenny, my best friend, yell, "Booksie! Run for the yellow hub! Nobody's watching it! We're going to gang bang them!" Jenny's such a sucker for paint ball. It was her turn to choose what to do for girls' night out, and this was her first choice.

With twenty points over our opponents, Jenny is satisfied when the game is over an hour later. "You wanna go for another round?" Wendy, Jenny's sister, asks. We give her a look like she's just sprouted an extra head. "Well, that only killed an hour and a half...what else are we going to do with the rest of the night?" We're standing in the parking lot of the paint ball warehouse; what's left of our team, anyway. The other three girls went home. Wendy looks across the street, about half a block down. "Shit. Did you guys know there's a strip joint here?" her eyes bug out.

"Forget it," I say, flat out. I have a boyfriend at home, and I'm sure he wouldn't be pleased knowing I went out to watch naked guys prance around in a poorly lit environment.

"Why not, Booksie? We have to check one out before Jenny's bachelorette anyway, right?"

Shit, she's got me there.

"I wanna go." Jenny says matter-of-factly. "Why don't you want to go, Books?"

My friends have called me Booksie forever. It's a playful poke at the fact that I'm always at home reading or studying. The point is that my nose is always in a book.

"Why do I need to go to a place like that, anyway? I have Mark at home."

Jenny places an arm around my shoulders. "Which is precisely why you need to go. I love you, babe, but Mark is more of a nerd than you are. Don't you want to go somewhere where the hot guys beg for your attention, and make your toes curl? Does *Mark* make your toes curl?"

"Does Brandon make *your* toes curl?" I ask too quickly.

"Hell, yes!" Jenny answers, which doesn't shock me. Brandon is so dreamy I kick myself for not introducing myself to him first. "Now, quit arguing. Mark isn't expecting you home until after midnight. We have hours to kill. Let's go."

"I really don't want to go." I whine. "We look like a bunch of freaks with all this paint in our hair, and I've sweat like a pig under the paint ball gear."

She gives me a look. "I have a brush and a deodorant stick in my car. We're going."

"Seriously?"

"Seriously. And it's my car so you're shit outta luck, Booksie."

I knew she'd play that card if she got desperate. Jenny means well. But ever since she and Brandon got engaged, she's become Bridezilla. Just the mention of something to do with the wedding, and she's all over it.

Ten minutes later, after a deodorant bath and us each taking a turn with Jenny's wedding makeup samples, we enter the strip joint. All of us wore interchangeable clothes to paint ball, not knowing exactly what we'd be doing afterward. Never dreamed we'd end up at a place like this. An arrow, or at least what I thought was an arrow, instead it was a crooked neon penis, led us to the upstairs portion of the building, where the naked men are. The downstairs is a sex toy shop...shocker.

At least the music is promising. As we enter the club, paying a handsome fee of ten dollars per person, I see the dance floor is full. There are no strippers in sight yet, to my relief. It's just a load of girls dancing and having a good time. *Perhaps this won't be as bad as I thought.* "You want me to the be the designated driver, sis?" Wendy asks Jenny thoughtfully.

"No, I want to check this place out with a clear mind."

Eye roll.

"I need a drink." I say, surprising myself.

"I'll get us white wine?" Jenny offers.

"Sounds good."

Two minutes later I've finished my first drink. "Go get her another." Jenny instructs Wendy.

"It's not like you to drink, Books. I like this side of you." Jenny elbows me. "It's about time you unclenched for five minutes."

"You should do the same." I say, taking my second drink from Wendy. We're standing by the bar, which is not much bigger than my walk-in closet. The whole club is no bigger than a small church. The dance floor is a square at one end of the club, with an archway covered in glinting beads being used as a makeshift door on the wall end. The dance floor is flanked with old wooden chairs that look like they've been bought at a garage sale. The round tables are slightly warped but appear clean. The floor isn't sticky, and neither is the bar, which is a plus, considering I thought this place would be one that you'd have to wipe any surface off first before touching it.

Jenny is about to rebuke when we hear an announcer come over the speakers. He asks us all to take our seats as some hottie is about to grace us with his presence. And he's not kidding. Some guy dressed as a firefighter suddenly appears from behind the beaded archway. He's decked out in everything, including the oxygen tank, impressing me. *Maybe he's a real firefighter and he does this on the side.* I let

4

myself think that as the second glass of wine takes effect. "Woohoo!" I screech as Jenny and Wendy exchange a look. They're impressed, too.

He comes out, at first just grooving to *The Bee Gees' 'Stayin' Alive'*. Making his appearance throughout the whole dance floor. When the song reaches the first chorus, as it goes 'Stayin' aliiiiiiiiiiive', he pulls off his jacket slowly as the stage lights flash. A few girls whistle, encouraging him to remove more. Underneath his jacket is a tank top over a set of wicked pecks and memorable shoulders and biceps. He looks oiled up under the lights. He continues, wiggling his eyebrows and pulling at the suspenders holding his pants up, which I notice are a couple sizes too big on him. His short blonde hair is slightly curly, and his green eyes sparkle in the light.

It's not long before he's wearing just his tank top and a pair of shorts. He leaves his fireman's hat on while he gyrates to the extended version of the popular disco tune. I can't take my eyes off him. He's beautiful and toned and has the moves that suggest he's a god in bed. When he finally rips off his shorts, the audience roars and my eyes go straight to his, well...you know. He's well endowed. He fills the G-string very well. My thighs are instantly damp and warm. Ten seconds later, he rips, and I mean literally, rips off his tank top from the center of the dance floor, under the stage lights. He's so hot my insides melt.

"Here, I grabbed some bills from the bar." Jenny says, handing me a bunch. "Go see what he'll do to you with that."

"What? Why me?" I bark, thinking I'd rather just sit here and drool, the wallflower that I am.

"Please." She says flatly, "What happens at the strip joint stays at the strip joint. Go have some fun. You deserve it."

"What about Wendy?"

"You can both go."

I look at Wendy and she shrugs and gestures with

her hand for me to go ahead.

Girls are hovering around him. One of the bouncers brings him a chair. He's lifting his leg up and dancing provocatively, I gather so his manly bits will look more pronounced....as if they need to be. He's more man than I've ever seen. As Wendy and I approach, we have to almost push through the throng of horny women vying for his attention. He's doing his thing; dancing and bulging out his biceps and abs so the girls can drool over him. With a G-string covered in bills, he walks towards the tables that aren't abandoned, spreading himself around.

"I guess we'll catch the next one." Wendy says. Just as she says that, the tune changes to Donna Summer's *'Hot Stuff'*, and another stripper appears. This one is in a white tuxedo complete with tail and top hat. He's steaming hot; tall and built as well as the fireman, but this one has an olive skin tone with deep blue eyes and short hair. I can't believe they make men that look like this. It's almost like a fairy tale.

Wendy guides me back to our table and we notice the fireman is making his rounds at each table. "Maybe he'll come back to ours." She says. "You want another wine?"

"Sure." I say, watching tuxedo man remove his jacket and drape it over his shoulder like he's a runway model. Hell, I'll take it. He looks good enough to eat. His dress pants are snug around his rear, which is also tight. I have to supress the urge to go over and take a bite out of his ass. It looks like two scoops of ice cream. My underwear is soaked, and I have to cross my legs to try and slow the blood flow. We stay in our seats this time as we wait for tuxedo man, who is slowing becoming tuxedo-less man, come our way.

His shirt barely contains his biceps as he undoes the buttons. When he stands there in just his suit pants, I count his six pack abs, drooling over each one. I want to touch them, kiss them, suck his hard nipples. God, this is the hottest thing I've ever seen. Wendy hands me another drink and I take a slow sip of it as I watch tuxedo man come closer to us. He rips off his pants, which I now realize are tearaways, and I look...there. Holy fuck. He's bigger than the fireman. This place is doing things to me. These men are doing things to me. This wine is also doing things to me.

Next thing I know, tuxedo man is standing within a foot of me. I take a dollar bill and blindly place it in his G-string, not taking my eyes off his. He's a monster compared to me. But he has such innocent eyes. "Go ahead, I won't bite." He says as I tuck the bill in. He touches the side of my face with his hand and my insides turn to syrup. As he dances away from me, I realize my mouth is wide open.

"Are you okay?" Wendy says, half-laughing. "You look like you're going to puke or something."

I shake my head no and toss down the rest of my wine. "I think I'm in love." I say, not meaning to say it aloud.

Jenny barks out a laugh. "Me, too, sister. This place is definitely on the list for my bachelorette. I've gotta find out the names of these guys and make sure they're here that night."

"I'll be there." I say, still entranced.

"Totally." Wendy says.

When another stripper comes out, I'm numb. I've never seen anything like this before. It's like 'Let's Make a Deal' of penises. I'll pick whatever door any of these angels comes out of. I watch the fireman make his way towards us. "Hey, did you know there's a VIP room in this place?" Wendy says. "I asked the bartender." She looks at me. "You wanna take one of these hotties to the VIP room?"

"Why? Does Jenny want me to test it out?" My tone is intentionally facetious as I speak like my best friend isn't sitting right next to me.

"Go." She ignores the jibe, chuckling. "You won't last sixty seconds in a room alone with one of these guys."

"Oh yeah?"

"Yeah," she guffaws, almost spewing Pepsi out of her nose.

"Is that a dare?"

"Double dare."

Chapter 2

Booksie

The first last time

'I'll show them', I say inside my head, as fuzzy as it is. Rising, ever so clumsily from my chair, I stick my tongue out at both Wendy and Jenny and get a laugh. Walking over towards the fireman, I see that he's standing, talking to a woman who looks old enough to be his mother. *Maybe it is his mother.* And I just about lose my nerve, when he sees me and smiles. "Hi, can I help you?" he asks in an Australian accent, which makes my toes curl. *God, could he be any hotter?* "Wha...aaa....are you busy?"

"Naw, not really, love. I don't go back on tonight. What can I do for ya?" His reaction surprises me. I have no idea how this strip joint industry works.

"Oh, okay. Well, I don't want to bother you." I say, walking away.

"Did you or your friends want the VIP room?" he looks at me blankly, as though he offered me a slice of cheese from a cheese platter he's holding. My hesitation is obvious, and he smiles. "Come on, I'll take you." He grabs my hand, making my insides like hot molten lava. Leading me through the throng of horny women, we end up at a small bank of pods, almost like changing rooms that you see in a department store. Inside each room is a small cushioned seating area fit for two (or one and a half, really) in cheesy red velveteen. The walls are painted the same dark red.

I almost have to laugh at the décor, even though I should talk; my couch at home is canary yellow and I still have my Judy Jetson bedsheets on the bed in the spare room. "Classy enough for ya?" he winks, inviting me to have a seat. The music from the stage carries well into the area, but it is muted enough that one can have a conversation. He smells lovely; like wood and spice.

"It's fine." I say, not knowing what to say next. It's surprisingly difficult to talk to a guy who's sitting next to you in a G-string. "Should I pay you?"

He waves. "Not to worry. My name is Dan." He offers me his hand to shake.

"Booksie." I shake his hand. This feels like a sexy job interview.

He rises, standing over me. His package is almost in my face and my heart jumps out of my chest before I realize he's going to squat so we're at eye level. *Phew!* "Well, you can relax, Booksie." He strokes the side of my face with his hand, looking at me like I'm an angel. "I'll be gentle." He kisses the side of my neck, sending shivers down my spine. The stubble on his face lightly scratches my skin deliciously. He then kisses my collar bone and pulls back to look at me. "Do you mind if I kiss you on the lips?" he murmurs. The tone is sexy as hell.

I don't even blink, but I shake my head no and close my eyes. At first, he kisses me softly with just slight contact. I don't respond right away until I feel his warm hands on my face, cupping me gently. My heart is racing, and I can feel my heartbeat...there. "Just relax." He whispers against my lips, before opening his mouth, gently forcing his warm tongue inside. I let my body take over, forgetting I have a boyfriend at home...for a minute.

As his mouth makes love to mine, I feel like I've suddenly turned to pudding. I couldn't pick Mark out of a lineup. He gently pushes me against the wall, as his hands go to my breasts and I begin to rear up, letting him have full access. My head is spinning with wine and hormones as my nipples bud from his touch. He uses his hand to pull my hand to his...stuff, and it feels like a steel rod begging to be released from its prison. His hand keeps my hand in place. I don't dare move.

I'm in a tailspin of drunkenness, hormones and confusion when voices blurt into the area, interrupting us. Giggles and girly squeals are heard, entering, and then they stop when they see the curtain between us drawn. When they leave, Dan, my sexy guest, takes a seat and rakes his hands through his hair. "I'm not supposed to do all this to ya anyway, love. I'm just supposed to dance for ya."

"Oh, I'm sorry. I'm new at this." I get up and adjust my shirt, and then sit back down again.

"Me too. This is my first week."

"Oh," *Gee, you'd never know it. Was he just born sexy?*

"Yeah," he chuckles. "Boss man finds out I'm out here makin' out with you it could be my last week, too."

"Do you want to go back to the other room?"

He waves and shakes his head. "Not really."

I feel brave, suddenly. Like finally I'm not the only person who doesn't know what they're doing. "Do you like it here?"

"Not really, no. But I have to do something to pay the bills. I used to be a bus boy and a host at a restaurant, plus I worked nights hauling bags of grain," he points to his bulging biceps, "that's how I got these. But I couldn't make nearly what I'm making here holding down three jobs."

"Don't you have an education?"

"I was working on it back in Australia, but some unexpected things happened, and I had to move here and give up school for a while." He presses his lips together. "I'll be going back once my troubles are settled here. This is just temporary."

"What are you going to school for?"

"Engineering. I'm working on my master's degree."

"Jesus." I'm shocked. "Well, I hope I didn't get you in trouble. I won't tell anyone. Besides, I've got a boyfriend at home, so the less I say the better."

"You're sweet." He grabs my hand. "C'mon. I'll take ya back."

As we're walking, the alcohol is beginning to wear off, and I have a burning question. Before he bids me adieu at the entrance door, I hand him the money I owe him and ask, "How come you wanted to...um...blur the lines...with me?"

He smiles. "You mean how come I took a risk with you?"

"Yeah,"

He leans in and holds both my hands in his. "Whoever this boyfriend of yours is who's at home, without you, I hope he knows how lucky he is." He winks and walks away, looking back to salute me farewell.

As he walks away in his G-string, all I can think of is...wherever he's going, I sure hope they have pants for him.

An hour later I'm sober and walking towards the front door, arriving home good and horny...and two hours early.

...and I walk into the biggest shock of my life.

***

The house is quiet and dark, and I think how perfect this is. I'll get into the bedroom, find my sexy negligee and surprise Mark in bed. Inwardly I know I'll be picturing Dan the whole time, but how is Mark going to know that? He'll have the best sex of his life, so he won't complain. Tiptoeing through the door, I don't even bother to turn on the kitchen light. Closing the kitchen door quietly, I place my purse on the table. My paint ball bag I left in Jenny's car. I'll get it from her tomorrow.

Removing my shoes, my bare feet tap gently on the linoleum floor. The living room lights are all off, and so are all the hallway lights. A small, sensor light that doubles as a flashlight is illuminating the hallway, and as I enter the bedroom, the room is lit with about six pillar candles. At first I think this is the moment I've been waiting for; Mark and I have been together for two years and while saving for a house, we rent this one so I can finish my studies and so he can help save up for a down payment. So, it wouldn't be at all strange to come home and find our bedroom filled with candles and Mark waiting for me on bended knee, asking for my hand in marriage.

...except that this is not that moment.

My loving boyfriend is on his back, in our bed, and some blonde tart is riding him, rearing her head back in the ecstasy I've always craved and never received from him. They're so into their sexy escapade that they don't even hear my gasp. On impulse, I take the candle closest to me and throw it at Mark, causing the fire and hot wax to instantly burn him. He screams like a girl, jolting up so quickly he knocks his slutty friend over and she falls onto the floor with a big thud. She's not even pretty; she's slightly overweight and bigger than me, with mussed up shoulder length bottled blonde hair, mascara smudged across her eyes and smeared lipstick. With another candle conveniently inches from my hand, I lift it a whip it at her. She raises her hand defensively and rises from the floor, naked.

Glaring at my beloved, I say nothing, as he quickly runs around, dick whittled down to nothing, and snuffs out the candles. He grabs his underwear off the floor, helping the slut gather up her clothes. I don't wait for him to give me some lame excuse. "I hope she gives you gonorrhea." I seethe as I walk out of the bedroom, grabbing my book bag off the floor in my wake.

Chapter 3

Wade

Worst Night Ever

I'm hitting the high notes bang on tonight. Who would have known the acoustics in a trash can like this would be so awesome? Normally I wouldn't play in a dump, but it's been slow at home in North Carolina, so I took the gig for the bread. The chicks here dig me, so it's cool. The guys are grooving to the tunes as well, so it's all good. It should be pretty easy getting action tonight, too, based on the looks I'm getting. It's never a challenge for me in that department. Being a rock and roll artist is a turn-on for most women.

My brothers, all four of them, hate it that I'm a singer. Well, not so much that I'm a singer so much as the fact that I play in armpit establishments. But it's all I've got. That's what it takes to make it in the industry. You've got to do your time before you hit it big. Like a rite of passage. I'm cool with it. Hell, I've been at this for years now, since I was seventeen and fresh out of high school. It's all I've ever done. It's all I've ever wanted to do. Yeah, my basement apartment's a hole, but it's *my* hole. At least I'm doing it on my own, without any help from my rich siblings. I've never asked them for a dime and I never intend to, either.

This one chick is all but flashing me in the audience. She's got long blonde hair and legs up to her neck. It doesn't look like she's with anyone, but I'll find out in a minute when I play the next song: a slow ballad. The boys hate it when I change the routine for the night based on what the chicks are doing. But hell, I'm the captain of this ship. As we change gears and play a cover of *Jeff Healey's 'Angel Eyes'*, I wiggle my finger in the air, looking straight at the blonde, indicating for her to come up to the stage. Obliging, this sexy woman approaches. I stick my hand out to help her up on the stage, and I place my free hand around her waist.

She laps it up, snaking her arms around my neck, making love to me with her eyes as she dances with me and I sing to her. She's running her hands through my hair, like we've known each other for years. Most women love this kind of shit. Looking around, I see some of the other single girls turning green with envy. It's kind of heady. When the song comes to a close, the blonde kisses me on the lips and winks at me. Before the next song starts, she whispers in my ear "You going on a break?" her expression says she wants to do more than dance.

Removing the mic from my face I answer, "I can go for a break anytime I want, darlin', I'm the lead singer."

"Storage closet." She mouths as I help her down off the stage.

The boys are ready for a break, so I announce it while pre-recorded music starts playing from the speakers.

Following the blonde, I see her open the storage closet door. I enter the dark room as she turns on the light. There's a lock on the door, which she engages. Then she grabs me and kisses me, tongue and all, until I can't breathe. "Easy, easy," I say, almost laughing.

She's wearing a black minidress with spaghetti straps. Her high heels are black with a gold heel so tall I'm not sure how she keeps her balance. While salaciously gazing at me, she lowers one of her spaghetti straps, revealing herself. When she takes down the other one, both her tits are sticking out, hard nipples and all. My dick turns to steel. They're small but real, and so pert I can't help but want to suck on them.

"Well, are you just going to stand there and stare or are you gonna touch them?" she asks, purring.

I've never had sex in a storage closet, nor have I ever wanted to. Especially this one; which has smelly garbage bags and various chemical cleaning products in it. I just figured we would make out; I had no idea this chick was going to start undressing. "You don't...like...charge by the hour, do you?" I joke.

She lowers herself and reaches for my zipper. "Whoaaa," I say, "Hey, take it easy. I'm not getting naked in here. What's your deal, anyway? Are you a hooker?"

"I'm whatever you want me to be, baby." She winks. *Fuck, I'm outta here.*

"Uh, yeah, thanks, but no thanks." I say, unlocking the door, not waiting for her to pull her dress back up.

Walking by a bouncer, I point the blonde out. "Get her out of here, man. She's a prostitute."

He nods as I step back on stage and watch her get politely escorted out.

I see my brother Jack walk in the front door. He lives a half hour from here, so he said he might show up. Usually Colton, one of my other brothers, comes with me to gigs—he's a bouncer—but he's away right now.

Jack waves at me and takes a seat by the bar, as we start back up with a fast tune on stage. I remove my hand from the standing mic so I can wave back. A brunette approaches Jack and asks him to dance. He's a pretty decent guy so I'm not surprised. He has a ponytail and tattoos, and hey, he works out, so there's not much challenge for him with the ladies, either. Problem is, he's stupid and lets the women find out he has money. When that happens for me, I'll *never* tell.

A pack of girls enters the bar. One is wearing a banner across her body that says, 'Bride to Be', and the others are wearing matching t-shirts labeled with their position in the bridal party. *Oh, goody...another bridal party.* Chicks that are getting married, and their friends, are loud, cheap and obnoxious. And usually already drunk, so they barely drink anything, which pisses the owner off. There is no cover for women here, and it works like a magnet. They choose a table in the back, away from the crowd. I watch them. There's one chick that looks so pasted together, like she spends every cent on plastic surgery. Her eyebrows are tattooed on. Another is really overweight but has a pretty face. The bride is hot, kind of a Courteney Cox look alike, with dark hair and blue eyes and a body. They're all looking at me with goo-goo eyes from the table, except the last one, a redhead, who's rolling her eyes, looking unimpressed.

The waitress stops and takes their drink orders. The redhead gets up and walks to the bathroom. I watch her. She's staring at the floor with each step. Her hair is tied back in a bun and she's got black pants on and her t-shirt says 'Bridesmaid', and she's got long, dangly earrings that glint under the bar lighting. When she finally looks up, I wink at her. A sour look crosses her face, as if to say, 'what the hell do you want, asshole?' as she pushes the door open to the lady's room.

My drummer signals to me that he needs to take a break. I announce to the crowd that we'll be back in ten minutes, and pre-recorded music starts playing from the speakers again. When I put the mic back on the stand, I realize I need to use the bathroom pretty bad. I see Jack lined up at the bar and I signal to him to get me a beer. He nods as I walk into the men's room. After I relieve myself, I head into the green room beside the washroom, knowing Jack will come back there, and as I walk to the room, I bump straight into the redhead.

"Oh, shit, pardon me." I say.

"Why don't you watch where you're going?" she says, and then recognition comes to her face as she realizes who I am. "What's the matter? Being up on stage, you lose your balance when you're back on the floor?" her tone is condescending.

"Hey, look, I said I was sorry. What's the problem?" I lift my arms in defence. *What's wrong with this chick? PMS?*

"There's no problem. I just don't like being molested when I walk out of the lady's room."

"I didn't *molest* you, lady. I accidentally bumped into you. I said I was sorry."

She guffaws. "What's the matter? Are you so used to women throwing themselves at you, you can't handle it when one doesn't *like* your attention?"

I lift a brow. "Look, lady. I don't know if you've got PMS, if you're some kind of man-hater, or if you've just been recently dumped—can't imagine why," I cock my head sideways in mock disbelief, "but like I said, it was an accident, and I've apologized. What more do you want? What, you want me to buy you a beer? Buy your friends a round of drinks? What?"

"Don't flatter yourself," she says, just as Jack approaches.

"What's the problem here?" he says, carrying our beers.

"Oh, great, pretty boy has an army." She comments sarcastically.

"Not that it's any of your business, but this is my brother." I say, taking my proffered beer.

"Yeah, I bet you have lots of 'brothers'." She air-quotes.

This chick is psycho

I take a sip of my beer. "I do, actually. Four if you really care to know."

"I *don't* care." She spits.

"You must care seeing as you're still standing here." I spit back. I've just about had enough of this shit hole.

"You're an asshole."

"You're a bitch." I chuckle. "Or a dyke, one of the two."

"For your information," she stops herself, lifting a hand. "Never mind. You're not worth it."

"Apparently I am, since you're still here, fighting with me." I laugh sarcastically. Jack is enjoying this. He's smiling as his gaze goes from me to the redhead, like he's watching a tennis match.

"God, where do assholes like you come from, anyway? Your kind seems to follow me everywhere." She says to herself, as if she's taking stock.

"North Carolina, you?" I ask, playing along sardonically.

"Oh, that's great."

"Why? You from North Carolina, too?" I laugh,

almost feeling sorry for this crusty chick.

She rolls her eyes. "Fuck."

"Oh, she's got a potty mouth, too." I say, spurring her on. "Well, I tell you what..." I trail off, gesturing to her with my hand, testing her to see if she'll tell me her name.

"Kendra,"

"Yeah, sure, we'll call you Kendra. I'm sure that's your real name."

"Mine's Bob." Jack supplies, lifting his beer with a wink.

"Well, Kendra, you stay away from my side of town," I tell her where that is, "and we'll get along just fine." I laugh. "By the way, I'm Wade...Wade Ford." Jack and I are killing ourselves laughing, knowing that our real names sound like stage names, when they're not. Colton, Dalton, Jack, Wade and Garrett Ford...how much more stagey can names get?

"Fuck you," she says as she stomps away, huffing.

Jack takes another sip of beer and places an arm over my shoulders. "You'll be married to her in six months."

After the women I've run into tonight, I'll never get married.

Little do I know this is just the beginning.

Chapter 4

Wade

The night just keeps getting better

I laugh at Jack's joke and guzzle my beer so I can head back on stage. For the next hour I sing my heart out and the dance floor is full. Jack salutes me goodbye as I take another break. Bitchy girl and her clan are gone, too. But a whole new set of patrons have filled the place. There are still a couple of hours left to kill as I check my watch, downing another beer on my break. One of the bouncers calls my name, "You're Wade, right?"

I nod, "Who's asking?" *God, what now?*

The bouncer gestures to a girl; I can only see her head through the crowd. When she approaches, I notice she's sporting a pregnant belly. She has short, wavy brown hair, glasses, and is wearing a sour expression on her face. I have no idea who she is or what she wants with me, but she tips her head sideways expectantly. "Let me guess...you don't know who I am." It's not a question.

"As a matter of fact, no, should I know you?" I ask, trying for equally cocky and condescending.

She looks around for a moment. "Do you think we can go somewhere private and talk?" her tone is cutting.

"Can you tell me who you are first?" I guffaw.

"Not that it would make a bit of difference, but I'm Priscilla. The last time I was here was about six months ago, which was around the same time you were here last." She rubs her swelling belly, and the hairs on my arm stand up on end.

"Err...we can go in the back room." I say, leading her. The bouncer stares at me and mouths 'you okay?'; the same bouncer that escorted the hooker out earlier. I nod yes. He nods his understanding but remains there, folding his arms across his chest.

When we arrive in the green room, I close the door. "So, what can I do for you, Priscilla?" *This ought to be good.*

She doesn't sit on the couch, probably because it looks like it might be infested with some sort of vermin. And I don't offer, either, since I don't even want to sit on it.

"Do you remember me, Wade?" her tone suggests she's irritated.

"Nope. Why don't you refresh my memory?"

She looks at the couch, "I used to have long black hair? I was about thirty pounds lighter?" she points at the couch. "I believe we christened that couch a few times, and the wall, and the floor?" she says, clearly not proud of it.

"Not ringing any bells, Priscilla."

A hand goes to her hip. "Jesus, how many women do you screw a night?"

"I don't think that's any of your business."

She puffs out a breath of air, "Well, remember me or not, I'm carrying your child, Wade."

My neck cranes back. "Bullshit."

This chick is nuts! What is it with this place? Remind me never to come here again! Jesus Christ, this place should be called 'Enter at Your Own Risk'!

"Deny it if you like, but it's yours." She is matter-of-fact. "And since there are dozens of Fords in South Carolina, I couldn't find you. Until I heard through the grapevine that you were playing here tonight. That's why I'm here."

I wasn't about to share with her that I don't live in South Carolina, that I live in North Carolina. The least this psycho knows about me the better.

I look at my hands, trying to buy time. "Well, I can tell you, Priscilla, that I didn't sleep with anyone when I was here last. This place is about as clean as a dumpster and despite what you *think* you know of me, I have standards."

I'll admit I was considering doing the blonde in my car later, before I knew what her deal was, but not now, and not in this dive.

"Well, like it or not, Wade Ford, you're going to owe me...big time." She says, handing me a manila envelope. "I'll see you in court." She speaks to me like I'm a joke and walks out of the room.

When I open the envelope, my eyes widen. Despite her telling me that she couldn't find me, she'd somehow tracked down my address and phone number.

For the life of me, I don't remember this woman. But something tells me she's going to be in my memory for a long time.

Chapter 5

Wade

Just when I think it's bad, it's worse

Having barely slept, I stare at this piece of paper that has now become my nightmare, and I have to fight the urge to tear it up. The legal jargon looks legit, but how the hell would I know? The only piece of paper I ever saw that had anything legal on it was my dad's will after he died. Even that was thoroughly explained by the Estate Attorney who dealt with my dad's last wishes. I don't have a lawyer; my brothers do, but I've never had a need for one, being the only Ford boy who doesn't have any inheritance. That's a long story. I don't like to talk about it.

If I tell my brothers about this, they'll think I'm a fool. I've never as much as touched a woman without having a box of condoms handy. Yeah, I know, birth control isn't one hundred percent effective, but hell, I'm careful. And there's no way in hell that I knocked this chick up. I remember every girl I've ever slept with. Guaranteed the name Priscilla is not on my list. I can't even decipher what she's trying to get out of me from this document. Good luck, because I've got *nothing*.

I quickly Google lawyers in the North Carolina area and realize I'm kidding myself. There's no way a decent lawyer is going to give away free legal advice. I can't ask any of my friends for help; they'll razz me worse than my brothers. There's only one person who can help me who won't judge me.

...

The phone rings at Mingles, the bar where I sing at in North Carolina, and I cross my fingers that Blake, the bartender, is there. He picks up on the third ring, slightly winded.

"Hey, Blake. It's Wade. Am I catching you at a bad time?"

"No, I was just sweeping the floor in the back. Had to run for the phone." He answers cheerily. "What can I do for you?"

"Hey, can I ask you something? And I need you to keep this between us."

"Sure. What's up?"

"Last night I was playing at that armpit of a club out in South Carolina."

"Aw, shit. That place? What are you going there for?"

I sigh. "Just...let me finish."

"Alright." He says reasonably.

"Well, this pregnant chick comes up to me, says I'm the father of her child, and hands me this legal document, and walks away." I pause. "I don't know what to do."

I then explain that I'd never seen her before in my life, and I don't know anyone named Priscilla.

"What's the document say? She suing you? Shit, the kid's not even born yet. She ain't even given you the option for child support."

Fuck...child support?

"Oh, man, you're scaring me, Blake." I say honestly.

"Well, Wade, it ain't no secret that your family is rich. Anyone who looks the name Ford up in the North Carolina area will see who you are. I'm surprised this hasn't happened sooner, frankly."

"But I don't have a dime!" I slam my fist on my thigh.

"Well, she don't know that."

I sigh. "What the hell do I do?"

"You have a lawyer?"

"No," I whine.

"And I'm guessing you can't afford one, and you don't want to tell your brothers, which is why you're asking me."

"Yep." I make a popping sound with the 'p', marking my 'I'm so screwed' attitude.

"You ever heard of 'pro bono'?"

"What the hell's that?"

"It's when a lawyer does cases for free."

"Why would they do that?"

"Some do it for charity, and for some it's like volunteer work to get experience. They're out there."

"Really? And they're legit?"

"Sure. Look it up. You just need one for legal advice at this point. For all you know this document is fake. Was it done on letterhead with a logo and all? Mind you, someone can copy that off the internet and paste it if they're real clever. You'd be surprised what kind of documents people can muster up out there. Some real slime balls in the world, Wade."

"Jesus, Blake. How do you know all this stuff?"

Blake chuckles. "When you've worked in a bar for as long as I have, you learn things."

"What I don't get is how she even got my contact information. She said she couldn't find me, that's why she came to the bar when she heard I was in town."

"Ah," Blake grumbles. "That was for dramatic effect. If she was serious, she'd a had you served by a dude carrying a clipboard. You'd a had to sign for the envelope and everything."

"So, you think this is phony?"

"Probably. But I'd still get an opinion on it. If for nothing else for protection. Be one step ahead of people like that. There'll be lots of them for you boys especially."

"Thanks, Blake. Hey, remember to keep this between us, eh?"

"I'll take it to my grave, son."

Chapter 6

Wade

The shock

Turns out Blake was right. I found a lawyer that does pro bono cases right here in North Carolina. The firm isn't large; there are only three lawyers, and what's odd is that the one that agreed to see me isn't even in the firm's name. Some K. MacGregor, and the firm is Stockwell, Lamb and Birkin. The receptionist set up the meeting a few days ago, and so I put on my best suit and tie and hopped in my car for the appointment. The building is small but just the law firm embodies it. There is parking on the street in front of the building but nowhere else, so I exercise my shitty parallel parking skills and nail it on the fifth try.

When I announce myself, I'm led into a small office that only fits a desk and two chairs, and I'm told that it will be just a few minutes. My nails are bitten to the quick and the manila envelope has been folded and fussed with so many times it's as wrinkled as a shirt that's sat in the bottom of a laundry bin for a month. I can feel the sweat collecting in my armpits and I suddenly feel very conscious of the pit stains that have likely formed under my arms.

I hear voices in the hallway and then a single knock on the door. As I'm about to answer, 'come in', a lady enters with her back turned to me, and she's facing someone in the hallway, finishing a conversation. When she enters the room completely, she closes the door softly and turns to face me. Both our jaws drop.

...It's the redhead from the bar the other night.

Fuck...me!

Her red hair isn't tied up in a bun, but it's in a topknot, held with some weird clasp that looks like something my grandmother would wear. She's wearing different glasses; wired ones, and a freshly pressed pants suit; black pants and a pink top with half sleeves.

"Well...this is a shock." She says. Her expression is part shock, part embarrassment, part 'ah-ha, what kind of trouble did this loser get himself into?'.

"Shows how well you stay on top of your appointments." I comment. "Didn't check to see who you were seeing next?"

She sits down behind the desk. "As a matter of fact, no. The receptionist double-booked me and I didn't get a chance to prepare." There's the embarrassed look again.

"Did you know the other night who I was?" I ask, suddenly feeling skeptical of all women, especially because of my experience at the bar the other night.

"Not until you mentioned it, no." she admits. I don't know whether or not to believe her.

"Am I wasting my time here? I mean, I'm pretty much a sitting duck, based on the opinion you clearly formed of me the other night. At this point it doesn't matter why I'm here, you're not going to help me, right?"

She's not impressed but barks out a phony laugh. "There are plenty of lawyers in North Carolina, but not many who do pro bono cases. You're welcome to try someone else, but it was your dumb luck that you found one who has room in her schedule. You'll be hard pressed. It's up to you. I'm a professional."

"What the hell does 'pro bono' mean, anyway? Why do you want to do cases for free?" I ask, sensing this woman is not the gracious type.

She steeples her fingers together. "Because I'm not fully licenced yet." Her tone is protective. She's got something to hide. "I can still offer legal advice and do all the legwork and administrative tasks, but I can't defend a client or approach a judge on a client's behalf or do the plethora of other things like notarizations and such."

"So, you wouldn't be able to sue someone." I say it as more of a statement.

"I can arrange all the documentation, but I can't sign it. One of the partners would have to."

Suddenly some chick storms into the room, carrying a wedding dress, and she has a very sour look on her face. The room is so small that both me and the redhead rise, startled. "Booksie, just what the hell were you thinking?!" she shouts.

Booksie?

"Jenny, this really isn't a good time." The redhead laughs without a trace of humor. "I'm in the middle of something."

"In the middle of ruining my wedding, yes." The girl guffaws, jamming a defiant hand into her hip. "You were supposed to give the caterer the final head count yesterday, and I haven't been able to get in touch with you...*you* have the final head count!"

The redhead turns towards me. "Can you excuse us for a minute?"

And suddenly it's like I exist. The crazy chick gives me an evaluating glance. "Hey, she's out a date for my wedding next Saturday. You'll do. You wanna come?"

Wow...cock a doodle do...she's nuts.

Redhead raises a finger to me before I have a chance to respond or to wipe the stunned look off my face. "I'll just be a minute." She whispers, thoroughly humiliated.

These two chicks should wear a sign that says, 'you don't have to be crazy to be my friend. I'll train you'.

Both girls leave the room and close the door. Outside I hear muffled hisses for a minute, and I'm about to leave, thinking I've been a fool to stay for as long as I have, when the redhead reappears, this time with her cheeks almost as crimson as her hair. "Sorry about that. Do you have sisters?"

"A sister-in-law," I say, scrunching my face.

"That's my best friend, Jenny. In case you didn't figure it out, she's getting married."

"You don't owe me an explanation. I was just about to leave anyway."

She bites her lip. "That's fair."

Something in her eyes changes. *Is it a tear? Shit, is she going to cry?*

"Is your name Booksie?" I'm suddenly inclined to ask, since the appointment said I would be seeing a 'K. MacGregor'.

Looking up at the ceiling, she sighs. "That's a nickname my friends have used since high school. My real name is Kendra, Kendra MacGregor." She holds out her hand for me to shake. "We didn't even get a proper introduction." There's that nervous laugh again. "Look, why don't you tell me why you need legal advice, and well, maybe I can help you, even though it seems that you're hell bent on leaving." The look in her eyes is gone.

And why wouldn't I leave? First, you lose your shit on me the other night at the bar for nothing, then your friend storms in here like a lunatic...why should I trust that you'll even have an ounce of helpful advice for me when you yourself seem like a Class A freak, and all you're likely going to do is judge me based on why I'm here.

She studies me and cocks her head to the side. "You're welcome to try somewhere else if you're put off by me. Frankly, I'd leave if I were you, too. But based on your performance in that seedy club and the fact that you have a shirt on that's two sizes too big and unmatched socks, I'd say that you can't afford anything other than what you've got." She pauses, steepling her fingers together and leaning her lips on to her fingers. "Is your situation time-sensitive?"

I picture the pregnant chick about to burst. "Kind of."

"Then you better fire it off to me, because anyone else who's doing pro bono cases in this town is six months out."

I don't like it, but I know she's right. "Can I sign something, so I know that anything I say to you is confidential?"

"Even though I'm not licenced yet, I'm still obligated to keep my clients' details privileged. It's implied." She gestures for me to continue.

She's so arrogant. Her manner is as condescending as it was the other night. "Fine." I give her the abridged version. She listens with an impassive expression, which is somewhat comforting. Then I hand her the document and she reviews it. I watch her eyes scanning it, and then she lifts the lid to the laptop on her computer.

"Is the lawyer legit?" I ask.

"The lawyer is legitimate, yes, but I'm not sure that the document is."

I peer at the ceiling, feeling slight relief. As she pecks away at her keyboard, I silently pray to myself.

"She could have a friend who works for the lawyer and has access to the letterhead." Kendra explains. "You're Wade Ford, right?"

"Yes,"

She pauses and scans something on the screen. My heart is beating a mile a minute. "The document is fake."

"Are you sure?"

"Yes," she says, pulling the laptop around so I can see it. "A couple of things raised a red flag." She explains. "First, the 'encl.' notation at the bottom is incorrect. There is no person with those initials at that firm. Second, the document makes mention of a criminal code that I had to look up since it's pretty obscure." She references what the code is and what it means. "It doesn't exist, but I had to check the section number to be sure."

I sit back and interlace my hands behind my head, breathing a sigh of relief.

"I wouldn't be too relaxed over this, Mr. Ford." She warns. "There's a reason this woman came after you." She bites her lip. "Do you have money?" she asks in a concerned tone.

"No. Not right now, anyway."

She cocks her head to the side.

"Everything said in this room is confidential, you

said, right?"

Kendra nods. "That's correct."

"My father was Wren Ford, the owner of an airline in South Carolina. When he died, he left my brothers a handsome sum of money, but he kept my share in trust."

"So, you have money coming to you when certain conditions are met." She intervenes, following along. "What do your brothers do?"

I count on my fingers, "Horse rancher, pilot, CEO of my dad's airline, and CFO of my dad's airline."

"It's probably no secret then that your family has money. It wouldn't be difficult for someone to figure that out." she surmises. "Have your brothers had any problems like this?"

"Not that I'm aware of."

"This woman sees you as a target. She might have been following you around or she has an insider." Kendra continues. "Do you have a manager?"

"Yeah,"

"An accountant?"

"No. But I could have my brother check out my finances if I ever had the need."

Lifting her chin, she gestures towards me. "Do you have online access to your finances?"

"Yeah, why?"

"Do you mind if I take a look?"

I hesitate. "Why do you need to look at that?"

"I just want to rule something out." her expression is flat, like when your doctor asks you to drop your pants but can keep a straight face about it when your dick is the size of a gherkin.

"Okay." Pulling my cell phone out of my pocket, I access my banking information and show it to her.

After examining it closely she asks. "Do you keep a spreadsheet with your earnings and what cut your manager and your bandmates are getting?"

Jack showed me how to prepare and maintain a budget years ago using an Excel spreadsheet. That's the only way I've stayed afloat all this time. "Yeah, I have it saved on my phone, too."

"Can I see that?"

"Sure," Opening up my One Drive, I show her my budget.

"Does anyone else look at your finances?"

"No. Just me."

"Have you ever been hacked? Like into your bank or your records?"

"No. I don't think so."

She's quiet for a moment as she closely examines my stuff, taking a scan of it for her records. It makes me nervous how quiet she is.

Her expression changes as I receive a text message, and then another. The screen on my phone isn't hidden, so she can see the message. "I see you have a fan club." It looks like she's irritated but it's hard to tell.

"Sorry," I say, taking my phone back. Of course, it's a girl I hooked up with a couple of months ago. Haven't spoken to her since. Why she chose now to contact me is a mystery.

"That's okay." She says but says it like 'really it's not'.

I pick up on the tone. "So, it's okay for you to have an interruption, but not me."

"It's fine," she huffs, holding her hand out for the phone. Just as I hand it back to her, it beeps again, and another message appears on the screen. She rolls her eyes.

My blood begins to boil, both at the inopportune interruptions and at her reaction to them. "Look, I'll just go, okay? Clearly you have a one-way opinion of me already. This is just a waste of time."

"Well, you got your answer." She says facetiously.

"That's right." I bark. "Should I get a second opinion? Did you even tell me the truth?!" I spit, feeling exposed and frustrated, silencing my phone and stuffing it into my pocket. "I mean, you did say that you're not even fucking licenced yet! I'll bet I know why, too!"

Glaring at me, she rises. "I'll thank you for not swearing in my office, Mr. Ford. And I'll thank you for leaving, too." Her face is red with anger.

"Gladly!" I shout, walking towards the door. She rises, too, to see me out.

As I leave, I look at her once more, giving her my toughest glare. She looks back at me, and it's like looking into a mirror. I hate her. I've never hated anyone in my life.

...was that a tear I saw in her eye?

Chapter 7

Kendra

The camel's back

After the escapade with Mark, I went straight to my parent's place. My old bedroom hasn't changed. Some of my clothes are still there, too. I had to hold my dad down when he found out what Mark did to me, he was about to drive over there and have a 'word' with him, which in translation means he was going to kick his ass. My dad is not the type to mess with. He loves his guns and is never afraid to threaten anyone...especially someone who messes with his only daughter. Mom is more refined. Disappointment was marked all over her face, but she pasted on a smile anyway and told me that this was God's way of leading me to something better.

Jenny's outburst was the last straw. It was sheer luck that none of the partners witnessed the scene. Melinda, the receptionist, was not pleased with Jenny's behavior, but I begged her to keep it quiet by treating her to lunch. The rest of my day was a blur and I couldn't wait to get home to deal with the other half of my messed-up life: moving my stuff out of Mark's house. Once I got home and had a bite to eat, I became enraged thinking about my best friend. Everything was about her and this god forsaken wedding. Her reaction when I told her what happened with Mark was so self-centered. All she said was that I better find another date for the wedding. Classy.

Jumping in my car I drive over to Jenny's. Fortunately, her car is in the driveway and Brandon's is not. We're alone. When I knock at the door, she says to come in. As I walk in, I see that she's ankle deep in what looks like tiny white netting, little colored beads and pre-cut blue ribbon bits. Her floor looks like a

Kindergarten class went section five all over it. She looks at me and doesn't even say hello. "You can sack the almonds and I'll tie the ribbons on. You're way better at that than I am."

I slam the door, which makes her put her little sack down. "What the hell, Booksie!"

"Yeah, 'what the hell' is right!" I shout. "You know you had no right bursting into my office like that today, dammit! I could have lost my job!"

She waves. "Oh, please,"

I take a step towards her, not bothering to remove my shoes, even though I know she's a clean freak, especially with her wedding stuff vomited all over the clean floor. Jenny gives me an unsettled look. "Do you think the world revolves around your wedding? Do you think that the lawyers at the firm don't notice some crazed Bridezilla crashing into their office in the middle of the day?! Just who do you think you are?!"

"Booksie, you're irrational." She mutters.

"I'm irrational?!" I state as if it's the most ridiculous thing I've ever heard. "You think the sun doesn't rise unless it says, 'Jenny & Brandon' on it!"

"Look, unless you can help me bag these almonds, you should go and calm down elsewhere. I have two hundred and fifty of these things to do...and Brandon just stormed out of here, so he's not here to help me."

"Shocker! Why did he storm out?! 'Cause you're a crazed wedding freak?! This whole thing has gotten completely out of hand, Jenny!"

She's exasperated. "The caterer needed the final count, Bookie. You weren't answering your phone and I had to give it to him, otherwise—"

I interrupt. "Otherwise what? You'd give it to him a day late? What's the big deal? I have a job! I'm trying to be a goddamn lawyer, not a fucking hairdresser!"

Her eyes widen. I never swear and certainly never use the 'f' bomb.

"And where do you get off inviting a total stranger to be my guest? He's a fucking client, Jenny! You're lucky he didn't file a complaint and get me disbarred!"

"You're not even 'barred' yet, Booksie." She minimizes.

That hit a nerve. "You fucking inconsiderate, self-centered...psycho." I seethe. "You know what? Forget about me bringing a guest...and forget about me coming at all, too!"

I'm about to leave when she stops me. "Wait, Booksie, come on. This is ridiculous." She whines.

Taking a step towards her I lift a finger and glare at her. "I stood by you when you and Brandon had trouble. I've been to every wedding-related event you asked me to, including missing my own personal appointments. My boyfriend betrayed me and all you were worried about was that you were down a guest for your wedding." I can feel the veins in my neck pop out. "I wouldn't be surprised if your fiancé walks out on you, too, because I sure as hell am. You should be ashamed of yourself for the way you've been treating people since you started wearing that damn ring. You don't deserve a beautiful wedding because you've turned ugly inside. Weddings are meant for princesses, not for frogs, you ungrateful, disloyal bitch!"

I stomp on a pile of her almonds, feeling them crack under my shoes. Jenny's jaw is on the ground as I walk out, slamming the door so hard I feel the earth shake underfoot. As I walk to my car, I see Wendy's car pull up. When she sees the angry puss on my face, a 'v' forms between her eyes. She walks out of the car. "What's going on, you look pissed."

"I am pissed. I just told your sister I'm done with her. I'm not coming to the wedding. That's the end of it all." I slice the air with my hand for emphasis.

Wendy's face falls. "Jesus. What happened?"

I explain to her and she shakes her head. "Wow. This is such a mess. I'm so sorry Jenny's being such a pill. I'll straighten things out, I promise."

"There's no need. I'm done with her."

"Don't say that." Wendy cocks her head sideways; her

voice is as soft as satin. "You guys have been best friends for too long. She's just nutty because of the wedding. Since she got engaged, she's...so OCD about everything. I read something about that. The article said that sometimes when the bride-to-be is obsessed with perfection, it can mean that the relationship is less than perfect. Kinda like when a guy has a teeny weenie, but he has a great big truck to compensate."

"Well if that's the case she better get a grip. Brandon's obviously feeling it, too. If she's not careful, she'll lose everyone before the wedding is even here. She's only got a couple of weeks left."

Wendy places her hands together in mock prayer. "I'll talk to her. Can you please just think about coming to the wedding? I promise I'll make things right. You mean a lot to her; you know that. She loves you. It would break her heart if you weren't part of the wedding. Deep down I know you'll regret it, too. I know you don't feel that way right now, but you will once you've cooled off. Please? Can you just think about it?"

Drawing in a deep breath, I say, "Fine. I'll think about it. But I'm not making any promises."

Lifting a hand, Wendy says. "That's all I ask." Then she changes the subject. "Hey, did you get into trouble at work for her barging in like that? For real?"

Thinking about Wade, my mind wanders right to his eyes, and I give my head a shake. I hate this guy. Aside from Mark, I've never hated a guy more in my life. Why am I thinking about his eyes? His lips? The way he sings and moves his body with the music? What the hell is wrong with me? The guy is an egomaniac, womanizing jackass. Why is he suddenly on my mind?

"Not with the client. Thankfully it was a pro bono case and I'd already given an answer. A favorable one." Then my thoughts slip back to his finances, and the fact that I might have seen something, but I was too angry to say anything. The file I created for him only included the piece about the phony lawsuit. "I'll admit her timing was impeccable; had it been a paying client I could have kissed my retainer goodbye."

"I'm so sorry, Booksie. I know she didn't mean it." Wendy's hand covers mine. I almost feel sorry for her. Jenny should be thankful she has such a great sister and Maid of Honor. "I should go and try to work things out. Will you be home later?"

"I'm not sure." I answer honestly.

She gives me a quick hug and says goodbye.

As I drive back to my parent's place, my thoughts are being pulled in all different directions. Should I forgive Jenny for behaving so badly? How am I going to get my stuff out of Mark's house without seeing the prick? And finally, do I leave well enough alone with Wade Ford, or do I tell him what I think I saw?

Chapter 8

Priscilla

One Month Ago
Nice Guys Finish Last

I hear him shout my name from the back of the house we rent together. "Priscilla! That you?" Leonard, my boyfriend, is home while I was out putting together things for a little project we're doing. He and I have been together for ten years, raising hell, and we've never been caught, so I guess that's pretty good. Before I answer, he's at the top of the basement stairs. "Oh, I thought I heard someone coming in." he embraces me, kissing me on the mouth. "Hi, baby. How did it go?"

"Pretty good. I got the stuff." I smile.

"All of it?"

I nod and his face breaks into an ear-to-ear smile. "God, we're meant for each other." he gushes. Leonard is nearly a foot taller than me, but we're both skinny and dirty blonde haired, which could make us pass for both a couple and siblings; not like we haven't used both scenarios before. It's come in handy for a couple of jobs we've done.

"Baby, if we can pull this one off, we're gonna retire. In the Bahamas."

"I'll go anywhere as long as it's with you, baby." I say.

He kisses me again. "Well, let's see it. I can hardly wait."

I'd taken my big purse, so I lift it in the air, teasing him. I pull out what looks like a pillow in the shape of half an egg, with a flexible belt hanging from either side. "This will be perfect. All I need is to stuff my bra a little and I'm set."

Leonard is impressed. "And the other?"

"Oh, that was easy." I brag. "You'd be amazed how

many legal secretaries leave their cabinets unlocked when they're away from their post. Idiots."

"You're my hero, baby." Leonard says, taking the bag out of my hands and placing it on the floor. He embraces me again. "I found out you were right about Wade's big brother, Colton. He's away overseas for eight weeks. Left four weeks ago."

"Really?" my eyes widen.

"And that's not all, baby." Leonard continues. "Wade's playing in that seedy joint in South Carolina this Saturday. Perfect place to take him down."

We both look like the Cheshire Cat. "And you? How did you do?"

"Took some doing, but you'd be amazed what kind of legal jargon you can find on the internet."

"You think he'll buy it?"

Leonard kisses my forehead. "Baby, the man's a whore and he's stupid. He's probably banged every chick at Mingles and more. The women hear his talentless voice and pine over him. When big brother's not around he's a sitting duck. This is our time."

"But we know he doesn't have the money. We've seen his hole of an apartment and his shitty car. He doesn't have enough money to get a decent shirt or a pair of jeans."

"Yeah, but there's something there, Priscilla. You and I both know it. He's the youngest Ford boy and they've probably got his money tied up somewhere until he's older. They'll either use their money to cut his loose or give him their own. Those Ford boys are all loaded, except for Wade. They won't want a lawsuit souring the family's reputation. Ain't no Ford's ever been sued before. And they'll give in, especially when they find out it's to do with a Ford baby."

"But what if they ask for a paternity test?"

Leonard waves. "They'll want to settle before that happens. They'll want this kept real quiet, and they can afford to do that."

"I love you, babe."

"I love you, too, baby." Leonard begins kissing my neck. "You want to make a real baby?" he teases, pulling me towards him.

"Oh, you know I hate kids, Leonard. But...I think we've got time to mess around." I say, pulling my shirt over my head. His eyes drink in my breasts. The expression on his face makes my thighs damp.

"You're so perfect, baby. I love your tits." He says, massaging them. His hands are so warm and experienced, I moan.

I can see his hardness growing in his jeans. His zipper is down and as I undo his button, he pulls his shirt over his head. The tattoo of my name on his chest makes me instantly hot. "Kiss me, baby." I beg.

His tongue thrusts into my mouth, making me whimper with need. "That tattoo's the best money I ever spent, baby." Leonard says between breaths.

We're a mess of wet, needy kisses as he unfastens my bra and pulls me close. I can feel his hardness on my belly, and I pull his jeans and underwear down, and then my own. We're standing in the kitchen, naked and kissing voraciously. Leonard pulls me up on the kitchen table and spreads my legs as my back meets the cold, hard wood. With one move he slithers inside my warm wetness and I cry out, pushing his rear with my hands, wanting to feel him all the way in. "Oh, baby, you're so wet and ready. You're so perfect." He says, pleasure is painted across his face like an erotic masterpiece as he glides in and out rhythmically.

"You're so good, baby." I breathe as I feel myself climbing. "Mmm...go faster, lover."

"You want it, baby?" he asks rhetorically. "I'll give it to you." He speeds up, beginning to pant. The table is rocking slightly with our movement. We've done it a hundred times on this table, so I know it'll hold up. It's one of those clunky, solid wood tables that you can only find at an antique store. My grandmother owned it. Granny Rumbolt would roll over in her grave if she knew what we did on it.

Leonard kisses my breasts, causing me to rear up from the table. "Oh, Leonard." I whine. "I love your lips."

"Mmmm...I love yours, too. Both sets." He kisses me hungrily and says. "Mmmm, these ones." And then he pumps me harder. "And these ones, too. You have the perfect slit, baby."

He hits a spot high in me with his hardness, and I cry out. "Oh, God, Leonard!" I can feel myself reaching the edge.

"I know that cry, baby. Are you gonna come?"

"Come with me, lover." I beg, squeezing around him with my Kiegel muscles.

He hisses through his teeth. "Oh, Priscilla. I love it and I hate it when you do that." He pauses as the veins pop out of his neck. Then he lets go, as I feel his warm seed wash inside me. I explode with him, feeling my orgasm rip through me like a hurricane. He pumps me faster, riding the waves of pleasure with me as we both groan with ecstasy.

As we lay in afterglow, half on the table, half off, Leonard kisses my breast. "We're like Bonnie and Clyde, you and I, baby. We fit together like a glove both in bed and in all the other nasty things we do."

He pushes up with his hands and helps me off the table. "You still got that freaky wig you use when we're under cover?"

I nod. "Of course."

"Good. We'll put the letter together today and get everything ready. We'll leave Friday night and make a weekend of it. Just you and I."

"Just you and I."

He kisses me and then we get dressed. "You think this'll work?"

Leonard looks at me and smiles. "If it doesn't, I've got something else in mind. Something we've never done before."

Half of me wishes it doesn't work out. I'm very intrigued...

Chapter 9

Wade

The following Saturday, back at Mingles

Saturdays at Mingles aren't the same without my older brother, Colton. That's why Jack's been hanging around. My other brothers are around often enough, too; we seem to support each other evenly together. When I was out in South Carolina last weekend, I saw my other brothers Dalton and Garrett, too. But tonight, none of my brothers are around, and it's kind of lonely, I'll admit. Nights like this I get the urge to sing a couple of the songs I wrote for the short time I served the country, like the rest of my brothers. Colton, the longest. He was fighting for nearly ten years.

It was our father's idea. I figured joining the military would sway dad's thoughts of me; they seemed to work for Colton, but it didn't seem to matter. Anyway, I was only on a peace-keeping mission. There was never any real combat where I was, even though I did get injured enough to be sent home for good. However, I still had to do all the basic training any other soldier does. That was ball-busting work. It's thanks to that that my body is the way it is. Before I left for the military, I was what you would call a ninety-five-pound weakling. I couldn't fight my way out of a wet paper bag before I went to the army. After...what a difference. I've kept that figure up pretty well since.

Tonight, as I sing a catchy, mid-rhythm tune that has guests on the dance floor, but not pumping like they would be if it were a dance tune, I see the ladies looking at me differently. Can't put my finger on what it is, but I suppose it has something to do with the lyrics. It's difficult to look at a man like he's a piece of meat when he's singing about serving in Afghanistan. I don't actually use those words, but they get the idea.

As the song comes to a close, I change my tune and sing a slower song. The dance floor fills up with couples, and I see the redhead come in through the front doors. She's alone, not with her bridal party friends, like when I saw her in South Carolina. She's also not dressed in what you would call 'party clothes', she's wearing a pair of black dress pants and a red blouse. If she weren't a total psycho bitch, I'd say she looked hot. Hotter if she'd let her red locks down. The librarian look doesn't cut it for me. Then again, she could be in a string bikini and I wouldn't look twice at the freak. She catches the cold stare I'm giving her during the guitar solo and she looks away. What the hell is she doing here, anyway? Hope she's not going to turn out to be one of those stalker bitches. Hello, restraining order? Yeah, check out the chick at table three.

Sitting at a table, one of the waitresses, Liz, who also happens to be my sister-in-law's sister, takes her drink order. A minute later, Liz serves her water with a slice of lime. *Badass.* I feel completely on display while she watches me intently from the table. Sipping her drink slowly, she's probably anticipating how she's going to skin me alive this time. While I'm set to take a break in five minutes, I ride it out for two more songs, making her wait like a slave. *Want to screw me over? Take a number, bitch.* When my drummer signals to me that he needs to take a leak, I relent and announce our break.

Rude, I don't even stop by her table, even though we both know I've known she's been there the whole time. As I walk to the washroom, I hear her call me from behind. "Wade!" she shouts. Making a meal out of this, I rake my hand through my hair and slowly turn around, disinterested.

"Yeah,"

"Listen, I...I didn't get to finish our um...meeting the other day."

"Oh, I disagree. We were done, lady." I guffaw.

She ignores my jibe. "Have you heard from...anyone?"

I draw in a deep breath, "Nope. Not a word."

"Well, that's a good sign."

"Yep. Hey, listen. I gotta pee really bad and I've only got a short break."

"Sure. Okay, yeah." It looks like she's going to say something, but she refrains.

Turning around, I go to the bathroom. When I leave the men's room, to my dismay, she's still standing there. "Hey, look who's still here?" I say with obvious, pasted-on excitement. "What do you want? You know yourself I don't have any money...you don't want, like, compensation for the other day, do you? Because you didn't send me a bill or anything."

"No," she rolls her eyes, "I just wanted to give you some advice on what to do...should they follow up."

"Oh," Well, that's reasonable. "Okay. Should I just call her bluff?"

"I'd go one step further." She hands me an envelope. I look at it. "What's this?"

"It's a letter, on company letterhead, signed by one of the attorneys at the firm, indemnifying you from any fiduciary responsibility to her, pending a positive paternity test."

I lift a brow. "Okay, that...only in English, please."

She smiles. *I didn't know she could do that.* Not bad.

"It just means that she can't pursue you unless she can prove to you legally that the child is yours."

Frowning, impressed, I nod. "Well, Booksie, or Kendra, or whatever your name is...thanks. You didn't have to do that."

A girl walks by and grazes my shoulder with her hand. "Wade," she purrs.

"Hey," I say. The girl is smoking hot with long blonde hair and a grabbable ass. I've seen her many times here at Mingles, and I've wanted to do her for a while, but she's always with some guy. Doesn't look like he's around tonight. I give her my best bedroom eyes and she winks at me.

Kendra clears her throat, interrupting the seduction.

"Err...sorry, I was just..." I'm lost for words.

"Shopping? Yeah, I know." Kendra is irritated. "Listen, I wanted to tell you something else, but I'd rather do it in private." She looks around, as if all eyes are on her. They probably are, too. With her 'all business' attire and stance, she sticks out like a sore thumb in a place like this, where all the girls are dressed in miniskirts or tight shorts and painted-on faces. "Is there anywhere here that we can talk for a minute alone?"

I don't usually take girls to the green room unless it's to prime them for later, but I'll make an exception. "Sure, I've got a few more minutes." I say, half to get rid of her, and half because sometimes this has a great effect on the other girls who are in line for me: girls tend to get jealous and it ups the ante.

The green room is just a room filled with extra sound equipment, a couch for when we're between sets, and a small, hotel-sized refrigerator, usually filled with water for the pansies who don't want to drink beer on breaks. Opening the locked door with my key, I switch the light on and offer her a water from the fridge, which she declines. Taking a seat on the couch, I gesture for her to join me. The couch is tall and bulky; I've slept on it many times when I'm too drunk to drive home and Colton's not around.

"So, what's up?" I say, raking a hand through my hair.

I notice her perfume; it's kind of nice, but I try not to let myself be attracted to her, despite the fact that being this close to her is a little unsettling below the belt. She may be a psycho bitch, but a psycho bitch with a great body is still nice to look at. Behind her glasses, her green eyes are clear and large, and her ginger eyelashes are cute. It's hard to tell how long her hair is all tied up in that bun, but I remember the last time I saw her, it was down to her mid-back. It'd be nice if she wore it all out. Like Julia Roberts in *Pretty Woman*.

"Mr. Ford, I'll be blunt with you."

Go on, I'm pretty used to it by now

"I think your manager is the reason you're having financial trouble. He may be the reason why you're not getting any offers for gigs anywhere else."

Hold the phone

"What?" I squeal.

"I did some digging. I hope you don't mind."

"What?" I guffaw.

She licks her lips and speaks frankly. "Your manager doesn't have the credentials he claims to have. I checked it out. He's never represented anyone before you. And he hasn't represented anyone *except* you. He's a fake, and he's also skimming from you. I saw it in your financial records. He's supposed to be taking thirty percent, but he's taking at least fifty and making it look like he's absorbing it in other costs"

"How do you know all this shit?" I'm flabbergasted, and I don't believe her for a minute. Not sure why she's pulling this shit on me, but I don't like it. This woman is a nutcase.

"Mr. Ford, I examined your financial records and made some background calls. Mr. Midel is a fraud. I'm very sorry to have to tell you this."

My eyes widen and my voice is a bark. "Yeah, you seem real upset!"

"You don't believe me." she states flatly.

"No, I don't believe you!" I yell, slamming my fist on the couch. "Chuck has been my manager for two years and he tells me all the time that he's gotta pay for this and that! When I do gigs out of town, it's not free, lady!"

"Well, tell me this...has he had any recording agents come to hear you play?"

A 'v' forms between my eyes. "No, of course not! I've only been doing this gig for two years! You have any idea how long you have to be doing this shit before a recording studio'll even look at you?!" I shout. "You know nothing about this business!"

"As a matter of fact, I do, Mr. Ford." Her voice raises an octave, stifling me. "If an artist is good, and they have the right people behind them, they can go far…fast." Her voice is laced with strong conviction. She rises from the couch. "But if you don't believe me and don't care to see any proof of what's going on right under your nose, then there isn't anything I can do about it." her chest heaves. *Wow, either she's nuts or she really does care.*

I rise so we're face-to-face. My chin tips upward. "Why did you do this?" I wiggle the envelope in the air.

"Because I…"

"Wait…you think I'm good?" my head tilts sideways in disbelief. The 'v' is still between my brows.

Her nose points to the ceiling, as if it's painful to admit that the man she hates, she also thinks has talent. "Yes,"

Well, this is a bit of a game-changer.

"And you believe that I should be doing better in my career?"

Her nose points to the floor, sheepishly, like when your mother asks you if you ate the last cookie, when you both know that you did. "That's right." She murmurs, so low I can barely hear her.

In all the time I've been singing, I've never actually heard anyone tell me that I'm good. All the women who fawn over me, it's just the rock star lifestyle that's appealing to them. It's got nothing to do with what or how I sing. As long as I sing. Hell, I could have laryngitis, and as long as I'm on the stage with a mic in my face and a guitar in my hand, they'll get wet over me.

Suddenly, my phone beeps, and Kendra laughs without a trace of humor. I know that laugh; I heard it in her office the other day when my phone went off then. Picking it out of my pocket, I see that yes, it's another girl. Kendra reads the expression on my face like she's psychic. A huff comes from her chest and she turns her head away from me, shaking it indignantly.

"You know, I—"

She's about to say something condescending, but I break her concentration by tossing my phone on the couch, and grabbing her face, cupping it with my hands. I take two steps, forcing her into the wall, and I impulsively kiss her like her lips will burst into flames if I don't. I half expect her to pull away and punch me in the face, but she opens her mouth, accepting my tongue. Pulling the pin from the back of her bun, I can feel her hair as it pools around her shoulders. Grabbing a handful of it from behind her neck, I lift my mouth off hers for a second, taking a breath, and slide my tongue into her mouth again. A small groan comes from her throat as we're both breathless. Her hands rake through my hair and my dick hardens instantly from her touch. I never knew hating someone so much could be so hot.

Her body is rigid against mine, and I can feel her belly quiver as if she's got so much untamed lust inside her, it's just bursting to come out. From her raw reaction to me, it seems like she hasn't come in months...maybe never, at least not properly, anyway. The feeling of power over her is heady. I want to go further, but I know she won't allow it. She's too by-the-book, probably a daddy's girl. I wouldn't be surprised if she was still a virgin, but I doubt it.

Suddenly she pulls away, escaping from the wall by squeezing out sideways from me. Both our chests heave from lust. "God, I can't believe I let you do that." She wipes her mouth as if I've poisoned her. "I *refuse* to be another notch in your bedpost."

I say nothing, but wipe my mouth, too, and rake a hand through my hair. As she wraps her hair back up into the bun, I watch her with my hands at my sides, as if contemplating what cutting statement she's going to say to me. Then there's a tap at the door. "Wade? Wade, we're up, man." It's my drummer. Opening the door, Kendra is nose-to-nose with Dave. "Sorry, didn't mean to interrupt." He says. With the angry look on her face, he lifts his hands in the air defensively.

"That's fine, I was just leaving." Kendra says, her tone is cold. She looks back at me and gives me the once-over. Thank God my hard-on instantly shriveled the moment Dave knocked on the door. Silent, she blinks once, looks at Dave again, as if to ask him if he'd give us a moment, then she seems to think better of it, and stomps away.

Dave lifts a brow at me. "What the fuck was that all about?"

I guffaw. "Damned if I know."

Chapter 10

Kendra

My favorite mistake

As I ride home from Mingles, I chide myself for letting that happen. What the hell was I thinking? First, he's a client. Second, he's a musician, and an arrogant one. Third, he's a whore, and an obvious one. I try to think of a fourth reason, but it doesn't come. Wade Ford is no good for me. Not just for the three reasons, but also because I'm smack dab in the middle of getting out of a relationship. Getting back into one immediately following it would be stupid. What happened in that room was nothing more than Wade trying to gain power over me. I'm not some horny twenty-something groupie who falls in love with cute musicians the instant I see them.

I should have pulled away immediately. I should have smacked him across the face. I should have screamed at him and told him what a pig he is. But I didn't. Instead, I held on to his touch for a full two minutes...which felt like hours, yet it wasn't long enough. His warm, hard body pressed up against mine in a way that no man has ever pressed up against me before. The way he kissed me; it was like a full body preview of what Wade Ford must be like in bed. It was a mistake. It was my favorite mistake. It'll never happen again.

Wade's voice resonates with me. Beyond what I've already told him, he'll never know. He'll never know how his Bryan-Adams-meets-Jim-Cuddy voice gets to me. His original song writing skill is beautiful. I've heard both his cover songs and his own work, and both are brilliant. What's more, he makes love to the stage. It's his raw, virile talent that strikes a chord. It doesn't matter that he's dressed in tattered jeans and shirts that are missing buttons, it's part of his look and it suits him. I won't think about how he'd tear up the stage if he dressed better, but the thought of him in a snug-fitting pair of dress pants and a white linen shirt...makes me sweat.

The way his fingers strum the guitar as he sings and winks at his audience...it's no wonder women drool all over him. Too bad he lets it all go to his head. Too bad he sleeps with all the groupies and wannabe groupies. Too bad he's too stupid to pick up on the fact that he's being raked through the coals and taken for a cheap ride courtesy of his manager. I tried to tell him. But he only sees me as another conquest, not a woman with brains and a care in the world. You would think that, after being overseas, he would be more mature. More seasoned through life lessons. I suppose not every male goes to the military a boy and returns a man. Not Wade Ford, anyway.

Shame, really. With the talent, looks, breeding and promise Wade Ford has, he could really be something. But it looks like the only thing he'll have in life is women pawing him. He'll inherit his fortune when it's time, but he'll squander it on women, booze and Lord knows what else. A typical trust fund boy. His father clearly knew his son well. It's just too bad that his brothers couldn't teach him a thing or two about real life. Maybe it's not too late. Maybe he'll get a head on his shoulders before his inheritance comes due.

As I pull up to my parent's house, I see that the living room light is still on. Twenty-four years old and my folks still wait up for me. Turning the engine off, my dad's head appears in the doorway. He opens the door and lets me in the house. "Where've you been?" he asks cordially.

"I was out speaking with a client." I say honestly.

"The office stays open this late?"

"It wasn't at the office. The client is a musician. I met him at a club that he performs at."

Dad nods. "Mark came by earlier and dropped off a bunch of your stuff for you. That's why I stayed up."

"You didn't have to do that, dad. I'm a big girl."

He pats my back. "Your mother couldn't wait up any longer. I sent her to bed an hour ago. I put the stuff in the spare room, but I didn't know if you'd want to go through it tonight or not. Mark said there were some things in there that you needed right away."

"And he lived to tell?" I only half-joke.

"Who...Mark?" Dad feigns disinterest.

"Who else?" I guffaw.

Dad rubs his nose nervously. "I had a word with him." he says too casually.

"When you say 'word', do you mean he left bleeding, and I should expect a restraining order to appear on my desk?"

"I bought a new gun this morning." Dad changes the subject.

"How à propos." My tone is facetious.

"I showed it to him. Thought he might like this one."

"As opposed to the others, when he had to change his shorts after the tour?" I bark. "Strange Mark even showed up to the house. Did he know you were home?"

"I had your mother call him."

"And say what? That you wouldn't be home? Yet you were?"

"Your mother was home."

"Yeah, asleep. Did she suddenly get tired, or did you make her go to bed the minute the doorbell rang?"

Dad waves. "He got the point."

Suddenly I picture Mark's nose pressed up against the barrel of dad's latest toy. "I'm sure he did." I walk to my bedroom. Inside there is a box full of law books, and another box with various items in it, and I sigh, as I see the law book that I consider my Everest.

"Something wrong?" dad frowns, rubbing my back like he did when I was a little girl and needed dad's comfort. "Don't waste sadness on him, love. He's not worth it."

"It's not that, dad." I scratch my head and pull the textbook out. "This is the subject I just couldn't conquer. This is the reason…" I trail off.

"You'll get it, honey. Next time you'll kill it without breaking a sweat."

"I hope you're right." I say. "I don't want to spend my life defending pro bono cases."

"You won't. I know it looks bleak now but give it time." He pauses, "You need help with anything? I'm beat."

"I'm sure you are." I playfully hit him with the back of the textbook. "After having run a few rounds with Mark."

He lifts a brow and winks knowingly. "You let me know if the boy hasn't returned all your things, now."

"I'll take a personal inventory right now, dad." I chuckle.

Gotta love him. As dad leaves to go to bed, I start taking the stuff out of the box that doesn't have the books in it. Inside is my jewelry box, some toiletry items, clothing accessories, and at the very bottom I see an envelope with my name written on it. It's Mark's handwriting. Checking to see if dad went upstairs, I take a step outside the door. The coast is clear. But something inside my gut doesn't let me open it…yet.

Chapter 11

Wade

Only a fool believes

What the hell was I thinking, kissing that nutcase? God, I must have a problem...like a sex addiction or something. The last thing I need is for that witch to latch on to me like some parasite. It was weird. It was like...I had to shut her up and at the same time get something out of it. The woman drives me crazy. I've never felt like that about a chick before. It's always either she's like my sister, or she gives me a hard-on. There's no in-between. But her lips were so fucking soft and sweet. They didn't smell like cigarettes or booze or another guy, and she smells like fucking heaven, too.

Kendra doesn't know what she's talking about with Chuck, my manager. He's a good guy. He'd never steer me in the wrong direction. As a matter of fact, he's told me he knows a few guys in the business, but he says I'm not ready for that yet. I believe him. The songs that I've written and composed are good, but not great. Not radio or concert great, anyway. They sure get the audience going, but let's face it...I work in a bar. Most customers are drunk out of their minds and don't know the difference between good music and shit.

As I sit in my kitchen, lit only by the overhead fan light above my stove, scribbling on a sheet of music, I look around my living area; the back of the couch is facing me. My place is a studio apartment in the basement of some old chick's house. I swear she rented it out just so she'd have someone to watch it while she splits every winter. Why she doesn't rent out the top half or let me live up there I have no idea. Probably afraid I'll trash the joint; which is stupid, because my place is awesome. I'm not a pig. I keep the place clean and tidy. There's a tattered old pull-out couch in the living room that doubles as a bed, but it doesn't stink. The sink is always clear; I don't let dishes pile up, and my laundry is always done; that's a necessity, since I don't have a ton of clothes like most guys.

Then something occurs to me. Maybe I *could* be making more money doing what I'm doing. Maybe there is a shred of truth in what Kendra was rambling on about before I ravaged her against the wall. Jack would know. Without telling him what happened with that freak-show Priscilla, I could probably have him look at my books. I'll just tell him I'll punch him in the face if he says anything stupid or tells anyone, especially any of my other brothers. He's the one who showed me how to keep a budget and a spreadsheet, he won't mind giving me a few pointers on how to save money, too.

Sitting at my breakfast bar, I hear my cell phone beep. With my lifestyle, it isn't unusual to get text messages in the middle of the night, so I check it. It's my sister-in-law, Julia, asking if it's too late to call. She's so sweet. She's the best thing that ever happened to this family. I slide to her number in the contacts list and hear the phone ring on the other end.

"Hey, it's your favorite brother-in-law." I say, as my usual opener.

Her voice is faint and hoarse. "Wade, I need a favor."

The hair on my neck stands on end. She's sick. "What, sweetie. What's up?"

She clears her throat. "Mary, you know my friend from Florida? She's here in town for the bridal show."

"Yeah, I know. She's getting married next year, right?"

"Yes. Anyway, I promised I'd go with her to the show in the morning, but I've been kissing porcelain for the last two hours. She's asleep and I don't want her to miss out because I'm sick."

"Yeah? What do you want me to do?"

"Do you mind going with her? It's too late for her to get anyone else out here from Florida. I thought I'd call you, so you'd sleep at least a little before morning. It starts at ten. Can you do it?"

My brother, Colton, is away in Afghanistan. Julia is holding down the fort at the ranch while Colton's away. Mary, her best friend and Maid of Honor, is getting married next year, and asked Julia to be her Maid of Honor. It's a major chick thing, being a Maid of Honor. I know Julia isn't one to disappoint, and I also know Mary's not the type to do stuff alone. Her and Julia are all but joined at the hip. I've partied with her at the bar a few times when the girls come to hear me play. She's a good shit. I like her. We get along really great, and her fiancé is really cool.

Going to a bridal show sounds just a little promising. I'm not big on bridesmaids in bars, but bridesmaids at a bridal show might give me a whole new perspective. "Sure, yeah, I can take her."

"Wade, you're the best. Just come by here in the morning around nine and pick her up if you don't mind."

"Sure, that's cool."

"I owe you one."

"Don't mention it."

Staring at the clock, I see that it's past two in the morning. I'm not in the least bit tired. Sleep will not come. I start thinking about my brother Colton. Since he and Julia married, his life has improved ten-fold. When he was in combat in Afghanistan, I missed the hell out of him, and we worried, too, for his safety, even though he's one hell of a warrior. Now, he's no longer in combat, but he's pursuing his dream to design planes for the military. While he's away, he made me promise I would look after Julia. And I have. I stay close to her always, helping her with Colton's horses; Maya and Rebel, and I make sure the ranch hands are doing their job. Not that Julia can't handle doing all that, but she's a full-time high school teacher, so she doesn't always have the time.

Heading to my bed, I hear a rustling, and just about

scream like a girl. "What the fuck!" I have a keepsake bat and ball set from when I was a kid hanging on the wall. Grabbing the bat, I hit the bed with it, blindly, in the darkness. The effect is like hitting a pool of water with a two-by-four.

"Wade! Fuck!"

I walk over to the light switch by the kitchen and turn it on. "Jack? What the fuck are you doing here?"

My older brother is laying on my pull-out couch bed, fully dressed. He's rubbing his leg as he rises. "I was on my way to the bar to see you play and I got a wicked, fucking skull-splitting headache." Jack suffers from chronic migraines. He has to keep medication with him constantly. Colton says it's because of his stressful job: CFO of dad's airline. "Anyway, the pills started taking effect, and I couldn't make it to the bar or back home. So, I crashed here."

Raking a hand through my hair, I draw in a deep breath, feeling my heartbeat slow. "Shit. You okay? Fuck, you scared the crap out of me."

"Sorry, man. I was going to call you, but I was in too much fucking pain. I couldn't even see enough to look at my phone. Lucky you left your door open...fuck, what are you doing leaving your door unlocked?"

A bad habit of mine; never have grown out of it, and I have no reason to. There's nothing in my house that's worth anything. "I almost never lock my door, you know that. What the fuck are they gonna steal?" I ask, gesturing with my chin around my living room, which consists of a couch, a coffee table and a small dresser I use for clothes and storage. My kitchen is nothing but a breakfast bar, stove, refrigerator and a small countertop. Laundry is done from a small vestibule the old lady had built. It's at the top of the landing before you reach the upstairs. "You feeling any better?" I ask Jack.

"Yeah. Those pills are great, but they knock me out." he scrubs his face with his hand.

"Good. You want anything?" I ask, placing the music

sheets I was working on on the coffee table.

"Nah, thanks. Hey, what's that?" Jack asks, gesturing at the music. "Something new?"

"Yeah," I hesitate. "Hey, are you up for looking at something? A spreadsheet?"

Jack blinks, as if he has sand in his eyes. "Yeah, what have you got?"

I keep a small laptop on my coffee table. As I open the lid, Jack watches me. "You still keep that budget. Good man."

"Of course. That's the only reason I can afford to eat."

He rolls his eyes. "I told you I'd help you, Wade. Any of us will."

I wave him off, pulling up my budget. "Here. Take a look at this. Anything look fishy to you?"

Jack shifts the laptop a couple of inches so he can see it, as we both sit on the edge of my bed, next to each other. He studies it for a moment, navigating around a little, using the built-in mouse pad. Sliding his eyes over to me, he says, "Something tells me you already know what's going on here." He glances at the screen again. "Is that seriously how much you pay Chuck? No offence, but what the hell has he done for you, anyway?"

"So, you think he's riding the pony, too." I comment.

Jack is incredulous. "Hell, yes."

I punch the coffee table with the heel of my hand. "Fuck!" I shout as I rise, pacing in front of the coffee table. "So, she was right! The fucking redhead was right!" I scream before I can stop myself.

Jack places his hands over his ears, wincing.

"Shit, shit, sorry." I whisper. "Fuck, I'm sorry."

My older brother lifts one hand as if in surrender. "It's okay. I'd be pissed off, too."

I am quiet, feeling like shit for obviously causing Jack immense pain. "Can I get you something?" I ask quietly.

He takes his hands off his ears. "No, no, I'm fine. It's okay, little brother." He chuckles, shaking it off, trying to make light of the situation. "Who's the redhead?"

I press my eyelids together and lift my head towards the ceiling. "Shit," I mutter under my breath.

"Oh, boy," he says, shaking his head. "I'm already sitting down, Wade, so you might as well get it off your chest."

I give him the abridged version about Priscilla and Kendra, leaving out certain things like the kiss.

"Something like this happened to Garrett a while back. It wasn't a pregnant woman or anything, but it was equally unsettling."

"Oh, yeah? What did he do?"

"Doesn't matter now, it's over with. But shit like this is always going to happen as long as we have money. Just have to stick to your guns." He sniffs. "So, this redhead…"

"Kendra," I correct. He gives me a look that I can't decipher.

"Let me see the letter she gave you."

I walk to my dresser and fish it out of the bottom drawer. When I hand it to him, he scrubs his face before he reads it. "Looks good. I'd keep that in a better place. You might even want to mail it to the lawyer. Registered. Keep it legal and all. It'll scare them off."

"The whole thing is bogus. I don't see the point."

"Keep a copy of the original. Send it to the lawyer to cover your bases." Jack advises. "And as far as Chuck's concerned, I'd kick his ass to the curb. He's no good anyway. I never liked him to start."

I scrunch my face, "Why didn't you ever say anything?"

Jack shakes his head. "I could say the same thing to you, little brother." Then he hesitates, "Hey, wait a minute. Wasn't that redhead from last Saturday night named Kendra?"

How the fuck does he remember that?

"Err…yeah,". I can't hide the smirk.

Jack lifts a brow. "More and more is making sense by

the minute."

Chapter 12

Kendra

Forgiveness

My parents are nuts. They're already up and out of the house before seven in the morning. It's *Sunday*, people. They will make perfect senior citizens when their time comes. As I stuff the pillow over my head, trying to drown out the racket as my parents leave, I hear a soft knock at my door. "What?" I whine with my gravelly voice.

"Hey, Kendra." I hear someone call from my door. When I lift my head, I see Jenny and Wendy standing there.

"Great. The Dynamic Duo. Just what I need first thing on a Sunday morning." My voice drips with sarcasm. "To what do I owe the pleasure?" I paste an intentionally exaggerated sweet smile on my face.

Jenny's face is like stone, but the moment I look at her, her chin quivers.

Shit.

"Kendra," Oh Lord, this is serious. She's *never* called me Kendra since shortly after we met. "I'm so sorry I've been such a bitch to you. Really," her voice cracks and the rims of her eyes turn pink.

Double shit.

"Can we please just forget about it? I really really need you there. I want you there. Let's not do anything we'll both regret, okay? I had no idea how awful I was being until Brandon said he was leaving me."

"What?"

Wendy intervenes. "He called her from his parent's place and told her it was over.'"

"Jesus." I say, even though it isn't unbelievable. She

has been ruthless since their engagement. "Well, I assume all is well now, right?"

"With Brandon, yes. But it's conditional." Wendy glances at her sister. "He heard about what happened with you two. He said she had to make amends with anyone she's upset during the wedding planning."

Jenny bends down on her knees and takes my hands in hers. "But that's not the only reason I'm apologizing. I really am sorry. God, I didn't realize how terrible I've been. I'm so sorry." Full on tears. They're contagious.

I let her hold my hands in hers. The tears start to prick the backs of my eyes. I can't stay mad at her. She's my best friend. I love her like a sister. Both of them. "Hey," I say, lifting her chin up so she's looking at me. "I'll come to your wedding as long as you can do me a favor."

"Anything," she whimpers. My heart clenches.

Reaching over to the box Mark dropped off last night, I grab the letter he wrote and hand it to her. "Please read this. I just...I just can't do it."

Jenny looks at the envelope and then at me again. "Oh no, this isn't the proverbial 'breakup letter', is it?"

"I don't know. I haven't looked at it yet."

She wipes the tears from her eyes and takes a seat beside me on the bed. Wendy sits on the opposite side. Jenny leans her head into me affectionately as she tears open the letter. I rub her back as a gesture of forgiveness. As the letter is pulled from the sleeve, I close my eyes. Wendy begins rubbing my arm. "Don't worry, we'll get you through whatever it is." She says. "Us girls are indestructible together. You'll see."

Jenny scans the letter quickly and then puts it back in the envelope without comment. "You don't want to know what's in here right now, Books. Trust me."

What?

Wendy holds her hand out. "May I?" She asks, looking at me.

I shrug. "Knock yourself out."

Scanning it quickly, Wendy mutters under her

breath. "I'll kill him."

Jenny interrupts. "We'll kill him together...later."

"Guys, I gotta tell you, you're not making me feel any better right now." I say, rising. "Why the hell are you here so early, anyway?"

"The Bridal Show is today, remember?"

Crap. With all the events in the last few days I'd forgotten. "Isn't it too late to go now? Your wedding is around the corner."

"Not at all. I might see something better there. Plus, I still get all the freebies. Doesn't matter how close or how far away your wedding is."

Jenny continues. "I thought we'd go out for breakfast and hit it. It starts at ten. Your parents are meeting us there."

"What? Why?"

"Because I invited them." Jenny is pleased with herself.

"Why would you do that?"

"My parents will be there, too" Jenny explains. "This way I'll be able to look around without my mother breathing down my neck."

Wendy and Jenny high-five each other. "She's smart. I'll give her that." I say to myself.

"So, are you up for it?" Wendy asks me.

"I suppose so. It's one place I'm certainly not going to run into Mark at." I comment.

"You go on and get a shower. We'll make your bed and tidy your room while you get ready." Wendy says.

I turn my back to walk to the bathroom and I hear Jenny say to Wendy. "And burn that letter."

Chapter 13

Wade

Twins

No, I did not sleep with my brother, Jack. In case you are wondering. Jack slept on the pull-out couch and I slept on the floor. After I set my alarm on my phone to wake me up early enough that I could shower and avoid going to the damn Bridal Show smelling like a bar, I took my lumpy comforter off the bed, leaving Jack with the sheets, and went to sleep on my plush carpeting.

Jack is surprisingly quiet when he sleeps. Which is probably why I had no idea he was even there until I walked right up to the bed. He is so quiet, that I didn't even hear him when he left in the morning. When my alarm sounded, I jumped out of bed and went straight into the shower. Realizing I'm out of clean clothes, I throw a quick load in the washing machine while I have the last clean towel wrapped around my waist. I feel like friggin Tarzan walking around my place. Just as the dryer finally finishes, I scarf down the last of my fried eggs and bacon, and quickly wash the dishes. Tossing a pair of jeans and a t-shirt on, I hop in my car and drive over to Colton and Julia's place.

The ranch is very quiet as the warm morning suns beats down on it. Rebel and Maya are outside in the pasture grazing when I arrive. I go over to them and Maya is quick to trot over to me. Rebel is feeling a tad snobbish, so he ignores me while he eats grass. Maya whinnies happily as I pet her snout. "Hey, girl." I say, "Have you been fed yet?"

"Hey, good-lookin'." I hear from behind me, inside the stable.

Turning around I see Mary. She's dressed, like me, in a pair of jeans and a t-shirt. "Looks like we're both underdressed." I comment, turning to give her a hug hello.

"You didn't get my memo? I told you I was wearing jeans and a t-shirt. Jesus, we're gonna look like twins."

"Or freaks. Always go with freaks." I joke.

I gesture with my chin towards the house. "How's Julia?"

With a scrunch of her face she answers. "She looks like hell but she's sleeping now. Finally stopped barfing. I told her I could go by myself, but I don't think she trusts me alone with a credit card. My friends aren't driving all the way out here, either, so I'm guessing that's why she roped you into this. If you don't want to go it's cool, I can go, or I can skip it and go to the one later in the year at home."

"No, it's fine. Hey, this could be a really great place to meet chicks."

Mary lifts a brow. "Dude, they're gonna think we're getting married," she lifts her shirt slightly at the top, "it looks intentional that we're dressed like twins. All we need is a banner."

"Can you change?" I chuckle, shaking my head.

She loops her arm through mine. "Nah, I think it'll be funner this way. I'd like to know what it's like to be betrothed to a Ford boy."

I roll my eyes. "Oh, Lord."

***

Mary is really cool about giving me the low-down as we drive to this humongous warehouse in the heart of Raleigh. It's so big they should have golf carts to take customers to the main entrance. Parking is a problem, too. You'd think with so many bridal parties coming to an event like this, that they would carpool. Judging by the plethora of cars here I'd say they didn't consider that. Parking isn't free, either. But when I see some of the stuff that's being offered here, I figure these brides-to-be aren't worried about money.

The place is packed. I can't believe chicks are so nutty about getting married. Personally, I'm never tying the knot with anyone. Colton is the only Ford boy that's married, and I'd like to keep it that way. Chicks are only ever after your money or to get into your pants. At least, that's the experience I've had so far. I'm not a dating kind of guy, either. Getting in and getting out are all I'm interested in. Most of the time that's all the girls want, too. Easy come, easy go. I've never been in a relationship nor do I intend to be. Especially seeing these freaky chicks here. I can't believe girls are wasting so much bread on one stupid day. It's unreal.

They've got everything from ice sculptures to chocolate fondue fountains here. They've even got some company that does up specialty guest gifts called 'Bombonières', that I still can't pronounce. Mary can't stop laughing every time she teases me and asks me to say it. She's awesome. So much fun. It's my mission now to find something *she* can't pronounce. For fun, when vendors approach us, we play along and pretend that we're actually getting married. I can totally get why Mary's fiancé didn't want to go to this suarez, not that I asked.

Mary is having some long discussion about her dress with some designer when I happen to look over at a vendor across the hall...and I lock eyes with the redhead.

Chapter 14

Kendra

Moments like these

When we arrive at the Bridal Show, Jennifer grabs three copies of the map for the venue event from the front desk and studies it quickly. "Okay, this is almost an exact replica of the one they posted online." She grabs a black Sharpie marker from her back pocket and circles some key areas, using Wendy's back as a desk. "We need to hit all these vendors. These are where the freebies are. If we get there in time, we can hit all of them." She grabs a red Sharpie marker out of the other back pocket. "And these are the ones I'd like to see, but it isn't the end of the world if we miss out."

"I'm glad I wore my walking shoes." I comment, sticking my head into the main hall. It's so big you can't even see the center of the hall.

"Is there at least a wine vendor here that's giving out freebies?" Wendy asks. "Or what about one of those donut makers? I heard those are all the rage for weddings this year. I could go for a sugar crash."

"There's a make-your-own-wine vendor here, but it didn't advertise freebies. And you have a dress to fit into. No donuts for you." Jennifer chides.

"So, I'll just pair up with Darren at the wedding, right?" I ask. Darren is the Usher that is my partner in the Bridal Party. He's Brandon's best friend Jacob's brother. Brandon has known both Darren and Jacob since primary school.

"Darren's married, so once his duties are done, he'll be dancing with his wife." She says casually, with one eye staking out the first row of vendors inside the hall. We follow beside her, practically holding her hand, so we don't get lost.

"Maybe they have a rent-a-date here." Wendy jokes. I elbow her.

Jennifer guffaws. "I highly doubt you'll see any men in this place. Unless you count the poor grooms-to-be that got dragged here. Hell, I wouldn't even ask Brandon to come. That's just cruel."

Just then we see two men walk by. Actually, I wouldn't call it a *walk*; it is more like a stride. They are dressed in tight leather pants and bright pink shirts; one emblazoned on the front with 'bride-to-be-2019', the other with 'bride-to-be-2019'. As they pass us, we chuckle. "I guess you were wrong there, Jen!" Wendy snorts.

"I stand corrected." Jennifer is matter-of-fact. "Okay, you won't see any *available* men here." She gasps. "Oo! Here's the first freebie!"

It's a cupcake vendor. They make specialty cupcakes and place them on a wire-tiered racking system. It's a wedding cake alternative, and the best part is that the guest keepsakes are placed on top of each cupcake. The keepsakes are lame: charms in the shape of the bride and groom's initials. "Don't you already have a cake decorator?" I ask.

"Yeah, but I want something for the sweet table." Jennifer explains. "Plus," she lowers her voice, "they're free samples." She gestures with her eyes at the table full of a miniature version of the full-size cupcakes they make for weddings.

"We also offer the mini versions for weddings." A lady announces from the table, giving me a business card. I feel like telling her I'd rather just have the free cupcake. "Would you like to try one?" she asks, not waiting for my response as she hands us all a cupcake. "I can also make them gluten-free."

The cupcake is delicious. Best one I ever tasted. As I scarf it down, Wendy elbows me. "Looks like one poor bastard got dragged here." She points out a lone man standing beside his to-be wife. They're dressed identically in jeans and a white t-shirt. He's facing sideways to me, but I see enough to recognize him.

...it's Wade Ford.

He spots me before I can turn away from him.

Shit.

He does a double-take and nods hello once. I just stare at him. *Why the hell is he here? And who is he with? I didn't know he was getting married! What an asshole! He friggin kissed me for god sake!*

Wade says something under his breath to his wife-to-be as I pretend that I don't see him and feign reading a pamphlet from the stack of brochures at the side of the table. Both Wendy and Jennifer are oblivious, talking to one of the owners of the cupcake business. *Please don't come over here, please don't come over here.* I say over and over inside my head like a mantra. Ten seconds later, he's beside me. "Hey," he looks over at Jennifer. "So, I guess you've got a pretty high threshold for bullshit if you're here with your friend." He comments, referring to what happened the day he came to my office and Jennifer stormed in unannounced.

"Or a low threshold for forgiveness." I glare at him.

A 'v' forms between his brows, and then recognition comes to his face, as if a light bulb went off inside his head. "Oh, I get it." he looks over at his fiancé. "You think I'm here because I'm getting married." He laughs. "Yeah, that's about as likely as us both getting struck by lightning in this place." He shakes his head. "That's my sister-in-law's best friend. *She's* getting married. To *her* fiancé. Who's in Florida...where they live together." He accentuates every sentence. "She came down here to go to this show with Julia, my sister-in-law, but Julia's been sick all night and couldn't make it."

"Oh, okay." I nod, feeling my cheeks heat.

"So, you thought," he gestures to himself, and then to his friend. "Oh, man. You must've thought I was a real dirt bag. As if your opinion of me couldn't be any lower." He points out.

"Yeah, kinda." I admit.

His friend finishes with the vendor that she is talking

to, and she comes over to us. "Hey," she says to Wade.

"Mary, this is Kendra." He looks at me, searching my face, and continues. "My lawyer."

Mary lifts a brow and guffaws. "Well, I don't think I've ever been introduced to anyone like that before." She holds out her hand for me to shake. "Nice to meet you. Are you getting married?" I shake her hand.

"No," I nod quickly, cutting the air with my hand for emphasis. "My best friend is." I gesture to Jennifer and Wendy, who are still chatting with the vendor.

Satisfied, Mary addresses Wade. "What in the hell do you need a lawyer for? Is everything okay?"

Wade gives her the short version but leaves out the part where his manager is siphoning his money. "Jesus Christ, Wade. I'm so sorry about that." Mary is heartfelt and concerned, placing her hand on her chest.

"Ah, it's okay. We're handling it." he waves.

Jennifer and Wendy approach. I make the introductions. Jennifer quickly points at Wade. "Hey, you look familiar." She circles her index finger in the air, trying to place him in her memory. I was hoping to sidestep awkward explanations, but it looks like I won't be able to avoid this one. "Oh yeah, you were in Kendra's office when I—"

"Stormed in like a psycho." Wade interrupts, taking Jennifer's proffered hand and shaking it. He's flippant and recognition comes to her face.

"Oh yeah, sorry about that. I was a little..." she trails off, waving her hands by her head as if batting away a swarm of bees.

"Psycho." Wade assists, smiling.

"Yeah, I guess you can call it that."

"That's okay," Wade chuckles. "Kendra got the problem under control. That's all that matters."

"And I got them talking to each other again, as usual." Wendy intervenes. "I'm the peace-keeping sister."

"I've got a few brothers like that." Wade comments, nodding once. Wendy is wearing a short-sleeved shirt with two buttons at the top. She undoes one button. I lift a brow. *Is she trying to flirt with him?* Then I see her flash her 'you-can-eat-crackers-in-my-bed-anytime' smile at him. I know that smile. I saw it when we went to the strip joint. I look at Wade and expect to see him returning the goo-goo eyes, but he's not. *Hmmm....*

"Hey, listen," Wade addresses me, "Can I talk to you for a minute in private? It's about the legal issue."

Jennifer is quick to jump in, letting me know what vendor they're going to next, and offering to meet me there. "Oh, I'm going there, too. Wade, you can meet me there when you're done." Mary says, and then asks Jennifer and Wendy if they mind her tagging along. They both give a consenting smile and nod, but Wendy gives Wade a longing, toothy grin before walking away with her sister.

I'm kind of shocked. Wade is such a lady's man, I thought he jumped at the chance at getting a little bootie. Not to mention, I find it surprising that he's willing to come to a place like this, and evidently stand out like a sore thumb, plus spend the day with a girl that he has zero chance of getting laid with...all for his sister-in-law? Maybe Wade just puts that slutty, selfish impression of himself out there as part of his stage act. Maybe Wade isn't just a hormone with legs. "Err, sure. We can go out to the main hall where there isn't anyone around." I say. "I'm not especially comfortable discussing a case in public though."

"Oh, it'll only take a minute." Wade says, and then he completely shocks me by taking my hand. Let's face it, this place is a zoo, and if we want to get somewhere in a hurry without accidentally getting split up, that's the only way to do it, but still. I hesitate for a second, but I let him take my hand as he leads me to the main hallway. It's been a long time since a guy has held my hand. I forgot how nice it is. His hand is warm and soft, but he has calloused fingers, I'm guessing from strumming his guitar. They're not off-putting at all, in fact, I find it a little sexy, partly because I'm picturing him on stage, singing and playing his guitar. But I shake it off.

The hallway in the main lobby, where the entrance is, leads us to an empty corridor. We walk into the corridor and he lets my hand go. "Listen," he starts, "I followed your advice and had my brother Jack look at my financial records."

"Oh yeah? Good, I'm glad." I say, folding my arms over my chest, listening intently.

"And you were right," he says, "Chuck is fudging the numbers."

I tip my head to the side. "Well, I'm sorry to hear that it's true. Sometimes I do wish I was wrong. Despite what you might be thinking, I don't enjoy being right when it means someone is getting the shaft."

"Well, I just wanted you to know that. And I'm going to fire him. I was going to do it first thing this morning, but when Julia called me in the middle of the night, it kind of put things on hold."

"I understand. It was good of you to step up for your sister-in-law."

He dips his head towards the floor. "My brother's in Afghanistan. It's hard on her."

My face falls. "Wade, that must be hard on you, too."

"Me? Oh, I'm used to it. He's served a long time. Way longer than me and my other brothers." He chuckles softly, nervously looking at the door next to us. It's as if he doesn't know where to look. God, is he...nervous? I suppose I would be, too, if I were this far out of my element.

"Are you okay?" I ask, chuckling softly, mirroring his disposition.

"I'm fine. It's just...I'm thinking about Chuck. It really pisses me off. I can't believe he'd pull this kind of shit." He sniffs, chewing on the pad of his thumb, "I thought I could trust him. I thought I knew what he was doing every step of the way. And now...now, I don't know what I'm going to do. I don't have a manager. Jack says he never did anything for me, anyway, but still."

"Maybe you don't need a manager, Wade. Not for the immediate future." I supply, "If all he's been doing is booking garbage venues like that dive in South Carolina, you can handle that. You'd do a better job than him, anyway. This is likely a blessing in disguise, Wade."

He wipes his nose nervously. This conversation makes him uncomfortable. "Wade, you can do this. I've seen many artists like you tear up the stage with the right manager, in big ticket venues, too." I take it down a notch. "They weren't my clients, of course." I murmur jokingly.

He laughs softly. "Well, if those lawyers are half as generous as you are, I'm sure that's why."

"I wasn't generous. I was doing what's right."

"Same difference." He says, and then he looks at me. "You know, I think this is the first conversation we've had where we haven't had an argument."

"Well, don't let it happen again." I joke.

"Hey, I'm sorry about that...kiss before. I was out of line."

"You were." I say firmly. "But I accept your apology." I smile.

He looks at me and smiles. Wade is kind of cute. Like a little boy who's grown into a man, but still has his little boy features. I hold my hand out with a crooked smile and he shakes it. "Truce?"

"Truce." He clears his throat. "Hey, do you want to *be* my lawyer? Like for real?"

"I'm afraid I can't do that." I say after a beat. Partly because I'm not a lawyer yet, and partly for another reason that I haven't figured out.

"I understand. I probably couldn't afford you, anyway." He says, just as a couple walks through the entrance doors. *Oh shit.*

"Kendra?" my dad calls as he looks my way. "Is that you?"

"Hey, dad." I say, walking towards him. Wade follows

me. My mom is at the ticket window, paying for their entrance fee. I give dad a hug and then I introduce Wade. "He's the client who plays at Mingles." I explain.

"Pleased to meet you, sir." Wade says, giving dad a firm handshake. "I'm just here as a placeholder for my sister-in-law." He says matter-of-factly, probably wishing to dispel any misunderstanding that he is betrothed.

"Well, you're in good company." Dad says. "I think you and I and Jenny's dad will be the only three males here." He chuckles.

"That's not true, dad." I tell them about the homosexual couple we saw earlier.

Dad's eyes widen but he's impressed. "Well, I'll be damned." He laughs.

"You should come to Mingles some time, Mr. MacGregor. There are all kinds of couples there. I see it all the time."

Dad is lapping this up. He loves being referred to as 'Sir', or 'Mr. MacGregor'. Wade is scoring points with dad and doesn't even know it.

"What kind of music do you play, Wade?"

Wade tells him as I watch my poor mother stand in the long line up for tickets. If I'd known that they were coming, I would have purchased them online.

"Well, it sounds like you've got some talent. I hope your need for Kendra's services aren't too serious."

Oh, shit, change the subject, change the subject.

"Nah, my manager's giving me some trouble is all. It's all been dealt with." Wade answers.

Phew!

"Hey, you don't really want to go in there, do you, sir? Are you a beer man?"

Ding Ding Ding!

"As sure as the nose on my face, I am." Dad says, impressed.

"There's a beer tent in there, believe it or not. I saw it myself." Wade supplies.

Dad places his arm over Wade's shoulders. "Lead the

way, son."

And then it comes to me. The other reason why I can't be Wade's lawyer. Because my heart is telling me it might be a conflict of interest.

Chapter 15

Wade

Fathers and Daughters

At first, I thought Kendra was here because she was getting married, and my heart skipped a beat. I kissed her and I made a complete ass out of myself. I really should learn to keep my hands to myself and my lips off girls until I know for sure what their deal is. Then it occurs to me, the second I see her psycho friend, who stormed into the office the first day we met: they're here because of her. A slight feeling of relief washes over me. Mary is busy with some wedding dress lady, talking lace and measurements and all kinds of crap that I can't relate to. I whisper to her that I'll be right back, and she waves me off.

Kendra is completely stunned and looks as if she's going to punch me. Until I realize why. It's kind of funny, actually. I'm not the marrying type, so this is probably as close as I'll ever get to that whole deal. Making a meal out of Kendra's friend's little outburst at Kendra's office is fun, but she takes it in stride, and I'm glad because any other response would prove she's no friend to Kendra. The Chuck issue is grinding at me in the back of my mind, and I don't see any other way but to tell Kendra in person, so I ask politely if we can talk. When I go to take her hand, so we don't end up on opposite sides of this zoo, she acts like I've got a bad case of warts. I pull her hand towards me anyway. I'm not up for the drama today.

It's a little unsettling talking to this girl, since I know she probably thinks of me in the same manner as she thinks of dog shit on her shoe. So, when she shakes my hand and offers a truce, I'm surprised. She still doesn't want to be my lawyer, even if she could, but at least I know she doesn't hate me anymore. It bothers me that it bothers me this much. I'm not used to girls disliking me. I've gotten so used to girls crawling all over me the way I like it, so this is uncharted territory. When we're done with our little pow-wow, her dad shows up. He's super cool. I like him immediately. He's big and imposing, but you can tell that he's soft on the inside. Kendra gives me an odd look as I kidnap her father and take him to the beer tent. At this point I can't read her expressions, but she offers to hang out with Mary, so I assume she's not angry with me, or she wouldn't have offered to do me a favor.

Walking into the beer tent, Mr. MacGregor and I exchange sly grins. There are about fifty men sitting in the tent, all drinking like it's two-for-one-Tuesdays at the local watering hole. "Haha...looks like we found the hiding spot, Wade."

The tent is a covered area with about twenty, four-seater tables with attached chairs, kind of like what you'd see at an amusement park. Waitresses come around and take orders just like at Mingles. We order a pint. "Looks like it, sir."

"When you call me 'Sir', I look around for my drill Sergeant." Mr. MacGregor says. "Call me Peter."

"Will do, Peter. Where did you serve?"

We both share our military credentials and the waitress brings us a plastic pint full of beer and two plastic cups. I pour for Peter and myself, and we clink glasses. "To beer." I say.

"To beer." Peter says with a smile as we both down a healthy sip of the delicious brew. Peter puckers his lips and makes a smacking sound. "That's pretty good."

"Can't complain." I agree. "On tap is always better than by the bottle. I get that at Mingles all the time and it's just not the same."

"I have a tap at home." He brags. "My wife and I installed a wet bar for our twentieth anniversary. She prefers wine so we added a wine fridge for her. We've got a little cellar, too."

"Very cool. Do you make your own?"

Peter frowns. "Na, I just like drinking it. No, my passion is my gun collection. You have one of those?"

"Na, I've got my music as my passion. But my brother Garrett's got a pretty cool gun collection. He served as well. All my brothers did, in fact."

"Really." Peter is impressed.

"Yeah, Colton, one of my brothers, he's out in Afghanistan right now. He's learning how to design military aircraft using their technology. He's got a degree in Military Aerodynamics from his ten years of service."

"How interesting." Peter is nodding, very impressed. "So, tell me, Wade. Do you have a girlfriend?"

Yuck...I don't like where this is going...

"No, sir. I'm not a relationship kind of guy."

He nods his understanding. "With your line of work, it's probably difficult. You probably meet many women and don't know what to do with them."

Well, he's half right.

"To be honest with you, sir, yes I meet a lot of women. But they just see me as an artist, up there on stage, singing. It's never been about relationships. It's always casual. I don't desire much more than that, anyway, so it's fair."

"And I suppose that since you've been in the military, that also adds a certain something to your repertoire with women, too." He surmises, taking a sip of beer. "When I met Carol, my wife, she was nuts about me. It's the uniform, I suppose."

"That's true. And now I have the added bonus of girls figuring out that my family has money."

"That would make it more difficult. At least when I met Carol, I didn't have two cents to rub together."

"Well, that certainly makes it less complicated."

Peter clears his throat. "Level with me, Wade. Do you have any interest in my daughter?"

I bark out a laugh. "Sir, up until about five minutes ago, Kendra and I hated each other. We did not meet under ideal circumstances."

He hits the table, satisfied. "Good. Because the last thing she needs is for another man to muddy up her plans to be a lawyer." He sniffs, "She's so close. She's got another chance to write the bar exam coming up very soon."

Why is he telling me this?

"Well, I wish her luck, sir. She's one hell of a lawyer already, even with the little bit that she's done for me."

"She is. It's taken Carol and I many years to save up for her education. And she's earned every penny."

"I don't doubt it, sir."

Okay, getting awkward...

Suddenly, I see Mary appear at the front of the beer tent. I wave at her, hoping like hell that she'll come and rescue me from this conversation. She glances at the pint of beer and smiles, coming our way.

"Oh, man, just what I need." Mary says, taking my beer and downing it.

I make the introductions and Mary shakes Peter's hand, taking the seat beside me. "Really, I'm not cut out for this bride shit." She guffaws. "I'd sooner have a destination wedding in a secluded island with ten people than deal with all this." she looks at me. "That Jennifer chick is insane."

"Tell me about it." I agree.

Peter laughs. "They call her 'Bridezilla'."

"Ain't that the truth." Mary says, filling the glass with more beer and drinking it. "Seriously. I'm done." She raises her hands in the air, as if in defeat. "I'm telling Chris that we're having a tiny wedding. We'll go nuts on the honeymoon, but the wedding...I'm keeping it small. I don't even want a fancy wedding dress. I just spent ten minutes talking with another dress designer, and my head is spinning."

"Well, it's your decision." Peter supplies. "I've told Kendra the same. We already have some money put away for her wedding, whenever it happens, but if she wants to use it for her education or for a down payment on a house, that's fine, too."

"Well, she's lucky." Mary comments. "My parents didn't save a dime for my wedding or for my education. Not that I'm complaining."

"I don't have an education, but my dad was stinking rich, so I could have had one if I wanted it." I add. "How much do you hate me now?" I'm being flippant.

"It's never too late, Wade." Mary jibes. "Look at Colton. He's got a Master's Degree in Aerodynamics."

"Yeah, but can he sing?" I say, lifting my glass. I start belting out Bon Jovi's 'Livin' on a Prayer', "Whooaaa, we're halfway there....whooaaa, we're livin' on a prayer, take my hand, we'll make it I swear....whoaaa, we're livin' on a prayer!" I get a few odd glances, but also a few whistles from a couple of girls walking by outside of the tent.

Mary smiles. "You're a goon, but you've got a great voice."

"Thanks."

Peter pours himself another beer and offers to top Mary's up. It appears my beer has been Bogarted. She takes the beer and clinks glasses with Peter. "To beers, queers, tears and Happy New Year's." Mary says.

Peter giggles. "I don't' believe I've heard that one before." Then something catches his eye. It's the rest of the clan walking by the tent. "Come on in and take a break." He calls.

When they reach our table, Peter says, "You just missed Wade's little serenade. He's got quite a voice, this young man."

"Well, thank you, sir." I say, bowing my head. Mary claps, playing along. Kendra smiles as they all sit at the table next to us, which is conveniently empty. "So, it must be a madhouse out there, Mary's converted after her exposure to this place...she no longer wants a big wedding."

Mary smirks. Her expression says, 'he's got that right'.

Kendra introduces me to her mother, Carol, who is

basically an older version of Kendra, complete with the ginger hair. "Nice to meet you." She says, giving me a surprisingly firm handshake.

"Likewise." I reply. "Your husband tells me you prefer wine. It doesn't look like there's any of that here, otherwise I'd treat you to a drink."

"That's okay, I'm the designated driver, anyway." She grins affectionately at Peter and he winks at her. They remind me a little of Colton and Julia with the way that they interact.

"I saw you talking to that dress designer." Jennifer comments to Mary. "I can give you the name of my dress designer if you like. I know there is a location in Florida."

"Thanks. That'd be great." Mary says.

"Shall we order another pint?" Peter offers. "Anyone else up for some beer?"

Everyone except Carol raises a hand in the air, making Peter chuckle. I raise my hand for the waitress. When she arrives and I order the beer, I notice Kendra is watching me, despite the breakout conversation between the rest of the girls at the other table.

"You thoroughly bored yet?" I ask Kendra.

"I don't know how girls do this. I could have gone my entire life without coming to a place like this. The women are vultures. I had no idea."

I nod. "My sister-in-law and my brother got married at their ranch. It was really small; like forty people tops. They rode the horses down the aisle and had a local pastor provide the service, which lasted like ten minutes. It was perfect. She had it catered, rented a tent in case of inclement weather, and hired a photographer. That's it."

"Seems to me that's the way to do it." she snorts. "This place is like the insane asylum for brides and grooms-to-be."

Why does it seem like we're planning our wedding? 'Kay, this is too weird. Ah, perfect, more beer.

As the waitress delivers the second pint, she winks

as she gives me a new glass. "Thanks," I say.

"No problem," she purrs. "I heard you singing. Aren't you the guy who plays at Mingles?"

My face heats. "Yeah, I am. You been there?"

"A few times." She says as I hand her the money for the pint. "I'll see you this Saturday."

I nod but I feel like crawling into a hole. How embarrassing. I expect Peter to glare at me, but instead he folds his arms across his chest expectantly and says, "I see what you mean. You're like a local celebrity."

"Hardly," I guffaw, trying to be modest. I pour myself a glass and as I take a sip, I look over at Kendra.

She's staring off in the distance, as though she's a million miles away. "You okay?" I ask.

Kendra shakes it off. "Fine."

I'd give a million dollars to know what's going on inside that head of hers.

Chapter 16

Kendra

The Surprise

It's a Monday night and I have work in the morning, but something is driving me to the bar where Wade plays. Dad gives me a look as I leave the house at nine-thirty to go to Mingles. That's about the only thing I miss about living away from home: my social life is between me and my four walls, nobody else. It can be tough to answer to someone after living away from home for so long. Dad asks where I'm heading, and I tell him.

"Oh, I see." He checks his watch. "It's a bit late for a work night."

"I'll be fine, dad. I'm not staying out late. I just wanted to talk to him about something to do with the case."

Dad lifts a brow. "Why don't you invite him to meet you at the office, at a more decent hour? That would be more appropriate, don't you think?"

I sigh. "Dad. I need you to give me some space, okay? I'm just working a few things out, and I need you not to question me."

He tips his head sideways. "Is this a personal issue? Wade says that the two of you didn't get off to a great start. He says that you're not fond of one another."

Shit, he said that?

"He's right. We met at the bar the night I went out with Jennifer and Wendy and a few girls from high school. It wasn't pleasant. I was very rude to him and he and his brother were rude right back. We've ironed out our differences now, so it's okay."

"Isn't it against the rules to get personally involved with a client?" Dad warns.

"I've covered my bases, dad." I explain to him that

I've maintained my pro bono status with everything that I've done for Wade. Assuring him that I haven't drawn outside the lines or made any exceptions. "Don't worry. The bar exam is in soon. I'll be ready."

Dad kisses my forehead. "You let me know if I need to show the boy my gun collection." He half jokes. "Is Wade expecting you?"

I scoff. "No. At this point he probably thinks he'll never see me again."

Hesitating, dad rises and walks toward the bottom of the stairs. "I trust your judgment, Kendra. I always have."

"Thanks, dad. Love you."

"Be safe. Love you, too."

As I slide into the driver's seat, I look in the rearview mirror at myself. Deciding to perhaps blend in a little more tonight, I take my hair down from the bun that it's in, and I fish out a pot of the lip gloss that Jennifer gave me in hopes that I might actually use it one day. Using my right ring finger, I smear a little on my lips and run a hand through my hair. Looking down at my wardrobe I realize that my blouse will do, but I need to undo a couple of buttons to reveal the chemise underneath. The dress pants are fine and so are the shoes. That's one thing about working in a legal office; you always have to dress top notch to look the part, especially when you're working your way up like I am.

I'm not exactly sure why I'm going to Mingles, but I know that I want to talk to Wade. Partly because I want to make sure he has his ducks in a row when he fires his manager. Wade has a cocky mouth, and he could easily get himself into trouble with it, especially if he's firing someone for the first time. I realize how upset he is at Chuck, and I don't want to see Wade in my office again, for something I *really* can't help him with.

Pulling into the parking lot at Mingles, I see a car pull in ahead of me. The car is familiar, but it doesn't hit me until the passenger appears, who the person is. My heart starts to beat faster, and I look around to see if there are any witnesses.

Shit!

Hesitating to get out of the car, I freeze, but my late-night guest comes right up and taps on the glass of my driver's side window. Suddenly, I'm face-to-face with my ex-boyfriend, Mark. Rolling down my window and inch with the engine still running, I see in his eyes that he's expecting me to roll the window all the way down.

My voice is flat. "What the hell do you want?"

"Can we talk?" he taps on the glass again, as if I can't hear his voice when the window is down a couple of inches.

"I have nothing to say to you. Please leave." I roll the window back up.

"Kendra, please." He begs. He's wearing the pair of black Levi's jeans I bought him for Christmas, and the sweater with Sheldon and Leonard from Big Bang Theory on it that I bought him for his birthday last year. Suddenly I realize I've spent way too much money on this asshole. His brown hair looks like it needs trimming; he usually keeps it very tidy and freshly cut short. "I need to talk to you."

Rolling down the window an inch again, I say. "Did you follow me here?"

"I didn't want to run into your dad again. He nearly chopped my balls off when I dropped those boxes off at your house. Tell your mom I said thanks for setting me up for that."

"She didn't set you up, my dad did." I seethe. "Now get the hell away from me before I call the cops."

Mark takes a step back and sighs. "Kendra, please. Didn't you get my letter?"

"I didn't read it. I've wasted enough time on you. You're wasting my time again. Now go away."

"I love you, Kendra." He whimpers. "Please. I'm begging you. I never meant to hurt you." His chin is quivering. I almost feel sorry for him, until I picture him in bed with the slut again. "It's over with that other girl. It was one night. I haven't spoken to her since." He pleads. There are tears running down his face. "I need you, Kendra." He gasps. "I even bought you a ring. I was going to give it to you at Christmas."

Keep digging, buddy.

"I'll do anything. Anything at all. Please. I can't afford the house on my own. I'm going to have to move back with my parents."

Poor baby, what the hell do you think I had to do? Buy another villa in France?

"Ever heard of a roommate?" I spit. "Maybe you can ask your slutty friend to move in with you."

"I told you I haven't spoken to her since." He cries. "I mean it. She means nothing to me."

"Ha, yet she meant enough to risk losing our relationship."

"I didn't know you were coming home early, Kendra." He gasps. "I wish I never did it."

I hope you're impotent and have a bad case of Gonorrhea, asshole!

"You can't take it back." I comment. "What's done is done and can never be undone. I'll never forgive you for it, Mark. I can't even look at you right now. You make me sick."

The spot beside me is empty. Mark sits Indian-style on the asphalt and cries like a baby, with his face buried in his hands. Part of me wants to sit beside him and console him, but the other part of me that wants to back up and run him over, is beating the crap out of the first part. "What exactly did you think would happen, Mark? How many times did you screw around behind my back to think you could get away with it again?"

"Do you think I'm an idiot? That I would take you back after a cooling off period, an apology and a few tears? No, I'm worth way more than that. I gave you so much and I've been so patient with you and with us. I deserve way better than this. The fact that you did what you did proves that that's what you think I deserve."

"I hate you. I've never hated anyone before, but I know for sure that I hate you. Don't ever come around me or my house again, or the next time, I won't stop my dad from bringing out his gun collection. He's not afraid of going to jail. Remember, he's served in the military. You 'd be smart to stay away."

I pull out of the spot, spinning my tires until I hear them squeal, just to make sure that I kick up enough dust at him. As I check in my side view mirror, I see that he at least had enough dignity left to get up out of the empty spot and get back into his car. Finding another spot, I slide out of my car and walk to the entrance. It feels odd coming to a bar alone again. I've never done that before, but the bouncer seems to recognize me as he doesn't ask to see my identification and he doesn't charge me a cover fee. "Thanks." I say.

"Wade's in the back. His set hasn't started yet."

I nod and walk inside. The lights are brighter, kind of like at a convention center, and the strobe lights and disco ball are not illuminated. Light rock music plays at a moderate level from overhead speakers. I'm guessing the speakers on the dance floor are the ones that are used when the music gets pumping. Tables are peppered throughout the space, filled modestly with people eating pub food and conversing.

The bartender sees me and asks me what I'll have. "Nothing. Actually, I'm here to see Wade Ford."

The man nods once. "He expecting you?"

"Not exactly."

"His set hasn't started yet. He's in the back, talking to his manager."

My eyes widen. "Then I've come at the perfect time. I'm his lawyer." I half lie.

Recognition comes to his face. "Aw, damn. My apologies. Name's Blake." He offers me his hand to shake.

I shake it. "Kendra. Kendra MacGregor."

He lifts a brow. "Scottish or Irish?"

"Irish." I smile.

"That would explain the red hair." He says. "I'll go get Wade."

"Thanks."

He winks as he walks away, tossing the towel he was holding over his right shoulder. About thirty seconds later, Blake returns, shaking his head. "Y'all don't wanna go back there, ma'am. They're screaming so loud at each other they can't hear me knocking on the door."

"Is the door locked?"

He shakes his head. "No, ma'am."

I gesture with my finger towards the bank of doors in the back hallway, where Blake came from. "Do you mind?"

He lifts his hand as if in defeat. "Suit yourself. I wouldn't want to get caught in the line of fire."

"I think I can handle it." I say, giving Blake a slight grin as I walk away. He's right, I can hear the yelling from the hallway.

"Chuck! You lying son of a bitch! Stop lying to me now!" Wade screams.

"I ain't lying about shit!" Chuck bellows back. I approach the door and turn the handle. When I open the door, I see the same room where Wade kissed me. The couch is in the same spot, so is the refrigerator. The couch is to the left as I open the door slowly. Chuck is sitting on the couch, arms flailing, and Wade is standing in front of him, screaming loud enough to wake the dead. Neither one of them acknowledge my presence since I've only got the door open slightly.

"That fucking trip to South Carolina wasn't cheap, Wade! I told you it ain't worth it to go to that dump!"

I interrupt, startling them both. "Actually, your earnings would have been twice as much on that trip, but it seems you pocketed forty percent."

Chuck lifts a hand. "Who the fuck's this bitch?" he gives me an evaluating glance, looking me up and down, like I'm wearing an outfit made entirely out of aluminum foil.

Wade is about to lunge at him, but I run and grab him by the shoulders. "Don't do anything you'll regret,

Wade."

"She's my lawyer, asshole! You watch your mouth!"

Chuck cranes his head back. "Since when do *you* have a lawyer? You can't even afford a decent pair of shoes!"

"Yes," I retort. "Thanks to you and pocketing most of his earnings."

Pursing his lips, Chuck shakes his head. "You don't know nothin'."

"I know plenty, Mr. Midel. If it wasn't for the fact that you don't have a valid contract with the band, Mr. Ford here would have grounds to sue you."

"You're done, Chuck." Wade says, stiffening. "Get the hell out of here and don't ever come back."

"You'll never find a manager who'll put up with your shit, Wade, and you know it." Chuck argues. "Your whoring around and all...I set you up with half those chicks, man. All that drinking during a set...that ain't allowed in the real world. You won't get away with half the shit you do now if you go and get another manager." He scoffs. "And you ain't got shit for talent, neither. Ain't nobody's ever gonna give you a record deal or nothin'! You'll be stuck for the rest of your life singing in armpit bars around the state."

The muscles in Wade's jaw are clenched. His chest is heaving up and down and the veins in his neck are visible. He's about to blow and I have to stop it.

"Mr. Midel, you were politely asked to leave." My voice is firm. "I suggest you do so before I call the authorities, and have you removed."

Blake is at the door. I have no idea how long he's been there. "Chuck?"

Chuck looks up at Blake. "Yeah?"

Blake's face is like stone. "Get out." he says coldly. "Now."

Gingerly, Chuck rises, scratching his head as though trying to figure out what just happened. Wade stares at a spot on the floor while his now former manager walks out. Blake glares at Chuck as he walks past him to get through the door. Chuck just swallows, hesitating for a second, and leaves. Wade looks at Blake, walks over to him and fishes out a wad of cash from his pocket. "What's this for?" Blake asks, puzzled.

Wade turns, focuses on a spot on the wall. His nostrils flare and his fists ball up as his jaw clenches tightly. His right arm lifts as he drives a hard punch into the wall, causing a huge hole to appear. The contact sounds like a cannon. Drywall dust flakes to the floor as Wade stands there, lifts his arm again, and drives another punch into the wall beside the other hole. It sounds like fireworks going off on the fourth of July.

Before he does it again, I grasp his arm with my hand. "Wade, Wade, you're going to hurt yourself." I whisper, standing in front of him. We're practically nose to nose. His pupils are dilated, and his eyes are wild, the way a shooter's eyes look right after he pulls the trigger on his victim. "Nothing Chuck said is true. You...are a very talented artist. I would never have gone to the lengths that I have for you if I didn't believe that. Chuck just said that to get back at you. He knows he's in the wrong. He wanted to say that just to hurt you."

"She's right." Blake says. "I'd never let you play here if you didn't have talent. I always wondered why you never went any further, and I always thought it was your choice. Never knew it was because of Chuck."

Wade's chest begins to slow. He breaks eye contact to glance at his knuckles. They're red but not swollen yet.

"I'll get some ice." Blake says. "Be right back."

Wade is silent. As if in shock. His jaw muscles are still working. He swallows and blinks finally, as if coming out of a trance. He looks at the damage he's inflicted on the wall. I remain silent, letting what just happened sink in. I've seen this look before on my dad. I know to intervene only when necessary. Blake returns a minute later. Wade hasn't moved. Blake wraps the ice around Wade's knuckles, using a dish towel.

He looks at Wade and gives him a pat on the shoulder. "You think you can go on tonight? It's no trouble if you can't. It's pretty slow out there tonight being a Monday and all."

Wade licks his lips, staring at his hand. "Yeah. I can go on, just give me a minute."

"Take all the time you need." Blake says, patting him on the shoulder again, this time twice.

When we're alone, I remove the towel from Wade's hand. "Flatten your hand." I ask.

He does it without a problem.

"Close your fist."

No problem. I put the ice back on his hand. "I don't think you broke anything, but you're going to feel that tomorrow."

He says nothing. It's like he's catatonic. I carry on. "If Chuck comes after you just let me know. He can't sue you for wrongful dismissal since he wasn't employed by you. If you had hit him," I glance at the wall. "We would be having a different conversation." I clear my throat. "Why don't you have a seat...I'll get you some water."

He blinks again and backs up onto the couch. As I pull a bottle of water out of the mini fridge, I loosen the cap for him, and hand it to him. "Drink this. Take some deep breaths, and we'll check your hand again."

Wade does as he's instructed and downs half the bottle of water. I scooch down in front of him. "You're going to run into a lot of people like that in your life, Wade. People who are going to take advantage of you. Believe me, money or not, people can be vicious." I start to babble, believing that talking to him is calming him down. "You think they're looking after you, that you're all on the same team, and next thing you know..." I look up at him, he's staring at a spot on the floor. I continue, "they're not."

"Even—"

Wade interrupts. "Kendra? Why are you here?" he asks, as though I've just arrived.

I was prepared for this. "Because I knew you were going to talk to Chuck tonight. I wanted to make sure I didn't get a collect call from you...from jail." I gesture towards the wall. "Looks like I was right on the money."

"Kendra, I've been looking after myself for as long as I can remember. I looked after my brother Colton, when he came back from Afghanistan, broken and half-dead. I looked after my dad before he died...I don't need anyone to look after me."

My focus is divided between both his eyes as I'm still squatting in front of him on the couch. "Maybe you're right. Maybe you don't need anyone to look after you. But maybe it's okay to have someone on your side to help you. Maybe it's okay to have someone on your team, rooting for you. Maybe it's okay to have someone who..." I look away.

Why am I getting so intense over this?

With his left hand, he takes my chin and directs it back towards his face. When our eyes are level, he continues. "Who what?" he asks, his gaze isn't sexual or antagonizing. He just wants to know what I'm thinking.

"Who believes in you." I say with conviction.

He lets that sink in for a minute, releasing my chin from his grasp. My legs have turned to jelly from squatting for so long, so I rise and sit beside him on the couch. "How's it feel?" I ask, gesturing with my chin towards his hand.

"Fine." He answers, back in a trance. He tightens the hold on the towel, so it's closer to his knuckles. He swallows and looks over at me. His voice is soft. "I've got four brothers, a couple of uncles, some bandmates, some bar co-workers, but until tonight, I never had a friend...especially a female one."

My voice is equally soft. "Girls are good to have around for more than just sex, Wade."

"I suppose you're right." He smiles and leans into me affectionately. I push him playfully, making him have to bend over to the other side of the couch. Then he changes tack. "So, who's the guy?" he gestures at me with his chin.

A 'v' forms between my brows. "What guy?" I guffaw.

"All that talk about people taking advantage and you thinking that they're looking after you and all...you couldn't have been talking about a girl."

I'm half impressed that he was actually listening, and half embarrassed. "So, you *were* paying attention."

He shrugs. "If I've learned nothing else from being a singer, it's to pay attention to your audience."

Sighing, I chew the inside of my mouth, buying time. "A couple of weeks ago I came home to find my live-in boyfriend doing some ugly slut in our bed."

"Ouch."

"Yeah."

"So, what did you do?"

"Threw hot candle wax at them both. Moved back in with my parents."

"Yowza!" Wade points at the wall. "I've got a pretty mean punch. You want me to go beat him up? I'll do it." he tips his head sideways, as if to say, 'I'm not kidding'.

"That's okay. I left him sobbing in the parking lot earlier. He followed me here to beg for my forgiveness."

"Now that's one thing I've never done...cheated on a girl."

I lean into him. "That's because you've never been in a relationship long enough to cheat, Wade." I'm matter-of-fact.

"This is true. But still, I've never done that before. A lot of guys have."

"Very noble." I'm facetious. "How many girls have you slept with and then never called them again?"

He stares at the floor sheepishly.

I point at him and smile. "Judging by how many times your phone goes off, I'd say that happens a lot."

"Busted." He admits, as he looks at his watch. "Shoot, I better get out there. You staying to watch?"

"For a little while, but I have to work in the morning."

"Okay." He looks at my lips and leans in. His kiss is soft, enveloping my bottom lip between both his lips, and it lingers for a second, making a smacking sound. "Thanks. For being here tonight." He whispers against my lips.

My heart beats wildly as I sit in shock, the most shocking part being...I kissed him back. Although it only lasted a few seconds, they were the most passionate three seconds I've ever had in my life. "You're welcome." I say, surprised I can speak after that.

As he rises, he slides his left hand over my ear and under my chin. His gaze doesn't leave mine until he leaves the room.

...I kissed him back.

Chapter 17

Wade

My fist hurts like hell but it was worth it. If Kendra hadn't been there, I would have probably ripped Chuck to shreds. I was already primed to punch him before she arrived. When he called her a bitch, that was it. He was history. It's pretty amazing how she's being such a great supporter when we haven't slept together. I thought women only felt that bond with a guy after sex. Maybe some of the things my dad taught me about women weren't the best lessons. Since my mom left, I suppose my dad was a little biased. Shit like that trickles down over the years. But even if Kendra and I never see each other again after today, at least she's shown me something way more valuable than my parents ever did.

But I definitely want to see her. She's great. It's amazing what a difference a day makes. Twenty-four hours ago, we were each other's nemeses. Now we're good friends. Except that I kissed her. Not sure if that was right or not, but it felt right. She didn't punch me or slap me, or even tell me off. In fact, if I recall correctly, she kissed me back. Oh yeah, she kissed me back. Now, she might tell me later that it was a bad idea, and not to let it happen again, but if so, I'm cool with it.

Blake is really cool; he's set up a spare table for Kendra so she can sit right up at the stage. Never done that before. I'm singing my heart out, trying to ignore the screaming pain in my hand, as I keep in close eye contact with Kendra. A blonde walks by the stage and gives me goo-goo eyes, but I don't pay much attention. I don't want to piss Kendra off. She's watching intently and I saw the icy stare she gave the blonde as she passed by her table. I like that look. It's hot.

As I hit some high notes, Kendra gives me a thumbs

up, as she literally grooves away at the table. She's so cool. In some moments, it kind of feels like it's just her and I here tonight. When a slow song is up next, I ask her over the mic if she wants to come up on stage, but she shakes her head no. I try to coax her but she's adamant. So, I sing, to her mostly, as I feel my hand swelling by the minute. It's getting difficult to play my guitar without hitting multiple strings. It's starting to sound like shit, so I take a break after the slow song, and Kendra goes to get me more ice.

Blake sees my knuckles, which have swollen to nearly twice their normal size and he shakes his head. "Wade, call it a night. It's slow anyway, and you've been up there over an hour. It's cool."

I feel bad, shortchanging Blake, but it's true...I sound like shit playing the guitar and a lot of my songs are guitar-based. "Sorry, man."

"No apologies necessary." Blake nods. "Y'all let me know how you are tomorrow. If you need to take a couple of days off, so be it. Get to the doctor if that gets much worse." He says to both me and Kendra.

"Will do." Kendra says to Blake, and then she addresses me. "Do you need to get anything?"

"No, the guys'll store my stuff for me."

"Have a good one, Wade, Kendra." Blake says.

"Goodnight, Blake." We both say.

"My car's in the back." I say. "How about we go get it and I'll drive you over to your car in the front?

"Sounds good. Lead the way."

My hand was throbbing before the ice, but now it's starting to calm down. As we approach my shit box, I try to fish my keys out of my pocket. "Ah, fuck!" I hiss, wincing from the pain of using my injured right hand to get the keys out of my right pocket.

I laugh, but it isn't really funny. "Kendra, you're gonna have to help me out here. Can you get my keys out of my pocket, please?"

She closes one eye. "What a guy won't do." She jokes.

I know this is going to be tricky. Did I mention these are cheap jeans? With really deep pockets? Like...pockets that go down way past my...stuff?

"Okay, I'll try to be a grownup here, but you're going to have to dig." I show her how far down my keys are. Of course, they're literally right beside the bulge.

She shrugs. "I can handle it. Can you?"

I'm impressed. "I can if you can." I purse my lips together. I try to push the keys over with my other hand first, but she gets impatient.

"Geez, Wade, just let me do it." she whines, frustrated.

I close one eye, mirroring her expression a few moments ago. "What a girl won't do."

That gets an eye roll. "Hardy har, come here."

Before I know it, she shoves her hand down my pocket, into my pants, hitting a tickle spot I didn't know existed. "Ah!" I shriek.

"What? Did I touch...it?" she gasps, freezing.

"Kendra, I assure you, if you touched it, I wouldn't have just screamed like a girl. You just...tickled me."

She looks at me. "Wade Ford is ticklish?"

"Yeah, don't spread it around." I say, as she starts fishing down further. "Keep your hand to the right, Kendra." I joke.

"Very funny."

She grasps them and pulls them out, just lightly touching my bits from the side. It doesn't give me a hard-on, but the gentle way she fixes my pocket afterward, does. "You...um...didn't have to do that."

"Well that annoys the crap out of me when *my* pants do that." She's matter-of-fact and adamant.

I push the key fob to unlock the door, and I use my left hand to open the passenger side door for her. "Why thank you, Mr. Ford."

"You're welcome, Ms. MacGregor." I play along.

As I slide into the driver's side, Kendra offers to put the key into the ignition for me. When she turns the key, the car hesitates. "Am I doing it wrong?" she asks.

"You turned the key, right?" I say, equally confused.

She tries again. Just the dashboard light comes on. "Did I break your car?"

"No." I chuckle, thinking this normally would be an easy situation to rectify. I'd just go back into the bar and either get a ride from one of the band members or crash on the couch. But it's only after ten o'clock. Nobody's leaving the bar for a few hours yet.

"Well, um, do you want me to give you a ride home?" Kendra offers.

I consider my options. "Yeah, I guess that would work. You sure it's not out of the way?"

"No, not at all." She says.

Her car is way nicer than mine. I drive a twelve-year-old Kia Sportage, she drives a four year old Toyota Rav4. "This is bitchin'!" I say, climbing into the passenger side.

"I bought it off a lease. It's been in a minor accident. That's how I got it so cheap." She admits. "That and my dad started sharing fun facts about guns with the car salesman."

I bark out a laugh. "Man, me and your dad think alike." She puts the car into drive, and I continue. "Tell me something."

"What?" We pull out of the parking lot and begin the trek to my house.

"How the hell did that shithead you were living with get past your dad? Did you not tell your dad what happened with him and the slut?"

She gives me a knowing look and smiles like the Cheshire Cat. "Dad took him on a personal tour of his gun collection when I wasn't home."

I slap my leg, laughing. "I think I'm gonna do that. Get me a gun collection. Show it to my daughter's dates and boyfriends. That'll work." I frown, nodding once, satisfied. "My dad had boys, so it's kind of on the receiving end here. Except we always had the 'don't get girls pregnant' speech."

"And you never worry? About getting someone pregnant? Weren't you terrified when Priscilla approached you?"

Her cadence is disarming. For the first time in forever I feel like it's safe to let my guard down. "You wanna know the truth?"

"Yeah,"

"I don't sleep with that many women at all." I admit. "I like people to think I do, because it's the whole 'rock star' persona." I air quote. "But the truth is, it doesn't happen a lot. It's better when people think I do, though."

"Why?"

"Sex, drugs, and rock & roll, baby. That's how we roll in the industry. And I don't do drugs, so if I don't have a lot of sex, what the hell else is there?"

"So...when was the last time you....?" She trails off.

"Now that's getting personal, counsellor." I joke.

"I'll tell you if you tell me."

"Six months ago." I admit after a beat. "But I'm making you sign one of those NDA things for that."

She nods, as if keeping our personal sharing a secret is inherent. "Now I don't feel so bad. That's about how long it's been for me."

"Who was the rejector and who was the rejectee?" I ask, feeling bold.

"Surprisingly, neither of us." She scoffs. "We seemed to have lost our fizz once we moved in together. At least that's what I told myself. He was probably messing around then, anyway. I'm not even sure why he agreed to move in with me if he was cheating. What's the point?"

"Half off rent and living expenses, sex from the live-in when the sluts aren't around. I, at least, live alone. I don't inflict my life on anyone else."

"Well, once I pass the bar exam, things are going to be a lot better. My parents aren't asking me for rent, so I've been socking away everything, saving for a house. But it's tough doing it alone."

We reach my house and she puts her car into park.

"I know what you mean. But hey, you're going to be

a lawyer, lawyers make a ton of money, right?"

I see the shadow of a grimace cross her face. "What's that look for?"

"You still have that NDA?" she half jokes.

"Sure," I shrug. "I've shown you my cards in confidence. Feel free to show me yours."

"Truth is. I don't think I really want to be a lawyer." She looks at me, as if silently pleading me not to judge her. "At least not a sit-down-and-do-law-stuff-forty-hours-a-week kind. I think that's why I failed the bar the first time."

Reaching for her face, I shake my head. "More and more about you is making sense every minute." I release her.

"What do you mean?"

"When we first met, you were so uptight and pissed off over nothing. Now I know why. Because some dickhead dumped on you the day before. You were the same way when I came into your office, and now I know why. You're never going to be happy with your life until you're in a happy place, Kendra." I pause. "My happy place is on stage. I love what I do, and I don't care how much or how little I make doing it. Truth is, I'm more pissed off that Chuck betrayed me than I am about how much money he sucked out of me. Another piece of truth is," I lick my lips as a pause, and lift a finger, "We still got that NDA out, right?"

She nods. "My dad left me millions, just like my brothers. I don't get it until I'm thirty or married, whichever comes first. Nobody, and I mean nobody, knows that. I'm a goddamn trust fund kid. But as far as I'm concerned, none of that shit means anything to me, because I'm already richer than any rich guy, because I'm doing what I love, every day. Nobody is ever going to take that away from me, or take advantage of me, ever again, so long as I can help it."

"It shows, Wade." She nods. "That you love what you do. You have this Blue Rodeo-meets Bryan Adams-meets Bon Jovi kind of voice, and it's beautiful. I envy you. I really do. Not many people love what they do or have the opportunity to do what they love to do. That's a true gift. And I'm happy that you have it. You deserve it."

"And you're bright, driven, completely self-confident and self-sufficient, and even if you don't love it, you make one hell of a lawyer. No lawyer would go the distance that you have for me. And you do it without making money at it. It's amazing."

Looking at my house, Kendra gestures towards it. "This isn't bad."

I chuckle. "Don't get too excited. I live in the basement."

"Oh, shoot, I'm sorry."

"Don't be. It's really not bad at all." I undo my seatbelt. "Have you got five minutes? Come on in, I can show you."

She hesitates for a second. "Five minutes? Remember, I've got to work in the morning."

"At least help me unlock my door." I chuckle, lifting my right hand.

"Okay." She relents.

But I haven't locked my door in five years.

Chapter 18

Kendra

Oh, man. The second I left my parent's place tonight I knew that something had crossed over in me. Now that Wade and I have this...connection, there's no turning back. But is it so bad? Honestly, Mark and I had an intellectual connection; we were both nerds and into trivia and challenging one another on intelligent topics, but this is different. Wade has a lot of street smarts, and up until now, I didn't realize how much of that I have, too. This man is more than meets the eye, and it's kind of scary, but it's also refreshing. I've never had this type of connection before with the opposite sex.

Realizing how much he cares about his music, and the fact that his mission in life isn't to bang as many girls as humanly possible, it gives me a whole new perspective of him. What's also reassuring is that he isn't superficial; he has feelings and isn't materialistic. I kind of had that impression based on his wardrobe and the fact that he couldn't afford a real lawyer, but in reality, he doesn't really care about the money that is due to him. That is worth it's weight in gold. Male or female, I don't know anyone who cares less about money than Wade Ford.

When I stuck my hand in his pocket, it was kind of exciting, but at the same time it was completely embarrassing. For him and for me. There's a story we can tell for a long time to come. At least he wasn't lewd about it, as I'm sure, given the same opportunity, any other guy would have behaved inappropriately. Wade has invited me into his house, but the way he positioned his invitation didn't seem threatening. He asked if I had five minutes, which clearly means he doesn't intend for me to stay any longer than that. What harm can come of this? We're friends. But that kiss...actually, since we're counting...both kisses.... Ironically, the second one seemed hotter than the first one. I haven't been able to get either one out of my head.

Wade hands me his keys and I open the door for him. It's the side entrance of the house, and it has a small mudroom behind the outside door. From outside, I can see a small laundry room with an almost empty laundry basket sitting on top of the stackable washer. The house is a two-storey detached dwelling. It has cream-white siding all the way up to the smoke-colored roof. The front of the house would be bland if not for the hanging baskets of what I can only guess are artificial flowers that sit on the windowsills of the double-paned bay window. The window blinds are closed, but the slats have a subtle flower pattern painted on them, that matches nicely with the artificial flowers.

Wade chuckles. "To be honest, I can't actually remember if I locked my door or not. My brother Jack was razzing me about that the other day.

Just as he says this, the door latch disengages, and the door opens. "Ah, I guess I did lock it after all."

As we step inside, the linoleum floor is shiny and clean, with just a pair of shoes tucked neatly by the doorway. "The same key works for that door." Wade says, gesturing at the wooden door on the other side of the mudroom. I tuck the key inside the hole, but nothing disengages.

"Oh, I guess I didn't bother to lock that one." Wade says, giving the door a push from behind me. His arm grazes my side as he opens the door, and he places it on my hip after he opens the door in front of me. "Watch your step." He says, indicating the stairs below. Using his injured hand, he flips the light switch at the top of the stairs, illuminating a small set of wooden stairs with a plastic, notched runner spanning all the way down to the bottom floor. "After you."

As I walk down the stairs, I can smell the faint scent of Wade's shower soap. He doesn't wear cologne, but the shower soap smells equally nice. I was expecting to smell mildew or sweat from a guy's apartment, so I'm pleasantly surprised. The door at the bottom of the stairs isn't locked because there is no keyhole, it just has a knob. I open it and he flips the light on from the wall. His apartment is small but very cozy and cute.

"It's not much, but it's mine." He says, tossing his keys on the breakfast bar that is just a few steps from the door. There are two bar stools under the breakfast bar, which is just a bump-out from the kitchen itself, that runs along the main wall about three feet from the door. The kitchen has a small, single metal sink with a gooseneck faucet, cupboards above and below the sink, which is immediately after the breakfast bar, closest to the door. There is no stove, just a cooktop range with a floating hood vent above. A large, glass encrusted light hangs above the kitchen, which is clearly on a dimmer switch, since I see Wade turning it up brighter. "I usually leave the lights low for when I come home at ungodly hours."

To the right of the door is the refrigerator and garbage can, and then a door that leads to what I assume is the washroom. The living room is tiny with just a pull-out couch that faces the sliding glass doors that lead to the backyard, and a dresser to the left of the couch, and a coffee table that is off to the side, against the wall. "Good thing I pulled out the couch before I left. I usually do, anyway."

"You mean you don't have a real bed?" I ask, horrified.

"No, sugar, I don't. This is a studio apartment. There is no bedroom."

"Well, I hope your bathroom kicks ass." I joke.

"It's...clean." He states, looking for another word but he clearly can't find it. "You can go check it out yourself."

I take two steps and can see it all. He has a glass-enclosed shower, a white, pedestal sink, and a white porcelain toilet to match. There is a small, square-shaped stool along the main wall. "Is that where you keep your linens?"

"And toiletries and stuff." He explains.

"Well, for the little space you have, you sure do a great job keeping it clean." I comment.

"You are my witness." He says, taking a bow. "You want anything to drink? I've got some beer and stuff in the fridge."

"No, I'm fine. Thanks." I say, looking at his hand. "Do you have ice?"

He catches my gaze and lifts his hand up. The towel is soaked through with melted ice. "Yeah. I've got lots. I'll change this."

"No, let me." I say, taking the towel. I lift his hand to inspect it. The swelling has come down a lot, and it's only red now because of the ice. "Looks a lot better."

"Yeah, I can still punch that ex-boyfriend of yours out if you want."

I cock my head to the side. "You do have a mean streak in you, don't you." I comment.

"Na, I just have low tolerance for bullshit." His voice is low as he looks at me.

The charge in the air changes. I clear my throat. "Do you have any Advil or something for the pain?"

"Na, I don't need anything. It doesn't hurt anymore."

"You'll feel it in the morning." I say, taking the towel from him and walking towards the fridge. The top part is a freezer. I open the door and pull out a plastic ice tray.

"You've mentioned that before." He adds. "It's not like a hangover. I'll probably be fine in the morning. I'm fine now, but I want to keep the ice on as a precaution. I mean, let's face it, my hands and my voice are what keep me fed."

When I'm done refilling the towel with ice and re-wrapping it, I bring it over to Wade and help him re-wrap his knuckles. "Feel better?" I ask, unable to hide the smirk on my face.

He catches on. One side of his face lifts into a crooked smile that's adorable. "What's the look for?"

"Nothing." I lie.

"Well, I was just going to test how good you feel, since I can't stand a big baby." I say as I reach into my pocket, and pull out the extra ice cube I saved just for the occasion, tossing it through the neck of his shirt.

He immediately jumps, pushing his torso backward to avoid the ice cube coming into contact with his skin. But it's too late. He winces, "Ah....cold! Cold!" he laughs. I'm laughing so hard, not trying to help him at all, even though he's trying to get the ice cube out using one hand. "You're cruel," he laughs. He can't get the ice cube. It's impossible to do with one hand. He looks like a contortionist. "Just keep laughing, lady." He mock-warns, "Your turn is coming." He grunts as he makes one last attempt to try and retrieve the ice cube from inside his shirt. "Is this like with the keys? Do you want to slip your hand in there and get the ice out? Or am I going to have to untuck my shirt and do it the easy way?"

I guffaw. "Well, I'm not sticking my hand in there."

He pulls at his shirt and part of it lifts out of his pants. The ice cube falls to the floor. He looks at it, and then at me, as if prompting me to pick it up before he does and tosses it down my shirt. "Don't even try it." I warn, laughing.

His shirt is soaked since the ice was in there for so long. He pulls it over his head with his left arm and picks up the ice cube off the floor with his shirt. "I'll get you back." He says.

But I can't stop staring. Wade Ford is cut as good as those strippers I saw with Jennifer and Wendy. He sees the look of shock in my eyes. "Sorry. I'll go put another shirt on." But I don't want him to. He has a beautiful body. Six pack abs, a tight stomach, and his belly button is flat. His shoulders are perfectly toned, and he has one tiny tattoo on the left side of his chest. It's what I guess is Chinese script. He watches my gaze. "I have no idea what it means, I just liked the pattern. Sounds stupid, I know."

As he turns his back to me, I bite my lip. His back is

beautiful, too. The muscles move every time he does. I can't take my eyes off him. He's looking for something as he heads over to the dresser. He seems to sense that I'm watching him. "You okay?"

"I...I just wondered...how do you stay in such good shape? Do you have a gym down here or something?"

He bends down to the third drawer in his dresser. "No, I've got a gym membership. I work out just about every day. What about you?"

"Yeah, I go to the gym, too. It's kind of a requirement unless I want to have a pancake ass. Desk jobs will do that to you."

"I guess you're right there. Shoot, my shirts are all in the dryer upstairs." He says as he closes the drawer. He walks by me and I have to all but remind myself to close my mouth. "I'll be right back." He says, touching my cheek. Instinctively, I close my eyes. His feet don't move. My eyes open when I realize he's still there. "You sure you're okay?" he whispers.

"Yeah," I murmur. "I just...I never knew you...looked like that underneath."

"Was it easier picturing me with a flabby gut and man breasts?" he smiles, still whispering.

"Yeah,"

"Well, then I'm one up on you." His voice is low and sultry. "I keep picturing you with warts all over. I'm sure glad I didn't put an ice cube down your shirt to find out what *you* look like underneath. I think I'd just about die. And what a way to go."

His eyes are so blue I can't take it. His hair is mussed from taking his shirt off. I want to run my fingers through it to straighten it out...or mess it up more...not sure what would be sexier. My hormones are raging through my bloodstream like lightning. I'm inches from his body and I can feel the heat of it. I swallow and stare at his lips. He watches my gaze.

"I'm not going to make a move on you, Kendra. The ball's in your court this time." He murmurs. His hand is still on my face as his thumb brushes the side of my cheek. Those full lips are silently begging me to kiss them, and I try like hell to take a step back, but I can't. Wade Ford is what I want. He's everything I've wanted. I just didn't know it until now. I wait only a split second more before I lean into him and envelope his lips with mine.

A sexy grunt comes from his throat as he wraps his arms around me and lifts my feet from the ground, kissing me back like if he didn't, his life would end. "Your hand," I whisper against his lips.

"It's fine." He says, as he gently tucks his tongue inside my mouth. I tip my head sideways so I can take it all in. He's one hell of a kisser. It's not even a kiss. It's more like he's making love to my mouth. His strong, naked arms around me and his rugged chest against me, it's like an all-encompassing body kiss. He slowly walks, carrying me in his arms, to the couch, and lowers me down onto it. Briefly, he breaks contact, as he stares at me. "Nothing is going to happen unless you want it to." He says, kissing me softly. "You just say the word, Kendra, and it stops."

But I don't want him to stop. Ever. He's barely touched me and it's like my body has burst into flames. Every inch of me that he's touched is heated and throbbing. I run my fingers through his hair, deciding it looks better messy, and pull him towards me, feeling hungry once again for his touch. His kisses are deeper as I feel his weight on me. With his shirt off, I feel his soft skin and hard muscles, and it's such a sexy combination. My fingertips gently claw at his skin as he continues to kiss me in a way that leaves me breathless.

His hands find my sides, and he begins cupping my body all the way up. He undoes the buttons on my blouse and pulls the material open, revealing my chemise underneath. "Take it off," I request, wanting desperately to feel his skin on mine.

"Are you sure?" he breathes, kissing the side of my neck.

"God, yes." I beg, pulling at the lapel, as if my shirt is

on fire.

Wrapping my arm around his neck, he pulls me up so I can get one sleeve off, and then we make it a team effort to do the same on the other side. He tosses my blouse over the side of the couch as we're nose-to-nose. His long eyelashes brush his cheeks as he gazes at me as though I'm some beautiful work of art that needs examining. "You're so beautiful, Kendra." He whispers. "I've never met anyone more beautiful."

Any other girl would think that's a line, but his voice is so intense and full of conviction, I know he means it. The comment spurs me on. I take his lips in mine, kissing him deeply. I can feel his hardness below his belt, and it makes my thighs throb with need. I want to know what he's like under the zipper. It's a hot thought that forces me to push my hand down there. He leans up a little to give me access. "Mmmm...." He purrs, feeling the pressure of my hand against his most sensitive area. He cups my breast and begins pressing his lips against my nipple from under the chemise. Even under two layers, the contact is heavenly. I rear my chest up, letting him have full access. "I'd love to take this shirt off...are you okay with that?" he asks, like a gentleman. It's so hot.

In answer to his question, I use my hands to pull the chemise up from my dress pants. He helps by pulling the shirt over my head and placing it on top of my blouse. "Take this off, too." I say, struggling to find the fasteners to my bra at my back.

"No, not yet." He murmurs, cupping my breasts in his hands, as if savoring them. Kissing the soft flesh that is spilling out from my bra, he's driving me insane.

"Wade, I'm dying." I beg. "Take the bra off."

"If you say so." He says against my skin, as he kisses closer and impossibly closer to my nipple, and he inches his hands behind my back, reaching for the fastener. When he undoes it, he lifts my bra up, revealing my breasts. "God, Kendra. I didn't think it could get any better."

"My chest isn't nearly as beautiful as yours." I say breathlessly as he takes my nipple in his mouth, kneading it with his lips pressed up against his teeth, using his lips as a sheath. The feeling is my undoing. I moan and he reaches his hand down between my legs, pulsing the heel of his hand against me. As he flicks my nipple with the tip of his tongue, I just about lose it. Pushing my hand down to the button of my pants, I undo them and unzip the zipper.

He lifts so he can see my face. His voice is sexy as hell; not quite a whisper, but loud enough for only my ears. "Are you sure you want to take those off? After that, there's no turning back." I don't even hesitate. I begin pulling my pants down with some effort. He kisses the tip of my nose and then rises, helping me pull them off. Then he does something that both surprises and excites me. Wade drapes my pants over the rest of my clothes, and unbuttons his pants, gazing at me with such a burning intensity, I bite my lip.

As he unzips the zipper, he lowers his pants down just enough so I can see a fraction of the head of his penis. "I'll warn you...I'm not wearing any underwear. I can't compete with those frilly things." He says, looking at my panties. Why I wore my fanciest ones, I have no idea. As he pulls his jeans down, exposing himself fully, I lick my lips instinctively. He's beautiful. It's perfect. I sit up, and he removes his socks, then he bends down and removes mine. "Do you want me to take those off?" he asks, glancing at my underwear.

I look at his hardened penis and whisper. "Hell, yeah."

He walks over to the dresser and opens the bottom drawer, lifting a box of condoms out. Removing one, he tosses the box back into the drawer and closes it. I don't want to seem like I'm easy, but I figure I should tell him the truth. "Wade."

"Yeah," he lifts his head, walking back to me. Him walking with an erect penis is so freaking hot.

"I'm on the pill. And I've had a physical recently."

"Oh. Me, too." he doesn't know how to react. "Do you want to still use one, just as back up?"

I don't really want to. I've never been a fan of condoms, hence going on the pill. "It's up to you. I've never missed a pill."

He tosses it on top of my clothes. "I'll leave it up to you then."

Placing his hands on my waist, he pulls at the lace on the waistband of my panties, and slowly lowers them. As he does, he kisses my belly, and just about every inch of flesh he can find as he exposes me fully. He continues to kiss all the way down my legs and on the insides of my thighs. I giggle and flinch as he hits my tickle spot. "Ah, I found one." He whispers against my skin. I can feel him smile.

"Mmmm..." I moan as he moves up and sucks the flesh by my underwear area. He's not hit the jackpot yet, but he's close, and he's teasing me. Blowing on my hairs he kisses me...there. "Oh, god, Wade." I whine.

"What do you want?" He asks, teasing me again, like he's dangling a carrot in front of me.

"Oh, you're cruel." I chuckle.

He laughs softly against my throbbing flesh, and then sucks me...there. "Oh, god, Wade." I hiss, "I'm not sure if you want to do that. I'm a one orgasm kind of girl."

He pauses his sucking, but gently forces his index and middle finger inside. "Maybe with *him* you were." He comments, and then sucks again, this time as he pulses his fingers in and out. Sending a shockwave of pleasure through me. "I'm going to make you come once, really hard and fast. You ready?"

I'm writhing on the bed. My body is quickly responding to his movements. I'm at his mercy. He hasn't stopped pulsing his fingers inside my body. And he doesn't wait for my answer. He sucks and then licks rhythmically, doing one and then the other, while I grab hold of the sheets with both my hands. I'm climbing so fast my belly is compulsively pushing, as if I'm in labor.

I can feel the veins in my neck pop out. My back is arched. He stops sucking for a second. "Let it out Kendra. Don't hold back." He says quickly.

"Ohhhh!" I cry out, sounding more like an animal than a human. He speeds up, shooting me to the stars as I scream while my orgasm rips through me. I feel wet and all my muscles are pulsing, each one giving me mammoth pleasure. Wade doesn't stop until I beg him to.

"I think you still have one left in there." He says, slowing down only a fraction, and this time focusing more on using the top of his tongue against my flesh. I've never had two orgasms back to back,

"That's not possible, Wade." I pant, as my heart is pounding out of my chest. At first, when the orgasm is over, his contact is ticklish and overly sensitive, but when he changes pace and makes the pressure slightly stronger, it feels good, and I relax, letting him give it a try. "My, that does feel kind of good." He pumps it up a notch and moves his tongue quicker. "Oh, wow." I whisper, feeling myself climb a little. He's moving his fingers so they're right up against the upper wall of my pelvis. I can see his arm muscles working and it's so hot. I look down and see his tongue dancing up and down and around on my clit. I've never seen anything so sexy. His eyes meet mine and he winks. *Have mercy!*

He gently pulls his fingers out of me and with both his hands, he reaches up and places his index fingers and thumbs around my nipples, squeezing them deliciously and with the perfect amount of pressure. "Mmmmm.....oh, Wade." I can feel myself climbing fast with his warm touch. Then he moans against my skin, creating a vibration as he starts sucking my clit again. "I can't believe this, god, I'm on the edge again." He ramps his speed up again and I feel myself on the verge, as my second orgasm pounds through me. I cry out his name again, bucking against him. This time, as my orgasm ceases, he releases me, resting his head on the inside of my thigh.

My heart is beating so fast I'm afraid it's going to bust out of my chest. My body is vibrating, as if it's just been struck by lightning. He waits a moment, massaging my legs as I slowly let them unfold. As my breathing finally slows, he comes up and lays beside me. His body is still ready. I'm not sure I'm ready for more, until he envelopes my nipple with his mouth, deliciously slow. Unbelievably, it immediately wakes me up...there. I figured I was finished...after the first earth-shattering orgasm. Using his whole mouth, he takes my nipple and areola and gently sucks on it, cupping my other breast, and stroking the other nipple with his thumb.

"Good God, Wade. I don't know how you're doing it, but I'm completely turned on again."

Taking my hand in his, he places my hand on his rock-hard penis. It's so big and firm inside my hand, and I can feel the veins in it pulsing. "Mmmmm, oh, Kendra." He breathes as I tighten my grip. Just his sultry tone makes my body respond. I can't wait to hear him make all the sexy noises I just made. Hearing him respond to my touch is both fascinating and erotic.

"And what do you want?" I ask, my tone is like silk.

"Whatever. You. Want. To. Give. Me." he says, kissing me slowly after each word. I begin kneading the sensitive tip, feeling a bead of lubrication cover it. With Mark that part was always gross, but with Wade, it's so sexy. Strangely, it feels like a reward; proof that he's enjoying what I'm doing to him. "Oh, your hand is so soft, but you have a good grip, baby." He comments, bucking his hips with my rhythm." But I want more. It's great that I'm pleasuring him with my hand, but I want to feel what it's like to have this kind of girth inside me.

He stops when he feels my grip loosen. "You okay?"

"Yeah, I was just wondering if we can make this...real."

He tips his head sideways, as if trying to guess what I mean. "You mean...you want to take this to the next level?"

"Yeah." I answer, with only a moment's hesitation.

He kisses me softly and speaks in a whisper. "It's your choice, Kendra. You're steering this boat now."

His expression is intense as he gazes at me from on top. Taking my hands in his, he interlaces his hands with mine and lifts them over my head. His penis is so hard against my skin, and I'm so wet, I feel like it's just going to glide right inside me with no effort. As I shimmy towards it, he closes his eyes and leans his forehead against mine. "Are you okay?" I ask.

"Just bracing myself."

"Are you afraid it's going to hurt?"

He opens his eyes. "No. I've just...dreamed about this so many times, I know how good it's going to feel."

"You're adorable."

"Easy for you to say. You've already had two orgasms. I'm afraid I'll explode." He chuckles softly and the sound is sexy as hell.

"Don't sweat it". I say.

He gives me an intense stare. "Do you have any idea how sexy and beautiful you are? I don't know how men have been able to keep their hands off you."

I part my knees and pull him toward me, locking my ankles together behind him, to stifle him from saying anything more. He has no idea how sexy he is, and that makes him even sexier. I can't stand it. I want him. Now. I feel the head going in and he sucks in a breath of air. As he slowly eases in, he stops before he reaches the hilt. "Holy god, you're so tight." He hisses.

"I think it's more that you're so big."

"I'm not hurting you, am I?"

"No." I say, kissing him softly on the mouth. "You can move any time." I say, feigning impatience as I try to lighten the moment. He looks so intense.

"Oh yeah?" He says and begins to move. He gazes at me with a look that makes me come undone. "Like that?" His voice is sexy, as if it's a dare. I'm dying. He's so friggin hot.

"Yeah," I wrap my arms around his shoulders, feeling wrapped in all of him. He cups my face with his hands as he slowly moves. Watching his expression change is such a turn-on. "Ooooohhh, " He breathes, and I feel him pulse inside me.

"That feels good?"

"Feels amazing." He whispers.

Then I do something that I've always wanted to do.

Chapter 19

Wade

Is it possible for a girl's virginity to grow back? Because I think Kendra's did. She's so tight it feels *too* good. I know I came off like a stallion just now, making her come twice with little effort, but now I'm afraid I'll be completely deflated by coming in under a minute. She's so unbelievably beautiful I can't stand it. And what's surprising is that she's fun. How many girls do I know that are fun? When she let go and let me do what I did to her, it was so hot. I figured we would make out for a bit, but when she told me to take her bra off, I thought wow, this girl is *on.*

She's perfect. From head to toe. I've never met anyone with such an amazing body or one that responds so well to my touch. We fit together like a glove. But either I'm too big for her or she's just unnaturally tiny inside. I'd like to think it's the first one, but I'm a guy. As I move on top of her, I can feel her warmth both inside and out. I slow for a moment and take her pert nipple in my mouth. First, I suck it, then I flick it with my tongue. Kendra rears up and moans. She absolutely loves this. I love it too.

Her insides clench when I suck on her breasts. It's so sexy. As if I think she can't be any tighter, I feel her tighten, and she smiles. "Mmmmm...oh, man, that's so hot." I whisper, enveloping her mouth with mine. I slide my tongue inside her mouth, sweeping across, and she meets mine with hers. I've never had sex without a condom before. This is amazing. Surprising her, I bury myself in her, and her eyes roll back as they close. "Mmmm...you like that? It's all the way in."

"Oh, Wade. Jesus." She breathes. "It's so deep."

Lifting on my elbows, I start gently pounding into her, trying like hell not to come too fast. I can feel her tightening the faster I go. Our skin is softly slapping together as she meets me thrust for thrust. I'm breathless as I watch this beautiful woman come undone under me. Praying that the pullout couch holds, I knead her breasts as I continue pumping her, feeling myself climb. I can tell she's climbing too, feeling the waves of pleasure as she bucks her hips closer to me, taking it all in.

Leaning further back on my knees, I use my thumb to stroke her clit. She cries out a moan and I feel her clench, bringing me close to the edge. "Oh, Kendra." I hiss, feeling my dick get impossibly hard inside her. "I'm close." I say, half as a warning, and half gauging how close she is. It's always nice to come together, but it doesn't always happen that way, especially on the first try.

"Oooohhhhh," she says, pressing her body against my thumb. "Oh, God, Wade. You're going to make me come again."

I grunt an 'oh' as I hiss through my teeth. "Kendra, I'm going to come, too." Not daring to stop rubbing her clit with my finger, I watch her mouth form a large 'O' as she gasps, and I can feel her muscles pulse inside as she releases a third time. Her insides hug me impossibly tighter, throwing me over the edge. My breathing is ragged as I come like a rocket inside her. Even the aftershocks feel amazing as I empty completely in her.

Breathless and spent, we both lay on the bed; me still on top of her, trying not to place all my weight on her. I lift my head so I can see her. We're both panting like we've just run a race. Licking my lips, I brush the hair off the sides of her face and cup her face with my hands. "That was amazing."

"You don't have to tell me." she pants. "I was there."

I lay my head on her chest, as if defeated, and chuckle. "Jesus Christ. I think that's the best sex I ever had."

"I don't think...I *know* that's the best sex *I* ever had." She says, patting me on the back.

I kiss her on the forehead and lift, removing myself from her. And I lay down next to her. Both of us are completely naked, sprawled on my bed, still trying to catch our breath. She rolls over on top of me. I place a hand on her rear end, stroking it. "So, tell me, Wade. How come your phone hasn't rang all night? Am I your only groupie tonight?" she teases.

Twirling a piece of her hair through my fingers, I smile. "I changed my phone number. It was pissing me off with the phone ringing all the time."

"So, these girls that have been calling you...did you sleep with them all?"

She sniffs and pulls a lock of hair behind her ear, still naked and on top of me.

"Just one. But that was months ago." I explain honestly. "I give out my number a lot, but I almost never follow through."

"Really?" she lifts her brows. "All that chance for some bootie and you don't jump at it?"

"I'm too busy." I shake my head. "Seriously. When I'm not at the bar I'm writing songs, practicing, at the gym, or hanging out with my brothers. I don't have time for all that."

She raises one brow suggestively. "And now? You think you can make time for some of *my* bootie?"

I gently use my fingertips, stroking the soft flesh of her ass. "For this bootie, I'll make time."

Kissing my chest, she says. "I bet you say that to all the girls."

Chuckling softly, I kiss her forehead. "Be careful. You might start to like me."

"I already like you." She kisses me on the mouth. "So, it's too late."

I can tell she's stifling a yawn. "Tired?" I ask.

"God, what time is it?"

I remove my hand from her butt and look at my watch. "It's almost midnight."

"Damn. I have to go. I've got work in the morning."

"So, leave from here in the morning." I offer.

"I work at a lawyer's office, Wade. I can't show up wearing exactly what I wore yesterday. People will notice."

"Just stay a little while longer." I say, surprising myself.

"There's also another issue." She says, as if considering her options.

"What?"

"My dad." She purses her lips together. "He'll be waiting up for me. It'll be much easier to explain getting home late from seeing you than not at all."

"Shit." I grumble. "You really gotta get your own place."

"I know." She rolls her eyes, lifting off me. I watch her as she stands there, and I start getting hard again. Her body is so hot. She gets as far as picking up her sexy underwear and I grab her arm, forcing her back down. "Shit! Wade!" she squeals playfully. "I really have to go!" she laughs.

"Not so fast." I growl, pulling her body back onto mine.

She feels my hardened dick against her skin. "Wow. You're ready to go again?"

"I can't get enough of you." I whisper, pulling her hair behind her head and kissing her like I'll never see her again. She leans her weight on me, and parts her legs as she sinks down on my dick and lets it slide right in. "Have mercy, baby." I murmur against her lips. She begins pumping on top of me as my dick slides in and out of her rhythmically. I hold her hips and pump hard from under her as I revel in the fact that her breasts are within sucking distance.

"Oh, Wade. Jesus Christ." She hisses. "God, you're all the way in. It's so deep."

"Mmmmm...." I moan, feeling her all the way to the hilt. It's so goddamn hot I can feel myself climbing already. I suck and lick her breasts as she leans toward me, taking it all in. The bed is whining will all the weight off center, and I worry that it might give and collapse from under us. "Jesus, fuck, I have to get a real fuckin' bed!" I say in the throws of passion, as I feel her insides clench, hugging me tighter. Placing my hand against her pelvis, I begin stroking her clit with my thumb, noticing that when I do that or suck her breasts, it makes her come. So, I go one better: I do both.

"Ooohhhhh, God, don't stop!" she cries. *As if I would.*

I feel her insides pulse as she cries out, releasing while I'm inside her. My cock twitches once more before I feel myself empty inside her like a tidal wave. Grunting, I grind my hips into her, feeling my release. Breathless again, she rests her head on my chest. Then we make the biggest mistake ever.

...we fall asleep.

Chapter 20

Kendra

I feel awful for leaving Wade the way I did, but I woke up three hours later in a panic. He was still sleeping, spooning me from behind, when I slithered out of the bed without him noticing. It was two o'clock in the morning when I pulled into the driveway, making sure I turned my headlights off before actually turning into my spot. As I open the door, I can see a lamp on in the living room. Dad is sprawled on the recliner, asleep. He stirs when he sees me trying to tiptoe past.

"You okay? Just getting in now?"

"Yeah, dad. I'm fine."

"Did you have car trouble?"

"No. Everything is okay, dad."

He rises to walk upstairs with me, and notices that I've done up the buttons on my shirt incorrectly. He lifts a brow. "You didn't have your shirt like that all day, did you? Nobody said anything to you?"

I look down at my blouse. "No, I suppose not."

He lifts a brow but smiles. "Well, as long as you're okay." He winks. "See you in the morning."

"Goodnight dad."

I'm so exhausted I fall onto my bed but find the strength to take my clothes off and drape them over the bottom of my bed. My body is still humming from Wade. Even though I'm spent as I try to sleep, the events of the night keep playing back inside my head. His intense eyes, his body, the sultry way he talks during sex. The fact that he made me have four orgasms. Up until a few hours ago, I didn't think that was humanly possible. I expect to feel sore and tender but I'm not. Not even a little bit. He's such a gentle and focused lover. Six hours later I bolt out of bed and hit the shower quickly. I'm late for work but if I hurry, I'll only be a little late. Nobody will even notice since everyone is booked with appointments this morning.

Driving to work, I remember the note I left Wade on his jeans. Then as I smile, thinking of him, my phone rings. Pressing the answer button on my dashboard, I say hello.

"Good morning." Wade says in a silky tone.

"Good morning. How are you this morning?"

I can hear him sigh, like when you just finish a huge meal that you've been looking forward to. "Can't complain. How are you?"

"I'm good. A little tired, but good. How's your hand?"

"It's fine. The knuckles look a little bit bruised, but they don't hurt. I was lucky."

"You were."

"So was your dad up when you got home?"

"Not exactly. He was sleeping in the recliner but technically he was waiting up for me."

"Are my balls nailed to the wall?" He chuckles.

"A girl doesn't kiss and tell."

He guffaws. "We did a lot more than kiss."

"No need to worry. I'm a big girl." I clear my throat. "You're up early."

"This is what time I usually get up. I've got things to do."

"Oh yeah? You play tonight?"

"Yeah. What are you doing tonight?"

"I've got to go over to Jennifer's house. There's still a million things to do before Saturday."

"Oh yeah...forgot about that."

I half laugh. "I didn't. She won't let me."

"If she's getting married this Saturday, what the hell was she doing at the wedding show?"

"Because she's...crazy. I don't know." I giggle. "Listen, I've gotta go. I just pulled up at work. I'm already late."

He chuckles. The sound is so sexy. "Okay." He pauses. "Hey,"

"What?"

"Last night was...." He trails off.

"It was...wasn't it." I comment. Finishing his thought.

"Yeah," he says, satisfied. "I'll talk to you later."

"K. Have a good day."

"It already is." He clicks off. My heart gushes. How the hell I'm going to get any work done today is beyond me. But I manage to do it. Just as I'm about to leave for the day, Jennifer calls me and tells me to come over right after work, that her and Wendy ordered Chinese food. Luckily, I had some forethought and brought a pair of jeans and a t-shirt to change into, so I wouldn't have to sit in my stuffy work outfit all night.

"Hungry?" Jennifer asks as I walk into the house. "The food just arrived."

The house smells divine. "I'm famished. Just let me go change." I say, lifting my bag.

Five minutes later, we're sitting at the table, stuffing our faces. Something catches Wendy's eye as she watches me eat. "What did you do to your neck?" she asks, a 'v' forming between her eyes.

"What do you mean?" I ask, unconsciously placing my hand on either side of my neck.

She points at the right side. "There." She rises to take a closer look. "Is that a..." her eyes widen, which catches Jennifer's attention.

"What? What is it?" Jennifer says, suddenly very concerned. When she takes a closer look, she gasps. "Is that a hickey?"

"What? No!" I blurt, running to the bathroom to look in the mirror. They follow me. Thank God their parents aren't home. They'd probably think there was a stampede of elephants stomping through the house. As I approach the mirror and turn the light on, with my best friends standing beside me, as I live and breathe, I learn that I've experienced a first....my first hickey. "Jesus Christ." I say, thinking first that Jennifer is going to freak because it's going to stand out like a sore thumb with my dress at the wedding. And then I'm thankful that I wore a silk scarf around my neck to work; I'm so good at tying them now that I didn't even think to look as I did it.

But Jennifer just stands there and gawks. "That's not Mark's work, is it?" the color in her face has drained.

"God...no." I say flatly.

Relief washes over her. "Thank God."

"Oh," I squeak, "so you're not angry?"

Wendy interrupts. "She will be if you don't tell us whose work it is." A sly smile crosses her face.

I hesitate for a moment, but deep down I'm dying to tell the two girls who mean more to me than anything, what happened last night. "Wade."

Both their faces brighten. "Are you serious?" Jennifer is impressed. "I could tell he was into you."

"When...when you stormed into the office and told him he has to be my date at your wedding?" I jibe.

She doesn't take the bait and I love her for it. 'No, at the bridal show. He couldn't keep his eyes off you."

"Please. He still hated me then."

Wendy snorts. "Well, he doesn't hate you now."

I instinctively place my hand on my neck. "No, he doesn't...anymore."

Jennifer smiles and turns the light out, guiding us back into the living room. "Evidently there's a fine line between love and hate."

"Well, he doesn't *love* me, either. Don't be ridiculous." I scoff.

"So, did you guys like make out or something?" Wendy asks, sitting down and stuffing a chicken ball into her mouth.

"Not exactly." I answer sheepishly.

Jennifer, who was smiling, gives me a blank look. "Did you...." she gestures with her hand for me to continue.

Feeling righteous, I stick my chest out. "It's called sex, Jennifer. And yes, we had sex."

"Really?" they both look at each other, grinning from ear-to-ear.

"Yeah," I admit, not looking directly at them. I try to focus on my egg roll.

"Was it good?" Jennifer probes.

"Good doesn't cover it." my mouth is full. 'What's your record?" I ask both girls.

"Record for what?" Jennifer asks.

"Number of orgasms in one night."

Wendy had placed another chicken ball into her mouth, she begins choking on it. Jennifer smacks her on the back, and she gains control of the coughing.

"Let me get this straight." Jennifer is blunt. "You had more than *one* orgasm last night?"

"Four." I answer immediately.

Wendy chokes again and Jennifer ignores her. She places her chin on her hand and leans in closer to me. "Really." She says, in awe.

"Really."

"In one night?" Jennifer confirms as Wendy takes a drink of water.

"Yeah. Two straight away, another shortly after, and the last one not long after the third."

"Wow." Wendy says, her voice is cracking from choking. "I thought you could only do that in porno movies."

"I didn't think it was physically possible." I admit. "It was intense."

"And you're not like...walking funny or sore?" Wendy asks.

I shake my head. "It wasn't like jackrabbit sex, Wendy. He's very gentle."

"And here I was thinking the sex Brandon and I have is pretty good."

"Well, it probably is. I thought the sex I had with Mark was good, too. Not four orgasms good, but nice all the same."

"Are you seeing him again?" Wendy asks.

"I'd like to. But he's not really a relationship kind of guy." I shrug. "It's up to him. I left him my number. We'll see where it goes."

"Wow." Jennifer has folded her arms over her chest and is shaking her head. "Way to get over Mark. You go, girl." She high fives me.

"Speaking of which," I say, having a little fun being the center of attention, seeing as Jennifer has been ever since she got engaged. "Guess who pathetically followed me to Mingles last night...to beg me to come back to him...in the parking lot...sitting on his ass, crying."

Wendy's eyes bulge. "I'll kill him."

Jennifer's jaw is on the floor.

"I nearly did. It took every ounce of willpower not to put my car in reverse and drive over the son-of-a-bitch."

"You should have." Jennifer says as she rises to go answer her phone, which is ringing on the coffee table.

"That's what he wrote in that letter, you know." Wendy informs me. "That he's sorry and he wants you back. Loser."

"Yeah, well, he has a better chance of me sprouting a third arm than he has of me going back to him. I'd sooner see him dead."

"Oh my God!" Jennifer cries, raking her hand through her hair, as she talks on the phone. "No. Oh my God. Tell the family I'm so sorry. No, it's okay. It's okay. I'm so sorry. Thanks for calling." She hangs up. By this time, Wendy is on her left side and I'm on her right, trying to console her for what is obviously horrible news.

"Oh, I need to sit down." She breathes, clearly in shock.

"Sit, sit." Wendy coaxes. "What happened?" she rubs her sister's back and looks at me. The color has drained from my face.

As Jennifer sits, she places her head in her hands and begins to sob. "God..." she gasps. "What am I going to do now?"

"What? What's wrong, Jenny?" Wendy says.

"We can help. Whatever it is. We can get you through it." at this point, it could be anything from the caterer ordering the wrong meat, to an asteroid set to land in the church at the exact moment that she and Brandon are supposed to be exchanging vows.

"It's the band...the lead singer...he died this morning." She cries. "That was the manager, he was crying. It was awful."

"Jesus. He wasn't even that old, was he?" Wendy says.

"Apparently it was a freak accident. He's an electrician." Jennifer explains tearfully.

"That's just terrible." I say. "Before you booked them, you were talking about a disc jockey. Maybe you can call them and see if they're still available."

"No, they have an online calendar. I saw it this morning. They're booked." She explains. "What am I going to do?" she looks at Wendy and I through reddened eyes. "I guess I'll have to rent some sound equipment and go nuts downloading from iTunes." Her face scrunches, as if she's just eaten a lemon.

I pat her on the back. "Maybe I can help."

Chapter 21

Wade

After I hang up to Kendra, my phone rings, and I smile, recognizing the number immediately.

"Well, would you look at that? My favorite sister-in-law is calling me."

"It's your *only* sister-in-law." Julia says. "I didn't catch you at a bad time, did I?"

"No, not at all, I'm just getting ready to head out to practice in about an hour."

"Cool. I just wanted to thank you for taking Mary to the show. She had a great time. You got her all liquored up. She was half in the bag when you brought her back here."

"Then I did my job. How are you feeling?"

"So, so, but better. Listen. I won't keep you long. I just wanted to let you know that Colton's coming home next weekend. Thought you might want to come by for dinner. I'm inviting everyone; all the Ford boys and Charles, our neighbor."

"Charles, too? I'm there." I say. "Can I bring anything?"

"Na, but if you talk to your brothers before me, just make sure that they're free. Colton's desperate to see everyone."

"Will do." Then I hesitate. "Do you mind if I um...bring someone?"

"Why? You feel like jamming again with the band like the last time? Sure...that was fun."

"Err...no. It's a girl."

Long pause.

"Julia?"

"I'm still here." She giggles. "Um...Wade, this isn't like a...groupie or a 'chick from the bar', 'air quote', is it? Because Colton and Jack have told me all about those girls, and I'm not interested in having to sanitize my furniture or dishware after having one of those here."

I bark out a laugh. "Give me some credit." I take it down a notch. "Her name is Kendra. She's my lawyer. Well, not *just* my lawyer."

"You're sleeping with your lawyer?" Julia is shocked but she's also laughing. "You've got balls, Wade."

"Okay, she's not really my lawyer. Never mind. Anyway, do you mind if I bring her? If she wants to come, that is."

"Well, now she *has* to come." Julia barks out a laugh.

"What do you mean?" I laugh, playing along.

"Because you've never asked to bring a girl to a function...ever. At least for as long as I've known you, and for as long as Colton's known you....and Jack...and—"

I interrupt. "I get it, I get it." I pause. "Listen, don't go all nuts over her, because I don't even know how I feel about her yet."

"Oh, I think you do."

"Why do you say that?"

"For all the reasons I just said, Wade."

"Yeah. I suppose you're right. Anyway, I'll be there. If she says yes, she'll be there, too."

"Okay," her voice is singsong.

"What." My voice is flat.

"Nothing." Her tone says she knows something that I don't know.

"Whaaaat." I demand.

"Nothing. I just...."

"Shut up. Don't say it." I warn, playing along.

"Goodbye, Wade." Her voice is singsong again, mocking me.

"Shut up." I chuckle, and I hear her chuckle, too, before she clicks off.

***

After I got a ride over to Mingles to boost my car, me and the boys had a great practice, and I even got to hash out a new tune that I've been working on. Dave, my drummer, finally got his new drums, complete with a logo of our band's name 'Take Risks' emblazoned on the front. We could almost pass for a real band...if we had a manager. "So, what do we do now?" Dave asks as we bring our last practice song to a close. "About bookings, I mean. I know we've got our gigs at Mingles whenever we want, but what about branching out? That out of the picture now?"

"Na, I'll call around. Don't sweat it." I wave. "But we're not going back to that dive in South Carolina ever again." I cut the air with my hand for emphasis. "No more dumps like that anymore."

Dave high-fives me. "Here here," he agrees.

Griffin, the base guitarist, names off a few places. "We should try some of those. I heard they're looking for a band for some dates."

"Thanks, man. I'll look into them."

"You want me to call a few? I've got time." Grffin offers.

"Na, that's okay, man. I'll give it a go first."

"You sure?" Griffin continues. "'Cause you know you suck on the phone, right?" Griffin's an internet marketer during the day, working from home. "I think I could give it a better shot than you, man, no offence."

"Alright, you can give it a go. I'll give you a higher cut if you can get us into any of those places." I relent.

"Cool." Griffin is pleased.

After heading to the gym and going home for a little nap before hitting the stage tonight, as I'm laying in bed, thinking about Kendra, I hear my phone ring. I smile as soon as I see the number on the display. "Hey, I was just thinking about you." I say in greeting.

"You were?" she purrs.

"Of course."

"You're sweet." She pauses. "Listen, I'm just over at Jennifer's place, and...gosh, I don't even know how to ask you this, but, we're in kind of a bind."

"What's up?"

I explain to him what happened. He sniffs. "Holy shit, that's rough."

"I know you have your gig at Mingles on Saturday night, but I was just wondering if you'd be able to do this."

"Well, my gig at Mingles is a standing order. I've played there every Saturday night since the beginning. I'm not sure what Blake and the owner will do on short notice."

"I understand. It's okay." My guilt-meter is reaching its maximum capacity. "We can rent some sound equipment and play pre-recorded stuff."

"Well, now, hang on here." I lift my hand, thinking about the exposure to a new audience, and most of all, doing a favor for Kendra and her friends. "Let me talk to Blake and Tony and see what we can do." I pause. "I can't promise anything, but at least I can ask."

"I appreciate it. Let me know, okay?"

"For sure. I'll call you right back."

I hang up with Kendra and call Blake right away. "Blake, my man."

"Hey, Wade. How's the hand?"

"Oh, it's fine. A little bruised but it'll do." I clear my throat. "Hey, listen. Something's come up and a friend of mine just asked if I can play at a wedding on Saturday. Any chance you can get someone to cover for me?"

"Well, it's funny you should ask, Wade. I just booked someone to cover for you for tonight, since you hurt your hand and all. I can get them to cover for you Saturday if you like." He changes tack. "I do get calls every now and again for bookings, you know, Wade. You don't have to feel like you've always gotta play here. Especially with Chuck out of the picture and all...you can play elsewhere if you like."

"That's great, Blake. Yeah, sure. The boys have mentioned a couple of other places to play for a change. Maybe mixing it up a bit isn't such a bad thing."

"Never is, Wade."

"Okay, man. I'll see you tomorrow."

"See ya."

I dial Kendra's number. She answers on the first ring. "Hey, baby. It's all done. Me and the boys can cover the wedding."

Her happiness is palpable. "Are you serious?"

"Yep. Sure am."

"And you don't mind covering a wedding?"

"You mean is it beneath me to sing at an event that guarantees at least a hundred guests? Hell, no."

"Wade. You're awesome."

"So, I've heard." I joke. "I bet your friend there wants to me to high-tail it right over, right?"

"It doesn't have to be tonight."

"Does she have a plan? Like a song list and some openers...things like that?"

"Remember who this is, Wade." She says, but in a sweet tone, so it sounds like she isn't talking shit about her best friend who is probably standing right there.

"Gotcha. Give me the address and I'll scoot on over. I'll bring the boys up to speed later."

"Sounds good. See you shortly."

Before I hang up, she pauses, and it's like I can read her mind. "Hey, it's cool. I'll be all professional-like in front of your friends."

"I know." She says and I can hear the smile in her voice.

"See ya." I say before hanging up.

Chapter 22

Kendra

Good Lord I'm wet just from talking to him. His voice on the phone is so unbelievably sexy. And that he's willing to drop everything and rearrange his life for my best friend, it's just amazing. Jennifer finally stopped sobbing but now she's perilously going through all her stuff from the other band. "Jesus, I'm not sure if he's going to be able to sing all these songs."

"Jen, you've heard him yourself. He's very good. He can handle it."

Wendy intervenes. "The only issue here I think will be wardrobe. He's used to playing in bars. Do we get him to wear a suit?"

"I'm not sure if the music fits with a suit." I supply. "Maybe a white linen shirt and dress pants?"

Jennifer snaps her fingers and points at me. "Yeah. With a suit on they'll look like a bunch of penguins singing rock music"

"Exactly."

"Shit. Do we have any food left for him?" Wendy roots through our food.

"It's fine. We can order more." Jennifer offers.

Five minutes later I see Wade's car pull into the driveway and my heart begins to pound. I'm dying to kiss him but it's not appropriate in front of my friends, under the circumstances. I decide to bypass any awkward situation and meet him outside. "He's here. I'll be right back."

"You sure?" Wendy asks with a raised brow. "Should I call the fire department?"

"Shut up." I say, smiling.

Wade gets out of his car and looks at me. "Hey," he gives me an odd look, "whatcha doing out here?"

"I...I just wanted to..."

His gaze slides down to my lips. "You read my mind,

baby." He murmurs, placing his left hand on my side. He leans in and kisses me once, full on the mouth, using enough suction to make a smacking sound."

My knees turn to jelly. If Jen and Wendy weren't standing in the front window staring at us, I would take him right here in the driveway. Even though my back is to the window, I can sense their eyes, burning into the back of my head. I should never have told them about Wade and I, but now I have to face the humiliation.

He smells heavenly and he's wearing a pair of jeans that hug him in all the right spots. He gestures with his chin towards the front of the house. "So, I'm guessing you told your friends about us."

As I turn around, I see Wendy and Jennifer standing in the window, waving at us with guilty looks on their faces. Wade waves back as my face turns red. I face him again. "It was sort of unavoidable. You kind of branded me last night." I point nonchalantly to the hickey on my neck. "I had to tell them. They thought I got back together with shitface."

"Ooohh." Wade laughs knowingly. "Geez, I'm sorry. I didn't know I did that."

"It's okay." I wink. "It was worth it."

He winks back and gestures for me to go ahead of him. "After you." And he takes my hand until we get to the front door.

"Hi...Wade, is it?" Jennifer jokes.

"Yeah, that's me." Wade shakes her hand. "Sorry about the circumstances."

"Hey, shit happens. Thanks a million for stepping in."

"No problem." He looks at Wendy, whose face is redder than mine.

"Hi, I'm Wendy."

"Yeah, we met at the bridal show." Wade smiles, shaking her hand.

I want to smack the stupid smile off Wendy's face, but I know I've got nothing to worry about. Wade is the hottest man I've ever met, and he does turn a lot of heads. "Do you have a song list for Wade?" I say to Jennifer, breaking the tension.

"I do." Jennifer says.

"You been practicing saying that?" Wade jokes.

Jennifer catches that and laughs, handing Wade the song list. He studies it as we all sit down. Me beside Wade on the couch, Jennifer and Wendy on the floor. "Does the hall have a piano?" Wade asks.

"No, why?"

He lifts a hand. "No, it's okay. We've got a keyboard for the wedding song."

I never even looked at what Jennifer's wedding song was. "What is your wedding song, Jen? I forget." I lie.

"When I See You Smile by Bad English." Wade answers. I immediately picture Wade singing that and my heart melts. "There's a keyboard in that song, but I thought a piano might be really classy at a wedding."

"We could rent one." Jennifer says, but the tone in her voice says she doesn't really want one there.

"No, a keyboard is fine. We have one."

"Who plays it?" Jennifer asks.

"I do, but my guitarist does, too. He'll handle it for this one."

"And you have one of those fancy electric guitars, too?" Wendy asks.

"Yeah, I have a bass guitarist. He plays a bunch of stuff like me." he pauses. "I'll have to get sheet music for some of this, but it all looks doable." He nods, satisfied. "It doesn't look like there's enough here to cover the entire reception. Did you want pre-recorded music for some parts?"

"During dinner I'd like pre-recorded stuff. Maybe some golden oldies?" Jennifer says. "And we'll leave some room for requests, too."

"Sure. We can put that together for you."

"How do you feel about wearing black dress pants with a white shirt?" Jennifer asks. "I thought a suit might look odd since you're playing soft rock."

"Yeah, no, that's fine. We'll have to do a sound check

on Friday night, and the guys and I will have to practice some of these pieces, but I think this will go well."

"And you're not screwing over the guys at Mingles, are you?"

Wade frowns. "No. It's fine." He guffaws. "I've never played at a wedding before. I feel kinda like Adam Sandler in The Wedding Singer."

"It's not quite like that. We're expecting two hundred people."

I though it was a hundred and fifty?

Wade is impressed. "Do you have an MC? I'll have to meet with him, too. Make sure I don't step on any toes."

"Yeah. I'll give him your number if that's okay."

Wade nods. Jennifer tells him how much the job pays.

"Holy wow!" he rakes a hand through his hair. "I'm in the wrong business."

I rub his back and he looks at me for the first time in about three minutes. I've been watching how he interacts; his eyelashes as he speaks, his mouth, his eye contact. He's so sexy I could watch him all day. When I rub his back, he places a hand on my thigh and sits back, hooking his right foot on his left knee. God, even the way he sits is sexy.

"So, you don't have to clear this with your manager or anything?" Jennifer inquires, still not convinced that she's not putting him out.

Wade draws in a deep breath and I place my hand over his. "I gave my manager the boot, so I don't have anyone to answer to at the moment." I see his jaw clench and I stroke my finger down his hand. He unclenches.

"Oh. Sorry about that." Jennifer is embarrassed.

"Na, it's okay." He waves and looks at me intently. "Some things are meant to be...and some aren't."

I smile. He smiles back, and lifts his hand, cupping my face for a moment.

"So where did you learn to sing, Wade?" Jennifer asks.

"I've been singing since I could talk, but I did some formal lessons when I was a teenager. Just after my voice changed. I started writing my own music in high school. Started a band in high school, too. When I was old enough to sing in clubs, I started doing it professionally. The rest is history."

"Have you ever done a recording?"

"No, not yet. It costs an arm and a leg to rent a recording studio. Mind you, after this gig, I might be able to afford it." He chuckles.

"Do you have enough original music to record an album?"

He waves. "Oh yeah. I've got loads."

"You should do that." Wendy says.

"I will. Some day." He looks at both girls. "Do you have any more questions?"

"No. We'll be in touch with times and places." Jennifer says. Then she lifts a brow towards me. "I'm sure you guys have better things to do."

My eyes bulge.

"That's okay," Wade says, "We didn't have any plans." He smiles and winks at me. He's so cool. My friends' insinuation isn't getting under his skin.

"Make sure you get your deposit back from that band." I remind Jennifer.

She rolls her eyes. "Oh, God. I completely forgot!" She covers her mouth. "That's not at all awkward." She's facetious. Then she looks at Wade. "Oh, God! I need to give you a deposit!"

Wade shakes his head. "Not required. I've never asked for one and don't intend to, either." He rises, taking my hand in his. "If you have any other concerns, just give me a call. I'm available twenty-four-seven."

"Thank you," Jennifer gets up and shakes his hand again. "Thank you a million times over. You saved me. Truly."

"I'm happy to do it." he presses his lips into a smile. "I'll see you girls Friday night." he leads me to the door and addresses me. "I'm free the rest of the evening if you'd like to stop by." He says cordially to me, knowing Jennifer and Wendy are still in earshot.

"Um...sure. I'll just help the girls clean up and I'll stop by."

"No help needed!" Jennifer calls, loud enough that the neighbors can probably hear.

"Okay. I'll meet you at your place then." I say. He smiles and leans in to kiss me chastely on the cheek.

"I'll see you in a few." He whispers in my ear, sending shivers up my spine.

Fifteen minutes later, I pull up behind Wade's car. He's standing outside waiting for me. The way he's leaning on his car with one ankle over the other makes him look like James Dean...minus the cigarette. He walks over to me as I slide out of the driver's seat. As soon as I'm fully out of the car, he hooks his arm around my waist and pulls me toward him.

"God you look good." He says, enveloping his mouth over mine. His kiss lingers longer than the one he gave me in Jennifer's driveway earlier. But it's ten times hotter. I'm conscious of cars driving by so I don't encourage him to kiss me deeper.

"Wade." I chide playfully. "Your neighbors."

"Ah, I'm not worried." He says, kissing me again, this time more chastely.

"I can tell." I giggle. "Why don't we go inside."

"Enter at your own risk, baby." He teases, taking my hand in his.

We walk down to his apartment and he turns the light on. The place is spotless, even more so than it was last night. "Did you know I was coming over, or do you always keep your place this tidy?"

He tosses his keys and wallet on the counter. "It's always this clean. Why?"

"It's unnatural. Guys are supposed to be slobs."

Scooping me by the waist with his left hand, bringing me closer to him, he explains. "I was in the military. It kind of grows on you."

I'd forgotten. "Gotcha."

"No, I've got *you*." He says, sliding his gaze to my lips. He kisses me softly. "You looked like you swallowed a bird over at Jennifer's house."

"Did you not hear what she said?"

"Yeah, I heard. But I thought you had a much thicker skin than that."

"I do. I was just worried that your face would turn red the way mine did."

He kisses my nose. "Not to worry. I don't embarrass easily."

"Clearly."

Wade looks past my shoulder to the couch. "I'd offer to watch television or something, but I don't own one."

"Is that by choice?"

"Yeah. If I'm not sleeping, I'm practicing or writing music. Never had a need for a television."

"Well we don't need one now." I say, staring at his lips. "I think we can figure out how to entertain ourselves."

With that he lifts me onto the countertop. I squeal in surprise. He snuggles in between my legs so we're nose to nose. "I figured you might be sore from last night. Or too tired."

"I'll let you know when I'm sore or tired." I tug at his shirt by the waistband of his jeans. He leans back a little and lifts his arms as his shirt comes off over his head. Running my fingers through his dark hair, I watch him close his eyes, reveling in my touch. "It took everything in me not to tear this shirt off you when I saw you come out of your car at Jen's house."

He smiles, chuckling softly. "I've created a monster." He tugs at my shirt and gives me a knowing look. "Do I get to take yours off, too?"

His intense expression spurs me on. I pull my shirt off and toss it on the floor. He rests his head in between my breasts and breathes. "God, you're so perfect." Kissing the fleshy part of my breasts, one by one, I lean back, placing my hands on the counter. Inching his way inside my bra, Wade pulls the lacey cloth away, exposing my nipple. Taking one in his mouth, he envelopes my areola and I rear my head back, letting out a soft moan. Slowly reaching back to the snap on my bra, Wade whispers. "Can I take this off?"

"For future reference, you never have to ask." I say, pulling at the enclosure, helping him remove my bra. When my breasts are free, he cups both of them with his hands, and kisses them tenderly. I'm already dying, wanting him to suck and lick them like he did last night.

Looking at me with that intense expression, he murmurs. "Then I don't suppose you would mind me unzipping your pants."

In answer, I reach out to the button on his jeans, and undo it. "You first." My voice is sultry as I lower the zipper slowly, and slide my hand in, feeling his hardened penis. Again, he's not wearing underwear. "In a game of strip poker, you would lose, baby."

He closes his eyes with my touch and draws in a deep breath. "If I'm playing with you, I'd fold anyway."

As I stroke him, his breath is audible. He leans in and kisses me with his open mouth, plunging his tongue inside, making me moan again. "God, you're such a fantastic kisser."

"You ain't seen nothin' yet, baby." He whispers against my lips. His penis is incredibly hard against my hand, and I'm dying to feel it inside me. Pulling his pants down with my free hand, he helps me, and his jeans drop to the floor. He's standing in his kitchen, gloriously naked. "It appears you're a little overdressed." He says, taking my arms and wrapping them around his neck. Lifting me off the counter, he lowers me to the floor. Reaching down with a smouldering expression on his face, he undoes my pants and pulls them down. He glances at my underwear and lifts a brow. I read his mind and pull them down, too.

When I'm naked, he lifts me again, kissing me, tongue and all, as we walk to the free wall by his bed. "You tell me if any of this is uncomfortable, okay?" He says as he guides his penis to me. As he slides inside, my eyes close and my body relaxes against the wall. "How's your back?" He asks.

"Mmmm...." I murmur. He starts to move, lifting my hands up against the cold wall. Kissing me full on the mouth, he continues to fill me and slide out, as we make love in a rhythm against the wall. As I feel myself climbing, Wade goes deeper, as we're nose to nose, and his eyes are smouldering with need.

"You feel that, baby?" He whispers to me. "It's all the way in."

"I love your sex talk." I breathe. "It's so hot."

He chuckles softly and it's my undoing as he pulls me from the wall, still filling me, and brings me to the bed. "I can't imagine that being good for your back for too long." He explains, cupping my face with his hands as he covers my body with his on the bed. His strong, muscular arms that held me against the wall now surround me.

When he begins sucking my nipple and flicking it with his tongue, I lift my chest off the bed, giving him full contact. "You love this, don't you." He says against my skin.

"Mmmm....don't ever stop." I beg, feeling myself climb further.

"Ohhhh, I love it when you tighten like that." He hisses, pumping faster. "Just when I think you can't be any tighter...you tighten more." Then he makes a delicious humming sound as his breathing becomes more ragged. He lifts his body upward, filling me deeper and harder. His six pack abs are in full view. I touch them, wanting so badly to kiss them. My breasts are bouncing with his movement and he reaches down to gently pinch my nipples.

"Ohhh, God, Wade." I say as he lifts my knees up to my shoulders and begins thrusting slowly.

"Oh, baby, it's all the way in again. Feel it, Kendra." He grunts.

As he hooks my legs over his shoulders, he reaches

his right thumb to my clit and begins making circles, stroking my sensitive nub slowly. "Mmmm....oh, Wade. You're gonna make me come if you keep doing that."

He continues thrusting in and out while circling my clit. I feel myself climb fast and I watch Wade's face grow more and more intense as he watches me. "Oh, Kendra." He grunts, "Oh, baby, I'm getting close. You're so tight."

"Say it again." I beg, writhing under him, feeling his impossible hardness all the way inside me.

"Which part?" he pants.

"All of it."

"Oh.....oh, baby, mmmmmm..." he starts. "God, Kendra, I'm so close...." He hisses.

"Oh, don't stop, Wade." I cry out, feeling my orgasm crash through me like a tidal wave. "Oh, God....Wade!" I say through a ragged voice.

Wade doesn't stop stroking me as I feel him release inside me, "Ooooohhhhhh, God," he grunts. "Kendra, oooohhhhh," he breathes as he finds his release.

We're both coming together, and when the intense waves of pleasure cease, he gently pulls my legs off his shoulders and slowly sets them on the bed. Then he takes my hands in his and raises them above my head as he brings his nose to mine. "That was one hell of an orgasm, baby." He says, his voice is low and his breathing is still a little ragged.

"Mine too." I say, kissing him full on the mouth. He kisses me back, making a smacking noise. "Jesus, I've had five orgasms in less than twenty-four hours."

He lifts a brow. "And counting." He smiles and kisses me again, before he lifts off me and slides in beside me.

I giggle. "Man, I don't know if I'm going to be able to control myself when you sing that song on Saturday."

He plumps a pillow behind his head and faces me. I'm still laying on my back. "Which song is that?" he grunts sexily as he places a hand on my belly, stroking my skin.

"When I See You Smile." That is one of my favorites.

I turn towards him so we're face-to-face, using my hand as a makeshift pillow.

He starts to sing the first verse softly. *"Sometimes I wonder...if I'd ever make it through...through this world without havin' you...I just wouldn't have a clue."*

He touches my face, looking at me intently. His voice is so beautiful; soft yet rugged, and he has just a bit of a ring in the last note of each line. Like a songbird. I dare not interrupt him.

"'Cause sometimes it seems like this world's closin' in on me...and there's no way of breakin' free...and then I see you reach for me."

And then the weirdest thing happens. I feel tears prick the backs of my eyes. It's like I'm pretending he's singing the song that he created just for me...to me, which is silly. I interrupt him. "Stop." My voice cracks.

A 'v' forms between his brows as he lifts his head off the pillow. "What's the matter?" he asks with a genuine look of concern on his face.

"Nothing...it's just...you're making me cry." I swallow, trying to push the tears down.

He smiles warmly and lowers his head back on the pillow, as he brushes a lock of hair behind my ear. "You're so sweet." He whispers, dividing his glance between both my eyes.

Wiping a tear from the corner of my eye, I sniff. "This is what happens to a girl post-orgasm. We get emotional." I say, blaming it on the passion we just shared.

Still smiling, he reaches down to the blanket and together we pull it over us. He tucks it in around me and then snuggles in front of me, as if we're having a sleep-over and we're about to tell each other ghost stories. We just stare at each other, taking turns stroking each other's faces and raking hands through each other's hair. I'd almost forgotten how late it was until I must have fallen asleep, because I opened my eyes and saw that Wade's eyes were closed. He looks so young when he sleeps. Granted, we're both still in our twenties, but Wade looks like a little boy when he's asleep, especially when his manly body is all wrapped in blankets.

Remembering that I had booked tomorrow morning off months ago for wedding stuff, I snuggle in beside him and fall asleep, dreaming of his voice.

Chapter 23

Wade

I've never made a girl cry before. At least never by singing. I mean, back in the third grade I stole a Snickers bar off this really fat girl named Sally, and she cried, but until last night, that's the only time I ever made a girl squeeze out a tear. No girl I've slept with has ever cried before, during, or after sex with me. I wasn't quite sure what to make of it, but I think they were tears of happiness, so that's cool.

Waking up next to her was awesome. I mean, it wasn't like the first night we hooked up, when she flew the coop, and I was left wondering if she ever wanted to see me again. Thank God she left the note. I wanted to puke before I found it. This time she didn't split. I was worried her old man would freak out and hunt me down or something, but when she woke up she said she was a big girl and could deal with her father. She's right. But I still can't help but worry about Peter coming to my door, carrying a loaded rifle in his hand with a bullet earmarked for me.

Her hair is all messy when she wakes up. It's cute as hell. Her body is still smoking hot and all warm in the morning. I had serious wood when I woke up, but I figure I need to pace myself. I've been making most of the moves, especially last night, so I should let her make a few. I don't want her to think I'm a nymphomaniac or anything. She'd be making skid marks in my driveway real fast.

I look at my watch. "Shit, don't you have to go to work?"

"Nope. I booked this morning off months ago for Jen. I'm free until about ten."

"Are you hungry?" I kiss her, keeping the blankets as a good separation from her soft skin, which I've already felt, and it nearly had me begging her to go for another round. I know some people aren't into morning sex, either. So I'll let her choose the boundaries.

"Kind of."

Lifting, so I'm sitting up in bed, I run a hand through my hair. "I don't have anything here. I'll have to run out and pick up a couple of things."

"No, you don't have to do that. Besides, my car is behind yours."

I point to the window. "There's a store up the street. Ten minute walk max. You can take a shower or whatever you like while I'm gone. I'll hop in now." In the back of my mind I'm hoping she'll join me in a sexy co-ed shower, but I know there isn't enough room. I can barely fit in there alone.

"Okay. I've got an overnight bag in my car. Would you mind bringing it in with you?"

I lift a brow. "Did you know you'd be spending the night?"

"With Jen and Wendy, yes. That was the original plan." She admits. "When I go over there, I always bring an overnight bag. Come to think of it, that's probably where my dad thinks I am."

I snap my fingers together and make a clucking noise. "That's thinking." I lift off the bed, completely naked, and grab my clothes off the floor. She's watching me. "Like what you see?" I chuckle, knowing I still have partial wood.

"Oh...yeah." She says, her voice is silky.

"Easy, tiger." I wink as I hop in the shower. I know I won't be able to handle seeing her naked again before a cold shower. When I get out, she's got her shirt and underwear on, sitting on the bed, texting someone. "All okay?" I ask.

"Fine. Just letting the girls know I'll be on time."

I grab some clothes and put them on while she's still texting. When I'm done, I lean over and kiss her on the lips. "I'll be back."

"Do you want to take my car?" she offers.

"I'll be fine. Back in twenty minutes. The bathroom

is all yours. I'll bring your bag in."

"Okay." She says, kissing me again. "My car isn't locked."

"'Kay, baby. I'll see you in a few." I wink as she pulls my shirt at the bottom, begging me to stay with her. It's almost impossible to resist with her sitting there in just panties and a shirt. "I can't *not* feed you, babe. It's the least I can do."

She kisses me one last time. "Okay. But hurry back."

"I will." I kiss her forehead and grab my wallet, keys and phone before leaving. I think this is the first time I've ever left a girl in my apartment alone. As I grab her bag and walk it down, leaving it on the inside of the door, I can hear the shower running already. Walking down the street, I run through the song list in my head again, remembering all the eighties hairband songs Jennifer had chosen for her wedding. I can play just about anything, but part of me is glad she chose that genre. Most of my material is from that era so it fits well. As I reach the halfway point to the grocery store, I slap myself in the head. *Why the hell am I not taking her out for breakfast? What an asshole she must think I am!*

As I turn around, shaking my head at my own stupidity, I break into a trot until I reach my driveway. Entering the house, I can hear a radio playing, or at least what I think is a radio. Until I realize, as I'm about to open the downstairs door leading directly into my apartment, that there is no music playing, just a voice. *Her* voice. Standing there, I immediately recognize the song as Kendra sings the chorus to Pat Benatar's 'The Warrior'. Kendra is belting out the lyrics like she owes Ms. Benatar money. I had no idea she could sing. There is a rough edge to her voice just like the original artist herself, as she hits the notes on key and ends it perfectly, without so much as a crack.

I'm impressed. She must have her iPhone with her in the bathroom as she's getting ready, with earphones in her ears. She doesn't expect me back for a while, so I stand there and wait for the next song. And then it comes. *"How do IIIIII....get through one night without you....if I had to live without you...what kind of life would that be?...."* My gaze drops to the floor as my hand rises to my chest. *"Oh....IIIIIIII.....I need you in my arms, need you to hooold.....you're my world, my heart, my sooooul.....if you ever leeeeeeave....baby, you would take away everything good in my life...."* My Lord. Until this moment I'd never heard such a beautiful voice. Birds can't sing as beautifully as Kendra. Her ring is perfect, her tone is on key, and she's got naturally what most artists practice for years to achieve...heart *and* soul.

"And...tell...me...now......how do I live without you? I want to know....how do I breathe without you...if you ever go...how do I ever...ever surviiiiiive? How do I....how do I live....." Honest to God, Leann Rimes has nothing on Kendra. If she were in an American Idol competition and I was a judge, I'd hand her the first prize right now. My hand hasn't left my chest. Listening to her, I'm in complete awe. I can't believe she's never told me that she can sing. More than sing. My girl is making love to my ears right now. As if she couldn't be more perfect. As she goes into the second verse, I rest my shoulder against the door, bringing my ear closer to the small gap between the door and the frame, trying to hear as much as I can.

I don't want the song to end, but as it does, I'm about to enter when she opens the door, carrying a bag of garbage in her hand. Letting out a little squeal of terror, she accidentally drops the bag as she covers her mouth in shock. "Shit, I'm sorry, baby. I didn't mean to scare you." I say, picking the bag up.

Her chest heaves with fright. "I was just," she swallows, gaining her bearings, "your garbage was full. I was just going to take it out for you." Her headphones are still in her ears. "How long have you been standing there?" she asks, tilting her head sideways. A 'v' forms between her eyes.

Licking my lips, I place the bag on the floor and place

my hands on either side of her waist. "Long enough."
Stroking the side of her face with the back of my hand, I
divide my glance between both her eyes and murmur,
"Baby, no wonder you don't want to be a lawyer.
There's a songbird hiding inside your heart, just begging
to come out and be heard."

Her voice is a mere whisper, as she searches my
gaze. "You think so?"

"Yeah. You sound like an angel. And I'm not just
saying that. I didn't think you could be more beautiful.
Everything about you is beautiful, including your voice."

Letting that sink in a moment, she swallows. "I...I
didn't know you....you were listening."

"Sorry, I didn't mean to eavesdrop." I explain
apologetically. "I turned back when I realized how slimy
it is to not take you *out* for breakfast, and then I heard
you singing, and I...didn't want you to stop."

"Really?" she says, as if she didn't hear me the first
time.

"Really." I say, kissing her on the forehead. "When
did you learn to sing?"

She frowns, "I was in the choir at school forever, and
I sang in a couple of competitions when I was a
teenager. Won a few." She shrugs.

"Why didn't you ever pursue anything further?"

"My dad wanted me to be a lawyer. He started saving
double for me for college when I told him I wanted to be
one after I went through an obsession with legal
movies."

"And you never had any motivation to sing
anymore?"

She chuckles softly. "I sing all the time. Just not
when anyone can hear me. My car is my pretend
recording studio."

I smile, picking up on a note of embarrassment in
her voice. "Does this make you uncomfortable?"

She looks at me and gives me a warm smile back.
"Not with you."

***

"Jack, my brother." I say, clapping my older sibling on the back. "Thanks for stopping by."

"Hey, no problem. You want a beer?" he asks, summoning Blake to grab him a cold one while I'm taking a break from my set. It's the only set I've worked this week, and it'll be the last one until next week, since I'm doing a sound check for the wedding tomorrow night, and then the wedding itself the following night. The boys and I practiced yesterday and last night.

"No, not tonight." I say, knowing Kendra's stopping by shortly, and she's coming over to my place when my set is over.

He gives me a look like I've just sprouted a third eye. "You sick? Since when do you *not* want a beer on break?"

"Ah, not in the mood tonight." I lie. I'm in the mood for something, but it's not beer.

He lifts a brow. "Okay." Blake hands him a beer and Jack nods his thanks, throwing a ten dollar bill on the bar. "Did Julia get in touch with you?"

"Yeah,"

"Glad Colton's coming home. That's the last of that Afghanistan crap in our lives for good from what I understand."

"Amen," I say, "Hey, you see the bitchin' silk-screening Dave did to the drums?" I point to the stage, where the front of the drum now says, *'Take Risks'* in red, with an appearance akin to flames.

"Yeah," Jack hesitates. "Something wrong with you tonight?"

"No, why?"

He shakes his head, and then cranes his neck to the side. "Because that smoking hot blonde just walked by, totally checking you out, and you didn't even bat an eyelash. Dude, what gives?"

I look at him like he just called me a shithead, "Nothing."

"Yeah, right." Jack guffaws.

And then it's like a beacon. The front door opens, and I see her appear, looking for me. I wave my hand in the air so Kendra can see me at the bar.

Jack smiles. "Ah, there it is."

"There what is?" I chuckle.

"The reason why you're acting like you matured ten years overnight. Next thing I know you're going to be telling me you want to perform at weddings and do a duet with her. Christ."

I purse my lips together, trying to keep a straight face.

"You're fucking kidding me." he says, lowering his beer, shaking his head.

Kendra reaches us. She sees Jack and clams up. Ignoring her stiff stance, I lean in and kiss her full on the mouth...twice. I'd do more if he wasn't standing right there with his mouth hanging open in shock. "Jack, you remember Kendra." I say by way of introduction.

"Nice to meet you, again, Jack." Kendra says, offering him her hand to shake.

He shakes it and smiles with a knowing look. "Kendra. I've heard a lot about you."

She smiles back. "Same here."

"Lies. All lies." Jack jokes.

"Wade tells me you're an accountant?"

"Yeah, CFO for my dad's airline. But I'm sure you knew that already."

I can't stop looking at her. She let her hair out. It's pooling in loose curls on her shoulders. The red glints under the bar lights. Her eyelashes, which are naturally reddish-blonde, are painted with a touch of black mascara. It brings out the green in her eyes. A hint of pink lip gloss remains on her lips. It tastes like watermelon. I lick my lips and ignore the throbbing below the belt just from four seconds of contact with her. My hand reaches out to hold hers while she converses with Jack and I lose myself, watching her.

She's a natural with people. Even though Jack's throwing her some curve balls, commenting on his trouble-making little brother, Kendra can handle it. Stroking the inside of her deliciously soft hand, I realize I have a song in my head. Using my free hand, I take my phone out of my pocket. "I'll be right back. Two minutes." I say, leaving them alone. Walking down the hallway, I go into the green room and close the door. Activating my voice notes, I begin singing the first verse and the starting of a chorus. It's very rough and I stagger some of the words as I go, but at least the concept is there.

When I return, Dave signals to me that we're ready to finish our set. I look at Kendra. "Gotta go finish up, baby." I say, kissing her full on the mouth again. I look at her and she smiles.

"I'll sit with Jack." She says.

I lift my finger to my brother in mock warning. "Keep your hands off."

He smacks the side of my head and I smile, smoothing my hair down, winking at Kendra one last time. I want to kiss her again, but I feel like I'm being watched. As I climb on to the stage, Kendra starts whooping, and clapping her hands, and it immediately catches on. The whole bar begins whistling, clapping and making whooping noises. I look at her and she blows me a kiss. It takes everything in me not to walk down there and kiss her back like there's no tomorrow.

Standing in front of the mic, I take it and say, "Thanks. I'd like to introduce the band." I name each as I point them out. "And that's my big brother Jack over there, and my girl, Kendra."

Jack raises his hand in greeting, but Kendra just looks at me blankly. I'm not sure what to make of her expression. Maybe it's too early to call her my girl? Am I being too presumptuous? Or maybe she's just embarrassed. I'll have to ask her later. All I know is that we're not friends, we're not just lovers, either. It felt natural to call her 'my girl', because it feels like she's mine. I feel like I'm hers, too. Maybe Jack's right. Maybe I did mature overnight. Since I met Kendra, a lot of things have changed in me. I feel like a whole new door has been opened that was shut tight before.

As I sing, I'm looking at Kendra during almost all the lyrics. There are no other females in the bar. Well, there could be, but I don't notice any of them. She's the only female that matters. The way she looks at me is intense. Like she's studying me. But at the same time, she's grooving along, and I even catch her mouthing the words a few times. I'd love to have her come up and sing with me. I want to ask her to, but I know it'll only embarrass her. Maybe singing together is something we can do in private later.

We sing a slow song, one of my own that I wrote a couple of years ago. It's a song about feeling alone, minus a mom, but there's a lot of symbolism, so unless you're really paying attention to the lyrics, you think it's just about a girl being absent in your life. As I sing the chorus, the words are intense, and I have to hit a high note that is difficult for most male singers to reach. When I get there, the audience begins clapping and whistling, including Kendra. But I notice something about her that's different. Her eyes are glossy with tears. I wink at her and she blows me another kiss, wiping her eyes. Jack looks at her and asks if she's okay. She says something to him that I can't decipher, and he rubs her back. I know he's my brother, but him touching her bothers me. I'll have to pound on him later.

When the song ends, I begin with a catchier tune of my own, about not being able to decide which girl is right; it's kind of satirical and doesn't necessarily apply to just me: I make it about all men trying to make the choice. The dance floor fills up and people are grooving to the music. I see Kendra get up and go use the washroom. When she returns, her face is dark and flat. Something's wrong. I give her a look, but she ignores it. Jack picks up on the tension and questions her, but she waves him off.   Following Kendra's icy gaze, I see someone walk by the bar and shoot her an equally cold stare.

...Priscilla.

Chapter 24

Kendra

He called me his girl. It felt so good. Any woman can relate to that moment in a budding relationship when you ask yourself 'where is this going?'. I mean, sex with Wade is phenomenal; the best sex of my life. We have a bond outside the bedroom, too, I think, that is even tighter in some ways than the bond that I have with Jennifer. There are some things about Wade that are unlike any man I've ever known. He's tough and you don't want to mess with him, but he's got a really soft side, too. He puts my needs ahead of his, which is more than I can say for any other man I know, my father included.

When he sang the song about his mother, I couldn't stop crying. The pain that that poor man has felt in his life because of not having a mom is insurmountable. For someone who's been abandoned, he doesn't seem to have abandonment issues, which I'm glad for. I wouldn't leave him, and I think he knows that. He has an extraordinarily strong way of looking at the world, too. He's living in a shoebox, making next to nothing, but he's so blissfully happy because he's doing what he's always dreamed of doing. I admire him for that. He doesn't need a fancy car or house to prove anything to anyone. He proves something every time he walks on the stage.

At first, I was embarrassed that he heard me singing. I don't sing for anyone except myself, and for him to appreciate my voice and sincerely compliment me, it meant a lot. Wade wouldn't tell me something in vain, so I believe that he truly likes my voice. Maybe we can sing together when we're alone. That would be incredibly romantic.

Jack is a boy stuck in a man's body. He's forever young, which is probably why Wade and Jack are so close. I can't wait to meet all the brothers; I've heard so much about them. But that's being a little presumptuous. He's probably months away from even considering introducing me to the rest of his family. I mean, I met Jack purely by coincidence. He speaks so highly of Julia; I'd really love to meet her. She must be really special since he loves her so much. Mary is really cool, so Julia must be equally down-to-earth.

As I sat listening to my man (can I call him that?) singing his heart out on stage, I couldn't hold my bladder any longer, as much as I didn't want to miss a minute of Wade's performance. After I finished relieving myself, I realized I had a guest in the bathroom. A very pregnant guest. Judging the woman immediately, I thought it was a horribly inappropriate place for a woman expecting a child. She has short brown hair, which is so thick I consider the chance that it might be a wig. "Can I help you?" I say as I wash my hands in the sink, noticing her eyes are burning into my reflection.

"You're with Wade." She says it like it's an affliction.

"Do I know you?" I ask, trying to keep the irritation out of my voice.

"No, but if you've got anything to do with Wade, you're going to." Her tone is cutting.

I fold my arms on my chest. "Look, I don't know what your problem is, but I don't appreciate the threat."

"Are you fucking him?"

Before I can warn her to watch her mouth, she continues. "Because you should know that he was fucking me, too." She points to her belly. "This is his kid, as much as he denies it."

She looks like she's about eight months pregnant, and she's wearing a loose-fitting black dress that goes past her knees, with thick shoulder straps. There is a blue scarf tied loosely around her neck, and she's wearing big, round blue earrings, colored to match her scarf. The hoops are so big a bird could easily perch on them.

Recognition comes to my face. This is Priscilla, the woman who gave him the threatening letter. I'm not even sure what Wade did with the letter I drafted for him. I let her talk, being careful to say nothing and appear impassive.

"Well, aren't you gonna like freak out? He's carrying my child at the same time as he's fucking you, lady!" a line of spittle flies out of her mouth and lands on my arm. I gaze at my arm and walk over to the sink to wash it off with soap. Lord knows what kind of cheap scank this is who would pull a stunt like that.

She wipes her mouth as though it didn't happen. "I'm suing him you know...for child support."

I say nothing. I'm making a meal out of cleaning up my arm, even though the spittle is very scant.

"He hasn't even responded. The coward. I know where he lives. He's in some basement apartment. He ain't even got a proper bed," she scoffs, giving me the once-over, "But if you're fucking him, you probably already know that, don't you."

I grab a paper towel out of the dispenser and dry my arm.

"He fucked me in the green room in that tavern over in South Carolina, you know. I found out this is his regular gig, so that's why I'm here. I'm going to talk to him after the set. Find out why he hasn't given me my money yet."

"You stay away from Wade." Is all I say.

"You threatening me?" she points to herself.

"Just...leave him alone." I repeat.

"Why?" she barks. "What are you gonna do about it?"

Saying nothing, I walk away from her. She's smart to stay back. As I walk back to our table, I try to keep my face impassive, but I can see that Wade is already picking up on something. So is Jack.

"What's going on? You sick?" Jack asks.

"No. Everything is fine." I lie.

In the corner of my eye, I see Priscilla walk by,

pinning a glare on me like it's a contest. Trying to ignore her, I fold my hands in front of my mouth and look at Wade. His face turns pale when he sees Priscilla. Thank God his set is finished. He wraps up the song about ten seconds later and walks off the stage.

He kisses me quickly but wastes no time asking me what Priscilla wanted. "She didn't...touch you or anything, did she?"

I shake my head no. "She had a few choice words with me. I had very little exchange with her other than what was required."

"That the chick that's trying to sue you?" Jack asks.

"Yeah," Wade says, hooking his thumbs through the loops in his jeans. "Thought that ordeal was over." He lifts his hand and rubs my arm. "You okay?"

"Fine." I force a smile.

"I've got a cop friend I can get in touch with if you like." Jack offers. "I can get him to come keep watch."

"I don't know if that's necessary." Wade says.

"She knows where you live. I don't know if she's got an accomplice or if she's on her own." I say. "It might not be a bad idea."

"Baby, she's like eight months pregnant. What harm can she do? She's just some sick freak who found out my family has money. If I don't respond to her, she'll leave me alone." Wade rubs my arm with an earnest look on his face.

"Alright," I smile.

"You want to get out of here?" he says, glancing at my lips, making my belly tingle.

"Sure. Do you need to pack anything up?"

"Nope. I'm all set." He addresses Jack. "You want to stop by my place for a bit?" he offers.

"Nah, I'm sure you two want to be alone." He frowns. "I'll head home."

"You sure?" Wade grasps my hand in his.

"Yeah. I'll catch you on Sunday if you're not busy."

"Sure."

"Nice seeing you again, Kendra." Jack winks his Ford family wink and I can't help but smile. He smiles back and looks at Wade. "You call me if you need me."

"Will do, brother. Safe driving home."

We watch Jack walk out the door and the band members stop by, saying their goodbyes to Wade and I. Wade introduces me and they all smile as they carry their instruments to the back of the bar.

"Come on, baby. Let's go back to my place." Wade says as he places his hand on the side of my face, kissing me tenderly. His touch sends shivers down my spine. We hold hands as we exit to the parking lot. He walks me to my car and as I press the fob and open the door, he slides his hands around my waist from behind me. "I'm dying." He says, kissing the back of my neck.

"What's wrong?" I ask as I turn around, genuinely concerned.

He looks up at the darkened sky and exhales. "Not that kind of dying, babe." He says. He guides my hand down to his jeans, over the zipper area. He's as hard as a rock.

"Oh," I whisper, immediately wet. "*That* kind of dying." I don't know whether I should kiss him or not; I don't want to make it worse.

"This is almost embarrassing. I'm like a teenager around you." He comments.

"If it helps...I'm soaked just from touching you a second ago." I admit.

He lets out a soft groan. "Oh, baby, you're killing me." he laughs.

"Do you want to...do it in the car?" I ask, only half-joking.

"I can't make love to you in a car, sweetie." He says warmly. "Let's get out of here. Drive me over to my car so I don't leave it here."

Fifteen minutes later we're at his place. "I'm sure your dad has caught on by now." He says, tossing his keys on the breakfast bar.

"No, not really. He's assuming I'm staying at Jen and

Wendy's place. But my parents will be at the wedding."

"That I'm not worried about." Wade says, wrapping his arms around me. "I'll be singing so it won't be that obvious." He looks at me. "I called you my girl earlier at the bar, while I was up on stage. Should I not have done that?" He asks with his eyes slit halfway, as if treading carefully.

"No, I loved it. It felt great. It kind of...made it official." I kiss him on the nose. "It was sweet." I lean in and kiss him on the lips. "So, I'm your girl?"

He smiles shyly, cupping my face in his hands. "I guess you are." He whispers, and the tone is sexy as hell.

"Does that make you my man?" I giggle, and he giggles as he leans in and kisses my neck. He starts just below my ear and trails kisses all down the side of my neck, lifting my hair out of the way so he can get right in there. Still giggling, because it tickles, I reach down to his zipper area. He's hard as a rock again...or still. "We seem to have a problem." I say, my voice is like silk. "Do you need me to take care of this for you?"

He whispers in my ear softly, sending shivers down my spine. "It appears I need some special attention. Do *you* need special attention?" he asks, but before I can answer, he's undoing and unzipping my jeans, and sliding his hand inside. "Mmmm...my girl definitely needs attention." He whispers again as a soft groan escapes from my throat. His finger is gingerly circling my clit. The warmth from his strong arm and hand ignites my skin as though it's on fire. He stops for a moment, lowering my jeans and panties to the floor, as I lift his shirt off and begin sucking his one nipple while gently squeezing the other with the opposite hand. "Oh, Kendra," he hisses as he rears his head back. "Mmmm....that's the first time you've ever done that."

Suddenly a fan of doing things for the first time, I bend down and undo his jeans, pulling them down to the floor. He steps out of them and expects me to stand up again. When I don't, he looks down at me. I'm holding his hardened penis in my hand. I lick the head slowly, staring up at him. "Oh, Jesus," He whispers, scraping his face with his hand. Licking my palm, I sit on my knees, and wrap my moistened fingers around the hilt. Stuffing his penis into my mouth, I hear him suck in a breath of air.

"Oh, Lord, Jesus." He hisses as I begin to pump him slowly. Gripping the breakfast bar, Wade lowers his head and closes his eyes. "Baby, oh God, Kendra." He breathes as I find his rhythm, with the perfect suction, sheathing my lips over my teeth as I take him fully in my mouth, pumping at the perfect speed. His breathing is becoming ragged as I taste the salty pre-come slowly oozing from him. "Kendra, baby, I'm getting close." He pants. I swallow harder, sucking stronger, pumping faster, until he says quickly. "Kendra, if you don't stop it's gonna happen in your mouth, baby." He touches my arm, making sure I can hear his gentle warning.

I look up at him and his eyes widen. "Kendra, I'm gonna come." His voice rises an octave, as if fearful, and then he shuts his eyes tight and his mouth opens wide as I feel his seed shoot into my mouth in spurts while I suck him, taking in the hot liquid, as his head rears back, eyes shut tight, and he shouts out, "Oh.....God....*Fuck*....." he grunts as the veins in the sides of his neck protrude. I think that's the first time I ever heard an expletive uttered from him. He pants quickly, and grunts as I feel more seed shoot out of him. His chest is rising and falling so fast, as if he's just run a marathon. When I slow, he's still breathing ragged, feeling the aftershocks. His penis still twitches as I come to a stop.

Looking up at him, his eyes are closed. He swallows as I watch his Adam's Apple rise and fall. When he opens his eyes, I get up off my knees. He lifts me on to the counter and rests his head on my chest, breathing heavily. Running my hand through his hair, I kiss his head. "Sorry I swore." He whispers after a moment.

"It was that fucking good, wasn't it." I chuckle softly.

"You have no idea." He kisses my shirt. "I'm wrecked."

He lifts his head and looks at me. His eyes are hooded. "Are you okay...after...that?"

"What do you mean?"

"Well, you...swallowed."

"Yeah, I'm okay." I smile. "I've never done that before." I frown, impressed with myself. I'd given oral sex before, but never swallowed. "And by the way I *do* have an idea."

A 'v' forms between his brows. "When you did...that...to *me*. It was mind-blowing." I explain.

He lifts a brow, suggestively. "Was it now."

"Baby, it was." I say.

"But it wasn't 'f' bomb good." He points out.

"Maybe I don't 'f' bomb in bed." I argue softly, kissing his lips chastely.

He gives me a smouldering look. "I think I can fix that."

Chapter 25

Wade

I've died and gone to heaven. What Kendra just did to me was the single most satisfying thing I've ever felt in my life. Trying everything I could to make sure she knew I was ready, I was holding back as much as I could, until I couldn't. One can never be sure how a woman is going to feel about that. It's one thing to do that, an entirely different thing to see it through to the end. I was so afraid that she was going to freak out or panic...or choke. I wouldn't want to make her feel uncomfortable or to make her feel like she doesn't have choices.

The 'f' bomb completely slipped out. For a second it felt like I was having an out-of-body experience and my mouth and my brain lost the filter that would normally prevent slips like that at such a delicate moment. She didn't seem to mind. In fact, I think she took it as a compliment. As she sits on the counter, half-naked, I can think of only one thing to do to return the favor, and to see if I can do it as well as she did to me just a moment ago. "Are you cold?" I ask, touching her naked legs with my outstretched hands, covering as much of her skin with my palm as I can.

"Not with you here, baby." She whispers, kissing me full on the mouth. "You keep me warm."

What I want to do might not be so comfortable on the counter, but I'm a sucker for spontaneity. As I remove her shirt and bra, I kiss her breasts and nipples, listening to her breathe deeply, taking in the sensation of my lips on her body. I love the sounds she makes. She's not shy about expressing her pleasure vocally, the same way I just learned I am a moment ago. Crouching down slightly, I rest her knees on my shoulders.

"Oh, what are you doing, Wade?" she breathes a giggle; it sounds delicious.

I wink at her as I'm eye-level with the counter, and I spread her legs apart, taking in the beauty that is her body. Pink and perfect, I suck her outer labia, separating her tender folds with my lips. She leans back on her elbows, taking it all in. "Are you okay like that?" I ask softly.

"I'll let you know." She purrs.

I chuckle softly as I surround her most sensitive area with my mouth, as if I'm French-kissing her there. She murmurs a moan that makes my cock twitch. If I want to have the right effect here, I have to make her come hard and fast. I've seen her do it before when I use the right technique. I can see her clit sitting up already. Shoving my face right in, I take the whole mound in my mouth and suck moderately at first, and hold it long, rhythmically letting it slide out in tiny increments as she breathes in and moans out her breath.

Repeating the same procedure, I reach her nipples and gently pinch them between my thumb and my forefingers. She cries out a huge 'O' and I go in for the kill. Using just the tip of my tongue, I flick her now swollen clit repeatedly, as I feel her legs stiffen, her rear buck up and down, and her feet flatten as though getting ready for takeoff. As her breathing starts to get ragged, and I taste her wetness flowing, I angle up a breath higher, hitting right on the apex of her clit. Her head is reared backward, and her chest is heaving. "Oh, God Wade!!" she cries out. "Ooohhhh...don't stop! Don't stop!" she says as I feel and see her body pulse. I lick faster, helping her ride the waves of pleasure.

My dick is throbbing again, experiencing my girl crashing in the throws of passion at my touch. Her eyes are closed, and her mouth is wide as she says my name once more before pushing off her elbows and letting her back rest on the counter. It is a sight to behold; my baby laying on the counter, spent from an epic orgasm courtesy of me. I give her folds one last gentle suck before lifting myself up, while supporting her legs with my hands. Standing over her, I look down and smile.

"You okay?" I chuckle, knowing full well that she's way more than okay. I'm rubbing her legs to bring the circulation back.

"We need to sanitize this counter." She giggles breathlessly.

"Don't worry about that." I say, kissing her belly. I take her hands and help her rise, and then I wrap my arms around her as we enjoy a naked embrace. I kiss her full on the mouth once, twice, half a dozen times, making a smacking noise after each time. "I never get tired of kissing you." I say to her.

"Good. Don't ever stop."

Lifting her off the counter, I drape her legs around my waist and carry her over to the bed, gently laying her down. My weight is on her as we lay like pancakes. She takes her hands through my hair as we kiss endlessly. One after the next. Chaste yet deep. "Your back okay?" I ask her, stroking the side of her face.

"Fine. Are you legs okay?"

"That's not my leg, sweetheart." I joke.

She giggles. It's such a wonderful sound. It's contagious. We're giggling together in bed. Never done that with anyone else before. I rest my head on her chest while we continue to laugh together. When we're breathless, I look at her. "Do you have to go home tonight?"

Her face falls. "Yeah. And I'm spending the night at Jennifer's tomorrow night. After tonight I won't see you until the wedding." It seems like it's months away, but it's only a couple of days. "We have the rehearsal dinner on Friday night while you guys do your sound check. I might be able to see you if Jenn has any last-minute things to do at the hall, but chances are pretty slim. She's got all her ducks in a row."

The longing in her voice is adorable. "That's okay, sweetie. Maybe I'll meet you for lunch at work tomorrow."

"Baby, I'm in meetings all day tomorrow, and I'm off Friday to prepare for the wedding. We have to go pick up our dresses and run dozens of errands."

"I'll miss you." Three words I've never said to another woman before. Three other words are on the tip of my tongue, but I'm not sure if either of us are ready to hear them or to say them to each other yet.

She kisses me full on the lips. "I'll miss you like crazy, baby."

My gaze goes from her eyes, to her nose, lips, and back up to her eyes again. I want desperately to make love to her again, but it's late and I know she has to go home and get ready for work tomorrow. "As much as I hate like hell that you've got to go, I don't want you driving home late."

I get off her and we both get dressed. We kiss ten dozen times before we say goodbye for the night. I feel like a lovesick teenager. It's nuts. I don't want her to leave. It's like part of me is leaving with her. It's stupid. It's childish. I try to brush her departure off by forcing myself to have a beer, but I don't want it. Instead, I clean my apartment like a man possessed, to try to take my mind off my place being absent her. Once I'm done cleaning, I hop in bed and try not to think about Kendra's scent in my bedsheets. It doesn't work, and I end up laying there for hours thinking about her.

Chapter 26

Kendra

I have to admit; my best friend makes a beautiful bride. Her dress is perfect; not too flouncy or ornate, but classically styled in cream silk. The top is a simple lace design with a scoop neck and an empire waist, caught in the back with a lace bow. The front of the dress stops at her feet so they're visible, and the back is a short yet subtle silk train. Her light brown hair is in an upsweep with a braid that lays over half her head like a headband, and a tiny wisp of baby's breath is tucked inside the braid. She looks simple and elegant. Just like her.

Thankfully, our bridesmaid dresses are equally simple. We're all in mint green silk with empire waistlines and scoop necks, but our dresses have no train, are floor-length, and have a slit up the left side. Wendy, the Maid of Honor, has a sprig of baby's breath in her hair to match her sister's. My hair is curled and swept up at the sides, but out in the back. Thankfully with my red hair, green is a good color on me. I'm wearing contacts today; which I often do on special occasions where photographs are in order. My parents are here; my mom looks beautiful in an emerald green knee-length frock and heels colored to match. Dad has on a black suit with an emerald green tie to match mom's dress. They look fantastic.

As I stand up at the altar, I can't help but think about Wade. I miss him so much, even though we've talked on the phone a dozen times since we saw each other last. There was no time to see him last night after the rehearsal dinner. All of us bridesmaids slept at Jennifer's place last night. Jennifer's cousin Lindsay, the bridesmaid who's standing next to me, is trying not to laugh. Most people shake when they're nervous. She's trying not to bust a gut beside me. Wendy is trying to shush her, but it's only spurring her on. Before we realize it, the ceremony is over, and Jennifer and Brandon are kissing for the first time as husband and wife.

A stream of jealousy shoots through me. I want this, too. It's crazy to think how deeply Wade and I feel about each other after only a short time. It takes many couples months or years to feel what we feel. My heart aches for him. I can't wait to hold him and kiss him again. It will be my undoing watching and hearing him sing tonight, knowing I can't kiss him or touch him until after the reception is over. I can't wait to see him. As the outside pictures are done, we're driven by our rented limos to the reception hall for the rest of the pictures. I find myself searching for Wade's car, and when I see it, my heart begins to pound.

"I hope everything went well with the sound check." Jennifer comments as she sees a spare microphone being carried into the hall by one of the band members. I'm disappointed it isn't Wade.

"If anything went wrong, you would have been the first to know, I'm sure." I say.

"Quit worrying." Wendy whines. "They're professionals."

"I know. It's just...very important. If anything goes wrong with the music, the whole night will be ruined."

"It will be fine." I say as the limo driver opens the door. As us girls disembark, we're led by the photographer to an area inside the main hallway. The reception hall is ginormous; it has three separate reception areas, but Jennifer is using the largest portion. Inside is an area that's been cordoned off for pictures. The guests are starting to mill in here and there, peppering themselves throughout the dining area. The remainder of the pictures are being taken to the left of the dining area. But from a distance, I can see the sound stage. The drums are set up, along with all the other sound equipment. Cords are taped to the floor with duct tape for safety. It appears all ready to go, minus the band members.

An hour later, and after what feels like five thousand pictures have been taken, the photographer lets us assemble for introductions. Thirty minutes later, all the guests have arrived, and we've all been acquainted via the most boring receiving line ever. The din of people is a little intimidating. I've never been to a wedding with more than a hundred people.

"Okay, everyone, pair up. The MC is going to announce us and then you go to the head table." Jennifer says. I take my partner's hand, which is clammy and gross from him being pasted into a suit all day. He recognizes the repugnant look on my face, and decides to hook his arm through mine instead, giving me an apologetic look in the process.

When mine and my partner's names are announced, we walk in to the tune of a pre-recorded song, which I don't even notice, because the only thing I notice...is him. Like the other guests, he's standing up, clapping as each wedding party member walks in and takes their seats. He looks...stunning. He's wearing a cream white linen shirt, with the top two buttons undone, and black dress pants that hug him perfectly. He's wearing dress shoes that are so shiny I can probably see my reflection in them. I can't take my eyes off him. He winks at me and it's my undoing. God, I want him. I want him now. I've missed him so much it hurts.

He whistles at me, and a few others take it as a signal to whistle, too. He smiles at me and I smile back, as his eyes don't leave me while I'm released by my guest, and I take my spot at the head table, which is directly across from the stage. I have an almost perfect view of him from where I sit. It makes me ache. We're all standing as Lindsay and her guest come in, and then the bride and groom are given a huge welcome last, and then as we all sit, the band takes a seat in the table right next to the stage. As we listen to a couple of speeches, and a word from the MC, dinner is served. Our eyes have barely left each other, when Wendy says she needs to use the washroom, and wants me to go with her. She and I rise together, and Wade smiles at me and I smile back at him.

"God, I'm so glad this is almost over." Wendy says as she washes her hands in the washroom. "I'm exhausted."

"It's a long day, that's for sure." I say, washing my hands beside her. The bathroom is tucked inside a small hallway, where there is also a coat check and a few other unmarked doors. As we walk out of the washroom, I see Wade standing in the hallway with Dave, one of his bandmates, showing him some sort of sound contraption. Wendy says hi, and I catch his gaze.

"Hey there," he says to me, taking a step towards me. His hand is immediately in mine, and he turns his back to Wendy and Dave, kissing me full on the mouth while watching for other guests behind us.

"Hi," I say, after he kisses me. I'm weak in the knees already.

"You look so beautiful." He says, tucking his hands around my waist.

"You look so handsome." I compliment, looking down at his chest.

"Errr...Wade, so you think I can record us with this thing?" Dave asks.

We turn around to face them. Wade's hand hasn't left my waist. My hand is hooked on the top of his pants. "Yeah, that's sweet. Never even knew you could buy something like that."

"Like what?" Wendy asks, curious.

Dave sticks this square device out to show us. It has a round, cup-like thing on each side, almost like Mickey Mouse ears. "It's a sound recording device. Specially made to record music without any of the background noise." Dave explains. "I was hoping to record some of our music tonight and play it on YouTube or something. The videographer's going to grab some of our stuff, too, and we'll run it together. I know him from high school.

He's pretty cool."

"Sounds awesome." Wade says, rubbing my waist with his hand. I want to kiss him again, but I don't want to make Wendy or Dave uncomfortable. We hear voices from the hallway, and I turn around to see my parents. It's too late to let go of Wade without making it obvious. My mom breaks into a smile when she sees me. I feel immediate relief.

"Hey, we thought you kids might have escaped." Dad says with a grin. Wade is holding his ground or doesn't want to let me go, because his hand is still around my waist. He shakes my dad's hand with his free hand, but otherwise doesn't move from his spot next to me. "What have you got there, son?" Dad asks Dave.

"Sorry, my manners," Wade says. "Dave, this is Kendra's father, Peter," they shake hands and my mom takes a step toward them and introduces herself. Wade's hand interlaces with mine and he begins stroking the inside of my palm with his finger. I could burst into flames from his touch.

"It's a sound recording device, sir. I was going to record some of our material from tonight."

"That sounds like a good idea." Dad says, "Do you need any help?"

Dave frowns. "You can hang on to it if you want. I know the videographer is going to do some recording, too."

"I can get some footage if you'd like, too." Mom offers. "This is quite the to-do, isn't it?" She addresses Wade, "Have you played at a large venue like this before?"

"No, ma'am." He shakes his head no. The smile he gives her is so endearing I want to kiss him.

"Well, show me how it works, I'll come back with you." Dad offers.

"Sure, thanks," Dave follows dad. Dad leans into Wade before walking away. "I suppose you don't hate her now, do you." He winks. My face turns beet red.

"No, sir." He smiles, chuckling, knowing he's been figured out.

"Yeah, it sickens me." Dave says in jest.

Wade smiles as they all walk back towards the hall, Wendy too, leaving us alone.

"That could have been much worse." Wade comments, wrapping his arms around my waist. I drape my arms on his shoulders. He kisses me tenderly and then leans his forehead on mine. "God, you're so beautiful. You're eyes...my God. Are you wearing contacts?"

I nod. Kissing him a little deeper.

"Mmmm..." he breathes. "As much as I'd love to stay here with you, we should get back, baby."

"We should." I agree, kissing him one last time. He takes my hand as we walk back to the reception hall and part ways.

Then I have one of the most memorable nights of my life.

Chapter 27

Wade

Dinner was fantastic and now the bride is giving me the cue to start. My stomach is a little jittery. This isn't a bar full of drunken scanks tonight, it's real people with expectations. And one beautiful girl who I can't stop looking at or thinking about. The MC walks over to the mic and he does a two-minute shpeel on housekeeping and requests for me. He introduces me and the band and the lights dim as the overhead disco ball starts rotating. I grab the mic and say thanks to the MC for the nice introduction.

"Congratulations to Jennifer and Brandon." I say as the bride and groom make their way to the center of the dance floor and Griffin starts playing the piano intro to the song. A few whistles and woots are heard, prompting the bride and groom to kiss.

I take a deep breath and start. *"Sometimes I wonder if I'd ever make it through. Through this world without having you. I just wouldn't have a clue."* I'm looking directly at Kendra and she has to look away as Wendy starts crying, looking at her sister. *"'Cause sometimes it seems like this world is closing in on me, and there's no way of breaking free, and then I see you reach for me."*

I think about the other night after we made love, how she cried when I sang those words to her. She's looking at me now and I can tell she's crying. But she's also holding Wendy's hand, so I'm sure that's the reason for the emotion.

"Sometimes I wanna give up, wanna give in, I wanna...quit the fight...and then I see you baby, and everything's alright....every...thing's alright."

The bride and groom are embracing each other so tight we can't see their faces. Wendy is bawling. Kendra keeps wiping her eyes and I want so badly to go over there and comfort her. Instead, I sing to her.

"When I see you smile...I can face the world...ooohhhoooo....you know I can do anything. When I see you smiiiile...I see a ray of light....ooooohhhhoo....I see it shining right through the rain....when I see you smile....baby when I see you smile...at me."

The acoustics are great in here. We have the sound up just high enough, and the doors are open, so it doesn't sound like we're singing out of a tin can. The videographer is walking around the bride and groom, getting footage, and Peter is standing about ten feet away from me, recording the song.

I continue, and Kendra looks at me. *"Baby there's nothin' in this world that could ever do...what a touch of your hand can do....it's like nothin' that I ever knew....hey...and when the rain is fallin'....I don't feel it..'cause you're here with me now...and one look at you baby....is all I'll ever need...it's all I'll EVER neeeeed."*

As I lead into the chorus, her eyes are on me, and mine are on hers. I've never made love to anyone with my eyes, but if I were to describe what I'm doing right now, that would be it. Even from several feet away the sentiment is clear. I'm completely, madly, head-over-heels in love with this beauty. And I'm telling her that through song, because that's the safest way right now. I don't want her to feel pressure, just love. This is the second-best way I know how. The first way I'll show her later when we're alone.

She blows me a kiss and I wink at her. *"Sometimes I wanna give up...I wanna give in.....I wanna quit the fight....then when I look at you baby, and everything's alright....hey, everything's alright....it's alright!"*

As Kelvin goes into his guitar solo, I just stand there and drink her in. The bride and groom are kissing and dancing, and every now and again the groom tips her into a dip, which guests are loving. And for a moment I can see myself doing this. I can picture me and Kendra on the dance floor, her in a wedding gown. It's not scary. Now I can understand what Colton talks about. Marrying the right person and it just feels right. He must be right; they got married very quickly and they've been happily married for over two years now. Trying for a family and everything. It can't be that bad. Thinking of Kendra as my wife feels kind of good, actually. She'd probably run like hell if she knew what I was thinking right now. I'll be careful not to let her know. I'd never want to do anything to lose her. The thought sickens me.

As I sing the last verse, my girl hasn't stopped smiling at me. "*When I see you smiiilllle...oh yeah......baby when I see you.... smiiiiiile....smile...at me.*"

The bride and groom get a huge uproar of clapping, whistling and shouting. Jennifer and Brandon didn't want a lot of slow songs, so they chose the second song to go right into something more upbeat. As the dance floor fills, I can't see my girl anymore. I search for her and finally find her milling around with the guests. Her dress is incredible. I've never seen her in one and I could so get used to it. She has great legs and this dress has a slit up the side that accentuates her form. So beautiful.

Wedding crowds are a lot more fun than bar crowds. While equally drunk, there are no fights, and it's just generally family and friends dancing and having fun. Kendra disappears a lot, and when I see her again, she always smiles at me. I love it. Jennifer requested pre-recorded music about an hour after the set starts, playing mostly wedding tunes like the bird dance and lame stuff like that. When our break arrives, the MC, although very inebriated, comes to the mic and announces that we're all expected to make complete asses out of ourselves while the band takes a break. Verbatim.

Kendra brings me over a bottle of water, and she gives me a quick kiss, since her dad is right behind me. "I think this is working, Wade." He says.

I take a sip of water. "Thanks, Peter. It should be good. I saw the videographer getting good footage, too."

"Carol, too." He states.

Kendra rubs a hand over my face, wiping the sweat off me. "It's hot under those lights." I explain.

"You are amazing." She says, shaking her head as though in disbelief.

"Thanks, baby." I kiss her full on the mouth, not caring anymore if anyone is watching.

"Do you want to sit?" She offers.

"No, but I'll need a washroom break before I go back on."

She takes my hand as we walk to the bathroom. The bird dance is in full swing behind us. The hall is barren as everyone is lined up at the bar outside the hall. We're hand in hand until we reach the washroom area. Her smile could light up the night sky. "What?" I ask.

"I'm so proud of you. You really saved my best friend. You're so talented and yet you don't mind performing at a wedding. Nobody better ever say that you're not humble, because you are."

I don't know how to respond, so I just kiss her deeply, which seems to have the desired effect. She runs her hands through my hair, and then she wraps her arms around my shoulders. "Shoot. You had to use the washroom." She says after giving me a squeeze.

"I can wait." I say, not letting her go. "But I don't want you to get all sweaty from me." I say, pulling back a little. "Don't want to spoil your dress."

"I don't care." She guffaws, then leans in with a salacious grin. "Like I'm not going to beg you to rip it off me later."

Tilting my head slightly, my eyes are slit, as I let out a soft giggle. "My, my, my...just for that, I'm going to kiss you." I open my mouth and envelope hers with mine, plunging my tongue inside. She lets out a throaty moan and kisses me back, plunging her tongue into my mouth. Pulling back, I stroke her face. "By the way, there will be no begging later. You don't even have to ask."

Just as we're about to kiss again, Jennifer appears.

"Oh, you two, my God, you're showing me and my new husband up." She's slightly intoxicated, or exhausted, it's hard to tell.

I release Kendra only a little, and as we're both in each other's arms, we rest our heads together. "Oh my God! What a perfect picture! Don't move!" she says, raising her phone that she was carrying in her hand. This is our first picture, I think to myself. "Sweet. I'll send it to you, Kendra." She says.

"Make sure you send it to my *personal* phone, please." Kendra clarifies. "The last time you sent a picture to me you sent it to my work phone by mistake. I had a lot of explaining to do."

"This wasn't like...a naked picture, was it?" I ask, playing along.

"Not of me..." she lifts a brow.

"Well, you were in it." Jennifer points out.

"But I wasn't naked."

"*He* was." Jennifer adds, making Kendra's face turn red. It's adorable.

"Wait...who's he?" I jibe.

Jennifer comes over and places a hand on my shoulder. "This stripper guy she met at a strip joint a couple of weeks ago."

Kendra rolls her eyes. "Thanks, best friend."

I smile and wink at her, still holding her close.

"Puuullllease. Like Wade would get mad at you." She scoffs. "Look at him, look at you two. You're all over each other."

Okay, it's settled. She's drunk. "You need to use the washroom, there, Jennifer?" I ask, helping her along.

She looks at me as if a lightbulb just went on inside her head. "Oh, yeah..." she points at me, poking me in the chest. "What were we talking about?"

"Just the fact that you had to use the washroom." I point out as if it's the truth, and the other uncomfortable part of the conversation didn't happen. Kendra snorts out a laugh. Jennifer shrugs and walks into the men's washroom accidentally, and then walks back out. Dave walks out, nearly crashing into her.

"Yo, you ready to go back up?" Dave says to me.

I look at Kendra. "I guess I should get ready." I kiss her full on the mouth.

Dave rolls his eyes and walks away. "Gross."

"I should go make sure she's okay." "Kendra says.

"Hurry back." I wink, but say it in a way that means business.

"Why?"

"Just...you should hurry back." I wink again as I walk into the men's washroom.

She has no idea...

Chapter 28

Kendra

When Wade took the stage, I thought I was done. Luckily Wendy was immediately emotional over her sister dancing with her new husband for the first time. But really those tears I was crying were for Wade. His singing is so beautiful I almost can't handle it. My heart was beating so fast I thought I was going to die. As he went though the lyrics, seemingly singing them to me, I couldn't help but get misty-eyed. He's so beautiful behind that microphone. His hair and skin look gorgeous under the lights. His voice is heavenly; husky yet soft in all the right spots. The two buttons undone at his neck teased me incessantly. As his hair started to curl with the sweat beading on his forehead, it was all I could do not to drool.

Kissing him when he's all sweaty is so delicious. I didn't care if he got my dress soiled. He can do whatever he wants to it. My parents seeing us together put me slightly at ease. Neither of them had any comments when Wade went on stage. To be truthful, I'm not sure if either of them cared much for Mark. It shows. Dad really likes Wade; I can tell. Dad doesn't help anyone out unless he likes them. For him to spend an hour recording Wade without even being asked to, that says a lot.

Jennifer is quite intoxicated as I help her clean up after using the washroom. She accidentally dipped her bow in the toilet bowl, luckily it was *after* she'd flushed it. As we walk back into the reception hall, Wade is singing one of his own songs. It's the one where he can't decide which woman he wants. Every time the chorus says, 'you're the one for me', he points at me. It's kind of catchy, so the band takes advantage and stops playing in the middle of the chorus, allowing guests to sing it. By the second verse, they've got it, and everyone is pointing to their loved ones singing 'you're the one for me'. I get in there and point at him, singing the same. The quirky smile on Wade's face melts my heart. He's really in his element on stage.

As I go take a fun selfie with all the bridesmaids at Jennifer's request, Wade plays another catchy tune, another one of his, and when that song ends, the band pauses for a moment. Wade addresses the guests. "For the next song I'm gonna need a little help." I look at him, curious. The background music starts, and I immediately recognize the ballad. It's *'Almost Paradise'* by Mike Reno and Ann Wilson. My face drops. He sees my reaction and gives me a smile that I can't resist. "Kendra, do you mind coming up here and singing this with me?"

The guests go nuts. Whistling, shouting; it sounds like New Year's Eve right before the ball drops. As I approach the stage, he holds out his hand, as if to say, 'it's okay, it's safe, I've got you'. He doesn't let go of my hand. Dave hands me a mic, and suddenly I realize that this might have been planned. He removes the mic from his face and addresses me. "You okay?" he nods, assuring me that it's okay. I nod and he kisses my cheek.

When the first verse starts, he takes a breath and winks at me. *"I thought that dreams belonged to other men.....'cause each time I got close....they'd fall apart again."* His voice is almost too much. He nods, prompting me to sing.

I smile and breathe. *"I feared my heart would beat in secrecy...I faced the nights alone."* He's glowing watching and listening to me. Placing his hand on the small of my back, he sings with me. *"Oh, how could I have known? That all my life I only needed you?"*

The guests are whistling, and coaxing us, as if we need it. *"Oh, almost paradise...we're knocking on heaven's door...almost paradise....how could we ask for more? I swear that I can see forever in your eyes....paradise."*

I can see my mom off to the side. She's got tears rolling down her cheeks. My dad is beside her, recording, but he's smiling and shaking his head, like he never thought he'd hear me sing again. Wade interlaces his free hand through mine. *"It seems like perfect love's so hard to find. I'd almost given up. You must have read my miiiind."*

He winks at me, stroking the inside of my hand with his thumb, when it's my turn. *"And all these dreams I've saved for a rainy day. They're finally coming true."*

He lifts his head slightly and cocks his head, as if he means the lyrics. We sing together, *"I'll share them all with you. 'Cause now we hold the future in our hands. Oh, Almost Paradise."* The guests have filled the dance floor. Half of them are just watching us, but some are actually dancing. Jennifer's jaw is on the floor. She had no idea I could sing. Wendy has her hands cupped over her mouth in shock.

Wade leans in towards me a little, stroking the side of my face. *"and in your arms salvation's not so far away. It's getting closer,"*

He smiles at me and I smile back, *"closer every day, almost paradise. We're knocking on heaven's door...almost paradise....how could we ask for more?....I swear that I could see forever in your eyes....paradise,"* he strokes my hand and winks, *"paradise,"*

Everyone is clapping and whistling. Wade kisses me full on the lips and mouths to me over the din, "You did great, baby."

"You, too," I say. He kisses me again, which gets a loud whistle.

Dave speaks into the mic, "please don't encourage them." His comment receives a load of laughs and then a bunch of claps. Wade rests his forehead on mine and we both giggle.

"Let's give my girl a hand." Wade says into the mic and kisses me one last time as the guests clap and whistle another round. As I leave the stage area Wade starts another song. As I walk towards my mom, she holds her arms out to me.

"My God, Kendra. That was so beautiful!" She gushes. Dad kisses my cheek and smiles at me, speechless.

"He's a wonderful young man, Kendra." Mom comments, "He seems to bring out a lot of good in you."

Before I can respond, Jennifer approaches, holding her arm up, as if to rest it on my shoulder. "Girl, I had no idea you had a set of pipes!" She comments drunkenly, leaning on me. "Was that you up there?" she slurs.

"Yes, it was." I say, matter-of-factly. "Maybe someone should get her some coffee?" I mouth to Wendy, who is approaching.

"Yeah, poor Brandon. Never mind their wedding night. He's going to be holding her head over the toilet bowl all night from the look of it." Wendy comments. Then she addresses her sister. "You need to puke, Jenn?"

Jennifer waves. "Nahhhh," she says, and I have to use my hand to clear the air of her breath.

"What the hell has she been drinking?" I ask Wendy.

Wendy shrugs. "Everything. I'll go get her some coffee." She looks at her phone to check the time. "Wade's almost done. They'll play some pre-recorded stuff in twenty minutes."

Mom interjects. "Looks like half the guests are gone anyway."

I look around. She's right. There are still quite a few people here, but we started with two hundred, now we're down to about one hundred. Wade's song is half over. He looks at me and smiles. I can't get over the energy in him. Aside from being sweaty, he looks like he could sing all night without tiring. His enthusiasm hasn't wavered, nor has his voice. I admire him. I'm exhausted. My feet are aching in the heels I'm wearing. Half the girls are walking around barefoot. That looks like a great idea.

"Hey, Booksie, you want to give me a hand?" Wendy

asks, as she tries to take Jennifer to the washroom.

"Sure, I'll take a side." I giggle, grabbing hold of Jennifer's other shoulder, while Wendy takes her side. Wade sees us in the corner of his eye as his song comes to a close.

"Hey, thanks for having me here tonight. It's been a lot of fun." He says into the microphone. I clap along with the crowd as the band sets down their instruments and the pre-recorded stuff starts.

"Jesus, is she even going to be sober enough to do the garter toss?" I ask Wendy.

"Hey, quit talking about me like I'm not here!" Jennifer whines as we walk past the bar.

"Sorry, sweetie." I say.

"I don't even have to go to the bathroom." Jenn says. "Why are we going?"

"Because you need to sober up. I don't want you puking in front of all your guests. You'll never live it down." Jennifer states firmly.

As we reach the bathroom, I tell Wendy I'll go get Jennifer some coffee. As I turn around, I nearly run right into Wade. "Hey, baby." He says as he kisses me tenderly. "Everything okay?"

"Jennifer is *really* drunk." I say, "I'm just going to go get her some coffee."

"Oh, geez." Wade shakes his head. "Does Wendy need a hand with her?"

I sigh, wiping the sweat off his face. It's so freaking sexy I could die. "No, thanks, baby. She's not puking or passed out yet, but it won't be long unless we get some coffee into her." I pause. "You want a beer or something? Your set is over now."

He smiles. "No, that's okay. But I'll come with you." He takes my hand in his. As it turns out, the bar doesn't serve coffee, so we have to go to the kitchen and track down a server. As we walk into the barren hallway, Wade's hand is interlaced with mine. We track down a server and bring Jennifer a super-strong coffee. Thankfully it isn't too late.

"Are you okay here for a bit?" I ask Wendy, as Jennifer sips her coffee. Their mother has joined them in the bathroom, so I'm released of my bridesmaid duties for now.

As Wade and I walk back into the reception hall, hand-in-hand, my dad approaches. "Looks like I got everything here, Wade."

"Oh, that's great, sir. Thanks a lot. I really appreciate it." Wade says.

"Dave had a look and he says it's all good." Dad is proud of himself. It's adorable.

Gregory Abbott's 'Shake you Down' starts playing. The dance floor fills up immediately. Wade looks at me. "Would you rather sit? You tired? Or may I have this dance?" he holds out his hand to me and I absolutely can't resist, as much as my feet are begging me to get off them, I want so badly to be close to him.

"I'd love to dance." I say, as he leads me to the dance floor. He takes my hands and places them over his shoulders and behind his neck.

"I'm all sweaty." He chuckles. "Maybe this wasn't such a great idea."

"I love your sweat." I murmur, running my hands right into the curls on the back of his neck.

"Mmmmm..." he says, kissing me on the mouth, snaking his arms around my waist.

Raking a hand over the sweat in the hair by his ear, I smooth his hair over. It's like he's recently had a shower, and it's making me so hot. I can feel the moisture in the back of his shirt, and I can see it in front. Those two buttons on his shirt show just enough of his chest to make me beg for more. I'm dying to kiss his neck and more. We are surrounded by a lot of couples, many of them are making out while dancing. It's a little unsettling. I look around for my parents and see them by the doorway leading to the bar. They're talking to Jennifer's parents; probably trying to figure out a way to finagle their way through the garter toss, without the bride tossing her cookies. I see Brandon over with his groomsmen at the bar, drinking, and he looks just as pickled as his new wife.

"Man, I'm never doing that." I comment.

Wade lifts his forehead off mine. "Never doing what? Getting married?"

"Getting drunk at my own wedding." I guffaw. "Jenn's put so much into today, and now she won't remember half of it."

"She'll remember enough." Wade says, stroking the side of my face. It feels so good to be in his arms. I missed him so much these last couple of days. "It's amazing how fast you get drunk when you haven't eaten properly and you're exhausted, plus all the nerves. It doesn't take much."

"I guess you're right." I give him a quick kiss on the mouth. "I thought you drink beer when you're performing. I've seen you a couple of times between sets."

He shakes his head and frowns. "Not in the mood for it now."

"No?" I whisper against his lips. "What are you in the mood for?"

He takes a quick glance around before slowly enveloping his mouth over mine, and gently plunging his tongue inside. He slowly sweeps his tongue in once more and I meet his with mine, and then our lips part.

"Me too." I say, wanting more, but not only is it inappropriate, but it's also risky with so many people around. I would die if my parents walked by and saw us kissing like that. I bury my head in his neck while we dance to the rest of the song. His hand strokes my back slowly, and the feeling is exquisite. Being in his arms is such a wonderful feeling. I'll never get tired of it. When the song is over, we kiss full on the mouth once, and he takes my hand in his. "I should go check on Jennifer." I say.

"I'll come with you." He says, stating that he needs to use the washroom anyway. When I get there, Jennifer is halfway through her coffee, and already talking straight again.

"Well, I see you're feeling better." I say to Jennifer.

"There wasn't anything wrong with me to begin with." She states. "You guys are a bunch of worry warts." The bathroom is designed like a suite. There are stalls in the back, and plush armchairs plus vanity-style sinks and mirrors in the front. Wendy is sitting in a chair beside Jennifer. Jennifer is drinking her coffee and Wendy is massaging her feet. Linda, their mother, is standing over Jennifer, making sure she doesn't spill the coffee on herself. There is one more empty chair on the other side of the wall.

"Sit." Linda says. "Take your shoes off."

"If I do that, I'll never get them back on again." I chuckle. "My feet are so sore they're swollen." I can see the skin bulging slightly under the straps. The limp I'd been holding back while Wade and I were dancing is unavoidable now.

"You should take them off and elevate them for a few minutes. It might help." Linda advises.

I do as she says, grabbing the chair by the wall. As soon as I take the shoes off, I let out a huge groan of relief. The straps have left crease marks on my feet. Redness beats through the crevices where the straps were. My heels are twice their normal size and the dye from the shoes has transferred to parts of my feet.

"Looks like you've had a reaction to the dye." Linda says, glancing at my feet. Jennifer insisted that we have our shoes dyed to match our dresses exactly. Little did I know I'd be allergic to the dye. "You should wash that off and see if it helps."

I look at how far away the sink appears to be and say forget it. "I'll be fine."

Lindsay, Wendy and Jennifer's cousin, appears inside the washroom. "Hey, Brandon wants to do the bouquet and garter toss now." She says to Jennifer. "If you're up to it." she looks at me. "Your boyfriend is wondering if you're okay."

It's odd but sounds so good to hear Wade being

referred to as my boyfriend. "Okay, thanks."

Linda looks at her now half-drunken daughter. "Are you ready? Your guests and your new husband are waiting."

"Sure, mom." She tosses back the last of her coffee. I get up off the chair reluctantly, but I know I can't get my shoes back on, so I carry them in my hand. I try like hell not to limp, but it's almost impossible since my heels are so badly swollen. At least the cold floor feels good on my feet.

When I walk out of the bathroom, Wade is leaning on the wall with one ankle resting over the other. "God, you must be exhausted." I say, "Why don't you go sit down? You don't have to wait for me."

He ignores my statement, but he looks at my feet. "Jesus," concern washes over his face. "Are you okay?"

I take a step towards him and wince. "I'll be fine. Just my feet."

He shakes his head. "Those aren't feet, baby. Those are clubs."

Linda walks out and overhears. "I told her to wash the dye off and the swelling will go down." She lifts her arms as if in defeat.

I'm so tired I want to cry. I'm too tired to wash my feet. I'm too sore to try. The pain is making tears prick the backs of my eyes. It's like Wade can see right through me. "Anyone else in there?" he gestures with his chin towards the bathroom. I shake my head no, feeling my chin quiver.

Lifting off the wall, he points to the door. "Come on."

"What? No...Wade. I...can't." I'm fighting the tears.

"I can." He's not taking no for an answer.

"You don't have to do that."

He looks at me with so much conviction it scares me. "I flushed my big brother's gunshot wounds for six months when he came home from Afghanistan. I can handle washing my girlfriend's feet." He tips his head sideways. "Come on."

Walking inside the bathroom, Wade inspects the

counter and grabs a handful of paper towel from the metal receptacle attached to the wall. Wiping the water from the counter, he then places the soiled towels in the garbage, undoes the buttons of his shirt at the wrist, and rolls his sleeves up. The counter is a little high, so he places both his hands on either side of my waist and lifts me onto the counter, kissing me once in the process. Pulling my dress up so the material is clear of my lower legs, he tucks the silk under my bottom. The slit on the side is unforgiving, and my leg is almost completely exposed. Wade is so focused on helping me that he doesn't even notice I'm practically half-naked sitting there.

He checks the sink for cleanliness. When he's satisfied, he stuffs a wad of paper towel in the drain and turns the faucet on cold until the sink is almost full. Thankfully the soap is the expensive, natural-based kind. Wade takes my feet and gently places them in the cool water. "Temperature okay?" he asks softly.

"Yeah. Feels great." I whisper. I'm so tired I could fall asleep on the counter. Wade begins soaping up my feet and the dye comes off easily. The massaging feels incredible. I let out a moan of pleasure and he looks over at me, asking gently if I'm okay. "You're hired." I say, leaning my head on my knees, enjoying the sensation. My toes have stopped stinging already. When all the dye is off my feet, he lets the soiled water drain out of the sink and fills it again.

Half-asleep, I revel in his massaging my swollen, aching feet. I'm hugging my knees, leaning my head against my thighs. "You're wonderful." I breathe in thanks. He kisses my forehead as we hear someone enter the washroom.

"Kendra. Are you okay?" Lindsay asks, ignoring the fact that Wade is in here with me. "They're ready to do the bouquet and garter toss. You're needed in the reception hall."

"'Kay." I say sleepily. "I'll be right there."

"Are you going to be able to walk?" Wade asks, drying

my feet with paper towel.

"I'll be fine." I say as he helps me off the counter. My shoes are dangling from his fingers as he places a supportive hand on my waist and we slowly walk back to the reception hall. The band members have already left. Jennifer made an agreement with the reception hall; the boys are allowed to leave their equipment overnight, with the understanding that they would clear it out by the next afternoon.

Surprisingly, Jennifer is sober enough to throw the bouquet. Wade watches me from off to the side, as I make zero attempt to catch it. However, he doesn't participate in the garter toss; he didn't feel it was appropriate seeing as he wasn't actually a guest. My dad brings me my overnight bag as he and mom prepare to leave. No questions are asked as to where I'm sleeping tonight...thank God.

"I'll see you tomorrow, sweetie." Dad says.

Mom advises me to soak my feet again before bed. "I will, mom."

We bid them adieu and say goodbye to Jennifer, Brandon and the wedding party; Lindsay is leaving, too. Wendy will help bring all the stuff to the house in the morning. Wade walks me to the front of the reception hall and says he'll go get his car. He takes my bag with him, and a few minutes later I see him pull up to the front. I take one barefooted step out the door and he raises his hand, shaking his head no. As he slides out of the car, he opens the passenger side door and trots over to me. "It's dark out here, baby, and you've got nothing on your feet." He says, pointing to my swollen appendages.

"What do you suggest? You want me to fly to the car?" I chuckle.

We're nose-to-nose. "No," he says, mocking anger. He's so freakin' cute it kills me. "Hang on to my neck." He advises as he drapes my legs over his arms and carries me to the car from the reception hall doors. As he lowers me into the seat, he whispers. "I'm glad you didn't have any wedding cake."

I open my mouth, feigning shock and he chuckles, kissing me. "Just kidding." Being so close to him, I want to kiss him more, but I see guests coming out of the hall and realize I have to stay in control for just a few more minutes.

Chapter 29

Wade

Tonight has been one hell of an experience. I think I fell in love with my girl ten times over as we sang together on stage. She has an incredible voice, and she's so goddamn beautiful it hurts. Seeing her in that dress...I couldn't keep my eyes off her. I'd like to sue the asshole who used the bloody arsenic-laced dye on her shoes, though. I've never heard of that before, but I sure as hell have half a mind to file at least some sort of complaint over it. Kendra's feet were so swollen they didn't even look like feet. I could tell they hurt so bad; the look on her face tore my heart out.

As I got her in the car, she took my hand in hers and I couldn't wait to kiss her again. As soon as we pulled up to a stop light, I leaned over to kiss her, but the poor little angel had fallen asleep. Her forehead was pressed up against the glass and her mouth was open part way as she slumbered. I didn't even have the heart to wake her when we got to my place. Her car was parked on the street from when Jennifer had dropped her off with it earlier. I let her sleep another couple of minutes as I took her bag into my apartment and opened the doors. My plan was to carry her in, lay her right down on the bed and cover her up, but as soon as I opened her door, as gently as I did, she awoke.

"Hey, baby, we're at my place." I say, crouching down to her level, stroking the side of her face.

"Okay," she says groggily. "I've got a pair of shoes in my bag if you wouldn't mind passing it to me."

"I've already taken your bag downstairs, babe." I lean in and kiss her on the mouth.

"Okay." She lifts her torso up and shifts her feet over. When they hit the asphalt on the driveway, I take a small step back. I think she expects me to move out of the way so she can walk, because she guffaws. "What, are you going to carry me down the stairs?"

"At least to the door, baby. It's dark. You could step on something dangerous out here. Put your arms around my neck."

She does as she's instructed, and I close the car door. Draping her legs over my arms, I walk her to the open door and stop, looking at her. "You know something?"

"What?" she says, stroking my face with her free hand.

"I think I'm going to carry you down the stairs. It's more romantic, isn't it?"

"You're going to put your back out, Wade." She says, trying but failing to give me a cross look. "And we could both fall."

"Oh yeah?" I whisper on her lips.

"Yeah," she says, kissing me.

I start walking down the steps, kissing her full on the mouth, the way I've wanted to all night, plunging my tongue into her mouth gently. When we reach the bottom of the stairs our lips part. "You were saying." I point out, kissing her quickly once more. "I'll go close the door upstairs. Don't move."

When I return thirty seconds later, she's pulled the combs out of her hair, and she's fluffing her curly red locks. "I swear my *scalp* is swollen." She comments. Her hair is unbelievable. It's a pool of loose curls all over her shoulders. She's breathtaking. Where her combs were placed, I position my fingers and gently massage her head in a circular motion, letting her lean her head into my chest. Her hands rest on the waistband of my pants. "You're hired." She moans.

I chuckle. "You've said that once before."

Lifting her head, she looks in my eyes. "I mean it. You're too good to me."

Without answering, I kiss her full on the mouth chastely. She takes the kiss deeper, opening her mouth, plunging her tongue inside. Cupping her face with my hands, I caress her, softly kissing her, meeting her tongue with mine. When our lips part, I whisper against her lips. "I thought you'd be too tired."

"It's been two days. The second I saw you tonight I wanted you. The wait has been torture."

Dividing my glance between both her eyes, I murmur. "Well, I don't like to keep a lady waiting." I snake my arms around her back, feeling for the top of the zipper on her dress. When I find it, I slowly lower it, listening to the hiss as it loosens the dress all the way to her waist. Finding the slit on the side of her dress, I slide my hand in, feeling her warm flesh. She closes her eyes and I lean in, kissing her neck, as I stroke her exposed thigh with my thumb. I slowly kiss her from the bottom of her ear lobe to her shoulder.

She reaches for the top button on my shirt and begins undoing each one. "You. Look. So. Hot. In. This. I. Can't. Wait. To. Take. It. Off." She murmurs after she loosens each button. Reaching the bottom, she pulls the shirt out of my pants and skates her hands over my chest, and then leans in and kisses my neck from my ear to my shoulder. My cock twitches each time her lips and tongue suck my flesh. I softly moan, dragging my hands over her rear, pulling her into me so she can feel the effect she's having on me. My hands find the opening in the back of her dress and I pull it forward, revealing her bra. As I kiss the flesh that's spilling out of her bra, she reaches back and undoes it.

Her nipples are already hard, and it makes my cock harder. She removes her arms from the dress, and it drops to the floor, pooling at her feet. As she stands there in just a thong, I shake my head. "You're so goddamn beautiful, Kendra." I've never seen her in a thong, and it takes my breath away. I take a step around her, drinking in the lace against her cheeks. Crouching down, I suck and kiss the flesh on her rear as I reach around and slide a finger under the front of the thong.

"Mmmm..." she moans, spurring me on. I circle my

finger around her clit, sucking on her flesh from behind. "I want you naked." She breathes. I kiss her rear once more and take a step around to face her. As I begin to remove my shirt, she stops me. "No, I want to do it."

I wink at her and massage her breasts with one arm at a time as she slowly removes my shirt, tossing it on the floor beside her dress and bra. As I knead her nipples between my thumb and forefingers, she lets out another moan. *God, I love that sound.* She slides a hand inside my pants and feels my hardness pulsing against her. I close my eyes at her touch as she caresses my dick with her hand. Swallowing, I undo my pants, giving her full access. "It's so hot that you don't wear underwear, baby." She comments softly. "Makes my life easier."

Sliding my pants down my legs, I step out of them. Her hand is still around my hardened cock. Hooking my fingers around her thong, I pull her underwear down and she steps out of them. We're standing in the middle of my kitchen completely naked. Thank God the drapes are closed. Wrapping her arms around my neck, we're nose-to-nose. Placing my hands on her sides, I lift her up, she wraps her legs around my waist, and I gently impale her. She lets out a gasp and breathes out slowly as I focus deeply on her eyes, watching her reaction to me entering her.

Drawing in a deep breath, I close my eyes, feeling her warmth and wetness against my impossibly hard dick. As I push in and pull out slowly, she opens her mouth and I slide my tongue inside, cushioning her cry as I start to move, walking with her to the pullout couch. Hands supporting her rear, I pulse in and out, taking in her tightness against my most sensitive part. My breathing becomes ragged against her lips as we bathe each other in kisses, and as I suck and nip her lips, she meets my tongue with hers.

Wanting to go deeper, I lay Kendra on the bed and lift her legs so her knees rest against my hands. "You okay?" I breathe, as I enter her right to the hilt.

"Oh...God." she breathes, chest heaving. *I'll take that as a yes.*

"It's all the way in, baby. Feel it." I whisper through ragged breaths, as I slowly pump, being careful not to go too fast. "Mmmm...." I moan against her lips, kissing her deeply, feeling the deep thrusts with her.

Leaning back, I reach for her clit with my thumb and begin circling it, watching her mouth form a big 'O'. "Oh, God, Wade, you're going to make me come." She pants. She's not lying; I can feel her tightening, deliciously squeezing me, bringing me closer to the edge. Wanting her to come like thunder, I thrust deeper and circle faster, trying like hell not to come too fast. Her rear is bucking up and down, slapping against my balls, making it impossible not to come. It feels like heaven and she looks like a goddess, laying under me, with her back arched and her mouth wide open, begging me to let go with her.

Then I feel it, the rhythmic pulsing of her orgasm, sucking and hugging me, bringing me over the edge with her. She moans my name as her chest heaves, feeling her release rip through her. My seed jolts out of me into her like lightning, as I close my eyes tight, riding the waves of pure ecstasy like I've felt with nobody else. Even the aftershocks are heavenly with her. As I slow, feeling my heart beat out of my chest, I gently lean over her, kissing her forehead.

Breathlessly she asks. "Is sex supposed to be this good? I've never...." She trails off.

"Me neither, baby." I breathe, pressing my forehead on hers. Gently removing myself from her, I slide in the bed beside her, sideways, resting my head on my hand. Skating my fingers across her chest, I watch her as she practically falls asleep post-coital, completely satiated. Lifting the covers up, I tuck them on either side of her. As if startled, she quickly opens her eyes. "Sorry, baby." She says, kissing me on the lips.

I chuckle. "You're exhausted. Don't apologize." I kiss her lips and get up to go turn off the light. As I come back into bed, she lays on her side and I snuggle in behind her, spooning her. In seconds I can hear her shallow breathing and I know that she's asleep. The warmth and softness of her body after sex is so pleasing. I feel like I can burrow myself into her back and stay there forever. What must be a few hours later, I wake up to the sound of the water running in the bathroom. Lifting my head, I see that the door is closed. Kendra isn't beside me in bed.

Rising, I grab a pair of jeans out of my drawer and pull them on, leaving the top button undone. Barefoot, I walk over to the door and knock softly. She opens the door wearing nothing but my sweaty shirt. Her hair is tied up and her face is wet. "Sorry, sweetie. I didn't mean to wake you." she says as she moves out of the way so I can come in.

"Are you okay?" I ask, running a hand through my hair, yawning.

"Yeah. I woke up and saw the raccoon eyes, and realized I fell asleep with my contacts in. I figured I should probably wash this crap off my face. Plus, I had to soak my feet again, they were stinging like hell."

Lowering the lid on the toilet tank, I take a seat and glance at her feet. "They look better. Still red though in some spots."

"Yeah. I won't be a foot model anytime soon, but they feel better." She's brushing her teeth. I should probably do the same. Rising, I pull my toothbrush out of the cup on the sink and squeeze a dollop of toothpaste on the brush. "You forgot, too, huh."

"Yeah, I guess I was a little distracted." I wink, brushing my teeth.

She giggles. I love that sound. She's looking at me in the mirror, staring at my stomach. Her eyes linger to my jeans. I look down, feeling slightly self-conscious. "What's up?"

Spitting the toothpaste into the sink, she rinses her mouth and answers. "I was just admiring you."

"Admiring me, huh." She moves over so I can spit the

toothpaste out and rinse. "I see you like my dirty shirt, too."

"It smells like you."

"I'm sure it's ripe after last night. Sweating like a hog under those lights."

"It reminds me of how sexy you look and sound when you sing."

I smile and take a step towards her, kissing her chastely on the mouth. "You must be exhausted. It's like four o'clock in the morning."

She rubs her nose across mine. "Funny how seeing you standing here half-naked with your pants unbuttoned wakes me up."

Chapter 30

Kendra

He's so sexy I could die. With his hair all messed up from sex and sleep, no shirt on, and his tight jeans only half zipped, I'm all but drooling in the bathroom as I watch him in the mirror. When he leans over the sink, his six pack abs contract, making me bite my lip. It sounds twisted, but he has the sexiest scent. No cologne in the world could smell as hot as he does. I want to bottle his smell on this shirt.

"And you standing there, naked, under my shirt...it does things to me." he murmurs against my lips.

Enveloping his lips with mine, I plunge my tongue into his mouth. He lets out a soft moan, which I feel...there. We're still standing at the sink. Wade bends down and gently lifts my leg, propping my foot on the lip of the sink. "Do you have good balance?" he asks softly.

"I suppose so. Why?" I'm confused, thinking maybe he wants to tend to my feet again. Then he lifts the shirt and leans into me, sticking his nose...there. "What are you do—" before I can answer, he begins sucking on my labia, placing his hands on either side of my rear. The sensation is so unexpected; deep and sensual. I wouldn't have thought the angle would work, but the way he's plunging his tongue deep inside my folds, it's working...fast. He's circling around my clit so deliciously I can't help but cry out.

He moans into my body, bringing a new level of ecstasy. "Oh, God, Wade." I breathe, in disbelief of how fast I'm climbing. He licks faster, pushing my body towards him rhythmically, and it happens. My orgasm finds me so fast I gasp and cry out loudly. "Don't stop." I beg needlessly, since he doesn't stop or slow down unless I tell him. "Oh....my God." I pant, my heart is beating so fast. I didn't realize that I had one hand on the sink, and the other on his head, grabbing his hair. I giggle, removing my hand from his hair. "Sorry."

Kissing my inner thigh, he rises. "I thought you were going to take a handful with you." He chuckles, raking a hand through his mussed locks.

Then I see it. He's as hard as a rock under those jeans. It looks like he's stuffed a modest cucumber inside his Levi's. "Wow."

He looks down and blushes. "Nothing sexier in the world than pleasing you...evidently." He admits.

Leaning towards him, I slowly undo his pants, freeing him. "We need to do something about this." my voice is silky. "What do you want to do about it?"

He pulls them down and steps out of his jeans. "As long as I'm inside you, it's your preference, baby."

I thought about doing that thing I did to him before, that made him swear, but before I can act, he places his hands on my waist and lifts me. I wrap my legs around his waist as he kisses me voraciously. We are a mess of tongues and lips, breathlessly kissing as if we'll never see each other again, as he walks me over to the bed and lowers me, placing his full weight on me. His body on mine is so delicious. His hardness is against my belly and it twitches when I kiss him.

"I can't wait until the day I can make love to you on a real bed, baby." He whispers to me, brushing stray hairs off my face. My hair is still in a ponytail. He gently removes the elastic, freeing my red locks, and then he lifts onto his elbows, slowly undoing the buttons on the shirt I'm wearing. When he gets to the last one, he opens the shirt and begins kissing the flesh on my stomach and chest.

"As long as we're together, it doesn't matter where or what we make love on." I say, raking my hands through his hair as he kisses my body. When he reaches my nipples, I moan, arching my back.

"I love that sound." He whispers against my skin. His girth is at my entrance, and I part my legs wide, pushing against his tight rear end with my foot. "Are you ready for me?" he asks, kissing me tenderly.

"Always."

Instinctively, my eyes close as he enters me. In the silent darkness, all we can hear is each other's breathing as Wade begins moving inside me. He fills me to the hilt, kissing me full on the mouth while cupping the sides of my face with his hands. The bed begins to squeak as he picks up his pace. "I'm so afraid that this bed is going to give way." He says with a sort of breathless chuckle. "I hate to hold back on you, baby."

What? This is holding back???

I'm about to respond, when he lifts on his elbows, raising my knees. "I love it when you do that." I whisper, feeling him fill me deeper.

"Mmmm....." he moans, "I can tell...."

Climbing quickly, I can feel him getting impossibly harder inside me. "Oh, Wade...it's soooo gooood."

With a soft hiss, he slows, "You're so tight, Kendra." And then I'm not sure if it's him getting harder or me getting tighter, or both. He feels like steel inside, and I can feel every inch of him. His soft voice in the dark is such a turn-on. It doesn't matter if he calls me baby or by my name, but the way he whispers it in the heat of passion is so hot.

When he reaches down to circle my clit with his thumb, it's my undoing. "You know what that does to me, Wade." I whisper a sexy warning, bucking against his touch.

"Baby, you feel so ready." His breathing is becoming ragged. He's so sexy it kills me. "Feel it, baby. Come with me. That's it." he says, and it's as if he has that kind of power over me. Suddenly my muscles are clenching, throwing me over the edge as my orgasm washes through my entire body; so powerful it makes me cry out. I can feel Wade's seed rush through me as he arches his back and makes a grunt/hiss sound that's as sexy as hell.

As his climax softens, he gently leans down on me, and we're nose-to-nose. Kissing me noisily, he makes smacking sounds. "We're electric together, baby." He murmurs against my lips.

Completely satiated, I take a deep breath. "More like heaven and earth fucking collide when we're together."

He chuckles softly, leaning his forehead on mine. "Wait, did you just 'f' bomb in bed?"

"I suppose I did."

"Ten seconds ago, that would have been *really* cool." He jokes, carefully removing himself from me. Cradling his body against mine, he spoons me from behind as I turn over with my back to him. I feel him kiss my shoulder and I turn over, kissing him on the lips.

"Should I start locking the bathroom door?" I tease.

"Wild horses couldn't keep me away from you, baby." He exhales as I turn back over, giggling. "Get some sleep." He says, kissing my hair.

We must have slept for at least three or four hours, because when I hear my phone ring, the sun is peeking through the drapes. Wade is so crashed on the other side of the bed. His hair is so sexy, all over the place. He's so tired he doesn't hear my phone. He doesn't even move as I get out of bed to answer it. I've still got his shirt on from last night...or this morning. Fumbling through my purse, I see that it's my personal phone, not my work phone, that's ringing...it's my dad. "Hey, dad. Good morning."

"Morning, sweetheart. So, what do you say...meet in an hour?"

Am I missing something? I look at the display on my phone and roll my eyes. *I can't believe I forgot.* It's my dad's birthday today. We have a tradition, my dad and me. Since my dad is such a lover of guns, he likes to take me to the shooting range. He'd given up on presents when I was a teenager. This is what we've done together for so many years I've lost count. I should have put two and two together when he said he'd see me tomorrow as we were leaving the wedding last night. "Sure, dad. I'll see you there."

"Tell Wade I've sent the video to his cell phone. He

gave me the number last night."

"Okay, dad. See you soon."

Glad he glossed over the fact that I spent the night with Wade, I hang up the phone, grab my bag and jump in the shower. When I come out, freshly dressed and ready, Wade still hasn't moved. He must be completely exhausted from last night. Not having the heart to wake him to tell him I'm leaving, I simply walk over and bend down, kissing him on the cheek. He stirs, opening one eye. "Hey, baby...What time is it?" he speaks with a gravelly voice.

"It's just after nine. With all the wedding hoopla I forgot about my dad's birthday. I've gotta go slip out for a couple of hours and meet him, but I'll catch up with you later, okay? Get some sleep." I whisper, kissing his nose.

He swallows, and turns over on to his back, raking a hand through his hair. I watch him stretch, pulling his arms behind his head. I'm trying like hell not to drool. His abdominal muscles contracting is so sexy, just the way they did last night, right before Wade pleasured me in the bathroom. I feel my thighs warm just thinking about it. He leans over on his elbow and slides a finger down my cheek. "Come here." He says.

I smile, leaning in. "What?" I giggle.

The lower half of his body is covered with the sheets. I'm kneeling on the floor so I'm close to his face. His eyes are hooded, and the morning sunshine is beaming, making his eyes look impossibly blue. "I didn't want to say anything last night...just because of the wedding and then..." he gestures with his hand to the bathroom and to the bed, indicating all the sex we had. "I didn't want you to think I was just caught up in the moment."

A 'v' forms between my brows. Wade drapes a loose curl over my ear and then rests his hand on the back of my neck, under my hair, stroking my chin with his thumb. "I just wanted to tell you...." He gives me a look with so much conviction it scares me. It's like he's about to tell me he's only got six months left to live. "I love you," he swallows and exhales, "*so much.*" Those last two words he gives emphasis to, like the first three mean nothing unless he adds importance to them.

A ball forms in my throat. Tears prick the backs of my eyes. I gasp as his gaze is divided between both my eyes. "I love you, too, Wade." A tear falls down my cheek and he sweeps it away with his thumb. My heart is beating so fast and my breath is ragged as he pulls me close and kisses me full on the mouth...once....twice...three times...I lose count.

As our lips part he smiles. "You must love me...kissing me with all this morning breath and all."

I bark out a laugh. I hadn't noticed any morning breath. He's too friggin sexy. He could smell like a dumpster and I wouldn't care. "So, it's your dad's birthday?" he asks.

I sniff, wiping my tears with the back of my hand. "Yeah. He likes to go shoot rounds at the shooting range. It's tradition." I pause. "Dad says he sent you the video from last night to your phone."

"Already? Geez...he doesn't mess around."

"Nope." I chuckle. "On that note...I should get going."

"Okay." He leans in. "Come here." He kisses me again, full on the mouth. "Love you, baby." He whispers against my lips.

"Love you, too." I say, feeling my heart swell.

As I walk out of his apartment, I feel like it's one of those moments when my life is about to change.

...and it does....as I'm approached by a pregnant lady walking towards me. When I back up, I'm grabbed from behind as a covered hand slides over my mouth. I breathe in, and the world goes black.

Chapter 31

Priscilla

Four Nights Before

"Leonard! Oh, Leonard, you gotta hear this!" Priscilla's shrill voice is heard from down in the basement, where Leonard is watching a ball game from their satellite dish. A minute later he joins his lady love in the kitchen.

"What, he getting her off again?" Leonard asks, leaning towards Priscilla, who is holding a sound device.

"These two are like rabbits." Priscilla comments, impressed.

"No offence, baby, but this is getting sick. I can't listen anymore." Leonard whines, reaching into the fridge to grab a beer. "The point of bugging this dickwad's house wasn't to have live porn. He even mention anything about the lawsuit, or is he just dicking her constantly?"

"Man, this guy can fuck!" she barks as the clear sound of a woman reaching orgasm is heard from the speaker. The cries are so loud, Priscilla adjusts the volume level down a notch.

"What, are you getting off on this shit?" Leonard asks, irritated. "Look, Priscilla, we've got to focus here. I mean, the guy's obviously ignoring the lawsuit. If we want to strike him when he's down, we gotta figure out when that is. This is no time to be fucking around, sweetheart." He twists the cap off his beer and tosses it on the table. "I mean, the guy was stupid enough to leave his damn door unlocked. We could have ransacked the place any time."

"And you think he's got anything valuable in that shit hole?" Priscilla is snide. "You saw the place. He's fucking this whore on a fucking pullout couch...he ain't got any money nowhere. We gotta do something more drastic."

"Oh yeah? Like what?" Leonard's tone is snide now.

"We go to the fucktard's place and stake it out. I heard them talking about some wedding they're going to on the weekend. We can ransack the place then."

Considering her suggestion, Leonard stands by the fridge, sucking back his beer. "But you said yourself there ain't nothing worth taking in his rat hole. What would be the point?"

"Well, we've gotta do something, Leonard. Maybe we can steal his car or something."

Leonard waves with a sour expression on his face. "That beater ain't worth nothing. Fifteen hundred bucks maybe. After all the trouble we've been through putting this thing together, we need something worth more."

"Like how much more?" Priscilla is intrigued.

"Priscilla, honey, what was all that talk about before? Did you forget about us talking about retiring to some exotic island? I want this to be the big one, baby. This guy's family is worth billions."

"Yeah, but he obviously ain't." Priscilla counters. "Unless he's got his money hiding in some offshore bank account."

"Well, we know his family's loaded. His brother Colton owns that ranch, and his other brothers own a goddamn airline. Their father left all of them billions. There's gotta be a way to suck the bastard dry."

"Besides the way this whore's sucking him dry right now?" Priscilla teases, listening to a male voice moaning.

Annoyed, Leonard grabs the device off the table, and turns it off. "Enough of this horse shit, Priscilla. We're going to South Carolina. Pack your bags."

***

The Night of the Wedding

Priscilla watches Leonard stomp back to the car after pulling up two houses down from Wade's place. The darkened street is quiet. All the neighbors seem to have turned in for the night. There are virtually no lights on in any of the houses, Priscilla observes, as Leonard reaches the car. "Damn asshole locked his door this time. You bring the picks?"

Nodding, Priscilla reaches over to her large handbag. Fishing a small box out, she hands her partner the key picks. "There ain't nothing going on in this neighborhood tonight, baby. We picked a good night."

"That your way of telling me you wanna come in with me?" Leonard smiles.

"Sure. I'm bored sitting out here."

Gesturing with his head, Leonard signals for Priscilla to join him. It takes two minutes for Leonard to pick the lock on the first door. He grows irritated when he has to pick the one on the second door. "Jesus Christ. Who the hell needs *two* locks?"

"Maybe he's got something worthwhile in there now, baby." Priscilla's hope is showing. Once Leonard gets the second lock opened, they enter Wade's apartment. Leonard fishes his phone out from his back pocket and turns the flashlight on. Priscilla looks around. "It's clean. That I'll give him." she looks at Leonard. "Do we keep it clean or ransack the place?"

"Let's keep it clean this time, baby. I got something in mind." He says, keeping his voice low.

Priscilla fishes her cell phone out and turns her flashlight on, heading towards Wade's kitchen drawers. "I'll check these drawers. You head over to the dresser drawers."

"Good idea."

Two minutes later, Priscilla has gone through the drawers in Wade's tiny kitchen. "Nothing." She sighs. "How are you doing over there?"

Just as the question escapes her mouth, Leonard comes across an envelope. "What's this?" he says to himself, opening the envelope addressed from the law offices of Stockwell, Lamb & Birkin. Intrigued, Priscilla walks over. "Looks like he did take action, baby. He's gonna make you prove your kid is his before giving you a dime." He reaches over to Priscilla's flat belly. "Seems he's been playing us all along, baby."

"Dammit!" Priscilla balls her hands into fists. "So, what the hell do we do now?"

A toothy grin crosses Leonard's mouth. "I told you I had a plan b, baby." He winks.

***

The morning after the wedding

Priscilla yawns. "Fuck, this better be worth it." she whines. "I've been up all night, smelling like a fucking pool gone wild. I'm almost high on the fucking fumes."

"Well, if you had've put the lid back on the bleach properly, baby..." Leonard trails off. "It's not that bad. At least we got the Chloroform mixed properly."

"Yeah, well it better work. That bitch looks like she could take me out if she wanted to."

Leonard glances at his watch. "Hopefully this works. Hopefully these two ain't joined at the hip already."

"Never mind," she guffaws. "What the fuck do we do if she comes out and a neighbor sees? This is ridiculous and risky, Leonard. I think this is a waste of time."

Holding the listening device in his hand, Leonard shushes her, as the sound of a phone is heard. They listen to the conversation and a smile crosses both their faces. "You got the phony belly, baby?" he says. She nods. "Get it on...quick."

"What difference does it make if I'm pregnant or not?" Priscilla argues.

"For dramatic effect. I want that bitch to know who's taking her down while she passes out from the fumes."

Doing as instructed, Priscilla places the prosthetic on her belly and adjusts it under her shirt. "I'll get her from behind. You distract her from the front. Just like we discussed." Leonard says, pulling the bottle of Chloroform out of Priscilla's purse. They exit the car and walk to the side of Wade's house, where the side entrance is. "It's now or never, baby." Leonard says to Priscilla as he stands five feet behind the door, and she waits on the sidewalk, looking like she's lost her keys.

As Kendra exits Wade's apartment, Leonard wastes no time. Priscilla approaches with a scorned expression on her face, as Leonard wraps his hand over Kendra's mouth, administering the Chloroform to her through a soaked rag. In seconds, Kendra's body turns limp. The car is feet from the sidewalk. Dragging Kendra's drugged body to the car, Leonard waits for Priscilla to trot over to the back seat and open it for him. Sliding Kendra's body inside, Leonard pushes her feet off to the side and climbs in beside her, instructing Priscilla to drive slowly.

"Nobody saw us." Priscilla says, removing the bulge from under her shirt.

"Drive slow anyway, just in case." Leonard says, looking at Kendra, who is laying lengthwise across the back seat.

"How long you think she'll be out?" Priscilla asks.

"Not long. I'll tie her up while she's still out."

"Gag her, too. There's extra cloth back there." Priscilla suggests. "She's a screamer." She gives Leonard a knowing look.

"Jesus Christ." He mutters under his breath as he ties Kendra's ankles and wrists together, and ties a length of cloth around her head, cutting into her mouth.

"So, we head back to the motel?" Priscilla asks.

"Yeah," he says, "and get your gun out."

"You've got yours?"

Leonard nods. "That was part of plan b. Luckily we didn't have to use it."

"Yet." Priscilla warns. They're silent for a few minutes, as they approach the area where the motel is located. The block is hidden among a marshy strip of land close to a creek. It looks like it's rented by the hour, and there is no sign of life, or shouldn't be, since it appears that anyone patronizing this establishment wouldn't know what daylight is.

"Dammit. I was hoping she'd be awake before we got here." Leonard complains. "Now I have to carry her."

Priscilla shrugs. "Drag her." She exits the car and opens the back door. "Here, I'll take her feet."

"Never mind, baby. You go open the door." He says. A moment later, Priscilla returns and takes Kendra's feet, as Leonard drags her from under her arms. "Thank God we got a room in the back of this place."

"That was good thinking, baby." Priscilla compliments, winking at her beloved.

"You know it." Leonard says, entering the room. As soon as he places Kendra on the bed, she wakes up. "Morning, sunshine." He says, sucking his teeth. Kendra's eyes are glazed over at first, and then they widen as Priscilla places her prosthetic back on her belly.

"Remember me?" she asks Kendra.

"Hey, hey, don't freak her out, baby." Leonard chides. He then addresses Kendra. "I'm going to take this gag off so we can have a little chat, okay?" he lifts his brows as he leans over so he's eye level with her. Taking his gun out of his back pocket, he shows Kendra the barrel of his weapon. "Any screaming or funny business, and I use this, capiche?"

Kendra blinks and nods as Leonard removes the gag and helps her up onto the pillow, so she's sitting upright. "What do you want?" is the first thing Kendra says.

"Oh, we'll get to that." Leonard's tone is smoothe. "You got a cell phone in your purse?" he asks, as Priscilla lifts Kendra's handbag in the air.

"Who doesn't?" Kendra is snide. Leonard nods as Priscilla opens the handbag and pulls out an iPhone.

Priscilla tosses it to her on the bed. "Open it up."

"It's an iPhone. I need my thumb." Kendra spits.

"And if you had any brains, you would have lost the phone at Wade's house. Anyone can track me here. They'll have you surrounded in this dump."

"That's why we've got the guns, sweetheart." Leonard brags, dangling his pistol in the air.

"Please." Kendra guffaws. "I could dismantle that thing in the dark. You probably don't even know how to shoot it properly." She pauses. "Go ahead. I dare you."

Priscilla lifts a hand. "Don't do it. She's goading you, babe. They'll hear the shot and call the cops."

Kendra shakes her head. "Great. It's like the blind leading the blind." She sighs. "So, what do you want? Money, I'll assume. I know your little pregnancy plan didn't work out, since, well, you're not actually pregnant. And even if you were, it took me five seconds to realize that your little letter was a fake." Kendra laughs without a trace of humor. "Funniest thing here is that if you're after Wade's money, he doesn't have any."

"Yeah, but his family does." Leonard interjects. "And I betcha your lover boy will pay a king's ransom to get his little whore back."

Ignoring his statement, Kendra continues, mirth in her voice. "You really should ditch the phone. My dad runs on military time and I'm supposed to meet him. If I'm a second late he'll be calling me. You don't want to mess with him or my boyfriend. They'll eat you both for breakfast."

A fleeting look crosses Priscilla's face. "Should we ditch it and split, baby? Take her somewhere else?"

"Where the fuck're we gonna go? This ain't a road trip!"

Kendra starts laughing. "Dumb and dumber."

Leonard's face falls. He takes a step towards Kendra, pointing the gun at her face. "You should be nicer, Kendra. Maybe we'll leave you here and go after your boyfriend. Slice his dick off? You won't have anything to play with then, will you?"

Kendra's face is stone. "I'm not afraid of you,

asshole."

"You should be. I'll kill you if I have to." Leonard says, with less conviction than he wants.

"If anything, you'll kill me by accident. That's a Glock. There's no safety on it. How many times have you actually fired it…by the look of it I'll say never."

Just then, Kendra's phone rings, startling Priscilla. Kendra giggles.

"Don't answer that!" Priscilla screeches. Kendra glances at the display. It's her work phone; her boss is calling. Then she remembers that she turned the ringer to her personal phone off, so even if her dad does call, nobody will hear it. Kendra prays the idiots won't think to question if she has a secondary phone with her.

"Take a little trip and throw it out." Leonard instructs Priscilla.

"I ain't going out there!" Priscilla argues. "What if the cops come!"

Kendra interrupts. "Guys, I hate to tell you, but my car is still parked on Wade's street." She says, also remembering that Jennifer had come with her to drop the car off at Wade's house before going to the wedding. "He's going to see my car there and know something is wrong. The cops will trace my phone here and come."

"Wha…what if we pull the battery out?" Priscilla suggests. "Bust it all up. They won't be able to trace it if we do that, right?"

"Good thinking, baby." Leonard says, still pointing the gun at Kendra. "Oh, I'd hate to bust up your pretty face. But daddy's hungry for money, and I'll do what I have to to get it."

Kendra lifts a brow. "Good luck."

Chapter 32

Wade

That was the most rewarding first I've ever had with a girl. I've never told a girl I loved her before. Kendra's reaction made my heart melt. She's the sweetest thing I've ever met. I love her to death. As I get out of bed, feeling empty without her, I hop in the shower. When I get out, I decide to take a look at the video Peter sent to me. I don't get twenty minutes into it when my phone rings. It's Peter.

"Good morning, sir." I answer. "I'm just looking at the video. Looks great."

"Oh, good. Glad you got it." Peter says cheerily. "Listen, is Kendra still there? I see she's running a bit late."

"No, sir. She left right after you called. Maybe a few minutes after that."

"Hm. Maybe she got caught in traffic."

"She might have stopped for something to eat, sir. Regretfully, there's nothing in my place for breakfast and she left in a hurry."

"We were planning to have breakfast first, as a matter of fact." Peter says. "I'll try calling her cell phone again. I'm sure she's fine."

"Okay. I'll talk to you later."

"Bye, Wade."

As I hang up to Peter, I continue watching the video, but something doesn't feel right. My stomach is a little unsettled, and I realize I haven't eaten anything yet. Grabbing my keys and wallet, and stuffing my phone in my back pocket, I head out the door. The second I do, I know something is terribly wrong. Kendra's car is still parked on the street, and there is no sign of her.

My heart begins to pound. I immediately call her phone. It rings until it goes to voicemail. Raking my fingers through my hair, I think about what to do next.

Starting with the house on the farthest corner on my street, I begin walking over, as I bang on the door, I'm dialing nine-one-one. There is one car parked in the driveway. As I wait for my neighbor to answer the door, the emergency operator answers. "Nine-one-one, what is your emergency?" It's a female.

"My name is Wade Ford. My girlfriend is missing. I'm ninety percent sure she's been kidnapped."

"Okay, sir. What is your girlfriend's name?"

"It's Kendra MacGregor. She's about five foot eight, slim build, with medium-length curly red hair. She left my apartment thirty minutes ago, and she was supposed to have taken her car, but it's still here. She was supposed to meet her dad, but she hasn't made it."

"Is it possible she was picked up or that she walked?" There is no answer at the door, but I try knocking again.

"No, ma'am. Where she was meeting her dad, it's too far to walk. And there is a person of interest whom I believe might have taken her."

"Sir, what is your address?"

I reiterate the information, just as my neighbor answers the door. He's a guy about my age, wearing a bathrobe. "Hey, man, sorry to bother you." My tone is apologetic. It looks like I caught him in the shower. He's a little irritated. "Did you see my girlfriend...she's got red hair; she left my place about a half an hour ago? I think someone took her."

The nine-one-one operator is patiently listening as I keep the phone close to my mouth, avoiding the need to ask her to hold on.

"Sorry, man. I just got up." My neighbor says. I thank him and move on to the next house.

"Sir, I've just dispatched an officer." The operator says and the call is ended.

The next call I make is to Peter. As I walk to the next house and knock on the door, Peter answers his phone. "Peter, sir, I don't mean to alarm you, but something is wrong." I give him a twenty second explanation of Priscilla. "Kendra's car is still here. I just called the police; they're on their way over now. I'm canvassing my neighbors to see if anyone saw anything."

"Jesus." Peter says. "I'm on my way." He clicks off as my next neighbor answers the door. It's an older woman dressed in elastic waistband pants. Her shoulder-length white hair is in tidy curls and her perfume is so strong I have to take a step back from her. "Sorry to bother you, ma'am." I use the same explanation as I used with the last neighbor, only she answers with a concerned expression. "Oh, that young girl I saw yesterday? She came by to drop her car off and she left in a stretched limo."

"That's right, ma'am. We went to a wedding yesterday. Did you see anyone come by this morning? A pregnant lady perhaps?" I'm trying not to sound like a lunatic, and perhaps it's working, because this lady appears deeply concerned.

"There was a car on the street this morning, now that you mention it." she says.

"Oh yeah? What color was it?" I probe, nodding.

"Blue. Light blue. It was kind of like mine." She gestures towards her car in the driveway; it's a Toyota Yaris, only hers is white. "The car was there last night, too."

"Did you see if anyone was in it?"

"Sorry, my eyesight isn't great. It was on the other side of the street." She nods.

"That's alright, ma'am. You've been extremely helpful. Thank you." I say, leaving her. Walking to the next house, I dial Jack's number.

He answers on the first ring. "Shithead! What are you doing up before noon?"

I ignore the jibe. "Jack. I need you here pronto, brother. Someone's got Kendra."

"Shit. This something to do with that letter?"

"I'm pretty sure."

"It's nothing to do with Chuck, is it?"

"No. I don't think so. Not unless they're in cahoots, which I doubt."

Jack sighs. "Alright, I'm on my way."

I would have called Colton, since he's the closest, but I know he isn't home from overseas yet. As I try to think of who else I can call, I see a police cruiser turn onto my street. Walking over, I salute the officers who exit the vehicle. One is male, the other is female. Both are probably in their thirties if I had to guess. "You Wade Ford?" the male asks.

"I am." I say, giving a single nod to both officers, providing them with a rundown of what happened with Priscilla. "One of my neighbors saw a blue sedan parked on the street last night and again this morning. I'll continue canvassing the neighbors."

"What can you tell me about this Priscilla person...where is she from?" the female officer asks.

"From South Carolina, I believe."

"You think they might've taken her there?"

"I don't know, but I'd send an alert out just in case."

I give the male officer a description of Kendra, Priscilla and the possible vehicle, and he slides back into the cruiser to prepare the alert. Something catches my attention in the corner of my eye. "Hold on a second." I say, lifting a finger. As I jog over to my entrance door, I see a black bottle on the ground, and a couple of feet next to it is a crumpled rag. "Ma'am. Can you come take a look at this please?"

She comes over and looks at the bottle on the driveway. Turning back towards the cruiser, she gets some baggies and a pair of gloves. When she comes back, she picks the bottle up with a gloved hand and sniffs it. "Smells like bleach. They probably made Chloroform to subdue her."

My eyes widen. "What?" It suddenly hits me that Kendra's been kidnapped and is in serious danger. "Jesus Christ!" I rake a hand through my hair. Just then, I see Peter's car pull up. "Sh...she's got her cell phone. Can we not locate her with that?" I can't help the desperate tone in my voice.

Peter approaches. "This is Kendra's father, Mr.

MacGregor. She was supposed to meet up with him; that's why she left here."

"Peter," Peter says, introducing himself. "I've tried calling her several times and she doesn't pick up."

"I was just asking the officer if we can try to locate her using her cell phone." I address the female officer.

"Most of the time the criminals make the victim dump their phone, but we can try. What kind of phone is it?" she asks.

"It's an iPhone." I rattle off the number.

She radios in from the device clipped to her shoulder for backup. Then she punches some numbers into her phone and an address pops up. "If they haven't made her dump her phone, she's at a fleabag motel about ten minutes from here."

"Which one?" I ask. She rattles the name of it off and I look at Peter.

The officer looks at both of us, and we can tell by the look on her face that she's reading our minds. "I don't recommend you intervene. I've got backup coming. This kidnapper must have an accomplice. There's no way a woman, a pregnant woman at that, would be able to carry another woman without help."

A switch goes off in me. Up until this moment, I would never disobey or disrespect any kind of police officer or military personnel, but my heart is overriding my brain and I can't let another second pass knowing that I'm standing here while Kendra is in danger. Peter has the same look of determination on his face. He turns towards his car and I follow him, sliding into the passenger seat.

"Got a gun?" I ask, engaging my seatbelt.

"Does a bear shit in the woods?" he asks rhetorically, engaging his seatbelt. "There's a spare one in the glove compartment." he gestures with his eyes as he puts the car into drive. We speed off, squealing the tires in our wake.

"You kill anyone when you served?" Peter asks as we drive.

"I'm not proud of it, but yes, sir, I did." I pause. "I've never killed a woman before, but if she's so much as harmed a hair on Kendra's head…" I trail off.

Peter gives me a sideways glance. "You leave any killing up to me, son. Kendra's gonna want you around, and they'll put you in jail long before they put me in jail."

"Sir," I nod. A few turns and within seven minutes, we're right up the street from where we need to be. "There's a blue car right there." I point out. "My neighbor said she saw a blue car parked on my street last night and this morning."

"You remember your basic training?" Peter asks.

"I do, sir. Never forget that."

"Amen."

The next thirty seconds I'll take to the grave with me.

Chapter 33

Kendra

I hear my phone vibrate, but the two idiots are too busy fighting to hear it. So many things are running through my mind. Like how at least one of them is going to get shot or killed when the police arrive, which will be soon, based on the fact that neither of them have the brains to get rid of my phone or check to see if I have another one. For sure I've been located by now. It's just a matter of time. Now they are fighting over what to do next.

"Priscilla, we've got to get out of here. We'll leave her phone here and trick the police." Leonard says.

I interrupt. "That's assuming the police aren't already here."

That hit a nerve. Leonard approaches me with his thick, garlicky breath. "I've just about heard enough from you." He seethes, and then I feel a blow to the side of my head. I wake up, what I believe to be a couple of minutes later, and I have a massive headache. The side of my face feels wet, so I can assume he's hit me hard and broken skin. Priscilla is still yelling at Leonard.

"What did you have to hit her for, Leonard? Now we're gonna really get into trouble!" she whines.

"You guys are both going to jail. There's no way around it. Newsflash...Kidnapping is a felony."

"You keep your mouth shut or I'll give you another gash on the other side of your face to match." Leonard threatens, pointing the gun at my face again. I know he's not going to shoot me. I was more afraid when I sat in the huge classroom to write my bar exam than I am stuck in this motel room with these two morons. But I button up anyway, just because the more he yells, the more she yells, and my head is killing me.

"Why don't you just put the gag back on her?" Priscilla says, and I'm impressed that she's managed a decent idea for once.

"We can do that." Leonard grabs the cloth off the edge of the bed and ties it around my head, being careful to jam it in my mouth. I want to spit at him first, but frankly, I don't want him to hit me again. A smear of blood is on his hand from my face as he pulls back. He looks at it, winces, and wipes it on the bed. *What an ass.*

"Should we call him now? Get our ransom money before the cops get here?" Priscilla asks, nodding for emphasis.

Leonard thinks for a moment and then agrees. "Yeah, let's do that now." He looks at me and then at my phone. He lifts it and tosses it closer to me on the bed. "Dial your boyfriend's number."

I give him a look. *You have my hands bound together, genius.*

"Get her to open her phone with her thumb, Leonard. We can do the rest." Priscilla suggests. Leonard brings the phone over to the bed. *Oh, for Chrissake! I'll enter the passcode, moron! I was lying earlier!*

I feel like I've been babysitting two of the world's worst children, who have tied me up for sport, and I'm just humoring them until their parents get home. By some feat, I manage to flex my arm around and key in my passcode while Leonard finagles my phone up and down and around so I can hit all the necessary keys. When my phone is unlocked, he navigates through the recent calls and finds Wade's number. As he dials it, for once the room is quiet.

Then I hear it...from the other side of the door...a phone is ringing...Wade's.

A second later the door bursts open. First, I see my dad, holding a gun up at the ready, then I see Wade. He eyes me and runs to me.

"Put the gun down, asshole. Or your brains will be painted all over this cheap wall." Dad eyes the grimy wall. "Which will be an improvement."

"Jesus Christ." Wade says when I assume he sees

that I'm bleeding. *I'm okay, just get me the hell out of here...and get me an Advil.*

Leonard drops the gun and it lands on the puke green plush carpet with a thud. "Hands behind your head...both of you." Dad orders firmly.

Wade quickly fiddles with the gag and loosens it. "You okay, baby?" he asks, kissing me chastely.

"I'm fine. Just get me out of here." I say. He studies the gash on the side of my head and his eyes shut tight. "It's okay." I say.

Wade quickly struggles with the ties on my ankles and wrists, as we hear the sirens from afar. When I'm free, Wade wraps his arms around me on the bed, pulling me towards him with his hand placed firmly on my neck, the way my dad used to hold me when I was a little girl. "I'm so glad you're okay." He says.

"You two get out of here. I'll keep these two in here, so they don't try to make a run for it outside." Dad instructs.

"Just hang on a second." Wade says. He walks up to the two idiots. "Which one of you hit her?"

"It was Leonard, Moron number one." I answer.

Wade's fist balls up, and before I can stop him, he lifts his elbow in the air and delivers a powerful punch to Leonard's face. I hear the crack and wince as Leonard drops to the floor. Blood pours from his nose as Wade flexes his fingers in and out, taking a step back. "Be thankful I wasn't the one holding the gun, asshole." Then he glares at Priscilla. "I hope you rot in jail." He seethes, as three police officers enter the room.

A female police officer sees me and radios in using the device clipped to her shoulder. "We need a medic in here."

"You okay, ma'am?" she asks as Wade takes my hand.

"I'm fine. Just have a headache."

"You should still get checked out." she says, observing the gash. "Did you get hit with the pistol?"

"Yeah."

"Jesus Christ." Wade swears as the police officer directs us to the ambulance outside. "I should have shot the bastard." He says, adjusting the gun he had tucked in the waistband of his pants.

"I'm sure you broke his nose. We're even." I comment as a female paramedic gestures for me to come over. She cleans up the gash and places a large band-aid over it.

"You should have a CT Scan to make sure you haven't got a concussion." The paramedic advises.

"I'll take her right now." Wade says.

"No, you can hop into the ambulance. We'll take her. The police can take your statements from there." She insists.

Dad says he'll follow us over in his car as we watch Priscilla and Leonard get hauled off to the police station in a cruiser. Leonard's face is covered in blood, and it's all down his dirty shirt. It looks good on him.

Moments later, ss I sit in the bed in the emergency room, Wade won't let my hand go. "I'm so sorry that you had to go through this, baby." He says for the hundredth time, sandwiching my hand between his, endlessly stroking it.

"It's not your fault, Wade." I insist. "Quit blaming yourself."

"Wade?" a voice says from behind the curtain. I know it isn't dad or mom, as they just went to get some coffee and snacks.

"Yeah." Wade rises, opening the curtain a little. His brother Jack appears.

"Hey, I've been looking all over for you, man." Jack whispers, glancing quickly at me.

Gesturing towards me, Wade explains. "Yeah, sorry, we had to turn our phones off in here. How did you find us?"

Jack shrugs. "Put two and two together." he looks at me. "You alright, little lady?" a 'v' forms between his eyes when he sees the bruise forming on the side of my face. "Got you good, eh?"

"Don't worry, I pounded on him." Wade says, sitting down and taking my hand in his again.

"So, what are you going to do now?" Jack asks Wade, as Jack takes the seat next to Wade. I notice that Jack speaks as though I'm not here.

"We just have to wait for the results from her CT scan, and then we need to go eat something. None of us have eaten a thing all day."

"No, I mean, are you going back to your place?" Jack clarifies, just as mom and dad return, each carrying a brown paper bag with snacks from the donut shop outside the emergency department. Wade makes the introductions and then Jack prompts him to answer the question. "So, Wade, what are you going to do?"

It's like a spider is crawling down Wade's back. "I don't know, man. They've been through my place. I...I don't want to go back, but what am I supposed to do?"

"You can come stay with me." Jack offers. "I've got plenty of room."

"Nah, that's too far. I don't want to cramp your style, either."

Dad interjects. "Well, you can stay with us until you find another place. We have a spare room. My wife and I are going away anyhow for the next two weeks. Kendra will need the company."

Mom adds. "It's Peter's birthday gift."

"Thanks." Wade rakes a hand through his hair. "It didn't take long to find that place. I'm sure it won't take long to find another."

All I can think is...*playing house with Wade might be fun.*

Chapter 34

Wade

Peter and I were already at the door, in position, when my phone rang. I knew it was her. I kicked down the door and ran to her, half in fear, half in rage. If Peter hadn't been there with me, I would have killed the son-of-a-bitch...both of them. Peter being there was the only reason those two assholes lived. Aside from the blow to her head, Kendra was completely unscathed. That girl is a brave one. Her father raised her right. As if it were possible, I love Kendra even more after that.

Jack helped me move my stuff out of the old lady's basement. It's pathetic how all my belongings fit into two cars, including my pullout couch, which got tied to the bed of Jack's pickup truck. Kendra's parents are great. They let me put all my stuff in their garage, where Peter keeps most of his gun collection, so nobody will mess with any of my crap. Her mother had been feverishly packing for their trip in the morning, while Kendra and I snuggled in the basement by the fireplace.

"How are you feeling, baby?" I ask, sliding a hand through her hair as she lays on my chest. I'm laying on my back, on the couch.

"Fine. You?" she asks, as though my question is perfunctory.

"I'm with you. All is good." I kiss her head as we watch the flames lick the sides of the logs in the wood fireplace. The crackling is comforting, and the smell reminds me of my brother Colton's place. "You tired?" I'd barely seen her all day as Jack and I moved my stuff, and Kendra helped her mom pack.

"Just relaxed." She answers sleepily. "I could stay here all night."

"We can if you like." I offer, enjoying the feeling of my baby on me, as I stroke her back. It felt like punishment not sleeping with her last night, especially after all she'd been through yesterday. I stayed with her in her bed as long as I could; at least until I heard her parents getting ready for bed. She'd booked the day off work today months ago for Jennifer's wedding, but tomorrow she would be back to work.

"I'd love to, but I have to work tomorrow, and you have to take my parents to the airport in the morning."

"Whatever you like, baby." I kiss her head again. Then she sneezes and it's such a weird feeling, seeing as she's on top of me. "Bless you." I chuckle.

"Excuse me." she laughs, and then she sneezes again. "Sorry."

"Don't apologize." I chuckle again. "I'm slightly turned on by that." I joke.

That receives a playful smack on the shoulder. She lifts and sneezes again. "You're a genius." I tease.

"Shut up." She sniffles, getting off me to go to the washroom.

I giggle. "Are you getting sick?" I ask, hearing her blow her nose.

"No, but I have half a mind to call in sick tomorrow. This bruise on my face is going to cause some trouble. I'm sure the partners will love it that I look like I lost a bar fight."

"Wear your hair out. It'll be barely noticeable." I lie, trying to make her feel better.

She returns, lowering herself on top of me again. "I'd rather stay home with you. My parents are leaving. We'll have the whole house to ourselves...I sound like I'm in high school." She guffaws, lifting her head, laughing at herself.

I kiss her chastely on the mouth and smile. "Yeah, we could...like...have an open house party." I say, feigning a teenage voice.

Kendra laughs, leaning her head on mine. It's contagious. "It's so weird." I say, "I've never *not* had a hard-on sleeping with you, but last night it was like I pictured your dad barging into your room with one of his shotguns, ready to shoot me for banging his daughter."

I'm killing her. She's laughing so hard she has to wipe her eyes.

"Kryptonite." She cries with mirth. "Staying at my house is like kryptonite for you."

I chuckle. "Yeah, I can't do it at your parent's place. It's too weird."

Her laughter comes down a notch. "Well, what about when they're gone tomorrow?"

"I don't know." I sigh, still smiling at her.

"Wow, this is a whole different side of you, Wade." She sniffs, "I might have to put on something sexy after work tomorrow."

Lifting a brow, I interlace my fingers behind her back and frown, glancing at the ceiling. "Well, that might work."

***

It's odd kissing your girlfriend goodbye before she goes to work, when her parents are right there. It was like kissing her mom goodbye. I sent her an 'I love you' text afterward, since it felt so weird being intimate under her folks' watchful eye. When I took them to the airport, thankfully, it wasn't awkward. They talked about their pending trip, which they're both very excited about. Apparently, Kendra's parents had been saving since Peter's last birthday for this trip. I bid them adieu and drove over to Dave's house for our practice.

"Hey, buddy, you gotta see this." Dave says when I arrive. "I broke up the videos between all the songs we played at the wedding and posted them individually on YouTube. Look at the traffic, dude." Dave doesn't often get excited, and I don't recall ever actually seeing him pumped about anything, but this is definitely it. "We got like ten thousand views in two days, man. That's smoking."

"Really?" I'm in disbelief. "Which songs are getting more attention?"

"The duet with you and Kendra, and a couple others." He names them, opening the page on his computer and he scrolls down. "Look at the comments. They're loving it, man."

"Well, my girl's got a great set of pipes." I say, reading some of the comments.

"Yeah, and a great set of—"

"Hey!" I shout, shooting him a look. "You finish that sentence and it'll be your last." I warn, pointing at him.

He lifts his arms. "Hey, sorry man." He chuckles. "We always fuck around like that. What's the matter with you?"

"She's my girlfriend, asshole. Have some respect."

"What...do you like...love her now?" he's being glib.

"I do, so watch your mouth."

"Whoaaa....." he teases. "Wade's getting serious...oooooo."

"Grow up." I chide, "Where are the other guys?"

Dave shrugs. "They'll be here."

They show up ten minutes later, and we practice for most of the day. When it's four o'clock, we decide to wrap it up. I want to go pick something up so I can make Kendra a nice dinner. Which is a plus with a real, full-size kitchen for a change. On the way to the grocery store, I give my sister-in-law Julia a call, asking for one of Colton's recipes for pork chops.

"So, is she coming on Saturday? Do we finally get to meet this girl who's tamed the untameable Wade Ford?" Julia teases.

I smile, ignoring the gentle jibe. "Yeah, she's coming."

"Apparently Jack's bringing a girl, too."

"No kidding? He didn't mention anything to me."

"That's because you Ford boys don't tell each other anything, but you can't keep anything from me."

"That's true." I agree. "When does Colton get back?"

"Tomorrow. Oh, and my dad's coming Saturday, too." She adds.

"Oh, that's cool. I haven't seen your dad in a while."

"Yeah. Be careful not to grope this Kendra girl in front of him, eh? I don't want him to have a stroke."

"I'll behave." I play along. "Hey, I'm at the grocery store now. Thanks for the recipe."

"No problem. Let me know how it goes. See you Saturday."

"See ya."

***

It's official. I suck at cooking. Colton is the one with the cooking talent. The pork chops are burned, the potatoes are hard and lumpy, and the vegetables taste like ass. Thank God I have the sense to order a pizza right before Kendra gets home. She walks in and my heart swells just at the sight of her. It's odd, but I missed her. I kiss her chastely on the mouth and give her a warm hug. "I missed you, baby." I say as I hold her.

"Me too." She purrs, running her fingers through the hair at the back of my neck, giving me shivers.

"Well, I *tried* to cook."

"Oh yeah?" she looks around, seeing no dishes or sign of food, and she looks at me, lifting a brow.

"Let's just say the score is kitchen one, Wade zero." I frown. "There's a pizza on the way."

She giggles into my chest as I embrace her, kissing her head. "That's okay, Wade. You don't have to cook for me. I can manage that myself."

"Well, I wanted to. At least I get an A for effort."

She lifts her head and puckers her lips intentionally. I lean down and kiss her chastely. "How was your day?" I ask.

"Busy but good." She sighs, observing the music sheets on the table, and my guitar laying across the chair. "Were you cooking while you were practicing?"

"Yeah. I'm working on a new song."

"That could be the cause of your cuisine-a-geddon, baby." She chuckles.

"Could be."

The doorbell rings. "Oh, hey, perfect timing." I say, pulling my wallet out of my back pocket. I pay the guy and we eat pizza happily at the table.

"You play tonight?" she asks me as we finish eating.

"Yeah. I've got a short set tonight. Blake said for me to come for nine. Just until midnight. He closes early tonight until Thursday. You want to come?"

"Sure." she says. "You expect Jack tonight?"

"Probably not. He's got nowhere to crash anymore."

"He can stay here." She offers.

I frown, considering it. "Maybe I'll let him know later."

We start a fire and sit on the couch. I drape my arm around her back as she leans into my chest. Stroking her skin with my thumb, she makes circles on my belly with her index finer. "This doesn't tickle, does it?" she asks.

"No. It feels nice." I kiss her head.

She lifts her head so we're almost eye level. "So, what's the new song about?"

I kiss her quickly on the mouth and explain. "I don't really know yet. It's just a bit of lyrics right now. I usually jam stuff out with the guys to formulate something solid first. We worked on it a little today, but we didn't get to really hash it out yet."

"Why? Were you guys busy doing something else? Practicing and stuff?"

"Yeah, that, and we were talking about the videos from the wedding." I explain to her that they had received attention. "We're thinking it might be worthwhile to record one or two, but it costs a hell of a lot of money."

"Well, Wade, I've been saving for a house for a while. I don't mind helping out."

I smile at her and kiss her full on the mouth. "I appreciate that, baby, but I can't take your money. My brothers would kill me for starters; they've been trying to jam my pockets with their money for years."

"Wade, no offence, but it's not like you're buying a

moped or something frivolous. Think of this as an investment, like a nest egg. This is your future, sweetie. If your music has the audience it looks like it's garnering, you should take a chance with it. Not everyone gets a chance. You might not get another one."

"Yeah, and if I take someone else's money, I'll always see it like I didn't make the start on my own."

"Well, look at kids who go to college or university; they don't get that money on their own."

"Yeah, but that's different. They get the money from their parents."

"Well, where do you think your brother's money comes from? Didn't your dad leave them that money?"

I wince. This is one of the reasons why I never tell girls about my family and the money. "I don't like talking about this, Kendra. Really. I'm sorry."

She smiles and lifts, so we're almost nose-to-nose. "Hey, honey. I love you. I'm not here to tell you what to do, I'm here to support you. Whatever you choose to do is your decision. I'm here for you no matter what."

God, I love her. She's so the woman for me. I change the subject. "Did you know the most viewed video is our duet?"

She cranes her neck a little and a small smile forms on her face. "Really?"

I nod once. "Really really."

"Wow." She's impressed.

"So, what do you think, baby….do you want to learn some of my songs so we can sing them together?" I suggest, just to gauge her reaction.

She rolls her eyes. "God, Wade, I don't know." Her giggle is adorable. Leaning over, I kiss her full on the mouth. "Think about it." I whisper against her lips.

"How can I resist when you ask me like that?" she says salaciously.

I kiss her deeper and slower. "How about when I kiss you like this?"

"You keep that up and you'll have to toss out your

whole 'I don't do it at Kendra's parent's house' stance."
She warns gently.

I pause, lifting a brow. "Have you heard from them?
Did they arrive safely?"

"Safe and sound. This house is all ours for the next
fourteen days." Her tone is teasing. "I have a real bed
upstairs that's never been broken in."

"Really?"

She nods and licks her lips a little more than
casually; as if she knows something is on them. I
glance at her lips and she takes that as a cue. The
blouse she's wearing has buttons down the front. She
begins undoing them as I watch, feeling the blood
rushing out of my head, going south of my belt.
Removing it, she tosses her blouse on to the floor and
rises, unzipping her skirt, and it pools to the floor.
She's standing in the sexiest two-piece lace white thong
and bra set I've ever seen. "Wow." Is all I can manage.
This ultra-sexy combo includes a garter and stockings.
She unhooks the stockings and pulls them down,
pressing her arms together so her cleavage screams for
me to look at it. "God, you're killing me, baby." I
murmur and she smiles.

"I was hoping I would." She's matter-of-fact as she
takes a step towards me and pulls my shirt over my
head. "What I want to do requires you to be wearing
much less."

I let her have the floor in this sexy overtaking. She
bends down and undoes my pants, and I have mercy on
her by standing and removing them. She checks out my
naked, hardened cock. "Still no underwear, eh." She
points out.

"You want me to start wearing them?" I ask
rhetorically, knowing very well what the answer is.
She's very impressed that I go Commando all the time.
No answer comes, but she takes my hand and leads me
upstairs to her room. Watching her rear end ahead of
me, I'm almost drooling. Gently grasping her waist, I
stop her, embracing her from behind. "You didn't think

you were going to get this far without me touching you, did you?" I slide her hair away from her neck and kiss it, sucking her flesh. Trailing kisses down her back, I hit all her tender spots, and then stop at her rear. With my hands at her hips, I kiss and flick my tongue across her cheeks and she breathes deeply, taking it in.

Grasping her underwear with my thumbs, I pull them down and she steps out of them. Then I reach up and unhook her bra, letting her remove it from the front. She backs into me, feeling my hardness on her buttocks. Wrapping my arms around her, I embrace her, and drag my hands across her rib cage, reaching for her breasts. Kneading her nipples gently, I trail soft kisses across her shoulder. Kendra rears her head back as I watch her nipples bead from my touch.

"I can't stand it anymore." She says, turning to face me. Her arms snake around my neck, as she rakes her hands in my hair, giving me open-mouth kisses, plunging her tongue inside. Sucking my bottom lip, she gives it a little nip, and I gently pull away.

"Easy, baby." I breathe.

She covers her mouth with her hand, taking a step back. "Oh, I'm sorry. Did I hurt you?" the remorse is clear on her face.

"No, you couldn't hurt me, sweetie." I chuckle, feeling guilty that I've made her feel bad. "I just want to take things a little bit slow, that's all." I smile. "Come here." Tipping her chin towards me with my fingers, I kiss her tenderly on the mouth. "I love you, baby."

Her glance is divided between both my eyes. "I love it when you say that." Her voice is soft, and I notice that her eyes look glossy. I exhale, staring deeply into her eyes, as if telepathically saying those three words to her again. Swallowing, I clench my jaw, and then lean in and kiss her again, deeper. "I love you more than anything, Wade." She says as her voice cracks.

Tilting my head, I envelope her mouth with mine, gently dipping my tongue inside. She embraces me, holding me close, and I lift her by the waist, carrying her to her bed, and slowly lowering her down as my body hovers over her. Cupping her face with my hands, I kiss her more, as she wraps her legs around my body, hugging me with every inch of her body. It's sexy as hell but it's also very tender and intimate. I'm not even inside her yet, but she wants to feel all of me. Lowering myself onto her, we're nose-to-nose. A tear has fallen down the side of her face, soaking her hair where she got hit the other night. I kiss her softly where the tear lands, and then I trail kisses from her cheek to her lips, and it's like she's drinking me in. She's all but gasping each time our lips connect. "Sex is a lot different after 'I love you', isn't it, baby." I whisper, rubbing my nose against hers in a kind of Eskimo kiss.

She gives a little nod and kisses me more, like she's desperate, as though we haven't seen each other in months; the way Colton and Pam used to kiss when he'd been away in Afghanistan. It's deep and moving. Nobody has ever kissed me with so much heart before. I feel a little nudge on the back of my leg; she wants to connect completely, as intimate as two lovers can get. As I enter her, she exhales and then breathes in deeply, pressing her chest upward into me. I take that as a cue and suck her nipples tenderly, taking them in my mouth entirely, right up to the areola.

As I start to move inside her, sucking her breasts, she's meeting me thrust for thrust, slow and deep, as if we're savoring each other. Placing my hands on either side of her face, my eyes are hooded watching her expression as she starts climbing. As my breathing becomes ragged, I've got her attention, as she observes my face while I feel her start to tighten inside. Instinctively my eyes close as every thrust I'm in all the way to the hilt. "Ooohhhhh," I say, leaning my forehead against hers. "It's so good, baby." I whisper.

"Mmmmmm....." she moans, and I lean up, increasing speed. The bed starts to squeak a little. "Oh, that's it, baby." She says, as though I need encouragement. Her hands skate across my stomach, as I lean all the way up, plunging into her at a deeper angle. She lifts her upper body, and I bring my legs around, adjusting my position, so she's sitting on my thighs. Her kisses are deep as her legs lift her in rhythm with my thrusts from under her. If we were on the pullout couch right now, it would be giving up, collapsing from under us.

"My bed's way better than yours." She says semi-breathlessly.

"Oh, no contest." I grunt, giving her a wink. Helping her lift her body with both hands at her side, we've found the perfect rhythm together. Our skin is softly slapping together in the silence, and both our breathing is ragged. Leaning my pelvis into her more, we slow slightly, as I try for her g-spot. I can feel her tighten instantly. It feels amazing.

"Oh....Wade..." She pants, closing her eyes. "Mmmm...." She moans.

"Oooohhhhh, Kendra." I whisper, feeling closer to the edge, her moaning spurring me on. "Jesus Lord,"

The bed is thumping softly. Thank God nobody is downstairs because it probably sounds like we're jumping on the bed together. She kisses me, sucking on my tongue and then my bottom lip. "Oh, God, Kendra...." I beg breathlessly. The suction is delicious, reminding me of what she did to me with her mouth...below the belt...last week.

"Mmmm...you like that..." she murmurs salaciously.

"I like it too much." I say, and then I suck on her neck, and lift her up higher so I can suck her breasts.

"Oh, God, Wade....oooohhhh......" she calls my name, the last 'o' crescendos, and I can feel her getting impossibly tight.

She's so close to the edge, but I want her to come harder and stronger, so I lay on my back and grasp her waist, reaching my thumb over to her clit. As I circle it, she smiles. "Oh, you know what that does to me."

"Yes, I do." I say, enjoying watching her bounce up and down, riding me. She has no idea how beautiful and sexy she is. Leaning down towards me, she begins kissing me, plunging her tongue inside, while I circle her clit with my thumb. It feels so goddam fantastic that my orgasm suddenly sneaks up on me. I try to slow it but then I feel her muscles contracting, squeezing me, and I let go. It's like a lightning bolt. "Oh, Lord Jesus," I pant. "Oh," I grunt, feeling the veins in my neck pop. "Oh, baby." I breathe.

Her mouth is wide open, her eyes are shut tight, and she's holding her breath, feeling her release. When she exhales, she lets it go in bursts, murmuring 'o' deliciously. Watching her come on top of me is so freaking hot it kills me. We're both a breathless mess as she lays down on my chest and I kiss her head. My heart is beating like I've just run a marathon, and I can feel hers doing the same. Finally, I swallow, and take a cleansing breath, stroking her hair with my hand.

"Can I stay here forever?" she finally says.

"Definitely."

She lifts her head so we're nose-to-nose. "Am I too heavy?"

"Not even a little bit." I kiss her full on the mouth. I stroke her cheek with my hand and whisper. "I love you."

She kisses me. "I love you, too."

As we lay there in each other's arms, I stroke her back with one hand. She giggles when I get to a ticklish spot and it's contagious. "Does that tickle?"

She lifts her head. "Yeah, but it also feels nice." And she lowers her head back down on my chest. I love it that she's still got some innocence.

"So, do you think I can convince you to do a duet with me at Mingles tonight?"

She lifts her head again, this time propping it on her hand, resting her elbow on my shoulder. "You're not serious."

I nod once for emphasis and place my hands flat on her buttocks. "I am serious."

"I think it was different at the wedding. Don't you

think the audience at Mingles prefers it when you appear single? I see how the girls bat their eyelashes at you...among other things." She tries to keep her distaste hidden, but I can tell.

"Na, that's just at Mingles. I told you that the duet has more views than any other song on YouTube. Face it, baby, people love us together."

"So, then, what would be the point of us singing together tonight at the bar?"

"Because I love it when you sing. And I love singing with you. Music is part of who I am and the fact that you have musical talent just makes our stars align even more."

How can she say no to that?

Chapter 35

Kendra

God, here I am thinking I'm sooo hot and sexy in this little number under my clothes, and I end up a blubbering mess! Wade must love me for real, because any other guy would have stopped the seduction. I mean, how much of a turn-off is it when a girl starts *crying* in bed? Ugh! My sudden emotional state didn't seem to stifle him, though. Every time we're together it just gets better and better. The way he looks at me while we're making love sometimes is so intense, I almost can't handle it. He makes love with every part of his body, including his eyes. I love him so much it hurts.

So, when he asks me to sing a song with him tonight, how can I refuse? We take separate cars and he leaves first, just because he knows I have to work in the morning. For a Tuesday night, Mingles is pretty happening. When I arrive just after nine thirty, the dance floor is full, and Wade is singing away on stage; he seems to be using much of his own music lately, which I love, and so do the customers. He sees me and gives me a wink, right in the middle of the song. He's so freaking sexy I could die. The lights on him are perfect. His hair, his face, his eyes, his butt in those jeans...damn! I want to kiss him so bad, but I know I can't...yet.

Taking a seat at the bar, Blake sees me. "Hey...Kendra, is it?"

"That's right." I smile.

"Can I get you anything? It's on the house."

"Just water, thanks." I say. "Was the owner upset about the wall?" I ask, remembering how Wade drove his fist through it the night he fired Chuck, his former manager.

He hands me a bottle of water. "Nope. But that's

'cause he don't know about it yet."

"Oh. Well, do you want me to tell him?"

"Ain't necessary, sweetheart. I already fixed it myself." He grins.

"Oh, you're a doll. I'm sure Wade will appreciate that."

"It's no bother, love. In a former life I did a bit of drywall repair. Took me back a little. It's all the same to me." he winks.

I toss him a five for the water. Blake raises a hand. "Not necessary."

"Consider it a tip for your trouble." I say, smiling, as I walk away, and stand closer to the stage. Wade doesn't see me at first as he and the band are singing the chorus of a catchy tune. Dave is sharing the mic with Wade, singing in harmony. Wade is belting out the higher notes, making my toes curl. I can see the veins in his neck pop from the vocal exertion, and it reminds me of earlier when we were in bed. I bite my lip. He has a bead of sweat dripping down the side of his face. Even sweaty he looks like a god.

As the song comes to a close, he announces that they're taking a quick break. He sets down his guitar as the pre-recorded music begins playing from the speakers. Hopping off the stage. I wave at Wade and he comes over, an ear-to-ear smile appears on his face. He kisses me chastely but full on the mouth three times. "Hi, baby."

"Hi, yourself." I say, feeling dizzy from his touch. He takes my hand and leads me to the bar, ordering himself a bottle of water. "I really like that song you just sang. Especially the harmony in it. Very Def Leppard."

He rolls his eyes and lowers his head, shaking it. He lets out a laugh. "Oh, dear". Blake brings his water, and he drains half of it in one go.

"Sorry, did I offend you?" I ask, loving the sound of him laughing.

He coughs, still laughing a little. "No. Not at all." He pauses, as Dave approaches. "Dave, get a load of what

Kendra just said". He winks at me, indicating that I should repeat my statement.

When I do, Dave's eyes light up. "Thank you!" He high fives me. "I *like you*." He's being matter of fact. "When I wrote that song that's *exactly* the sound I was after. Thank you, Kendra, for your *astute* observation." His tone is forced, and judging by the glib look on Wade's face, this song has been a bone of contention between Wade and Dave for a while.

"He wrote it and none of us liked it." Wade adds.

"Oh, it's a great song." I say.

Wade leans over and kisses me. "You're lucky I love you."

Dave rolls his eyes. "I'll go get the hose." He says, walking away.

Wade chuckles again. Then he puts his hands on my waist. "So, what are you up for tonight, baby? You feel like something slow or do you want to shake it up a bit?"

I look around and see the energy in the bar tonight. "How about shaking it up?"

"Works for me. Do you want to do a cover, or one of my songs?"

"I like your songs. How about that one about not being able to make up your mind? The one you played at the wedding and you had the guests singing along at the chorus."

"Sure. We haven't played that one yet tonight. It's called '*Don't Want to Run*'."

"You better not." I tease, elbowing him in the ribs.

He tilts his head, lifting a brow. "The only running I'll be doing is *to* you, baby."

"You bet your ass." I say, kissing him. He cups my face in his hands and makes the kiss deeper, yet still chaste.

Griffin, the bass player walks up to us. "Dave's fingers are itchy, man. Are you ready to go back on?" he addresses Wade.

"Sure, you want to start with '*Don't Want to Run*'?

Kendra's going to sing it with me."

"Sure, I'll give her the extra mic." Griffin walks away.

Wade looks at me, flashing his eyes. "You excited?"

"Excited and a bit nervous."

"You'll be great, baby. The lyrics are so easy, but I've got the music written down on top of the speaker box." He points to the large plastic box in front of the mic stand. "With this song it's not even about the singing, it's about getting the audience to participate, and the regulars do all the time. They'll recognize the song as soon as it starts. It's very Queen-esque if you will." He winks.

I lift a brow.

He stomps twice and claps and then does it again in time. The song 'We Will Rock You' comes to mind. "Oh, okay."

He lifts a hand, indicating 'you got it', just as the pre-recorded song comes to a close. "You ready?"

I nod and he takes my hand, guiding me to the stage. The crowd starts to whoop and make other sounds of encouragement as we climb the stairs to the stage. It feels odd being led up there, but once I'm there, especially standing next to Wade, it doesn't feel so bad. "I want you all to put your hands together for my girl, Kendra, she and I are going to sing something together. Sing with us if you know it." he winks at me as the music starts up, gesturing to the sheet music that is right in front of us. The clapping is almost deafening, and I can see a load of people on the dance floor.

Wade was right, the people recognize the song right away. Some are clapping to the beat. As we start singing together, the chemistry is so natural. By the second verse we're singing in harmony as if we practiced for days together before this performance. His face is lit up like a Christmas tree as we sing. I love it. I've never met anyone so happy before. When Griffin does a guitar solo, Wade takes me by the waist, and we do a little dance together. He spins me around and we do a couple of two steps, and then he lifts me in the air and shifts me around, letting me back down softly on the opposite side. We receive some loud whistles and shouts for that. I laugh out loud it's so much fun.

When the song is over, the place is so loud with whistles and woohoos, I feel like a celebrity. I've never felt so alive. Wade kisses me full on the mouth, which makes the whistling and woohoos way worse. One guy actually howls like a dog, and another guy sounds like he's baying at the moon. It's hilarious and exhilarating, and the look on Wade's face is so incredibly sexy I could faint. He's so proud of me. My heart swells. "Come on, let's hear it for Kendra. Thanks, baby." He says, as if they need another reason to holler and make a ton of noise again. I start laughing so hard I have to bend at the waist. As I depart from the stage, I give a little wave, which encourages further pandemonium. I'm shaking my head as I leave the stage, smiling from ear-to-ear.

As I walk to the bar, Blake leans over to me. "There's a match made in heaven if I ever saw one."

I don't know how to react, so I just smile. He brings me another bottle of water. "Do you sing in a band?" he asks.

I guffaw. "No."

"Really." He was expecting me to have a different answer. "So, you don't do that on the side? You just practice law?"

"That's right. I write the bar exam in a little while...again." I add, even though I usually leave that part out. Somehow since I met Wade, I feel like I don't have to hide anything.

"I suppose some of us have multiple talents." He surmises as more people approach the bar to order drinks. He leaves me and I look over at Wade. I could watch him all night, and I would, if I didn't have to work in the morning. Guilt befalls me as I leave, giving Wade a wave on my way out. I don't want to leave, but I have to be at work early tomorrow, and the partners are not forgiving when it comes to tardiness.

Two hours later I hear the lock disengage downstairs.

My mom gave Wade her key to use while they're away. He's being so quiet I don't even hear him. All I hear is the shower running softly from the basement washroom. He slides into bed next to me so gently that if it weren't for him kissing my head, I wouldn't know he was even there. I look up at the clock. It's just after one o'clock. "You're back earlier than I thought."

"Oh, sorry, honey. I didn't mean to wake you." He whispers, spooning me from behind. "Go back to sleep."

He smells so fresh and his body is still damp from the shower. "I don't know why you bother to shower. I like it better when you're all sweaty."

"Oh, no...you would have insisted on it. Someone puked on me."

"Gross." I turn over to face him. "Are you okay?"

"My clothes aren't." he sighs. "I put them right in the washer and closed the lid. Don't open it, whatever you do. I'll run the machine in the morning. I didn't want to wake you...which I see I've done anyway." He chuckles, rubbing my back.

"That's okay. I'm a light sleeper. Always have been. I hear it when bugs crawl at night."

He chuckles softly. It sounds incredibly sexy. I run my fingers through his damp hair, and he swallows. My eyes have adjusted to the darkness. I see his eyes getting heavier each time I stroke his head. "Tired?" I ask.

"Exhausted." He whispers. "Sleep, baby."

"Okay." I murmur. "I love you."

He kisses my forehead, even though I want him to kiss my lips. He's too smart for that; he knows what his kisses do to me. "Love you, too, baby. With all my heart."

When he says that, something goes off inside me, and I want him even more. I kiss his lips, full. "Mmmm...." He says, lifting his head, opening his mouth and enveloping mine with his. At first, it's a somewhat chaste kiss, without tongue, as if he's gauging how far I want to go. Tilting my head, I gently dip my tongue inside his mouth, softly sweeping until I meet his tongue. His hand goes to the back of my neck, and his kiss becomes instantly deeper, deliciously deeper, and he tosses the blankets off us, and slowly climbs on top of me. Below the belt he's already like steel. I can see his beefy shoulders shimmering in the moonlight that's creeping in through the curtains. He looks like an Adonis.

My hands are all over his damp hair, as we feverishly kiss each other, tongues, lips, nipping, sucking, the whole lot of it. We're breathless in moments. He trails kisses down my neck, as my hands are still in his hair, raking, sweeping, tugging at him, and then he's at my breasts, taking them in his mouth, making love to them like they're some treasure he's just discovered. Arching my back, he cups each of my breasts, and I can feel what he's doing all the way to my toes, but especially...there. My muscles are contracting the same way they do when he's inside me. I had no idea that was possible, but he's working on both of them, kneading one while he's licking, sucking and nipping the other. I'm all but pulling handfuls of his hair out when I realize what he's doing is driving me to the edge. Half in shock, half in ecstasy I call his name when I feel my orgasm rip through me suddenly. My chest is heaving up and down as he continues flicking his tongue over my nipple while I ride the waves of pleasure. I'm in awe. This is a new experience for me.

He comes back up to kiss me full on the mouth, as I breathe heavily against his lips. Then he's gone, trailing his way down my stomach, kissing and sucking my flesh, which half tickles and half feels amazing with my skin all over-sensitive post-orgasm. Reaching my thighs, he places his warm, gentle hands on them, parting them, and I gasp inwardly as his lips touch my most sensitive spot. Grabbing hold of the sheets, I feel my body growing rigid as he begins sucking and licking my folds rhythmically, driving me closer to the edge again. The tip of his tongue is right at the apex of my clit, and it feels unbelievable, and I can't believe how quickly he's getting me there, but within a couple of minutes, I'm unconsciously bucking my hips, making noises akin to a porn video, sounding more animal than human. When my second orgasm crashes through me, my breathing is so ragged I don't know how I'm getting oxygen.

But he doesn't stop. He slows only slightly as my breathing evens. My body feels like it's made of rubber, and my insides feel like pudding. I don't know how he's continuing; how his tongue isn't sore or how he's hanging on without finding his release. And slowly my breathing starts to become ragged again, and I feel myself climbing. How the hell is he doing this? I feel him slide a finger inside me, rubbing my pelvic bone, and I gasp. It feels fantastic, and he moans, and I'm not sure if he's intentionally increasing the sensation with the vibration, or if he's just responding to the sounds and movements I'm making, but either way, it's such a turn-on and it's driving me close to the edge again. When he slides a second finger inside, it's my undoing. I hiss and buck my rear up so high as I feel my release. He moans more as I come, with so much need it's intense.

Finally, he stops, as he kisses the inside of my thighs before trailing kisses up my stomach, through my breasts and at my neck; like he's going backwards from where he came when he first started. I'm panting, out of breath, practically unconscious from three orgasms in a row. "God, you're going to kill me." I whisper breathlessly.

"Death by multiple orgasm. What a way to go." He murmurs against my lips. "Can you handle one more?" he asks salaciously, as he hovers his hardness around my entrance. He waits until I answer before he moves. "I think you've got one more in there with my name on it, baby." His voice is like silk.

"Four in one night. It reminds me of our first night together." I comment.

He chuckles softly, kissing me on the mouth. "You're not sore, are you?" he asks tenderly.

"God, no. You're so gentle." I say and mean it, as I place my foot on his rear, indicating that he can proceed. When he enters me, filling me to the hilt, it's like a whole other kind of delicious. After so many orgasms, I didn't think it would feel so intense, but it does. I feel like it's been all about me so far, so I ask. "What would you like? You want me on top? You want me to do some of the work at least?" I let out a little giggle.

He kisses me full on the lips and says as he moves slowly, deliciously. "I don't know...I think this is kind of nice." He says, lifting my legs, giving my knees a kiss. "I can do this,"

"Mmmm..." I moan, feeling him deeper.

"And then you make that sound." He chuckles playfully, and it's sexy as hell. It's like I'm his sexual puppet. And I like it. A lot. "And then I feel you do that inside." He whispers, kissing me deeply, sweeping his tongue in my mouth. He's moving faster. "Ooohhh," he whispers in the darkness, and then he makes a soft hissing sound, and I can feel him get impossibly hard inside me. He's held out for me this long, and I don't think he's going to last much longer. Leaning up slightly, he hits the spot at my pelvic bone, knowing that's what threw me over the edge the last time. "Oh, God, baby, I'm close already." He grunts. But it's just those words out of him that bring me closer.

As I watch his eyes shut tight, and I feel his warm seed shoot into me, I feel my release. His breathing is ragged as he moves faster, feeling his release and mine. "Oh, God, baby. Oh, Jesus." He breathes as he comes, and I call out his name, feeling the intense pleasure with him. We're a mess of panting and writhing as we climax together. He leans his forehead on mine when his last aftershock subsides. His heart is beating against mine while he's still inside me. Releasing my legs, he then strokes the sides of my face with his thumb. "You were great tonight." He sighs, trying to catch his breath.

"So were you." I answer salaciously. But I don't think we're talking about the same thing.

He snorts a laugh and takes a cleansing breath, saying, "Phew!"

"You okay?" I chuckle.

Removing himself from me, he lays on his side and rests his head on his hand, propping his elbow on the pillow. "That...was...intense."

"You're telling me." I'm matter-of-fact.

He pulls the sheets up, covering us both. "You should get some sleep, baby. I would hate to have you exhausted tomorrow."

"It was worth it." I say, kissing him.

"You're so sweet." He whispers against my lips. "I love you so much."

"I love you, too, baby."

He spoons me and I fall asleep instantly.

When my alarm goes off at five o'clock, it's painful getting up. Wade doesn't even move. Clearly, he's not a light sleeper. He's on the other side of the bed, on his stomach. His back is naked, and his arms are under the pillow. I'm so jealous I could cry. After I get ready for work; being careful to get dressed and do everything in the bathroom so I don't wake him, I tiptoe in and kiss him on the cheek goodbye. I leave an 'I Love You' note under his cell phone, which he left on the kitchen table.

At noon I get a call from him while I'm on my lunch. "Hey, baby, I've got some pretty cool news." Wade announces.

"Oh, yeah...what's that?" I ask, excited just to hear his voice, and him calling me 'baby' makes my toes curl.

"Dave's buddy recorded and posted some material from last night...you'll never guess what song is getting the most views." His statement is rhetorical.

"Really? That is pretty cool."

"Yeah, we're like Sonny and Cher or something." He's impressed and proud.

"Okay, I'll let you be Sonny."

He chuckles. "Thanks for the note this morning. It made my day."

"Well, you always make my day."

"Can't wait to see you later. Love you, babe."

"Me neither. Love you loads."

As I hang up to him, he immediately sends me a text of a pair of lips, as if to kiss me. I smile. I get the feeling this is just the tip of the iceberg for how many wonderful things are about to happen to me. And I think it's all going to start really soon.

Chapter 36

Wade

It's hard to tell, but I think Kendra's nervous about meeting my family. She's met my brother Jack, but today she'll meet the other three, plus Julia, my sister-in-law, and her family. I suppose it would be intimidating, even though I would never feel trepidation if I met all of her family at once. Mind you, being a performer, I suppose being extroverted comes natural to me. It would be more awkward for me if I was expected to sit in a room full of stuffy people and keep quiet. I'd be the first to crack and tell a stupid joke or make a quirky comment.

Her hand is clammy in mine as we drive to Colton's ranch. I stroke my finger across her palm, trying to calm her, but she keeps looking out the window, staring into the sky. "You okay?" I ask as we hit a stop light, afraid of the answer.

"I'm fine." She leans over and kisses me on the lips. I kiss her back twice and my eyes keep lingering to her lips as we wait for the light to change. "Behave." She giggles.

"Well, that isn't any fun." I tease, as the light turns green. "So, you're going to love Julia. But don't mention anything about starting a family if it comes up." I warn gently. "There's been more than a few embarrassing moments for some people when they bring up the word 'baby' around Julia."

"How come?"

"They've been trying to start a family since they got married a couple of years ago. No dice so far. Breaks my heart. Colton wants kids so bad it makes him ache. I've been hearing it from him for years. Julia is the same; she's wanted kids forever. She loves kids. She's a teacher."

"Oh, that's tough. Thanks for the heads up. I'll be

careful."

I kiss her hand. "I know you will. I just wanted to spare you any embarrassment."

"I appreciate that." She pauses. "I notice you brought your guitar with you."

"Yeah, we usually jam it up a little bit after supper, while we sit by the fire. You're cool with that, right?"

"Are you kidding me?" she's aghast. "That sounds like so much fun!"

"Yeah, it is. Especially if my brothers have a few beers. Colton won't sing unless he's tanked. Jack'll get into it after one or two, so will Garrett and Dalton, but when Colton sings, you know he's going to be kissing porcelain later."

She laughs. "And do they all stay at Colton's?"

"Na, they usually stay with me, but they got a room at the Hilton this time."

"They could have stayed with us, Wade. It's no problem."

He lifts his hands in mock defence. "I offered. They're weirdos. Don't sweat it."

"Okay."

As we pull up to Colton's ranch, Kendra's eyes widen. "Oh my God, Wade. Is this it?" she pulls her seatbelt off, looking at the acres of green grass, the gated pasture where the two horses are grazing, the stable, and the huge ranch ahead of her. "Wow. This is just...breathtaking."

"It is, isn't it? Sometimes I forget how beautiful it is." I pull my seatbelt off and clasp her hand in mine. "When Colton found this place, it was practically a pile of matchsticks. We helped him build this place and then he got the horses, Rebel and Maya, and the rest is history."

"This is unbelievable." She breathes.

"You haven't seen the inside." I'm matter-of-fact.

"If the inside is anything like the outside, it's gorgeous."

I let go of her hand. "Come here."

She leans in and I steal a few full-mouth kisses, when a knock on my window scares the dickens out of us. Both of us gasp. It's Jack, with a huge grin on his face. "Mind rolling down your window, son?" he jokes.

I open the door intentionally fast. "Jesus Christ, you moron!" I chuckle, lifting my fist, pretending that I'm going to hit him. He ducks for cover and laughs an ungracious apology to Kendra.

"What the hell are you two doing in there? Jesus, you have her folks' house to yourself! Why are you making out in the goddamn driveway?" he teases.

"To rub it in your nose how lonely and empty *your* life is." I shoot back.

Jack grabs his chest, acting like I hurt him badly. I ignore him, as Kendra walks to me and I take her hand in mine. "Where is everyone?" I ask Jack.

"In the house." He tilts his head towards the ranch. "I was just heading out to grab Julia something. I'll be right back."

"Take your time." I say, as if the longer he's gone the better.

Kendra looks at me and snorts a laugh. "What's so funny?"

"You. If you act anything like this with the rest of your brothers, I'm in for a lot of laughs."

I roll my eyes. "Great."

She hugs my arm as we walk into Colton's ranch. We walk in and there is a low din of conversation coming from the kitchen. Julia walks out of the kitchen with an expectant look on her face. "Oh, I thought I heard someone come in." she says. "Hey, Wade," she opens her arms and we embrace. She gives me a pat on the back, and I kiss her cheek. "You look good. Less pasty than usual." She winks.

I ignore her good-natured jibe. "Julia, this is Kendra." I gesture towards my girl, letting go of her hand.

In total Julia-style, she doesn't shake Kendra's hand, she gives her a hug. "It's so nice to finally meet you."

She says, giving Kendra a warm smile. And I think to myself that I have my two favorite women in the same room together. Life doesn't get any better than this.

"It's great to meet you. I've heard so much about you." Kendra says, and then she observes Julia's blouse, "I really like that."

Julia looks down. "Oh, thanks. Colton had a connecting flight and he bought it for me at this hoity-toity clothing store in the airport. I love it though. He's never bought me clothes before."

Colton dips his head out of the kitchen and sees me. "Hey, little brother!" he shouts. Walking over to me, he embraces me tightly and we both stand there hugging for a few moments, patting each other on the back. It's so good to see him again. He's so tanned he looks like he's been in a tarpit. His friggin eyes are creepy; they're ocean blue, way lighter in color than mine, and with his skin so dark it looks like they're glowing. "Jesus, you ever heard of sunscreen?" I ask, slapping his face playfully.

"You gonna introduce me to this lovely lady here, or what?" he asks, ignoring my comment.

"Colton, this is Kendra. Kendra, Colton. This is the brother I told you about who bounces at Mingles...when he's not in Afghanistan."

Colton sticks his hand out and she shakes it. "Nice to meet you" he says. "Anything he's told you about me so far is a lie, I assure you."

Kendra smiles. "Likewise."

"Well, come on in and meet the rest of the crew." Colton says to Kendra. I take the opportunity to grab her hand again, interlacing our fingers together. Dalton is marinating a steak, drinking the wine right from the bottle as he works, and Garrett is wrapping potatoes in aluminum foil. Colton speaks over the din. "Everybody, this is Kendra, Wade's new girlfriend." He points to her from over her head and nods, as if up until this point, there has been no proof that she actually exists.

"Whatever he's paying you I'll pay double." Dalton

jokes, placing the wine bottle on the counter. He takes a step forward to shake her hand. "Just kidding. It's nice to meet you, Kendra."

"This is Dalton, the *other* smartass Ford boy."

Kendra looks at me. "And I suppose you're the *original* smartass?"

I smile. This is a side of Kendra I've never seen. She's quick-witted. I like it.

"Wow, she's been here for thirty seconds and she already passed orientation." Garrett winks, shaking her hand.

"And this is my biggest brother, Garrett." I say.

"Oldest." He corrects. "Although neither makes me sound all that great; big or old...whatever." He shrugs.

Kendra smiles, and that's when I notice a strange female entering the room. "Oh, and this is Kelly, Jack's girlfriend." Colton introduces. "Kelly, this is my little brother Wade, and his girlfriend Kendra."

Kelly must have come from the washroom. Jack must not like her too much if he left her with the herd while he stepped out for Julia. I'd never leave Kendra with my family, not until she knows them really well. My brothers can be real dicks sometimes. Colton's pretty cool, and Garrett, my oldest brother, he's good too, but Dalton and Jack, forget it. Dalton has no idea how to act around women, and Jack can be kind of an asshole. This Kelly girl is very made up with tons of mascara and lipstick. She's like a barbie doll. Her eyebrows don't move. When she's introduced, she just presses her lips together in a tight smile. She looks like she'd rather be anywhere else.

"Wade, Kendra, you guys want a drink?" Julia offers as Jack walks back into the house, handing Julia a small bag; the logo on the bag is from the corner store a block away.

"Yeah, I brought the good beer, Wade." Dalton says. "It's in the other fridge. You want me to get you one?"

"Nah, I'll just have a water. What would you like, baby?" I ask Kendra.

Dalton feigns having a heart attack. "You'll have a WHAT?"

Jack shakes his head, walking over to Kelly, draping his arm around her waist. "I told you, man, he doesn't drink anymore. You didn't believe me, but I told you."

Dalton places a hand on Kendra's shoulder, and says pointedly. "You broke him, Kendra."

I remove his hand from her shoulder as if it's a diseased tree branch. "Hands off, buddy. Get your own."

"Na, she fixed him." Colton corrects, winking at her, draping his arm around Julia, sipping his beer.

I kiss her lips chastely, ignoring the banter. "What would you like to drink, baby?"

"I'm fine for now, thanks." She smiles, leaning in to me.

"So, Colton, are you all done overseas now?" I ask, rubbing Kendra's back.

"Yep. All done. I start at the airport next week."

"So, you're going to design airplanes now? No more bouncing at Mingles?"

"You got it." Colton smiles, kissing Julia.

"Julia, you must be over the moon about that." I say.

"Couldn't be happier." She comments, kissing Colton, smiling.

"Yeah, they come with *two* wings. Remember that, Colton. It's very difficult to fly one with a single wing; bad enough with a single engine." Garrett comments.

"Garrett's a pilot." I explain to Kendra.

"I got that." She giggles, nodding.

"Dalton and Jack run the back end of things at the airport; Dalton being the CEO, Jack being the CFO, and now Colton's going into design the aircraft."

"Yeah, Wade's the only misfit in this family." Garrett jests so only Kendra and I can hear, winking at Kendra. She and I both smile at him. "Least she's getting a better introduction to the family than poor Julia did, eh?" Garrett guffaws, lifting a brow.

"What was that?" Julia giggles. "What are you saying

about me over there?"

Oh, shit.

"Nothing, Julia. Trust me." I say, chuckling, grabbing hold of Kendra's arm, holding her close.

"Come on. You might as well share." Julia says good-naturedly.

Garrett raises his voice pointedly with a proud grin on his face. "I was just saying how Kendra here is getting a better introduction to the family than you got."

Julia licks her lips and turns beet red, hiding her face in Colton's chest. "It's alright, sweetie. We're all over it." Colton says, embracing her, chuckling.

"Evidently not." Julia says, her voice is muffled from speaking into Colton's chest.

We're all laughing, except Kelly and Kendra, who have no idea what's going on. "What am I missing?" Kendra chuckles.

Colton overhears. "Go ahead, Wade, you can take the floor for this one. I know you want to."

Dalton interrupts me before I even start. "So, we've only ever heard of Julia at this point, except for Wade; he'd met her a number of times already. We're all on our way over to Colton's to help him get ready for this fundraiser thing we do every year here at the ranch." He's addressing Kendra only, I notice. He's not paying any attention to Kelly.

"Anyway, Wade walks in first, and then me, Garrett and Jack...long story short, we caught these two," he points to Colton and Julia, "in bed together. Never met her before...we all walk into his bedroom...there they are." He's proud. Julia's face is still red, but Colton doesn't look rattled at all.

Kelly pipes up, I'm sensing it's to save Julia. "So, how long have you been married?"

"Two years, five months." Julia answers.

"And no kids yet?" Kelly asks conversationally. My face drops. Kendra glances at me and then looks at the floor. The room is silent.

Double shit.

"Nope. Not yet." Colton says. Julia looks at him and my heart drops to my feet. I could kill Jack for not giving Kelly the pre-emptive advice I gave Kendra. I see Julia's chest rise and fall as she takes in a deep breath. I want to go over and hug her, and tell her it's okay, but Colton looks at her and says. "Yet." Pointedly.

Something is wrong.

Julia wraps her arms around Colton's neck and buries his head into her shoulder. They embrace tenderly and I can tell Julia is crying. "Oh, man, sweetie. It's okay." I walk over and rub Julia's back. But I notice that Colton's getting misty-eyed, too. "Oh, damn, what's wrong?" my heart is beating fast. Kendra comes over, too, and it's like moths to a flame. Suddenly the entire family has gathered around Colton and Julia as they weep together. I feel myself getting a little emotional too. Kendra takes my hand and squeezes it.

"Nothing's wrong." Colton breathes, loosening his grip on his wife, wiping his eyes with the heel of his hand. "It's been really emotional since I got home a couple of days ago." He gasps, trying to get in control.

"Why? Is everything okay?" I ask, feeling morbidly worried. There is a ball in my throat. All I can think of is when Colton nearly died when he came home the last time from Afghanistan. What could be worse than that? Is *Julia* sick? Wait, I remember she was really sick a couple of weeks ago, when she couldn't go to the wedding show with Mary, and I had to go in her place. "Julia...is something wrong with Julia?" I place a hand on her back, and I feel tears pricking the backs of my eyes. If anything ever happened to Julia, I think I'd rather die first.

Pulling her away from his chest gently, he kisses her forehead. She's a weeping mess. "No, nothing is wrong with Julia." Colton says, lifting her chin so he can glance at her eyes. He wipes the tears from her eyes with his thumbs. "Right, baby?" he smiles at her, a tear falls down his cheek. She smiles, but gasps and a fresh set of tears fall down her cheeks.

"Oh, Jesus, what's going on?" Garrett says. "There's nothing we can't get through together, man. We've been through it all."

Colton draws in a deep breath, but he's so emotional, his breathing is ragged. "I was hoping you'd say that."

Oh my Lord. This is bad. Kendra is leaning on my shoulder, kissing my shirt, trying to comfort me, and I can tell she's holding Jack's hand, he's on the opposite side of me. She's glossy-eyed and fighting tears. I love her so much. She's just met my family and already it seems like she loves them all.

"'Cause we're going to need a lot of help raising two more Fords." Colton laugh/cries, pressing his lips together. He kisses Julia's swollen, wet lips once, twice, three times.

"Wait, what did you just say?" I ask, craning my neck. Kendra lifts her head and her eyes bulge.

"Did I hear right?" Jack asks, wiping his eyes with his thumb.

"You heard right. Julia is expecting twins." Colton looks at the ceiling, trying not to cry. "It's official. She's fourteen weeks, so we're past the first trimester."

"Are you serious?" I'm flabbergasted.

"Totally." Colton looks at me with his reddened eyes, and I can see the sheer happiness in them. "She told me the night I came home. She wanted to surprise me. Boy, that was the best surprise ever." His voice cracks. Julia widens the gap between her and Colton so I can give my brother a hug. Kendra is closest to Julia, so she gives Julia a hug and congratulates her. Then each of my other brothers takes a turn giving her a hug. When she finally gets to me, I shake my head. "Jesus, I thought you were sick or something." My voice cracks.

"Sorry, sweetie. I didn't mean to scare you. But to be honest, I was sick. Sick as hell for the first three months."

I embrace her tightly. Then I pull back and look at her. "Twins?"

"Yep. Two babies. Two for the price of one." She smiles. "You're going to be Uncle Wade times two."

"Oh, wow." I have an ear-to-ear smile. I hug her again and I see Kendra standing next to Colton. She's glowing watching this exchange. As if I didn't think I could love her more, I do.

Two hours later, we're sitting around the fire telling jokes and reminiscing. Jack had taken Kelly home after dinner. "So, your life isn't quite as lonely or empty as it was a week ago, Jack." I start, probing him for her story. She barely said two words during dinner. Either she's really shy and therefore totally with the wrong guy, or she's stuck up as hell.

"Yep." He grunts. "I've known her for a little while, but I figured it's time to start bringing her around."

"How'd you meet her?" Kendra asks. She's sitting beside me. Our hands are interlaced together.

"Mutual friends." Jack answers after swallowing his beer.

"You have friends?" I comment.

Dalton intervenes. "How did *you* two meet?" he addresses me and Kendra.

I look at her and she gestures for me to take the floor. "Okay, the short version is I showed up at her workplace a couple of weeks ago, and then I ran into her at a wedding show and things took off from there."

"Uh huh." Dalton says. "And the long version?"

Kendra intervenes. "I'm a pro bono lawyer and he's my client."

Colton covers his face with his hand. "Oh, Jesus. I knew there was more to this than you were letting on." He's being glib.

"Care to elaborate?" Garrett prompts, chuckling.

"Some woman showed up at this sleazy bar in South Carolina where Wade was playing, claiming Wade fathered her unborn child, threatening to sue him for child support. He came to see me, and the rest is history." She explains like a knife through butter.

"And what happened?" Colton asks, a 'v' has formed

between his brows.

"She and her partner are in jail." I answer.

Colton's eyes bulge as he shakes his head in disbelief. "I need a drink." He says, rising.

"Hey, I'll come with you." I say, taking Kendra's glass so I can get her another. I kiss her quickly on the lips before I rise.

I follow Colton into the kitchen and watch him get a beer from the fridge. We hear a knock at the door and Colton walks over to answer it. "Dad!" I hear him say, and I see Gregory Abbott, Julia's dad, at the door. He's dressed in a suit and tie. "So sorry I'm late, Colton. I had some business to attend to."

"No problem at all, sir. Come on in. Julia's just outside. We're having a bonfire."

Gregory sees me and I stick my hand out for him to shake. "Wade, how are you?"

"I'm great, sir, and you?"

"I'm wonderful." He looks at both me and Colton. "Did she make it official yet?"

Colton smiles warmly. "Yes, she did. Just before dinner. We all know you're going to be a grampa again."

"Isn't it lovely?" Gregory is glowing.

"It is, sir."

Gregory looks at Colton's beer. "Do you happen to have one to spare? I've had a rough day."

"Sure, let me get you one."

"My driver is coming to pick me up later, so I can indulge." Gregory explains.

Gregory owns a chain of golf resorts all over the country. He and Julia are originally from Florida, but he's been staying in North Carolina since Colton and Julia married.

"You can go see Julia if you like." Colton offers Gregory.

"I'll go say hi in a moment."

"So, you moved?" Colton asks me, opening a beer and handing it to Gregory. "You're living with Kendra?"

"Not exactly." I explain. "This nut job we were talking

about earlier busted into my place, so I had to get out of there. Her parents offered for me to stay with them, and they're away for two weeks, so I figured I should be able to find a place pretty quickly. This is just temporary." Although, if I'm honest with myself, even though it's only been a few days, I'm loving living with Kendra.

"You need a place?" Gregory intervenes.

I'm hesitant when I answer. "Yeah. I'm staying with my girlfriend right now, but her folks are cool with it."

"The resort I'm living on right now has plenty of room. In fact, I've got two houses vacant, you could have your pick." Gregory offers.

"Oh, sir, I couldn't do that."

"Why not?" Gregory insists. "Julia lives with Colton, Liz is stubborn like her father, and is on her own, and I've got these houses that I don't care to rent out. They're sitting vacant, completely furnished, not being used. It's a damn shame if you'll pardon my language."

Before I can refute and say I couldn't possibly afford the rent, he continues. "All you have to do is keep the place clean...and..." he frowns, thinking of something to add to sweeten the deal, "play at the club house when we have an event. You can even practice there. The golfers would love that around the social area."

"Geez. You're making it hard to say no." I say. Colton lifts a brow, agreeing with me.

"Wade, my boy, you're family. I wouldn't want anyone else except family to live in one of my houses. I built those two for my daughters and neither of them will ever use them."

"Really? I'm family?"

"Sure, you are. Your brother is married to my daughter." He's matter-of-fact. "Your girlfriend can live there, too."

Colton just about chokes on his beer.

My cheeks turn red. I hadn't thought of that, but the thought makes me happy. "You're going to *live* with her?" Colton says, "You've known her *how* long?"

I place a hand on his shoulder. "It's a Ford thing." I

say to him, and neither of us have to point out that Julia moved in with Colton within weeks of them meeting. They were married about two months later.

"Yeah, but Julia and I have been married for over two years, we were madly in love with each other when she moved in here."

My face falls. It's like stone. He looks at me and lowers his beer. "What, you...love her?"

I nod once. "I do."

"Does she know this?"

"She does."

"And I assume she loves you, too."

"She does."

He shakes his head, trying to process. "Jesus...are you sure?"

I remove my phone from my back pocket and scroll through to the video that was recorded of Kendra and I singing at the wedding. Playing it, both Colton and Gregory observe.

"So, she sings." Colton says, half impressed, but acting like he's not.

"You make quite a couple." Gregory comments. "Lots of talent, young boy."

I ignore Gregory and address Colton. "And she's caring, loving, she stopped me from killing Chuck last week, she's braver than any woman I know, and what's more is we hated each other when we first met."

Jack walks in then, hearing the last part of that sentence. "What, you and Kendra? Yeah, shit, I thought I was going to have to break up a fight between the two of them when she was there that night at the bar."

Colton lifts a hand. "Wait, I thought you said you met her at her office."

I explain to him how it technically happened; how she and her friends were at the bar in South Carolina, and then I ran into her at her office a few days later. Colton is satisfied with the explanation.

"And why did you hate her at first?" Colton asks.

"Well, I didn't know her boyfriend had just cheated on her, and her life was a pile of dog shit. We literally bumped into each other and she was all attitude."

Jack intervenes. "Yeah, and then I said to him that they'll be married in six months. Look at them now." He's impressed with himself. Colton gives him a look that wipes the smile off his face.

Suddenly Julia and Kendra walk in. "Hey, the fire's not the same without the whole gang. Julia sees her dad. "Dad! Hey, I didn't know you were here." She walks over and gives him a hug.

"Hi, sweetheart." Gregory says, kissing her cheek. "I just got here. Did you know Wade can sing?"

"Oh, yes, I do. He has a beautiful voice. I've heard him many times at the bar where he plays. And he's great on stage, too. Fans adore him."

"Oh, stop." I guffaw, feeling my cheeks heat again.

"It's true." Kendra adds. "He played at my best friend's wedding and he was a total hit."

"You're one to talk, baby." I say. "You should hear *her* sing."

Julia looks at Kendra and her face is alight. "You can sing too? Oh, that's so perfect!"

"Come and see this video, love." Gregory says to Julia. He gestures to me to start it again.

Colton pipes up. "It's on YouTube. Let me put it up on the television." He offers. I roll my eyes, but everyone gathers in the living room, including Kendra. As Colton cues the videos up, everyone takes a seat. For the next half hour, we watch the videos that have been recorded of us in the last couple of weeks.

When they're over, Gregory looks at me. "Wade, my boy, how come you never recorded any of these songs? They're excellent."

Coming from an old man I'm impressed that he's impressed. But I don't want to get into a conversation about this with a man whose wealth rivals my deceased father's wealth, especially with my rich brothers in the same room with him. "It's a long story." I say and leave it at that. Colton and all my brothers know my stance on this, so they're decent enough to stare at the floor and stay out of it. Julia must know, too, since she's staring at a spot on the wall.

Gregory picks up on the tension and changes the subject. "What do you say you and Kendra come with me and check out the resort? I can call my driver to take us over now if it suits you."

"I'd love to, sir, but I have to play tonight. I'm supposed to be there soon."

"What, Blake couldn't give you the night off?" Colton asks.

"I didn't ask for it off." I say, suddenly feeling like I don't want to be here anymore. Kendra's gazing at me like a deer looking at a set of headlights. "Come on, baby. You want to listen to me play tonight?"

She brightens with a smile. "Of course."

We say our goodbyes, thanking Julia and Colton for their hospitality, and I have Julia give me her dad's number. On the way back to Kendra's place, I'm curious what she's thinking as she stares out the window. "What did you think? Of my brothers, I mean."

"They're all fabulous. I'm jealous you guys are all so close. I never had any siblings; Jennifer has always been my pretend-a-sister."

I chuckle at that and then I sigh. "Julia's dad made me a pretty decent offer."

"Oh yeah? Does he want you to play for him somewhere?"

"Not exactly." I lick my lips. My hand is enveloping hers as I stroke the inside of her palm. I explain to her how Gregory owns golf resorts and he has a house available that he offered me to live in. "With you." I add, almost nonchalantly.

She blinks intentionally and I stay silent. I'm tempted to retract but I want to gauge her reaction first.

"Did you just say you want me to *live* with you?" she looks at me and a ghost of a smile creeps on her lips.

"Well I figure you were saving for a house anyway,

and I'm looking for a place. Mr. Abbott is itching for this house to have inhabitants from the sound of it. He has a clubhouse where me and the guys can practice, instead of using Dave's garage." I pause, letting her digest that for a moment. "But yeah, I want you to live with me." We stop at a light and I look at her. "We're great together in every way. And we love each other. What could be better than that?"

She gives me a toothy grin and I lean towards her to sneak a kiss before the light changes. "Nothing could be better." She agrees. "I'd love to live with you. But are you sure he wants us both there?"

"He offered for us to live there. He said specifically 'you and your girlfriend', I know because Colton almost choked on his beer when Gregory said that." I chuckle.

"Uh oh...does Colton not approve?" Kendra looks worried.

I lift my brows. "Listen, I don't need anyone's approval, least of all Colton's." I give a brief explanation of Colton and Julia's history. We're silent as we get closer to Kendra's place. "So, are you going to keep me in suspense?" I ask, trying to keep my teasing tone at bay.

"Maybe for a little while."

Chapter 37

Gregory

"You need a hand getting up, dad?" Colton offers his father-in-law as they turn the television off, after watching a couple of Wade's videos again, once he and Kendra left. Gregory had taken a spot on the floor to sit on, while offering his expecting daughter to take a seat.

"I'm fine, Colton, thank you." Gregory grunts as he rises from the floor, with minimal effort. "I'm still as spry as I was in my twenties. It's all the exercise I get having a private gym in my office. And all the walking I do while golfing, of course. It's rare that you see me with a cart."

"It's true." Julia confirms.

Once Gregory is on his feet, he dusts his pants with his hands and addresses Colton. "Explain to me why such a talented young boy like that Wade, wouldn't want to record any of his songs? He seemed to clam right up when I brought it up."

"Wade has no money and doesn't want any of ours. We've offered so often we're sick of it." Colton explains.

"And I imagine it costs quite a lot to record music?" Gregory asks.

"I'm not sure how much, but it must cost a load, otherwise he would have done it years ago. The boy's been writing music since he could draw stick people."

"He's barely watched a minute of television his entire life." Garrett adds. "He's either writing music, practicing, or singing. It's his passion."

"Well, then it's a darn shame." Gregory shakes his head. "Golf has always been my passion and look where I am. I started from nothing but a war bond my grandfather left me."

"It's okay, dad. Wade gets his share of the Ford empire when he gets married or turns thirty, whichever comes first. He's not far from either as he stands now."

"For pity sake." Gregory has a sour look on his face. "The poor boy's put up a wall on his future, just to prove a point it seems."

"He's stubborn. I'll give him that." Dalton says. "I've tried everything to help him. We all have. I think he hated dad so much he doesn't even really want the money, no matter how it comes to him."

Gregory purses his lips. "I hate to see young people squander away such a bright future."

"Well, now, maybe he'll decide to take your offer, dad." Julia interjects. "Maybe Kendra will be a good influence on him."

"She's already been a good influence." Jack adds. "Did you see him with her? He's not eying her like she's a grade A slice of beef, and he stopped drinking, he moved out of his armpit of an apartment, and he's singing with her."

"He says they love each other." Colton says.

"Oh, they totally do." Julia says. "They adore each other; you'd have to be blind not to see that." She addresses Colton. "You know he called and got your pork chop recipe so he could cook for her?"

Gregory smiles. "Well, I've heard all I need to hear. Julia, be sure to give Wade my number."

Julia lifts a brow. "Dad...you've got that look in your eye."

A 'v' forms between Gregory's brows.

"That look you get when you have an idea." Julia answers his questioning glance. "The same one you got when you invented that special Astroturf knockoff stuff for mini-golf courses."

Gregory gets his phone out and scrolls through it. "My dear, I don't know what you're talking about." He feigns irritation.

"Dad..." Julia warns good-naturedly. "Be careful. Wade can be a loose cannon. He's a great guy, but he's not one to tick off."

Gregory has a brief conversation with his driver,

explaining that he's ready to leave, and then he pushes his daughter's cheeks together, like he did when she was a little girl. "My dear, don't you worry. He's a loose cannon who's in love. That's a completely different animal."

Chapter 38

Kendra

Being in a room full of Fords is like being among calendar models. I felt like I'd walked into the set of a daytime soap opera. They're all gorgeous. I thought Wade was a beautiful man; his brothers are just as hot. Colton's eyes I could practically see from the driveway. With his Afghanistan tan he looks like a bronzed god. Great genetics in that family. Mercy. What's more; they've all got fantastic personalities. They all care deeply for one another, that's clear. They're also not the type to flaunt their riches. You'd never know they're all millionaires. Heck, we had a barbecue and a bonfire; how much more white trash can you get? It was awesome.

While he's in the shower, I get a call from Jennifer. When I see her name pop up on the screen, I lift a brow. "Aren't you supposed to be in Aruba on your honeymoon?"

"We had to cut it short. Brandon got really sick. Couldn't stop puking to save his life. He's at the hospital getting fluids through an IV."

"Oh, wow, sweetie. I'm so sorry to hear that. Is he going to be okay?"

"Yeah, the doctor says he picked up a nasty bug, but once they get him hydrated and get some Gravol into him, he'll be fine. He could have contracted it even before we left. Just thank God I didn't get it."

"So, are you going to go back? Weren't you supposed to be gone for like...three weeks?"

"No, we're going to go away again for Christmas. Aside from the puking, Aruba was boring. I'd rather do something a little more exciting with less hanging around the beach like a whale. You know me, hell, we go paint-balling for fun for chrissake!"

"Yeah, that's true." I guffaw. "So, how's married life

so far?"

"Not much different from anything else. I mean, it's nice to make it official, but aside from that, big whoop. How's things with Wade?"

I can't help the smile on my face.

"Booksie?" she has a teasing tone.

"It's wonderful. I've never had such joy in a relationship before. He tells me he loves me like ten times a day and I never get sick of it."

"Is he still giving you half a dozen orgasms a day?" she jokes.

"Shut up."

Jennifer chuckles. "Hell, I'd be bragging. The first night we arrived in Aruba was pretty hot, before he got sick that is, so I can't complain."

"Good."

"Are you with him now?"

"He's just in the shower. We're heading out soon."

"Where are you going?"

Oh geez...

"We're going to look at a place. He had to move out of his pretty quickly, so he's staying with me for now while my parents are away."

"Oh, wow...playing house, are you?"

"Shut up." I giggle.

"Are you still able to walk straight?" she teases.

"You're a pig."

I decide to get her opinion on this matter, even though she's being a tease. "He asked me to move in with him." I blurt.

"Oh, Lord. What did you say?"

"I haven't given him an answer yet."

"Well, it could go either way. But I've heard of relationships tanking whether they start slow or fast...look at you and Mark. These days, I don't think it makes much of a difference. What it comes down to is whether or not you're a good fit and you're happy together. Judging by how you two looked on stage, I'd say you won't find a better match. But what do I know?

I just got married and my husband's been puking his guts out ever since. We're not off to a great start." She guffaws.

"I think I'll let the thought gel a little longer." I decide. "My dad's going to kill me though."

"Your dad really likes him." Jennifer reminds.

"Yeah, but there's a difference, Jenn."

"Well, he's letting him stay with you, isn't he? That says something."

"I don't know." I sigh.

"Books, as long as you become a lawyer, I think you're in your dad's good books no matter what."

Don't go there.

I hear the water turn off and a few minutes later, Wade comes down the stairs. His jeans are half undone and he's shirtless. His wet hair is slicked back like he just dove into a pool and popped his head up out of the water. Curls drip from the back of his neck down his toned shoulders and trail down his spine. He looks at me and smiles, noticing that I'm on the phone. I smile back, only half-listening to Jennifer go on about how boring Aruba is. Wade goes to the sink and pours himself a glass of water from the faucet. I watch his Adam's Apple bob up and down as his head tilts back while he drinks. His ab muscles rise up and down a little during each breath. He's so sexy I could die. How did I find a man this beautiful? I have to turn away because my thighs are heating up and we have to leave in ten minutes.

As I turn my back, I hear him go down to the basement, and I hear the dryer door shut. When he comes back upstairs, he's wrestling his arms into a linen shirt. The same one he was wearing when he played last night. We *have to* get this man more clothing. He's recycling his clothes after each wearing. He does up the buttons as he glances my way. I see his eyes linger to my shirt. I was up hours ago studying while he slept. He got home a couple of hours after I did from the club. I'm writing the bar really soon and I still have so much material to cover.

Wade leaves the top two buttons of his shirt open and rakes a hand through his wet hair. He looks good enough to eat. I glance at his lips and he takes that as a cue to kiss me. I never have to ask twice. And I almost never have to verbally ask him. A look is all the signal he needs. He takes a step towards me and kisses me full on the mouth. Jennifer hears the smacking noise and says something vulgar. "Again...you're a pig." I say to her. Wade gives me a look as if to say, 'who is that?'

"It's Jennifer."

"Hi, Jennifer." He says into the phone. His voice is so hot, and his lips are so close to mine, I'm tempted to steal another kiss. He wraps his arms around me from behind and gives my neck a chaste kiss. Although any touch from him right now doesn't feel so chaste, since he looks so sexy. And I just notice how delicious he smells. *Oh Lord!* He's right behind me and his hands are inches from my breasts, even though what he's doing is perfectly PG.

"I should go." I say to Jennifer.

She says something else vulgar. "God, do you kiss your new husband with that mouth? We're not animals!"

I hang up on her, shaking my head. Wade chuckles. "Your friend is a bit of a vixen."

I turn towards him. "You looking like that so close to me and I'll be a vixen too."

"Me? What about you in this sexy blouse." He murmurs in my ear so slowly it's almost my undoing.

"What's wrong with this blouse?"

He lifts the neck up slightly, helping himself to a full view of my chest. "Absolutely nothing, baby."

I spin around, getting a full view of him. "If we didn't have to leave so soon, I'd do unmentionable things to you right now."

He wiggles his eyebrows and kisses me, this time not-so-chastely, dipping his tongue in slightly, but then he pulls back before I can ravish him with my mouth.

"Let's go now, before we get into trouble."

We make out at every stoplight, as if we're teenagers. When we pull up to the resort, we have to check in. Our names have been left at the concierge, so we're let in seamlessly. Gregory has been paged, we're told, and we're instructed as to where to park; at the clubhouse. Gregory appears from the clubhouse. A golf cart is at the side of the building. "Hello there!" Gregory calls, and approaches us, shaking both of our hands. "I'll take you to the area where the houses are and leave you to browse. I've got a meeting in about five minutes."

"Oh, should we come back?" Wade offers.

"Nonsense. You two can look at your leisure. I'll leave you the keys for both. Take as long as you like. You can come back whenever you want if you need to take measurements or pictures. Whatever you need. Take your pick of the two houses and if you decide to, you can move in as soon as you like. Today if you want." He chuckles.

We hop into the golf cart, and drive away from the clubhouse, through another parking lot to the country club, which is an enormous building with a wraparound patio, and then through part of the golf course, where we see people teeing off from a distance. The roadway is narrow; it's only for golf carts. "This portion is off limits to the public." Gregory explains as we drive into a green area with rolling hills and valleys. Off in the distance are two houses, about a hundred feet apart, separated only by a long set of well-manicured bushes. One house is ranch-style with a cream-colored picket fence surrounding it, the other is a two-storey with a wraparound porch, similar to the country club.

"The path that leads to the house from the road is just behind the houses. It's a private entrance. Wade, you could even practice in the garage, but the clubhouse has better acoustics." Gregory explains.

"Acoustics are good." Wade comments. His mouth is wide open as he stares at these two beautiful, huge homes. They would be classified more as mansions, not houses.

There is a smaller house, which looks more like a guest house by comparison, down a hill from the two houses. Gregory points to it. "That's my place. I don't like big houses; never have. If it bothers you that I'm so close, I can have another house built on the other side of the course. Plenty of room." He says it like he has to simply order a house and it'll be here in a couple of weeks.

"No, that's fine, sir. Thank you." Wade is in awe as the golf cart stops in front of the first house; the ranch-style one.

"Well, I'll drop you off here. Call me when you need someone to come pick you up. I'll arrange it for you."

"Thank you again, sir. This is awfully kind of you." Wade says, practically bowing in front of this generous man.

"It'll be nice to have someone live here. If I'm being honest, you're doing me a favor. It gets kind of lonely out here sometimes. Make all the noise you want, I don't mind. I only wish my daughters decided to live out here with me, but I'll take what I can get." He smiles and hands us the keys, indicating which key is for which one. Then he drives the cart away, waving as he drives off.

"He's such a wonderful man." I comment.

Wade is silent, staring at the house before us.

"Are you okay?" I ask, placing a hand on his arm.

"Yeah," he says, breaking himself out of his reverie. "Just thinking I wish more people were like that. He's practically begging us to live here. He has such a huge heart and I wouldn't want to hurt him."

I step in front of Wade. "Why don't you take a look inside before you start figuring out how to let him down?" I say gently.

He looks at me and I can't figure out what he's thinking. "Come on. Let's go inside." I coax, taking his hand. We fiddle with the keys until one works, and we walk into the dwelling. We are greeted by dark oak flooring throughout. It's open concept with cream marble flooring in the kitchen to the left, a large living room with a bay window to the right, and a narrow hallway leading to a bank of rooms in the center. The curtains are drawn, so the place is kind of dark. Walking over, I open the drapes and the home takes on a whole new perspective.

I walk to Wade and take his hand, leading him to the bedrooms. The bathroom is big enough to have a party in it; complete with hot tub, glass-enclosed stand-up shower, and double sinks, there are four other rooms, three are basically empty but the master bedroom has a huge, four-poster bed made of oak, and oak nightstands, dresser, and chest. The walk-in closet is big enough to have afternoon tea in.

Wade looks like he's being dragged through a women's clothing store. Or about as impressed. "You don't like it? You want to go look at the other one instead?" I ask.

"What do you think of it? Or does it matter...I mean, I don't want to push you or anything, but I want you to be happy, whether or not you decide to live here with me." he asks, dividing his glance between both my eyes.

My heart swells. He really does want me to live with him. Personally, as long as I'm with Wade, I don't care if we live in a shack in the woods. His apartment was a shoebox compared to this, and we were happy as clams there. "I think it's too big." I say, gauging his reaction. "For one person, anyway."

"Yeah," he says, looking at the floor, walking towards the bedroom window. The sadness in his voice is palpable.

"Maybe not too bad for two people." I watch his eyes slide over my way, but he doesn't meet my gaze.

"Maybe." He says, looking away, as though he's afraid to look at me.

It's breaking my heart seeing him so down. I don't ever want him to feel this way, especially if it's my doing.

He lifts his head, looking out the window. "You want to go look at the other one? I think that one's bigger though, so if you think this one is too big, you definitely won't like that one."

I can't stand it anymore. Walking over to him, I wrap my arms around his neck and kiss him, trying to brighten his mood. He kisses me back with vigor. Needy, open-mouthed kisses he returns with, yet Wade has a way of making even the deepest kisses chaste. I break away just enough to rest my nose on his. His eyes are still closed, like he's drinking me in. "I want to live with you." I whisper to him.

"I was hoping you would say that, baby." He whispers back. "This place wouldn't be the same without you."

"You're so sweet. I love you." I kiss his nose. "Let's go tell Gregory the good news."

"Love you, too, baby." He lifts a brow and looks at the bed.

...Wade's back.

Chapter 39

Wade

Dave gets the beat right on the drums as I hit the high note in my new song. It's a slow ballad that I've been working on for weeks, but I haven't been able to get it right. Mr. Abbott was right, the acoustics in the clubhouse are fabulous. We haven't practiced this well, ever. Kendra is holed up in the new place, in one of the rooms we made a study, as she studies for the bar exam coming up in two weeks. She's nervous as hell and there isn't a damn thing I can do to help, and it kills me.

Griffin kills it at the end with the electric guitar, and I decide that this song is as polished as it's going to get. Just as we finish up, we hear clapping coming from the entrance. Gregory walks in with three other gentlemen, all dressed in golfing attire. We had no idea we had an audience. "Well done, boys, very well done." Gregory boasts, walking up to us at the front of the clubhouse.

"Thank you, sir." I say, holding my hand out for Gregory to shake. "Did you need us to clear out of here?" I offer, sensing maybe he needs to have a meeting with these men.

"No, not at all, Wade. I was just bringing my friends over to hear you sing. I hope you don't mind."

"No, sir. Not at all. We can play something more if you'd like. We do our own music as well as plenty of cover songs. Do you have a request?" I sound like I'm grovelling, but I can't help it. This man has done so much for me in such a small amount of time. I feel like I owe him more than my fair share.

"This is Thomas Monroe, Jeffrey Pilston and Michael Angelo." Gregory introduces, gesturing to each man with his hand. They all look well-dressed and manicured. Money oozes from their appearance. Thomas could pass for Gregory's younger brother; tall and slim with short salt and pepper hair, Jeffrey is younger and wears aviator sunglasses that he removes, placing them on his crown. Michael is the oldest, with a little ponch in the front.

"Gregory showed us your video. Why don't you play *'Don't Want to Run'* for us?" Thomas asks.

"Sure. Wow, we'd love to." I say, motioning to the guys to play.

I had no idea Gregory enjoyed our music so much that he's even recommending it to his friends. This is awesome. The men pull up a chair and listen to us, tapping their toes and they even chime in during the chorus when prompted. These men seem very hip for older guys. I'm impressed. I thought golf guys were dry and boring, with too much money and time to kill. When we finish, they clap and rise.

"You're very talented boys." Gregory compliments.

Thomas observes the graphics on the drums. "You guys have a manager?"

I shake my head no. "Not at the moment."

"Okay, you guys ever perform in Vegas?"

"No. Why?"

"One of my acts just landed himself behind bars and I've been looking for a band to cover for a show next week. You interested?"

My eyes widen. "Oh my God, yes! We would absolutely love to! Wow, sir, thank you so much for the opportunity!" I shake his hand so much his hair jiggles at the top.

"I'll give Thomas your number." Gregory offers.

"Thank you, sir. Thank you so much." I'm so excited I can't wipe the smile off my face.

"My pleasure." Thomas says. "You don't happen to have anything recorded, do you?"

My face starts to fall but I catch it, making a thin-lipped grin. "No, sir. Not yet. I hope to some day."

"Fair enough." Thomas nods once. "I'll see you all on Saturday."

"Looking forward to it. Thanks again." I say, shaking

his hand again. When they leave I turn to the boys. They have half-hearted looks on their faces. "What's with the sour pusses, boys?" I ask, guffawing. "We just got the offer of a lifetime."

Dave is busy tapping away at his phone. Griffin pipes up. "Wade, it's a thirty-five hour drive from here, man. And how the hell are we going to truck all our gear there? He never mentioned anything about being paid, either. You know how much it costs to rent a U-Haul to go that distance? Plus lodging? I think we should have thought this through."

"Relax," I say, "Do I have to remind you that my family owns an airline? I'm sure my brothers would fall all over me if I finally called them for a favor."

"Hey," Dave says, looking up from his phone. "Was that one guy Jeffrey Pilston?" he spells his name out.

"I think that's what he said." Griffin answers.

Dave guffaws, scrubbing his hand over his face. "Jesus Christ," he laughs.

"What's the problem? Is he another owner of some millionaire company you'd love to have a stake in?" I tease. Dave's been schmoozing a little since we started practicing here, finding out the names of golfers who are only too conceited and impressed with themselves to advertise their names. For kicks, Dave looks them up and we poke fun at how stuffy they really are.

"He's a producer at a fucking record company, man." He cranes his neck back and smiles, as if a lightbulb just went off inside his head. He lifts his phone and shows me the image on Google; confirming that he is the guy we just met moments ago. We digest that information as Dave punches in the name of the other fellow who accompanied Thomas and Jeffrey. "Oh, and Michael Angelo is the *owner* of *another* recording company." He makes a sound like he's going to laugh or cry. "My God, Wade, we hit a fucking gold mine."

I don't know how to respond, except that I wish I wore something more appropriate for performing in front of, well, basically, Jesus and God in the recording industry. I'm so happy and nervous I could burst. Nobody has ever asked us to perform at a venue that didn't have a ten-dollar cover charge before. This is fantastic. All I can think is that I can't wait to tell Kendra. I'd love to take her with me if she can, and have her sing with me on stage, in front of the Las Vegas crowd. Based on the YouTube traffic from the video of our duet, I believe that at least part of this I have Kendra to thank for. If it wasn't for her, so many wonderful things would never have happened to me. My girl is a million blessings to me. I love her more than anything else.

"We should practice '*You*' again." Dave says, referring to the new song. "Definitely want to play that one in Vegas."

"Sure, you guys cool with that?" I ask, adjusting the mic.

"Hey, Wade?" Griffin says. "Are you sure you want to be practicing this one so open? What if Kendra hears?"

"Then she hears." I answer.

"Sure you're ready for that, man?" Dave asks.

"Why do you think I wrote the song?" I say matter-of-factly. "Besides, I plan on asking her to come to Vegas so we can sing a few songs together, anyway."

"You're brave." Dave says it more like he believes I'm a fool.

I ignore him and wait for the intro. When I get into the lyrics, I lose myself, closing my eyes, feeling the music. Thinking of my baby being here with me, and how she's so much a part of me, that she's all I can think about. How my life was nothing until now...Until *You*. When we finish, I'm certain that the song is perfect, except for one thing, which I can take care of before we pack for Vegas.

***

Kendra is elbow-deep in textbooks when I return from practicing and running a couple of errands. I don't want to disturb her, so I tiptoe past the study, and head to the bedroom, closing the door behind me. My guitar is leaning against a chair by the wall, so I pick it up and begin playing as I sit on the bed, knowing Kendra won't be able to hear me as long as I keep the door closed. As I start singing, I hear a soft knock, and then her beautiful face appears from the other side of the door. "Hey, baby. I didn't want to disturb you, so I just came in here." I say as she walks over to me. It feels like I haven't seen her in days, even though we only parted ways this morning. Placing my guitar on the bed, I rise and meet her halfway. Kissing her softly on the mouth, I drink her in.

"You're not disturbing me." she says, snaking her arms around my neck. "I could use a little break."

"How's the studying going?"

She sighs and rolls her eyes. "Oh, I'm living the dream." She pauses to kiss me again. "But I'm making headway. How did the practice go?"

"It was...great." I'm not sure if now is the time to tell her about Vegas. I don't want to break her concentration.

"Great? Did you finish with that new song you've been working on?"

"Sure did." I say, pressing my lips together, trying to hide the mile-wide smile that's hiding beneath the wimpy one.

"Can I hear it sometime? Has Dave made a video yet?"

"No, no video yet. But you can hear it. Maybe when you're done studying for the day. I can play the acoustic version if you like. Or you can wait until we practice again tomorrow and hear the regular version."

She narrows her eyes as she grins. "What? Something is different."

I kiss her on the lips. "Well that's an understatement." I kiss her again. "Lots of things are different. My life has changed so much since I met you."

"Mine too, baby." She gives me a warm smile.

My cell phone starts ringing from my back pocket. I check the display and see that it's Gregory. I tell Kendra who it is and answer it. "Hello, sir."

"Wade, my boy. I don't mean to disturb you while you're practicing."

"Oh, no, that's fine, sir. We're finished practicing for the day."

"Wonderful. I just didn't want you to worry about getting to Vegas. I know it's a terribly long drive so I was thinking we would go in my private jet."

No response comes. That's a sentence I've never heard before. "Um,"

"I wouldn't want you to trouble your brothers is all. My jet is free and ready any time."

Kendra is giving me a puzzled look. I rub her arm, so she knows everything is okay. "That's awfully kind of you, sir. Thank you."

"As long as you don't mind me joining you two...assuming Kendra is coming too."

"No, sir. The more the merrier. It would be an honor if you could come."

Now Kendra's looking at me like I have two heads. "Once again, thank you so much, sir. I can't thank you enough."

"Nonsense. I'm happy to help. I'll talk to you later."

"Sure thing. Bye for now."

I hang up and Kendra tilts her head. "Good news?"

I draw in a deep breath. "Very good news."

She's smiling already and she has no idea. When I tell her what's going on, her face lights up. "Are you serious???!!!!" Her volume has raised an octave.

I nod once and she bounces on her heels a couple of times, with her arms around my shoulders, jumping excitedly. She starts laughing and whooping and I laugh with her. "God, Wade, this is the best news ever!!"

I just smile.

"Aren't you out of your mind with excitement?"

"I am. I'm just enjoying watching your reaction." I grunt as I lift her up and spin her around. "There, is that better, baby?" I chuckle.

"Once more." She says, egging me on. I spin her again and when she lands, I kiss her chastely a half dozen times.

"Do you want to come with us?"

"Are you kidding? I'd love to!" She gushes. "I've never been to Vegas and I've always wanted to!"

"It's not going to interrupt your studying?"

"We're flying there, baby. I can double up."

"Okay." I look at her and sigh. "Do you want to sing with me?"

Her eyes bulge but a huge smile erupts. *I'll take that as a yes.*

"Is your new song a duet?"

"No, it's just a ballad."

"Like a slow song you mean, right?"

"Yeah," I rub her back, drawing her closer.

"Can I hear it?" She asks so sweetly I can't say no. I kiss her tenderly and rest my forehead on hers.

"Yeah, I'll play it for you." I murmur, saying a silent prayer to myself. Leading her to the bed I grab my guitar as she sits. I choose to stand to play the guitar for this one. As the music starts, my heart is beating a mile a minute. In the first verse she's caught on that the song is about her. Her eyes are already glassy with unshed tears.

Like a dream that became real
I finally know how it feels
To love someone with all your might
To love someone so much it's worth the fight

From the stars in the sky, through the nights and days
I know what my heart says
...it's yoooooooooou
...it's yoooooooooou

Her face is soaked with tears. My chest swells but I keep going, even though it feels like my heart is going to explode.

It's like I've known I've loved her all my life
It's like she came from the stars sent from up above
It's like the Lord made her to be my wife
It's like there's nobody else for me to love
...it's yooooooou
...it's yooooooou
...it's yooooooou

The ghost of a smile appears behind those tears, and I can't get to the end of the song because my voice is cracking with emotion. It's killing me. I have to go to her. She's still sitting on the bed, and I crouch to her level, wrapping my arms around her waist as I kneel between her knees. I close my eyes tight, trying to squeeze away the tears. It's so weird but it's contagious when she cries. As I swallow, I pull back, glancing at Kendra. "I started writing that song when we first met. I've re-written it so many times as our relationship has blossomed into what it is now...I added the wife part just after I said I love you." I look at her to gauge how much more I should say. She's listening intently, like I'm telling her something really important. "Whether it's now or ten years from now, I know you're the one who's meant to be my wife. It doesn't feel rushed to me because it isn't. My love for you doesn't have a time stamp. It's just how I feel, and it seems to get stronger every day, so I know it's real and I know it's meant to be."

Softly raking her hands through the sides of my hair, she looks at my lips, and I kiss her; good, long, deep kisses that convey the message that I love her. Drawing in a breath, she tries to speak, and I'm patient, staying silent. Her fingers play in the hair around my ears, as if buying time. Then she looks at me and whispers. "I feel the same, Wade."

I kiss her forehead tenderly, and then I leave her for a moment, going over to my side of the bed. Inside my nightstand I grab a package and go kneel back down where I was. I place the package in one of my hands and put my hands behind my back. "Pick one." I say, trying to lighten the mood a little.

She smiles, playing along, and chooses the left one; the correct choice. I hand her the small box and she purses her lips, trying like hell not to cry. Only half the battle is behind me now. I wait until she opens the box and then I ask her those four pivotal words that most women wait so long to hear. Not my girl. She deserves everything I can give her. Including a lifetime of happiness with me. "Will you marry me?" I whisper.

She nods immediately but I playfully hold the box, not letting her have it until she gives me a verbal answer. "Is that a yes?" I chuckle softly, wiping her tears with my thumb.

She gasps. "Yes!" And I take the ring out of the box and place it on her left ring finger. It fits perfectly and she looks at me, shaking her head. "How did you know my size?"

"I had help. Your mom pulled a ring out of your jewelry box for me."

She places her hands on her cheeks, as if in shock. "Oh my goodness! My parents know?!"

"Well, of course. I wasn't going to ask you without asking your parents first."

"Oh my gosh! What did they say?" She hisses, as though this should have been kept secret.

"Well, your mom seemed pretty happy about it. She jumped up and smiled, and then she went to your room. Two minutes later she came back with a ring." I chuckle. "It was a little intense being alone with your dad in those two minutes. Frankly, I was shaking like a leaf. But he just grinned and told me to keep his baby happy or he'll show me his gun collection. He laughed and then I laughed, and he patted me on the back."

Kendra giggles. "And they didn't say anything about it being so soon?"

I shake my head and frown. "They said nothing to

me."

She sighs and then looks at me. "My God, Wade...how did you ever find the money for this?" Her eyes gesture to the quarter carat diamond solitaire sitting on her finger.

"Again, I had help." I answer. "You'll remember my father's estate, right." I say as more of a comment than a question. She blinks but doesn't say anything. "Garrett is the executor of dad's estate, so he told me what I stand to inherit once we're married."

I take a breath and she interrupts me. "But I thought you didn't want any of it, Wade." She says with such concern in her voice.

"Well, baby...a man can change." I say simply. "I want to give you everything I can. I want you to be happy."

"I am happy." She gives me a warm smile.

I lift my hands in the air. "Mission accomplished."

She smiles again and squeezes my hair between her fingers, gently forcing me to her. Her kiss is tender and needy. I kiss her deeply and then our lips part. "Oh, and Julia helped with the ring, so if you don't like it. Talk to her."

"Does everyone know?" She barks out a laugh. "Am I the last?"

I admit I had a busy afternoon. "Gregory doesn't know. And Jack. But Dalton was with Garrett, and I told you Julia helped me, so Colton knows too. It's a family affair, what can I say?" I kiss her again.

"And nobody tried to convince you to hold off? Nobody's flipping out? I mean, we've only known each other for..."

She tries to tally it up in her head, but I interrupt. "Baby, we love each other. Nobody thinks it's too fast. Do you?"

"No." She shakes her head, but she still seems a little in shock.

"My parents got engaged and married quickly, and you know about Colton and Julia. I don't know...maybe it *is* just a Ford thing. We could be engaged for ten years if you think that's best. But I don't."

A fleeting look crosses her face. "It's not the money, is it baby?"

"No. Not at all." I shake my head and take her hands in mine. "I have a feeling that after we go to Vegas, money will be aplenty. After all, I'm used to pauper's wages playing at Mingles."

"You deserve so much more." She says with so much conviction I can't help but grasp her face and kiss her like I mean it. I can feel her pull me as she leans back on the bed. We're kissing madly as she crab-crawls to the pillows and I follow her, hovering on top of her as we stay attached by our lips. "You know what's going to be sexy as hell?"

"What?"

"You, singing with a wedding band on. The metal clinking against the mic. My God." She gushes.

I look at her like she just told me to start wearing women's underwear. "Really? Wedding bands are sexy?"

She nods emphatically and then gives me an open-mouthed kiss and sweeps her tongue so hungrily into my mouth that I'm instantly hard. Nipping her lower lip, I cup her face with my hands and then glance deeply into her eyes. "I love you so much, baby."

"I love you, too, Wade." She whispers, and then she looks at her new ring as it glints at her from the early evening sunshine coming in through the curtains. "It's hard to believe that mere weeks ago we hated each other, and now our love is so strong it's indestructible."

"That's right, baby." I say, kissing her tenderly on the lips. She leans up, gently pushing me off her. Rolling me over, she climbs on top and pulls her shirt off. Her breasts spill over her bra, begging me to kiss the flesh. Tugging at my shirt, she signals for me to lean up, and I do, kissing her in the process, as she slides my shirt over my head. I wrap my arms around her middle, hugging her while I sit upright. Her legs are cradled around my middle. I remove her bra, letting her breasts free, and kiss and suck them while she moans, rearing her head back.

"Oh, Wade, I have to get my pants off." She breathes.

"Let me help you with that." I murmur playfully against her breast as I gently push her onto her back and crouch on my knees, unzipping her pants, kissing her belly. She looks so sexy laying on the bed half naked. As I pull her pants from her waist, I kiss her below the navel and trail kisses down to her folds. She lets out a sultry moan that I feel below the belt as I begin separating her folds with my tongue. Giving her French kisses there, I listen to her start to breathe heavily.

"Oh, God, Wade. You're so good at that."

She pants and I can feel her legs already starting to go rigid. I insert a finger inside her and begin rhythmically pushing in and pulling out, being careful to press on the upper side of her pelvic bone. Writhing in sync with my touch, I can hear her breathing becoming more ragged. The sound is so sexy it feels like my dick is going to break through my pants. Licking her faster with a feather-like touch, her moans are getting louder and she pulls at the hair at the sides of my head. She's close. Very close. Placing a second finger inside her I give her a healthy suck and then lick extra fast. And she begs me not to stop. I would never stop unless she asked me to. Gripping my hair with both hands, she tugs as she moans my name. It's music to my ears. She releases her breath in spurts as she lets go, feeling intense pleasure. As her grip loosens, I unzip my jeans and remove them, crawling on top of Kendra

"Feel better, baby?" I ask.

"Mmmm...." She answers as I slowly rest my body on hers. "You think when we're married the sex will still be this good?"

"Better." I answer, kissing her lips. "Our sex is pretty tame so far. We haven't even scratched the surface."

"I don't think it can get any better, baby. You take my

breath away."

I wink. "You ain't seen nothin' yet." My kiss is deep and soft as I hover my hardness against her.

"Try me." she challenges as our lips part.

"What...like you want to try something we haven't done yet?"

"If you say the sex will be even better...maybe we should start being a little more adventurous." She lifts a brow.

"You're a little vixen, baby."

"Says he with a major hard-on." She teases.

"Alright, just for that." I grunt, laying beside her as if I'm going to spoon her. "I can handle challenge." She's still laying on her back. "Turn over that way." I point at the wall. I don't want to do anything that might make her uncomfortable, especially since this is a pretty special day. She does as she's instructed, so her back is to me. Sweeping her hair from her neck, my lips find her flesh and I begin kissing her from her ear to her shoulder, resting my head on my hand, propping it up with my elbow. Kendra leans her head back, taking in the contact, and she reaches for my hardened cock.

"Gosh, we seem to have a problem here."

"Not for long." I draw in a deep breath, taking in her hand, which is lightly stroking me. My hand finds her breast, and I begin kneading the nipple. It beads immediately when I touch it. "Oh, this could be fun."

"Well, so far, it is." She closes her hand around the head of my dick and begins rhythmically pumping it.

"Mmmm...that's nice, baby." I nip her ear lobe and give it a gentle suck. "I know you've got another orgasm in there. How about we do something about that?" I take her hand that's pleasuring me and place it in my hair, since I know how much she loves to pull on it. Thank God I've still got lots to spare. Sliding my hand in the space between her thighs I lift her leg and lean it against me. "If this doesn't work for you, just let me know, baby. We can try something else." I whisper in her ear as I find her entrance and fill her from behind.

She gasps softly at first. "You okay?" I speak into her ear as I slowly begin moving. My eyes close instinctively as I feel her warmth surround me.

"Oh, this *is* different." She states in a half moan, half hiss.

"Different *good*?" I ask, sliding my hand down her thigh, through to her clit, where I circle it with my middle finger. Her leg stays up with little effort.

"Oh...God...yes."

Picking up speed, I keep my finger busy as my cock slides in and out of her with ease. It feels...amazing. Kendra rears her head back and we kiss; our tongues tangle with each other and she gives me a little suck that makes me moan involuntarily. The sound spurs her on and I can feel her clench inside. "I love it when you do that." I pant.

The bed starts to squeak a bit with my pace. Luckily, it's a four-poster bed, so it's as solid as a rock. The only trouble we've had so far is with the headboard. It knocks against the wall if we get really crazy in bed, which we have a few times. Surprising me, she turns on to her side, facing me, and then she climbs on top. "I want to see your face." she explains breathlessly, holding my arms above my head.

"You do, do you..." I chuckle softly, as she fills herself with me.

"Yeah...your face is kinda sexy in bed. I don't want to miss it." she smiles, giving me a wink.

"You're the boss." I murmur salaciously, drawing in a breath, lifting my pelvis so I'm filling her completely.

"If we're getting married, you better get used to saying that." She jests, trying like hell to keep a straight face, but I can tell that what I'm doing to her feels too good. At this angle, I can lift and lower her body as she sits on top of me. Grabbing hold of her hips, I grunt softly as I move my pelvis up and down, enjoying the friction and watching her breasts bob up and down. But the best visual is her face. Her eyes are closed, her head is reared back, and her mouth is half open as she makes noises that can only convey one thing: that she's enjoying herself...a lot.

Her head comes down to my chest as she begins sucking my nipples. "Oh, my..." when she begins to flick them with her tongue, it increases the sensation on the part that's inside Kendra, ten-fold. My mouth forms a big 'o' as I let out a deep breath, feeling my dick turn to steel. "Mmmmmmm..." I breathe, as our speed increases, and the goddamn headboard starts slapping against the wall. "Oh, baby...I'm getting close."

Lifting her head, Kendra leans back, and I find her clit with my thumb, circling it. I'm deep inside her and as she lifts and lowers on me, I can feel her clenching. "Mmmmm...Wade." She breathes.

"Oooooooohhhhhh....mmmmmm....Kendra."

The bed is squeaking as we both make a hiss noise together, feeling our release seconds away. "Oh...God....Kendra." I grunt, as I feel her orgasm sucking me hard from inside her, begging a rush of seed out of me. I feel it shoot out and she cries, feeling it too. My pelvis involuntarily lifts as I come like thunder under her. Kendra's breathing is so ragged as she feels her release. It sounds so hot I almost can't handle it. When her muscles stop contracting, she rests her head on my chest, as I feel the last aftershock and shiver.

"Cold?" she asks, placing her hands on my arms.

"Na...just that last aftershock....wow."

Our hearts are beating so fast they seem like one. She lifts her head and kisses my lips. "Love you."

"I love you to the moon and back, baby." I kiss her back. "So, do you have to call anyone and do the girl thing?"

"What, you mean tell them we're engaged?" she giggles.

"Well, yeah. Isn't that what girls do?"

"Some girls. I'd rather just stay right here."

I chuckle softly, kissing her head.

I have no idea that within the next forty-eight hours, I'll be doing something so life-changing, even more so than what just happened in the last twelve hours.

Chapter 40

Kendra

My stomach is doing flip-flops I'm so excited. I'm going on a private jet to sing with my fiancé on stage in Vegas. Can you say HOLY SHIT!!! Wade has my hand cemented in his. I think he's just as excited. A record producer is supposedly going to be there, but Wade doesn't want to get his hopes up, just in case the guy is a no-show. I'm not sure why he thinks that things might fall through...I mean, what could possibly go wrong? We're going to Vegas...to perform live in front of I don't know how many people. Apparently, the YouTube videos have reached something like two million views collectively, which is one of the reasons why this Vegas guy asked Wade and the band to sing for him.

As we walk to the private jet on the runway, Wade kisses my hand. "This is all thanks to you, baby."

I smile. "That's so sweet." We kiss deep but chastely before boarding the plane. As we walk inside, Wade directs me to go first. Lifting my head, I hear clapping and whooping, and I look to see where the noise is coming from. My nervous face slides into a toothy smile as I see my parents, all of Wade's family, and Mr. Abbott, Julia's sister Liz, and nephew, Nate. Jennifer, Wendy and their parents are also here, plus Brandon, Jennifer's husband.

"Surprise!!!" They all shout. "Congratulations!!!"

I look at Wade, thinking he might have had something to do with this, but he looks just as surprised. "What the?" he says, grinning from ear to ear.

Gregory stands. "We thought you could use some moral support while you perform. So, I invited everybody to join us. I hope you don't mind."

I walk over to Gregory and give him a giant bear hug. "You...." She nods and then kisses him on the cheek, "are the most wonderful man."

"Oh, come now." He says, growing modest. "Come and say hello to everyone and tell them the big news."

Jennifer pipes up. "Yeah...your mom's been teasing me. What the hell's going on? You're not pregnant, are you?"

My eyes widen. "God NO!" I bark out a laugh. Pursing my lips together, I look at the ceiling and hold my hand out so she can see the ring.

"Whaaatttt!!!!!" she shrieks, "Is this what I think it is???" her face is alight with excitement.

"It is." I answer as Wade comes up behind me and embraces me. "We're engaged."

"Well, that breaks a record, I think." She comments. She hugs me and I go say hello to my parents and the rest of the family. Wendy just about cries when I reach her. Wade schmoozes as well, and then comes back to me a few minutes later, as if he missed me. He's so adorable I can't stand it.

Hours later, we're all helping set up for the concert. Wade and the band are real pros; they know how to plug everything in and where to position everything, so it sounds perfect. When they do the sound check, I can't keep my eyes off Wade. "I'm gonna sing that song I wrote for you tonight, baby." He winks, speaking into the mic. I smile at him and he smiles back. *Oh, my heart...*

Six hours later, after the concert has ended, Wade and the band *Take Risks* are offered a record contract. As we walk past a wedding chapel, eight hours later, Wade looks at me through the corner of his eye. "Everyone's here with us, baby. You want to take the plunge right now?"

This man isn't afraid of anything. He never ceases to amaze me. "Why don't you wait another week, baby." I grin. "You might need a pre-nup." I wink, teasing.

He takes my hand in his and kisses it, making a playful grunt noise. "Baby, you're lucky I love you to bits."

"I do too..." I say, kissing him.

Chapter 41

Garrett

Proposal Day

Wade walks into my office, and I can't help but feel a pang of jealousy and an ounce of regret, even though I try like hell not to show it. My little brother has been to hell and back in the last little while, and I should really show my support. After first having a potential law suit threatened on him, his manager betraying him, he fell in love with a wonderful girl who he at first hated, and then he saved her from dangerous criminals, and I'm proud of him, as much as it pains me to have memories brought back to the forefront of my mind.

My little brother works so goddamn hard at what he does, and he's spent the better part of ten years living below the poverty line. As much as he could have easily shifted out of that predicament with a simple request from any of us, he chose to take the high road and pave the way by himself. Good on him for doing that. But in this case, when he wants to propose to the one he loves, I don't blame him for wanting to shell out as much as he can so he can get her the most beautiful diamond ring.

"Hey," he says as he walks into my office. "Still in your uniform."

I look down at my white pilot's uniform, clad in the airline logo both on the left lapel, the hat and on the outside of my left pantleg. "Yeah," I pull off my hat, and leave it sitting on the desk. The visor makes it sit unevenly, so it teeters on the wooden surface. "I was going for a workout shortly," I explain.

With a soft thud, Wade sits on the guest chair. "I forgot how fancy this place is." He comments, having seldom visited. My office looks like the waiting room of a V.I.P. lounge at an airport, which is ironic, seeing as it is inside an airport. My office chair and both guest chairs are made of tufted Italian leather. The desk is solid oak, and the airport logo behind me is not cheaply painted on, rather, it's made of brass, and hung professionally on the wall. He's the only Ford boy who doesn't have any interest in the airline. He came here more often before dad died, but not much.

"It's my stomping grounds."

"Did you have a lot of flights today?" I can sense that he's a little uncomfortable being out of his element, seeing as he's broaching a topic that he knows nothing about, and has even less interest in.

"Yep. Domestic flights today. This weekend I'm flying to Italy."

"Ah, you'll miss Vegas then." He comments, disappointed.

"Yeah, sorry. Duty calls."

He waves. "No problem. I didn't give any notice."

"Next time."

"Yeah, hopefully there *is* a next time." he says by rote. With his line of work, Wade sometimes doesn't know where his next gig will be, aside from at Mingles, where he's paid a pittance for what he does.

"I'm sure after Vegas, there will be. That's a pretty serious place and I know you'll put on a kickass show."

He gives me a tight smile. "Thanks."

The look on his face reminds me of that same look that he had on his face a couple of days ago, when he came to my house. He hates it that he has to ask for money. It's a tough pill for him to swallow, but he's head-over-heels in love with Kendra, and he wants to propose to her. This came on very quickly, and I want like hell to try to talk him out of it, but I already know that I can't. Wade is very headstrong, and he'll propose to her with a goddamn pipe cleaner for a ring if he has to. Me giving him money is a moot point.

"So, are you going to make this awkward, or can you just hand it over?" he asks, getting to the point.

"Have you already got a ring picked out?" I ask, partly trying to stall him, and partly waiting for an interruption of some sort, but that only happens when it's poor timing, of course.

"Yeah. It's on hold at the store." He says. "I had to max out my credit cards to put a deposit on it."

I wince, good-naturedly. "At least you didn't have one custom-made."

Wade gives me a look. "I knew you were gonna go there."

Lifting a hand defensively, I say, "Sorry, just making conversation."

"Look, I know that this is painful for you, but you made it through Colton and Julia's wedding, and you can make it through me and Kendra's wedding, too."

"I know." I nod.

"I'm sorry about what happened, but...life goes on, man. Shit happened to me lately and I lived to tell, and so will you."

I chuckle shortly. "Look at you. Little brother giving big brother advice."

"Who woulda thunk it?" he says, being glib.

"You know how much you're getting once that ring is on your finger, man?" I ask bluntly.

"No. Do I *want* to know?"

"You need to have a plan for it, Wade. You can't just leave that sitting in your account like a paycheck." I explain. "You think you had troubles with people trying to con their way into your bank, you'll leave yourself vulnerable to way more if you go that route."

"Fuck, I don't want to talk about this right now." He's irritated.

"Fair enough." I lean forward, clasping my hands on the desk. "I just want to make sure that this is what you really want before taking the plunge."

"Man, I knew I should have gone to Jack for this instead of you." He whines. "Why do you have to be this way? I thought we talked everything through."

I place my hands, palm down, on the desk. "Now,

hang on a second. We *did* talk everything through. I just wanted to check, you know. A man can change his mind."

"I'm not going to change my mind, Garrett. I want to marry Kendra, and that's it. I'll do it with or without the loan."

I nod. "Okay." I pat the desk and rise. "You tell me how much you want, and I'll transfer it to your account."

He shakes his head. "You had me come all the way down here, when you could have done this without me here. I knew it. You just wanted me to come down here so that you could try to talk me out of it."

"Think what you want, Wade. It's valid." My voice is firm. "You just met Kendra, and now you're asking for a substantial amount of money to buy her a ring. It isn't unreasonable to be skeptical. Anyone else would be."

"Fuck you." He says, rising.

"Hey," I say as a 'v' forms between my brows. "Take it easy. You're acting like I said no. The money will be in your account in the next five minutes."

"Fine. Thanks." He spits out, like he's telling me where to go, but sugar coating it.

"Hey," I say, rising, catching him before he walks out the door.

"What." He almost shouts.

"Congratulations." I nod, trying to be reasonable.

He looks me up and down. "Yeah, thanks."

I watch him walk down the hallway towards the exit stairwell leading to the back parking lot, and then I walk to the window in my office, and watch him appear in the lot. He gets into his beat up old car and I smile. He's a good kid. He deserves everything he's getting, and he's waited long enough to get it.

Walking over to the wall, I pull away the framed photograph of my dad when I first got my pilot's license. In behind it is a combination safe. Turning the knob, I can feel my heart beating faster. Why the hell I do this to myself is beyond me. It's twisted and self-destructive.

And I know it. Somewhere in heaven my dad is chiding me, I just know it. I can feel a cold shiver every time I open this damn safe. Jack tells me it's because there is an actual draft inside, but it's impossible, since I know personally that the thing is insulated inside the wall.

The lock clicks and I pull the handle down, opening the door. Inside is a small, black velvet gift bag. And inside that is a black velvet box. Pulling the box out, a montage of memories flies through my head, and I almost drop the box as my mind races. She was the most beautiful woman in the world. She was perfect for me. But even as I stand here with the box in my hand, I hate her. I hate the box, and I hate everything that it stands for. I hate what's inside it, and I hate that I can't get rid of it.

What's worse is, I can't get rid of all these hateful feelings. What's worse is, I can't get rid of all these *loving* feelings, either.

I get to watch another Ford wedding, when dammit, mine should have been first. But God, why can't I let go? What happened between us was a pure mistake. The lie that ended us should never have happened. They say that the truth will set you free, but as sure as this box sits in my hand, that hasn't rang true for me.

...yet?

Ready to meet Garrett next? Read more
about him in...
Handle with Care

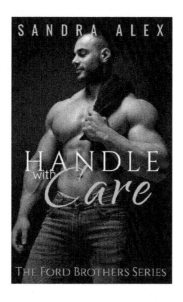

**The ex-military pilot. The bewitched single mother.
The plane crash that saves their lives.**

Getting pregnant by the wrong man and trying to make it right didn't serve me well. It's been years and we're not any closer to where we should be. Working night and day in an I.C.U. doesn't bode well for a relationship, either, but I'm doing my best. Tonight, the most beautiful man walks into the hospital. He's here for his father, who was just rushed in with a massive heart attack. If the man lives through the night, I'll be surprised. His son, Garrett Ford, is a pilot, and he's dressed like one. It's difficult to focus on my job with a man who is larger than life, and dressed to kill, with piercingly blue eyes and full lips. What's more, he's very polite and professional, which gets me. When his father wakes up for just a second and thinks I'm his estranged wife, Garrett looks at me in a way that I'll never forget.

***

She's hands down the most beautiful woman I've ever seen. Nora could stop traffic. What's more, she's smart, hard working, independent, and she's the best single parent I've ever met. Her kid's dad is a pill, but I have to turn the other cheek with him around, even though I know he'd rather see me crash and burn than see Nora and I together. I soon learn what lengths he'll go to to remove me from the picture. We'll see how far he gets. Trouble is, Nora sees him through a different set of eyes, and there is no convincing her that he is what he is. It's tough being the outsider in this three person relationship, and sometimes I feel like Nora's daughter Missy just puts up a front for me. I mean, what kid wouldn't want her natural father and mother to be together? Soon, it's clear just how much that is true...

HEA (Happily Ever After)
Second chance romance
Medical romance
Military romance
Medium heat

Course language
Mild cliffhanger ending
Third book in a complete 5 book standalone series

*****READ A FREE SAMPLE OF '*HANDLE WITH CARE*'
AT THE END OF THIS BOOK!*****

Keep in Touch!

Join my free newsletter and be the first to know when I have a new release out!

It's absolutely free, there are no strings attached, your information is completely confidential, and you can unsubscribe any time.

All you need is an email address.

To subscribe to my newsletter, please visit www.sandraalexbooks.com.

Extended Epilogue

Want to know what Wade and Kendra are up to in two years? Flash forward and check it out! Find out in this FREE **exclusive** Extended Epilogue that's <u>not available for purchase</u>.

To get your exclusive FREE Extended Epilogue, please visit www.sandraalexbooks.com.

Handle with Care - SAMPLE
Chapter 1

Garrett

The red light above the turbulence warning sign flashes on and off. "Well, that's not the light you want to see right now." I say to Leon, my co-pilot, flippantly. It's his first flight with me and he looks like he's about to vomit. "It's alright, man. Just hit that switch over there and we'll ease off on the altitude." He does as he's instructed but it doesn't seem to calm his nerves. The plane lowers slightly, away from the band of clouds we were flying through, and the vessel ceases shaking.

"There." I look at Leon. His face is less pasty, but he still looks like he needs to change his shorts. I'm not sure if this guy is cut out for being a pilot. He definitely needs to have a much thicker skin. I've seen it all from bringing a plane down in the middle of a wooded area, to landing in a shallow body of water. It's all about staying calm and keeping your head on straight. Also, remembering your training and crash-landing strategies. I've never been in a crash, but I'm sure prepared for it should it ever happen.

Lifting the radio, I give our coordinates and altitude reading to the control tower and wait for permission to land in the Greensboro airport...better known as home for me. The skies are clear, and the wind is calm. Aside from that little bit of minor turbulence, this was a textbook flight. The radio squawks at me to circle the airport once more so the runway can clear. I roger that and hang the radio back on the dashboard. Taking the interior radio in my hand, I push the call button and say, "We're coming in for a landing in the Greensboro airport. Please put your seatbelts on and follow the instructions from your flight attendant." I thank the passengers for flying with our airline and place that radio back on the dashboard.

After circling the runway, we have a clear landing. I pat Leon on the shoulder and congratulate him on his first flight.

"You drink, man?" Leon asks.

I frown. "Can't say I do."

"After this I need a scotch neat *real* bad." He guffaws.

I clap him on the back. "You'll do fine. Just need more practice."

Passengers disembark the plane and I wait for the flight attendants to clear out before leaving the aircraft. It's been a long few days. I've forgotten what my own bed feels like. It happens periodically. But I love what I do, and I'd never complain about it. I've been given a rare opportunity in life to fly, thanks to my dad, who once owned the airline that me and my two brothers now run. When he passed away, all five of us Ford boys inherited his millions, and he would be proud. We've all put it to good use.

I'm the oldest of the five boys. Dalton and Jack run the airline while I fly the planes, and one day Colton will design the aircraft when he's finished his mission in Afghanistan. We all served. Those were dad's orders. Since he served as a young adult, and then he raised five boys on his own, which was no easy task, we all served. Some as punishment, some as a rite of passage. It's made us all stronger men no matter which spin you put on it.

My office has everything I need in it, including a bed, which I've used on occasion, when I return from a flight and I'm way too wiped to even think about driving home. Or If Jack or Dalton aren't here to give me a lift. Turning the key in my office door I flip the lights on and see my desk phone flashing in the distance, indicating that there's a message waiting. The walls are painted a cream white and a large airline logo is all but a mural on the part of the wall where my desk is. It's hideous. But the marketing executives know best. The oak desk has been buffed to a shine and my assistant has kept the paperwork to a minimum. Only the most important documents sit in my inbox atop my desk. In front of my desk are two leather wing chairs and the door behind the chairs is where all my files are kept. The bed is in there, also, a shower stall, workout center, a collection of clean uniforms and a small kitchenette.

I'm starving, so I see what Maggie, my assistant, has packed in there for me. "Oooo..." I say to myself, eying the crab salad. Maggie knows I have a thing for seafood salad. Pulling it out of the fridge I then grab a fork from the drawer and sit at my desk, perusing the paperwork that awaits me. After munching while signing documents and reading notices, I rise and walk over to the wall safe. It's hidden behind a small picture of my dad and I from when I first received my pilot's licence. Flanking that photo are my framed degrees.

Turning the dial on the safe I hear my desk phone ring and realize I haven't bothered to check my messages yet. Ignoring the phone, I open the safe and pull out the tiny box I was checking on. Inside the box is a one and a half carat diamond solitaire ring. It's worth over fifty thousand dollars. I had it specially made for Nora, the love of my life. It's been my plan to propose to her tonight. It was one year ago today that I met her. It was one year ago today that my life changed forever. Nora is and will always be the greatest thing that ever happened to me.

It's been a little complicated, I'll admit. She has a daughter. Nora was very young when she had her, and the man who fathered Missy has had his share of trouble, but we'll get into that later. Nonetheless, I love Missy. Nora's a great mom, too, which bodes well for me. I want tons of kids. She wants more children, too. After having her first at age sixteen, child-rearing, for Nora, is a blur. Now that Missy is going on fourteen, Nora's been fighting the urge to have more kids...until I came along. As soon as that wedding band is on her finger, the baby-making factory is open.

Placing the velvet box in my back pocket, I hear my cell phone ring. I'd left it sitting on my desk. I see that it's Jack, one of my brothers. "Hey, bro, what's up?"

"I saw your flight landed like an hour ago. How come you're still here?" My brother can see my car parked in the staff lot from his office window.

"You're one to talk. Why're you still here?" It's past midnight.

"I might as well live here, man. You know how it is."

Jack is the CFO of the airline. He had some big shoes to fill when dad died. "You remember what killed dad, right?" I say, half joking.

"Yeah, I know. Anyway, you out for a couple of days now, or are you sticking around?"

I unconsciously grasp the small box in my pocket. "I'm heading out. But I'll be back the day after tomorrow." I know that Missy is away at a sleepover with friends tonight, and Nora is off work tomorrow. Missy knows I'm going to propose to her mom, so she agreed to give us the night alone. I'd considered doing a joint proposal, like the ones you see on Facebook a lot, where the guy plans a proposal with the child, but Missy's...not quite there yet. I'll get into that later, too.

Not noticing that I hadn't said anything in a couple of seconds, Jack asks if I'm still on the line. "Yeah, I'm here. Just have a lot on my mind."

"You okay, man? Need me to give you a lift home?"

"Nah. I'm not going home, anyway. I'm going to Nora's."

"At this time of night?"

"I've got a key. And she'll still be up." Nora is a nighthawk, which works well with my line of work. She's a nurse, and currently working the afternoon shift.

"I can drop you off if you want. I'll be driving right by her street." Jack offers.

"It's okay. Thanks."

Jack guffaws. "You're finally gonna do it, aren't you?"

"What?"

He chuckles. "You've got the ring in your pocket

right now, don't you." It's more of a statement than a question.

Jack found out about the ring by accident. I'd picked it up from the jewelry store earlier that day, and it fell out of my pocket, just as I was fumbling to put it in the safe. Jack walked into my office at an inopportune moment. He has a habit of not bothering to knock when it's after hours. The ring has been in my safe for a couple of months, since I was waiting for this particular day to come. My kid brother has been goading me ever since, accusing me of not having the balls to propose, otherwise I'd have done it that day.

"That's right. I told you today is the day. I told you months ago."

"I'd have done it that day if I met a girl half as awesome as Nora."

"Yeah, well, you've never been able to hold your wad for anything. That's probably why you can't meet decent women."

"Eat shit and die, man." Jack chuckles.

"After you." I say and hang up. He texts me two seconds later, wishing me luck. He's a good brother. They all are. Jack is the only one who knows about my plan to propose. I wanted to keep that to myself. After I shower and change into normal clothes, I grab my keys, wallet and phone, double-check to make sure the ring is in my pocket, and I drive over to Nora's. As I pull up to her place, I don't see her car parked in the driveway. This may work out better than expected.

I know she's not working tonight, and I also know that she's a sucker for candles. There is a drawer in her kitchen reserved especially for them. Planning for tonight, I brought a bag full of pillar candles, in hopes that I'd get the opportunity to use them. So I'm glad that I can. Hopping out of my car, I fish out my keys and unlock the door. I haven't heard from Nora since this afternoon, so she might be out at the movies with her sister or with friends. Either way, this is perfect.

Nora's house is a two-bedroom bungalow. It's small

but perfect for her and Missy. I've offered for both girls to live at my place; I have plenty of space, but Nora's a little old-fashioned, which is one of the things that I absolutely love about her, so she wants to wait before living together. Maybe after this she will change her mind. My house is far too big for one person. When I bought it, the realtor snowed me over, I admit. He knew I had money and I was a sucker. He saw me coming. It was my foolishness really, telling him that I'm a pilot and that there is no budget for my house. Dalton warned me to exercise a little restraint...and in no uncertain terms, to keep my mouth shut.

Though small, her house is immaculate. One would never know that Nora is a single mother, raising a teenager, working shifts as an ICU nurse. As I make my way to her bedroom, with the bag in my hand, I pray that she still has a lighter in her nightstand. Checking, I see that she does, and I begin making quick work of assembling the candles in all the right spots. Usually Nora does this, when she's feeling romantic, but I've been paying attention and I know exactly how to place them and where. I set the candles in varying heights on the nightstand, bed, dresser, and I finish off with a handful of rose petals strewn on the bed. I kept an extra bunch of roses for Nora.

Looking at the clock, I see that it's going on one o'clock in the morning. Where on earth could Nora be? I try texting her, but she doesn't answer. Nora knows I'm flying back tonight, and we do have plans to be together tomorrow, on her day off. Just as I begin to worry, I hear the key turn in the front door. Hurriedly I light the candles. She knows I'm here because my car is parked in the driveway. She doesn't immediately come into the room. I quickly place the ring box on the bed, opened, so she can see what my intentions are. I saved a bouquet of roses to hold up just as she enters the bedroom.

As I see and hear the bedroom door open, my beautiful Nora's face appears from the other side. Her long dirty blonde hair is swept up and clipped in the back, the way she always wears it. She's wearing the red blouse I bought her for her birthday, and the black jeans that I love so much on her. Nora is beautiful without a trace of makeup. When her hair is down it reaches her mid back. Her body is perfect. At least in my eyes. I can't wait to kiss her and ask her to be my wife. I am the luckiest man alive to have found her and have her love me back. When I'm with her, my life is complete.

Normally clear and unscathed, Nora's face only wavers when she's lost a patient that has grown dear to her. When my father suffered a massive heart attack, she was one of the nurses who watched over him before he died. In his final days, dad was a different man. Usually cold and unfeeling, dad shared heartwarming stories with me and Nora about my estranged mother. Though my other brothers couldn't handle it, Nora and I listened intently to the man on his deathbed, speaking of the woman he loved more than life itself, who left him and gave no reason for it.

My brothers, especially Wade, who was a toddler when she left, didn't care to hear about the mother who didn't care enough to stay. It is my belief that my dad's success was the major reason for my mother leaving. Oftentimes, dad didn't have time for any of us boys, so I can well imagine how much time he was able to spare for my mother. Sometimes I understand the why, but I still have a difficult time understanding the *how* she left. By no means is Missy my daughter, nor do I treat her as much, but in the short time that I've known her, I couldn't imagine leaving her. She's a tough teenager, but I remember Wade, and how much crap he put my dad through, and I realize that it's all just part of the package.

When I look at Nora and think about how much of a devoted mother she is, it makes me love her even more. Despite the drama that Missy has inflicted on her mother, Nora loves her to death. And I love her for it.

Not many single mothers can pull it off the way that she does. I admire her. Nora deserves nothing but the best, and the best I'll give her. It's tough making time for each other with both of our hectic jobs, but we make it work. The key is compromise and understanding, also, remembering that it's about quality time and not quantity. When we're together we make it count. We go to special places, do special things, make love like it's the last time ever, or the first time, and it's...wonderful.

As she walks into the bedroom, her sweet face appears sullen. I know she's lost a patient and my heart bleeds for her. When she has those days, it's always best not to bring attention to it unless she needs to be held and wants to talk about it. Instead, on bended knee I say, "Hi, sweetie. I love you more than anything else in the world. Will you marry me?" I hold the flowers out to her and reach for the ring box. Her face is like stone. She's completely shocked. I smile. It's been a tough day for her. As I rise, I go to embrace her and she takes a step back, as if she doesn't know who I am. As if I'm some stranger who has broken into her room and vandalized it. "Don't...touch me." She seethes.

A 'v' forms between my eyes because I'm completely confused. "What's wrong, Nora?" I whisper, making a second attempt to hold her. She lifts her arms as I reach for them, as if I'm made of poison, and the mere proximity to me is toxic.

"Get out." Her voice cracks as tears form inside her eyes. "Now." She says so low it scares me.

"I...I don't understand." I say, shaking my head. I feel dizzy with dread. The seafood salad I ate earlier is sitting at the back of my throat, threatening to spew all over the wall. "What...why? What happened?" My hands are trembling as I place the ring in my pocket, out of sight.

She eyes me like I'm an intruder and she's holding a gun to my head. "Missy told me what you did to her...you son of a bitch."

My eyes widen. My heart starts to beat out of my

chest. "What...oh my God...what's wrong with Missy? What happened?"

She turns her face from me. "I can't even look at you...you sick, disgusting pervert." She turns her head and shoves me with both hands. I fall back a step. My breath is cut off. I feel like I'm drowning. The shock and horror are insurmountable. "Get out before I do something I'll regret." She shouts. Nora has never shouted at me before. I feel it in my chest. She might as well have stabbed me. My eyes are so wide I feel like I can't close them. My breathing is ragged, and I'm fighting the strong urge to hug her and tell her that everything is going to be alright. Judging by the look on her face, I risk a blow if I attempt to do that again.

Resigned, I swallow. "I don't know what's going on, Nora. Tell me what's going on." I beg, as though I was deaf to the unspeakable accusations the first time they were uttered.

"Missy told me what you did to her." Angry tears wash over her face. Her jaw is clenched, and her voice is a mere whisper.

A hand goes to my mouth as what I'm being accused of registers. Tears prick the backs of my eyes as I realize what my beloved thinks I did to her daughter, the girl I love just like my own. "God, Nora, I couldn't imagine doing anything to hurt Missy." I say, my voice cracking.

She looks at me with sheer hatred in her eyes. I can't look at her. I can't place that expression in my memory. I'd rather see a dismembered body than the woman I love glancing at me like that. My eyes go to the carpet. "Get out." She says one last time. I realize that there is nothing more I can do. Nothing I can say is going to help. The longer I stay, the worse it gets. Keeping my head down I walk out of her bedroom and out the front door.

I sit in the driveway, trying to process what just happened. The love of my life just shattered me into pieces. I've been accused of doing unspeakable things to someone I love. And in the process, I've just lost the love of my life. She hates me. She never even gave me a chance. My whole life has just been ruined in less than sixty seconds. I want to walk back into the house and say something; sometimes they say you have to fight for what's worth fighting for, but I know that this case is an exception. This is truly sensitive and must be handled with kid gloves. If I go back in there right now, I'll just upset Nora more.

Taking deep breaths, I try to calm my nerves before turning the engine over. Wiping my eyes with the backs of my hands I put the car into reverse. The drive home is a blur. By the time I turn the key in the front door, I can't even remember how I got there. My phone beeps with a text message from Jack, reminding me of something I have to do before my next flight the day after tomorrow. I text him back, saying that I got it, and it's already been dealt with.

The phone rings. "So, I guess you chickened out after all." His tone is facetious.

"Now's not a good time."

There is a pause. "What's going on? Who died?"

"I can't...I can't...talk about it right now." I rub a hand over my face.

"Oh shit. That bad, huh."

"Yeah,"

"Okay, man. You know where to find me." He hangs up.

Placing my phone on the entrance table, I walk towards the kitchen. Looking up on the top of my refrigerator, I see a lone bottle of whiskey that Dalton left here once when we had a poker game. Never a man to drink, the bottle has remained there ever since. Staring at it, I walk over and stretch up, reaching for it.

I don't remember the last time a drop of alcohol touched my lips.

...but a man can change.

Chapter 2

Nora

One Year and One Month Ago

The phone rings and my colleague, Stella, picks it up. She nods and says okay, and then hangs up. "We've got one coming in now." Stella addresses me, "Massive heart attack, critical condition. Paramedics have resuscitated twice already. We need to get doctor Bryson here ASAP for assessment."

"I'll call Bryson. You get room three ready. Mrs. Mathers has been removed and sent to the morgue already." I instruct as I dial Dr. Bryson's extension and explain the situation. Within three minutes I see the gurney come off the elevator. The paramedic isn't on top of the patient, pumping his chest, so that's a good sign. It looks like the patient is stabilized to some degree. Rising, I meet the paramedic team and instruct them as to which room to place the patient. I'm given his stats and information as they carefully lift the male patient on to the bed.

I begin making quick work of setting up the equipment. The intravenous tube has already been administered. Dr. Bryson trots into the room, closes the door, and begins his assessment. I hear a knock at the door and see one of the volunteers appear. "The family is here." She announces. "Should I let them come up?"

I look at Dr. Bryson. He nods, looking at me over his half-glasses, and I know what that means. Patients don't generally come here for rehabilitation, and if they do, they almost certainly go downstairs for testing or to the operating room first. If no diagnostics are ordered, the doctor has determined that there is nothing further that can be done. I look up at the oxygen saturation meter reading, and I'm surprised that the patient has survived the few short minutes that he's been here. He clearly isn't strong enough to undergo any procedure, diagnostic or otherwise. He's barely breathing on his own. It's like Bryson is reading my mind. He ups the oxygen to help keep the patient alive for a short time so his family can say their goodbyes. As I exit the room, I see the elevator door open and the most gorgeous man in the entire world appears. In this line of work, the very last thing on my mind is the opposite sex, but this man is *that* beautiful, *that* unmistakably, unapologetically handsome, that I can't help but look at him. He's in uniform. I'm guessing it's a pilot's uniform, because he has one of those flat caps with a visor on. He's head-to-toe in white; his suit has an airline logo emblazoned on the left breast pocket. His eyes stand out a mile they're so blue. His hair is cut short on the sides, all the way around, and it's slightly longer on top. A shock of it sticks out from under the front of the cap. He's so tall I have to crane my neck upward to achieve eye contact. His arms look imposing under his uniform, as he removes his cap, placing it under his arm as a sign of respect.

His face is like stone. Hardened with concern. It's clear that it's his father who's just been admitted. "I'm here for Wren Ford. I believe he's just arrived." He says. His tone is gentle yet direct.

"I take it you're family?" I ask, as part of hospital protocol.

"Yes, I'm his eldest son, Garrett." He gives a slight nod.

"The doctor is with him now, sir. Please have a seat." I gesture to the small bank of chairs along the wall by the nurse's station. He does as he's instructed as I return to my post at the nurse's station.

Miraculously, an hour later, Wren Ford is still alive. As I enter the room to check on him, Garrett is still there. Trying not to interrupt their time together, I benignly check his monitors. "How's he doing?" Garrett asks. He's sitting on the guest chair with his knees parted and his elbows resting on his knees. His hat sits on the second chair and he rakes a hand through his hair. The man looks beat; like he's been flying for two days straight without breaks.

I tell a half-lie. "He's doing okay. His vitals are stable."

"How many guests are allowed in here at once?"

Wren isn't expected to survive the night, so for all I care, they can have a party in here. "As many as the patient can handle. But normally it's two."

"So, in other words, if the patient has a prayer, they can have two guests. If they're the walking dead, it's unlimited." His tone is slightly facetious, but I've heard it all in this line of work. It's an emotional time when a loved one is dying. "Sorry." He lifts his hand and says after a beat.

Wren stirs, opening his eyes. He looks up at me and sees me fiddling with a monitor.

"Dad?" Garrett says softly. "It's Garrett. I'm here."

Wren removes the oxygen mask. "Where is Dalton?" he asks. His voice is gravelly and barely audible.

"He's on his way. He had to go pick up Wade."

"What about Jack and Colton?"

"Jack we can't get in touch with, Dalton keeps trying. And dad, Colton's still in Afghanistan."

"Why can't *you* find Jack?" the man is talking in gasps. I encourage him to put the mask back on, but he bats my hand away like it's a fly.

"He's been in off-site meetings. I can't call him from in here because you're not allowed cell phones, dad."

"How much time have I got?" Wren is being belligerent, lifting his hands in the air.

"I don't know, dad." Garrett is frustrated. "Just try to relax."

Leaning over, I gently place the mask back on Wren's face. "This will help you breathe, sir."

Wren scowls at me. "Who the hell are you?"

"Dad, watch your language." Garrett chides.

"My name is Nora. I'm a nurse, sir." I talk to him as though he's a child.

Wren's face softens slightly. "Nora. That's such a lovely name."

"Thank you. It was my grandmother's name." I chuckle. "And my mother's middle name. My family doesn't score many points in the originality department, I suppose."

"I'm named after my great-grandfather on my father's side." Wren boasts. "And if we had a girl, my wife and I were going to name her Nora, as a matter of fact."

"But you ended up with boys, right?" I say, adjusting another monitor and checking his intravenous fluid bag.

"Five." He answers. Garrett looks up at me and gives a tight smile. "I raised them myself." Wren is hoarse.

"That must have been quite a task." I play along.

He ignores my comment. "My wife was beautiful. The most beautiful woman." He shakes his head but says no more.

"I'll be back in a little while to check on you." I say.

Garrett rises. "I'll be right back, dad."

He follows me out the door. "Is he in any pain or anything?"

"He shouldn't be. He's on a mild sedative to keep him calm and comfortable." I nod. I can't stop looking at his eyes. I try not to look at his full lips, but it's difficult. I've never had a man this handsome standing in front of me, talking to me before. It feels like I'm in some romantic dream. *If I am, don't wake me up.*

Two hours later, three more of Wren's sons appear. I'm almost thankful I'm pulling a double shift today, because these boys are unbelievable. It's like I'm stuck in a room with male models. They're all gorgeous. Garrett is still in his uniform; he hasn't left his father's side. Wren is more talkative as I enter the room to check on him. He's talking more about his wife, and I notice that the youngest son leaves when the subject is broached.

The other boys only stay a short time and then leave, but Garrett remains. He must be the closest to his father. It's very late, and the man hasn't so much as gone for a bathroom break. Just as I'm about to encourage him to take five, an alarm sounds in Wren's room. A fleeting look crosses Garrett's face as I run to the room, asking Garrett to stay back. As I enter the room, I see that Wren's heart has stopped. The heart monitor is flatlining. Two other nurses come running, and I hear one of them paging the doctor.

Wren does not have a DNR waiver, so I begin initiating CPR immediately. As Dr. Bryson arrives, he coaches me as we try to resuscitate Mr. Ford a third time. But every second that the heart monitor flatlines is another second that Wren is facing his demise. After a third attempt at the procedure, Dr. Bryson cuts the air with his hand, indicating for me to stop. The drapes in the window are closed, so Garrett can't see what's going on in here. But he can hear most certainly hear what's going on.

Dr. Bryson makes another attempt to bring the man back, but it's in vain. All the monitors have stopped registering, and one of the other nurses finally switches off the heart monitor. Bryson pulls the clipboard off the bottom of the bed and writes some notes before opening the door. I see Garrett sitting on one of the chairs outside the room. His knees are parted, and his head is resting in his hands. My heart bleeds for him. I'm not sure how close he was to his dad, but it looks like they were very close. The other boys, I'm not so sure. I watch Bryson approach Garrett, patting him on the back, before the door closes.

***

Hours later, when my shift has ended, I walk towards the back parking lot, passing the 'cell phones allowed' zone, and see Garrett pacing, talking on his phone. He's not saying much, just perfunctory responses. He's still in his uniform, but his jacket is unbuttoned, and a white t-shirt is poking through. His hat lays on a chair beside him. You could shoot a cannon through the room; there is nobody in sight. It's also three o'clock in the morning. When he sees me, he asks his caller to hold.

"Excuse me. Do you know when I can go up and make...arrangements?" he says, gesturing with his hand, as though the word 'funeral' is an expletive.

"I'm sure you can go up now. The coroner has been in." I explain.

He nods and holds a finger up, asking me to wait. "I'll have to call you back." He says to the caller and ends the conversation.

"Hey, listen, thanks for putting up with my dad. He's not the easiest person to get along with." Garrett says, shaking my hand, as though his father dying in my care completes some transaction between us.

"It's no problem. That's my job." I smile.

He smiles and I realize how fantastically handsome he is. "So, you're a pilot?" I ask, trying to change the subject.

He looks at his hat on the chair, as though his uniform doesn't give it away. "Err...yes, for the Greensboro Airport. My dad is...err...was...the CEO." He licks his lips and then bites his lower lip, in thought. As though it just occurred to him that his father is gone.

"I see." I say, gauging whether or not I should end the conversation and leave, or stay. It's hard to tell what he's going to do next. He's not looking at me, he's staring at a spot on the wall. "Are you okay?"

He lifts a hand, breaking himself out of his reverie. "Yeah," he pauses, and then shakes his head slightly, as though in disbelief. "Funny how when my dad calls meetings, all his associates come running. When the man is on his deathbed, nobody cares." He guffaws. "This will be the smallest funeral ever, evidently."

I don't know what to say, except, "Is there anything I can do to help?"

He looks at the floor, shaking his head. "No. It seems my own brothers couldn't stay long enough to see their old man off, either. What a shit show this is turning out to be." He lifts his hand. "Excuse my language."

I chuckle. "Oh, Mr. Ford, if you only knew what I've heard, you wouldn't be apologizing."

He tilts his head. "I guess when people get caught up in the moment, they let their guards down, huh."

I nod. "Something like that."

A colleague walks by and asks me something to do with work, just as Garrett's phone rings. His face falls and I ask my friend to hold on a moment. "Are you okay, Mr. Ford?"

"Yeah. It's my brother Colton...calling from Afghanistan. What a call this is going to be." He says, pushing his hand down his face. He answers the call and I inch my way over to my friend, giving him privacy.

"Nora, when are you on again?" my friend Judy asks. She's just coming in to start her shift.

I tell her and she starts chatting about mundane, work-related things. But I'm only half-listening. I'm paying more attention to Garrett's conversation. I hear him tell his brother that their dad is gone. It's a short conversation, and when he hangs up, I see him turn his back, so he's facing the other direction. His head moves forward, and one hand goes to his face. I'm not sure if he's rubbing his eyes or clearing tears.

As Judy ends the conversation and walks away, I approach Garrett. His eyes are reddened with tears and exhaustion. My tone is gentle; the same tone I use on my daughter Missy when she's upset. "Is there anyone I can call for you?" my heart bleeds for him. He's dealing with all this alone.

He sniffs and draws in a deep breath. When he speaks, his voice cracks. "No...," he sighs, "thanks,"

Then I do something I almost never do to someone related to work.

...I hug him.

Chapter 3

Garrett

(Three Months Later)
One Year Ago

Attempting to leave the airport after my last flight of the day, I pull my keys out of my back pocket, and walk towards the exit. There are signs posted all over the place that the exit is closed for repairs. The janitor is cleaning the windows at the other staff exit, and I don't have the heart to interrupt, so I do the unthinkable and walk towards the main exit doors. It's a beautiful day, so I don't mind walking outside to the back. I'm in normal clothes, so I blend in nicely. There's nothing more unsettling than walking through the main entrance dressed in my uniform. I stand out like a sore thumb.

Walking towards the exit, I bump into Jack, who is standing in line to get the good coffee. I smack him on the shoulder. "I don't know why you don't just order the good stuff to go in your office, man. It's not like they won't deliver, you know." I tease.

"Yeah, well, this way I don't have to make it myself." He admits. "You heading home?"

"Yeah, I'm gonna go get some shut-eye. Are you going to see some sunlight today, or have you completely turned into a vampire." I say it as a statement more than a question.

He looks at his watch. "I've been here since six. Was here until eleven last night. Dad kept much the same schedule." He's matter-of-fact.

Just as I'm about to rebuke, a lady walks by, rolling a suitcase in her wake. One of the wheels gives and the suitcase falls to the floor, making an obvious scraping noise. She stops and assesses the situation.

"Shit, she looks familiar." I say, and then recognition comes to my face. "I'll be right back."

As I approach her, she's frustrated and embarrassed, judging by the look on her face. "Nora...is it?" I ask.

"Yeah...that's my—" she stops and gives me an odd smile. "Mr...Ford, right?" she lifts a finger to me.

"Yes, Garrett...Garrett Ford." I nod. "Can I give you a hand?"

Nora looks at her broken suitcase and chuckles without a trace of humor. "Well, I guess I do. Unless I scrape this thing across the floor."

I lift the suitcase. "No need. Lead the way to your car."

"Why don't I just get a cart?"

"It's the middle of the day. Good luck with that." I guffaw. "Show me to your car." I nod to Jack and he gives me a wink. I give him a sour look back.

As she walks to her car, I walk alongside her.

"Thanks so much for this. I really appreciate it."

"No problem. Are you coming back from vacation?"

"Not exactly. My friend had a destination wedding. Her second. If she expects a gift, too, I'll use the money and cash it in for a new friend."

I chuckle. "Can't blame you there."

"So, how are you doing? I mean...since your dad passed away?"

I shrug. "I'm doing okay, I suppose. My brother Dalton is having the most trouble adjusting. He's filled my dad's old role. Jack's not much different; he works day and night. It's no wonder my dad worked himself to death."

"I see that all the time, unfortunately. But I'm one to talk. I work all hours of the day and night. Sometimes my daughter forgets who I am."

"Oh, you have a daughter?" I ask, as we approach the Park & Fly parking lot.

"Yeah, she's thirteen. Her name's Missy."

"Thirteen? Wow, you don't look old enough to have a teenager." Fact, she doesn't look old enough to have kids at all. I didn't realize how pretty she was until I take another look. Her long dirty-blonde hair is swaying in the wind. She has sunglasses on, but they're tucked up on her crown, giving her a youthful glow. Her dress flows gently, revealing her left leg through a slit that runs up past her knee. The dress is cream white with a floral pattern.

"Well, I had her very young." She says, and I sense that it's not a topic she's comfortable with, so I drop it.

"So I take it your husband didn't go with you to this wedding?"

As we reach her car, she gives me a thin smile. "I'm not married. Go ahead and judge. I was a fool when I was sixteen; thought sleeping with this really cool guy would get me places, but the only thing it got me was pregnant. I raised her with my mother's help, and my mom passed away two years ago. What can I say? Life gives you lemons, you make lemonade." She lifts her arms as if in defeat, and presses the fob on her keyring. "Anything else you want to know?" she asks, with an almost snarky tone.

I ignore the tone and ask her something, surprising myself. "Are you free for dinner tonight?"

***

Do you know how long it's been since I asked a girl out? I've never really dated if I'm honest. In high school I was friends with a girl for a long time, but it never amounted to anything, to my dismay. I can't say that I was in love with her, I mean, if I had to choose between learning to fly and going out with her, well, you know how that turned out. In college, I had a few casual relationships, but no girl ever pulled my chains in a way that made me want more. So, when I asked Nora out, it was very out of my element. Jack's jaw dropped when I told him who I was going out with.

"Are you nuts? The nurse? Isn't that...like...incest or something?" he teases.

"She was dad's nurse, not his second cousin, dickwad." I say as I tie up my tie, trying like hell not to drop the phone in the process. "and you should talk, mister 'I can't stop jerking off to my teacher's sister's picture'."

"Hey, that was in college." Jack refutes. "and she was hot...like *hot.*"

"And how did you get the picture...stalker."

"Hey, I can't help it if I'm a closet Facebook geek." Jack hacked into his college professor's Facebook page and at the time, he was rather proud of himself.

"You're a closet something, but I wouldn't give any intellectual weight to it, Jack." I add, giving up and putting him on speakerphone.

"Hey, where are you taking her, anyway? Jokes aside."

"Out to a romantic restaurant and then to a movie, why?"

"Cool. Make sure you kiss her though." He advises.

"If it feels right I will."

"No, man, trust me. You don't kiss a girl on the first date, you'll end up in the friend zone again. Those were the days, eh buddy?" he teases, reminding me of that girl in high school I mentioned.

I hesitate and he takes that as an admission that he's right. "I'll expect a full report tomorrow."

"Fine. I gotta go." I hang up on him.

Fifteen minutes later I pull up to this stuffy restaurant that I'm not so sure about. From the outside it looks like it belongs in a regency romance novel. And for a second, I'm thankful that I told her where we were going. I'd hate for her to feel underdressed and embarrassed thanks to me not giving her a pre-emptive tip. It almost feels like a mistake, since we're going to a movie afterward. We're going to look like a bunch of penguins showing up all dressed like we're expecting a visit from the queen at the Cineplex.

But when I see her walk towards me, my jaw drops. She's in a body-hugging black dress that goes just above her knees. It's strapless but has a small jacket to cover her shoulders. Her heels accentuate her calves, making me think un-Christian things about my dad's nurse. I almost feel bad for not picking her up, but she insisted on meeting me here. I suppose it's an escape tactic in case the date goes sour. As she recognizes me, she smiles.

"Hey there," she says, taking a spin. "I'm not used to dressing like this." She giggles. "I found this tucked beneath my dozens of scrubs."

"You look beautiful." I smile but I'm careful to be matter-of-fact, not wishy-washy in any way. After all, we barely know each other.

"Thank you." She says. "This place looks like it should have a stable in the back."

I chuckle. "I was just thinking that. Do you want to go somewhere else? I really should have researched this place a little better. My apologies."

She waves. "No, it'll be fine. Besides, I'm starving."

"Hopefully the food is good." I tuck my arm inside hers as we walk into the restaurant.

"You sure look different without your uniform." She comments. "When I saw you earlier at the airport in regular clothes, I almost didn't recognize you."

"And you without your scrubs. I had to look twice." I look at her and notice how beautiful her eyes are. They're like a bluey green, and her lashes are so long. I steal a glance at her lips and she quickly looks at mine, but we both quickly look somewhere else a second later.

The hostess seats us immediately and luckily the food comes fast and is amazing. Nora is definitely a lover of food. She is like a closet food critic, but she's completely impressed by the cuisine. Her comments are astute, and I actually learned a little something about the steak I ate. Colton's the cook in the family; the best I ever did was make a baked potato with sour cream and bacon bits. Real bacon, too.

"So, what made you decide to be an ICU nurse?" I ask, after taking the last bite of my steak. She also chose steak, but she's only halfway through hers.

"I knew I wanted to be a nurse, and for some time I also worked in a trauma unit, and I guess I figured an ICU nurse was a good middle ground. I love it, despite the crazy hours."

"I hear you on that."

"And I suppose your dad is the reason you became a pilot?"

"He's part of the reason, but not the only reason." I counter. "I've always had an interest in flying. I used to watch all the fighter jets in old war movies and I couldn't get enough."

"Well that was lucky for you, then." She smiles. "So how come you didn't join the Air Force?"

My eyebrows lift. "I did, actually. Before I flew for the airline, I was in the Air Force."

"Really?" she seems impressed.

"Yes." I nod. Her face changes. She looks down at my lips again and it makes me squirm. I'm feeling the urge to lean over and kiss her, but I'm afraid it's inappropriate here.

"So, do you have any kids?" she asks me.

I shake my head. "No. But I want to have kids for sure some day."

"Yeah? Most guys say that but don't mean it."

I crane my neck. "Nora, I'm not a liar. And I don't play games, either."

She considers my statement for a moment. "I believe you." She pauses. "For the record, I don't play games, either. But I do sometimes have to lie."

I lift a brow.

"Like I had to lie tonight. To my daughter."

"Why?"

"When you're a single mother, you have to tell the odd lie, especially if you're going on a date."

"Ah, hence you insisting on meeting me at the restaurant." I say. "How did you explain the dress?"

"Oh, don't worry, I turn back into a pumpkin before I go home. I changed in a bathroom at a donut shop before I arrived here."

I laugh. "You didn't."

"I did."

"So, where does she think you are?"

"Out with a friend from work."

The waitress asks Nora if she's finished with her meal, since her plate has been untouched for the last five minutes. Nora asks her to wrap it up for her and the waitress takes our plates away.

"So, do you still want to go see a movie, or would you like a different option?"

She interlaces her fingers under her chin. "What else did you have in mind?"

"Well, since we're both dressed in our monkey suits, and you have a change of clothes, I thought instead of going to a movie, I have a large screen television at my place, and plenty of unwatched movies. I'll keep my hands to myself and I promise to make sure you get home in time to stay in the good graces of your daughter."

Nora doesn't even hesitate. "Done."

***

She follows from behind me as we drive to my place. The cobblestone wraparound driveway is clear, and I gesture to her to park anywhere she likes. I park my Audi furthest from the door, giving her access to the full area. When she exits her car, carrying her bag, she looks up at my house. "Jesus, are you a Rockefeller?" she chuckles.

My cheeks heat. The house is imposing from the outside, I admit. There are two large pillars out front, flanking the double entrance doors. Above the doors is a glass window that leads all the way up to the second floor, highlighting my spiral staircase and glass chandelier. There are eight bedrooms inside. This was the Ford family home once, and dad left it to me when he died. All the décor was done long ago, and I've changed nothing since I took possession. I still sleep in the same room I slept in as a child. I considered selling this house and keeping my own, but I thought there were too many memories here, and I'd only lived in my own house for about seven years. Maybe some day I will part with this place, but in the meantime, it's home.

"I inherited it when my dad died." Is all the explanation I can muster.

"Ah," she says, nodding her understanding.

"Well, my place is a shack compared to this, but I won't judge if you don't."

I lift my hand in surrender. "No judgment here." Pulling my keys out of my pocket, I unlock the door and gesture for her to enter. The sensor lights come on automatically, illuminating the front foyer. The stairs are directly in front of us. Nora takes a step towards the stairs, observing the chandelier. "I've always loved these things." It has tear-shaped crystals that plunge downward in a spiral fashion, kind of like the inside of a rose. The crystals reach down about ten feet from the ceiling.

"My dad's decorator had it imported from Italy, I think."

"It's beautiful."

"Come on. I'll show you the rest of the house." She's about to remove her shoes. "No, it's okay. You can leave them on."

"Oh, please, have mercy." She laughs, taking them off, massaging her foot with her hand.

"It's just that the floors are cold." I say, gesturing to the cream marble flooring throughout the foyer.

She waves and walks to me. Without her heels on she's about a foot shorter than me. "Do you want to change first?" I ask, offering to take her bag.

"Sure, let's do that first."

"Would you prefer a bathroom or a bedroom?"

"How many bathrooms do you have?" she's humored.

"Five. Two upstairs, two downstairs, and an ensuite in my dad's old room.

"A bathroom is fine." She smiles, trying but failing to hide a smirk.

Showing her to the main bathroom on the first floor, I turn the light on and tell her I'll meet her in the living room. Pointing to the room to our left, she nods, and I hand her the bag.

I quickly trot upstairs and change into jeans and a linen shirt, carefully hanging my suit in the closet, and giving my underarms the sniff test. Suddenly I realize that there's a potentially naked woman in my bathroom. And I feel the urge to take a cold shower before joining her. Well, I feel other urges, but a shower would take care of that. Should I take Jack's advice and kiss her? Or should I let her take the reigns? It's been so long since I've been near a woman, I've forgotten protocol. I hear the plumbing from the bathroom downstairs and then I hear the door open. My heart starts to beat faster. I'm almost too nervous to go downstairs, and I find myself thinking of conversation starters to allay my sudden urges.

Then I hear her calling me from the bottom of the stairs.

...time's up, mister. Let's fly this plane.

Chapter 4

Nora

When I pulled up to the restaurant, I almost lost my nerve. I could see Garrett standing at the entrance, looking like James Bond in his suit and tie. My plain black frock couldn't do his specially tailored suit justice. We looked like rags to riches standing next to each other. But when he looked at me with those big blue eyes, I nearly melted. He's such a distinguished gentleman it's unnerving. When he offered for me to go back to his place, he said it so innocently, I knew it was safe. There's no way this man is going to pull any kind of stunt on me.

His place is a mansion. He calls it a house, but it certainly isn't. I'm standing in his bathroom, and it's as big as my living room. We're going to watch a movie together, and I'm so nervous I could die. I don't know why I even accepted this date. My mouth just flapped out the word yes when he asked. No rhyme or reason. It flapped also when he asked me to go back to his place. What is wrong with me? I have too much going on in my life to be involved with anyone. Between my job and my daughter, and my ex...whatever Missy's dad is, I have enough to keep me busy until I die.

But I'm standing in this gorgeous man's bathroom, changing into a pair of jeans and a shirt, something too comfortable for this place, and I'm about to be alone with a man who looks like he belongs on the cover of GQ Magazine. Why is he even interested in me? Why did he ask me out on a date? I'm totally not in his league, and he's way out of mine. I tended to his father on his deathbed, for God sake. Why does he want to see me again?

That embrace at the hospital was definitely notable. His arms gripped my body so tight I almost gasped. He's built like nobody I've ever known. How he finds the time to work out when he's flying so often is beyond me, but he must. Nobody is that built naturally. As I placed my hand on his shoulder, I looked into his eyes and he saw what my intention was. He accepted by placing his hands on my waist and slowly, gradually snaking his arms around me. It was delicious, and I chide myself for even thinking that way; the man was a mess. He lay his head against mine and for a few seconds, he took in the comfort I offered him. He needed it. Maybe I needed it too...I'm not sure. But it felt wonderful, and to be truthful, I was hoping I'd see him again after that.

There is only one way to deal with my nerves here; take it head on. As I shove my dress into my bag and give my hair a shake, I open the bathroom door and walk to the foot of the stairs, calling for Garrett.

"Hey, yeah, I'll be right there." He calls. I can see him walking around the upstairs landing, making his way to the stairs.

"I was a little nervous being down here alone." I half-joke as I watch him trot down the stairs. He's wearing butt-hugging jeans and a white linen button-down shirt. He looks good enough to spread on a cracker. He gives me a strange look as he tilts his head away from the bottom of the chandelier; he's so tall he barely clears it. I have no idea why, but the way he tilts his head is hot. Is he for real?

"Nothing to be nervous about." He says simply as he reaches the bottom of the stairs. "Do you want something to drink or a snack?"

"After that meal we just ate? Good Lord," I laugh.

"You're right. Well, what are you into? Comedy, action, romance, thriller?" he gestures towards the living room, which is a complete understatement. We could throw a cocktail party in here it's so large. The L-shaped brown leather couch is so big it had to have been custom made. Ten people could sleep on it easily. In the center of the couch is a huge, square-shaped glass-enclosed coffee table. The picture window runs from the middle of the wall to the ceiling, definitely custom made as well, and the drapes are cream, gauze-like material. Along the main wall is the biggest television I've ever seen. It's so big it looks like it's part of the wall.

"Missy's been making me watch a lot of horror movies and thrillers lately, so anything but that."

We both look at the couch and it seems like he doesn't know where to sit. "Which one is your spot, Garrett?" I say, not hiding the teasing tone.

He chuckles. "I usually sit right in the center, closest to the television."

"Then sit there." I smile, laughing. "It's not like I'm going to move your water dish."

He laughs, shaking his head. "Sit...where you want." And he sits in his spot, grabbing the remote from the coffee table. "You don't have any issues with Netflix, do you?"

"Not at all, that's what I have." I sit a couple of feet away from him. He rests his feet on the coffee table, and I mirror him. He smiles at me. "You don't mind if I put my feet there, too, do you?"

"Nope." He glances at my lips for a second, but then he turns his head towards the television. *God, that look...*

He starts flicking through the new releases and finds something we both haven't seen before. It's a comedy show, but it turns out to be not funny at all, but I don't want to say anything, so I just keep quiet. Except that the couch is so freaking comfortable that I feel myself nodding off. I feel him stroke my arm. "Well, that's not a good sign." He says, his tone is low, and his head is resting on the back of the couch, glancing in my direction. "When your date falls asleep." He looks so goddamn sexy I can't help but hold his gaze.

"Sorry, I didn't want to say that the movie was boring, and this couch is lethal. Plus, I'm still a little jetlagged."

"Didn't help that you ate a huge steak for dinner, too.

Food coma." He chuckles.

"Yeah, I forgot about that." I grunt as I get up and stretch a little. "I should go. I'm beat."

"Okay." He says, rising with me. He gestures for me to go ahead to the doorway. "I'm flying out of town tomorrow and the next day. But are you busy Friday night?" he asks as I approach the door.

"Sure, yeah. I'm off Saturday and I think my shift ends at seven on Friday night." I answer, feeling mighty awkward. I hate this part of a date...the *end.* You never know what's acceptable. There is always a fine line between 'is he into me? And 'he's just setting up another date, so I'm not crushed'. "Thanks for dinner, by the way, and thanks for the crappy movie." I joke.

He chuckles and takes a step towards me. *Oh, God, he's going to kiss me.* "Just so I don't end up in the friend zone." He says softly before leaning in and giving me a soft, chaste, yet lingering kiss on the lips. As he pulls back slightly, he glances at me, and my eyes go to his lips. He takes that as permission to kiss me again. This time I kiss him back, opening my mouth slightly. *Don't do that! What are you doing??* He makes the kiss less chaste by tilting his head a little. My heart is beating so fast, and my hormones are quickly taking over. It's been so long, I can't remember the last time I was kissed by a male...especially one this sexy. *Never...*

His hands go to my waist as my hands snake around his shoulders and caress his neck. I kiss him deeply, without tongue, and he envelopes my lips with his, keeping his tongue where it belongs. He's being so polite; not getting too sexual, but my body is wanting more. I try to pull away, but I'm like a magnet to him. The next kiss I plunge my tongue into his mouth, and he lets out a soft grunt that I feel in all the right places. His head tilts further, accepting the contact. His arms grasp me tighter as our tongues connect. I can feel his breath on my cheek; warm and ragged, as his soft, virile tongue meets mine.

He pulls back, kissing me once more on the mouth.

"I suppose I'm clear of the friend zone." He chuckles, and it's as sexy as hell.

"Not yet." I jest, wanting more. His eyes go to my lips again...yes, *that* look. And he opens his mouth, dipping his warm tongue inside again. This time I let out a soft moan; hungry, eager for more. I can't seem to stop myself. It feels like it's been a hundred years since I've had physical contact with a man. And it probably has been. I've never established boundaries because since Missy was born, I never dated. I know it's generally not lady-like to get to second base on the first date, but Garrett is an exceptional kisser, and up until now he's been completely gallant. Which is almost too much to handle. If he'd copped a feel earlier when he had the chance, it might have been easier to stop, but he hasn't, and my body wants it. Craves it. It's like physically I've been on a diet of bread and water for the past thirteen years, and this kissing is an appetizer.

He pulls me closer to him and as I pull myself onto my tippy toes, I feel him bend slightly and lift me, so our faces are level. *God!* His manly arms surround my body in warmth and strength as his lips envelope mine and his tongue caresses the inside of my mouth. My breasts are throbbing against his chest, dying for contact. A strong pulse is beating between my legs, as if just the amount of friction against his body is enough to drive me over the edge. I haven't so much as masturbated in years.

His teeth gently nip my bottom lip and I let out a soft cry, begging for more, feeling his touch everywhere. Lowering my head, I kiss his neck, sucking his earlobe, and he makes an "Mmmm..." kind of a grunt that makes me want to strip him down naked right here in his hallway.

We're both breathing ragged, and he lifts his lips off mine for a second. "God, Nora," he pants, "how long has it been for you?" he asks, as though he's comparing notes.

"Thirteen years," I breathe, and then I give him an

open-mouthed kiss.

"Jesus." He kisses me once more, with this look on his face like that kind of time without sex is absolutely ridiculous. "Let me put you out of your misery." He says and doesn't wait for me to argue. He lifts me higher, so my feet are clear off the floor, and he walks over to the couch, lowering me onto it. He undoes the top three buttons on his shirt and lifts it over his head.

"Oh, God, Garrett." I whisper, looking at him, half-naked. He's stunning. He has a washboard stomach, tight pectoral muscles, and biceps and triceps that are begging to be kissed. I can see he's hard as a rock under those jeans, and I bite my lip noticing how well endowed he is. My thighs are pelting together, as if just the sight of him is going to bring me to orgasm.

I pull my shirt over my head and he lowers himself onto me. Just the contact makes me moan. He parts my legs and rests his hardness in the spot where it counts, and my eyes roll back into my head. "You're close already, aren't you." He comments; his voice is so low, laced with sex. He lowers his lips to my breast and it's all I can do not to come right there. As he gives open-mouthed kisses to the flesh on my breasts, I rear up, taking in the contact. When he reaches my nipple, the moment he sucks it, I lose control.

"Let it go," he says, licking my nipple, as I feel a floodgate of pleasure wash through me. It feels phenomenal as I've lost control of my voice and my breath, making noises that I've never heard come out of me before, in my entire life. He licks and sucks for what feels like minutes, gently pressing his hardness into me in pulses, like what he would be doing to me if he were inside me. I cry out the Lord's name as I feel the waves of pleasure that have been lingering in me for more than a decade.

When the last wave ceases, I realize how embarrassing this is. He's barely touched me, and I've already finished. My bra is still on; he hasn't removed it. I giggle, but somehow, he doesn't think this is funny.

The look on his face is so intense I wonder for a second if he's angry. Then I realize he isn't finished with me yet. He inches his way down to my thighs and he undoes my jeans, pulling them down my legs. My panties are soaked and I almost shy away until something stops me...him, removing his pants, too. He's so big the head of his penis sticks out of the top of his underwear. I feel myself climbing again just looking at it behind the material. As he pulls down his underwear, I can't stop looking at it. I've never seen a penis that large before. I'm throbbing and soaked again as he lowers my panties and slides them off.

Closing the gap between us, Garrett slides his hands behind my back, removing my bra. He kisses and sucks one breast while kneading the other gently with his free hand. I feel myself climbing with the wonderful pressure and friction of his tongue and lips against my aching flesh. His penis is inches from my hand, and I don't stop myself from grasping it. It's warm and hard and throbbing from my touch, and it twitches in response to my caresses and stroking. Garrett's breathing becomes ragged as my strokes pick up the pace.

"It's been a while for me, too, Nora." He says, his tone slightly warning. As he licks my breast more, I feel him reach for himself, grasping my hand in his. With his hand, he guides me to my clitoris, and rubs it with the head of his penis, making me moan aloud. "Stroke it, just like that." He instructs gently, showing me that we can enjoy mutual sensation as my hand strokes him while at the same time the head of his penis strokes my clitoris. It feels phenomenal, and I think that this man is a sexual genius.

His sexy grunts make me feel him more, as he feels what I'm doing to him more. It's so heady. Then he inches kisses down my stomach, trailing them through my thighs, as he parts my legs and envelopes my folds with his lips. The force of pleasure makes me involuntarily cry out. He sucks my clitoris and it feels so unbelievable I almost can't stand it. Garrett is going to have to scrape me off the ceiling later. Just when I think that what he's doing couldn't get any better, he begins licking me in the most sensitive spot, sending me to the moon. I'm writhing under him as he flicks my clitoris with his tongue, while reaching for my nipples, gently squeezing them between his thumb and forefinger. I'm a complete ball of lust, at his mercy, moaning, crying, making sounds that I've never made before.

When it feels so good, I feel like I could die, my back arches and my pelvis involuntarily lifts in rhythm to his touch, and another wave of pleasure crashes through me, as my body pulses and contracts inside, sending me to heaven and back...again. My heart is racing, my chest is rising and falling so fast I can't keep up, and my body is so rigid I feel like I could break in two. Coming down from the height of ecstasy, Garrett softly kisses the inside of my thigh: one and then the other, and inches his way back up to my face.

His hardness is resting on my belly, and as if I thought I couldn't feel any more, he moves slightly, so he's back in the spot that counts. "Feel better?" he asks, his voice is still laced with sex.

"A million times better." I whisper, but I still want more. I want to feel...him. It's been so long since I've felt a man inside me. "But I don't think we're done yet." My tone is direct.

"Well...we might have to be." He gives me a thin smile. "I don't have any...condoms." He kisses me full on the mouth, sending delicious shivers through my body.

"I think it's safe...I just finished my..." I trail off, feeling a little embarrassed that I'm doing period math when the sexiest man alive is naked and on top of me.

"And neither of us have had sex in a very long time." He adds. "Are you sure?"

His penis twitches; both of us feel it and both of us know we feel it, and his embarrassed grin is so cute I can't handle it. "Hell yeah." I whisper, pushing my foot against his rear, indicating that I want him.

"Okay" he whispers, and he kisses me hungrily, plunging his tongue into my mouth, and I feel a whole new wave of desire. He sucks my lip and trails kisses down my neck and down to my breast. As he nips and licks my breast, I arch my back and he thrusts into me, shooting a blast of pleasure through me. His head lowers and he draws in a deep breath, as if the feeling is too much. "Oooohhhh," he breathes, and his sounds are my undoing.

Filling me, he falls into a slow rhythm, as he glides in and out, sending rushes of sensation through me with each thrust. I grasp his shoulders, raking my hands up his neck as he closes his eyes, feeling the friction. He lifts slightly, filling me to the hilt, and I'm climbing faster, feeling my body clenching. He makes a hissing noise as I tighten around him inside. "Oh, Nora...mmmm...." He moans, and it sounds so sexy I want to mentally record it for all those moments when I'm feeling...edgy. "Mmmm...you're getting close again." He breathes, telling me he can feel me hugging him tighter from inside, as if he's reading my mind.

"Are you getting close?" I ask, feeling him hard as a rock as he continues to thrust.

"Oh," he whispers, kissing me deeply, "it feels fantastic...yeah, I'm close." And the excitement is such a rush; this incredibly sexy, gorgeous man is going to have an orgasm right here, with me. It's intense, and it just about throws me over the edge, until he grasps my knees, parting my legs further, and lifts, filling me right to the hilt.

"Oh, God, Garrett," I cry out as he picks up speed and grunts, right before I feel his seed shoot out into me.

"Oh, God...oh," he moans, breathing deeply through his mouth, as I watch the veins in his neck protrude and his head raises then lowers as he climbs to the reaches of ecstasy with me. His breathing is ragged, almost a pant as he feels the same blast of pleasure I feel. As he slows, his breathing is still in spurts, until he stops and lowers himself on me, releasing my knees. "That was...phenomenal." He whispers, still breathing heavily, resting his head on my shoulder. His heart beats against mine a mile a minute as we both try to catch our breath.

I swallow. "That's a record for me."

He lifts so we're nose-to-nose. "What, for how long you've gone without?"

I chuckle. "No, for most consecutive orgasms. I've never had more than one...I didn't think I could have three in a row."

"That's what happens when you go without for so many years." He explains softly. "If it hadn't been that long for me, and I could hold out longer, there might be one or two more for you if I worked for it."

I laugh and he gives up and laughs with me. "That's kind of a record for me, too."

"Like how many orgasms you've given a woman in one go?"

He smiles. "No...I've never had sex on a first date before."

"Me neither."

I look at his lips and he gives me a long, lingering kiss, and then a quicker, softer one. "When are you expected to be home?" he asks, stroking the side of my face with the back of his hand.

"I didn't really give a time. My neighbor is sitting with Missy."

"Okay." He says. "I was going to ask if you want to spend the night, but I don't want you to feel obligated."

I kiss him on the mouth. "I'd love to, but I can't. It's...complicated."

He nods. "I understand." He lifts off me and slides on the couch beside me. I'm amazed how much room this couch has. "I've never had sex on this couch before, either." He says conversationally.

"I've never had sex on *a couch* before"

339

"Well, I would have taken you upstairs to my bedroom, but I wasn't sure if you were going to make it."

I chuckle. "Good call."

"Next time." He lifts a thumb and winks, grunting sexily as he rests his head on his hand. "God, I could at least get a blanket or something...hang on." He says, lifting on to his feet. I watch him trot over to a nearby chest of drawers. He pulls out a large afghan and brings it over, draping it over me.

"You're too sexy for words." I comment and he guffaws as his cheeks turn pink. "and now you're too cute for words."

He says nothing but he snuggles in beside me, kissing me on the mouth. "Keep it up and I might have to ravage you again." He wiggles his eyebrows, making me melt.

"Well, that's the sexiest form of punishment I've ever heard of."

He draws in a deep breath. "Oh, my. You and I...we could get into a lot of trouble together." He kisses me again, gazing at me intently.

"Yeah...we could." I agree, and then that thing I swore I'd never do again with another man...I do. I let myself start to feel more than a physical connection to him.

Chapter 5

Garrett

I keep playing it over and over again in my mind; trying to figure out if I made any mistakes. After listening to my brother, I figure he was right about kissing her goodbye, and I was careful to keep it PG, but she seemed to want more, and I was sure as hell willing to give it to her. Nora's body was literally trembling as we kissed. The poor girl was suffering badly, and I think she's grateful that I helped her release all that...tension. Before Nora, it had been a couple of years since my last sexual encounter, and that was a disaster, turning me off from doing that again. But the moment I met Nora, I knew there was something about her I wanted to explore further.

The fact that she has a teenager doesn't bother me at all. Nora seems very well put together and grounded. She's motivated and career-driven, which is important, because it's tough to stay devoted to your career when your partner isn't devoted to their career. For a relationship to be successful, there has to be some balance. One would say that she was too forward, having slept with me on the first date, but sometimes I think our bodies don't give us much of a choice. I have every intention of pursuing a relationship with her; to me, this is certainly not a one-night-stand. I've done the one-night-stand thing, and it was a mistake in the past.

As I dress in my uniform, starting with the bottoms, I hear the front doorbell. Trotting down the stairs, I sneak a peek at the driveway, and I see Dalton's truck parked out front. I open the door and give him a look. "Why didn't you use your key?"

"Jack said you had a date last night. I didn't want to interrupt if anyone was still here."

I poke my head out the door and look in both

directions intentionally. "Do you *see* any other vehicles here?"

A 'v' forms between his eyes. "How do I know you didn't drive her here? Why are you so crusty? Did things not go well?"

"How do you know she was even here?" I probe.

Dalton shrugs. "I don't know. Was she?"

I guffaw. "Yeah,"

"Well, then." He walks in, removing his shoes. "Got any grub in this joint?"

"Do you not know how to grocery shop?" I don't hide the sarcastic tone.

He ignores my comment as he walks right into the kitchen and opens the fridge, grabbing an apple from the bottom drawer. He takes a bite and speaks with his mouth full. "So, how did it go?"

"What?" I ask, starting up the coffee maker.

"Your date, stupid. What the hell do you think I'm talking about?"

"Oh...it was...great. She's great."

He nods, swallowing. "You gonna see her again?"

Adding instant coffee to the machine, I answer. "Yeah...tomorrow night."

"What's her story?" he takes another bite of his apple.

I fold my arms across my chest and drape one leg over the other as I lean on the counter. "She's a single mom, and I'm guessing Jack told you she was one of the nurses that looked after dad. She's...beautiful and smart."

The coffee starts to brew, making a sound akin to someone peeing in my kitchen. Dalton throws the apple core into the bin on the counter and opens my fridge again. "You do know that this isn't dad's place anymore. I don't just stock food for you."

"I'm hungry." Dalton says, grabbing a carton of eggs off the top shelf. "You up for scrambled?"

I shrug. "Sure."

Bread is kept in one of the cupboards, so I grab a loaf

and start putting pieces into the toaster as Dalton pulls the frying pan out. The butter is in a container on the counter. I hand it to him with the flipper from the drawer beside me. He tosses a dollop of butter into the pan and as soon as he turns the element on, it starts to sizzle. Dalton takes a bowl out of an overhead cupboard and breaks six eggs into it, while I grab the milk and a whisk.

"Her name's Nora, right?"

"Yeah,"

"Jack's such a pig," Dalton guffaws. "He said he told you to slip her the tongue to make sure you two don't end up 'just friends'," he air-quotes, "like that chick you pined over in high school."

"Yeah," my face turns pink and I turn away, thankful that the coffee is finished brewing. I hand Dalton his coffee and he glances at me.

"Why do *you* look so guilty?" he chuckles, and then he takes a sip of his black coffee, while I grab the ketchup bottle out of the fridge and set it on the counter.

"I don't look guilty, loser."

"Your face is as red as that ketchup bottle." He comments matter-of-factly. "You've never been able to hide anything in your life. What happened? Did you sleep with her?"

"No," I say unconvincingly.

"You're such a liar." He chuckles, teasing me. He lets the subject sit for a minute, and then continues. "Wow...that's not like you, Garrett. So, who made the first move...you or...Noooooooraaaa?" he purposely accentuates her name to taunt me.

"Like I'm going to tell *you*, moron."

"I bet *she* did. You're too much of a pussy."

"Fuck you." I'm irritated. "You're just jealous because you haven't been laid since Dana the ditz from dad's gala two years ago."

"And you're so different...it's been that long for you, too. Who was it...oh, yeah, that redhead you met at the bar the night we had dad's buddy's retirement party."

"Yeah..." I say, and then I hear the front door open.

"Hey, shitheads!" Jack shouts. "Ooohhhh....foood!" he says, walking into the kitchen. "Oh, man...you guys got enough for me? I'm fucking starved."

"I can throw more on." Dalton says, grabbing the eggs and milk.

Jack helps himself to a coffee while I grab the plates from the cupboard.

"So, what's the scoop?" Jack asks, pulling his cell phone out of his pocket before sitting at the table.

"Garrett got laid last night." Dalton's voice is flat. He lifts his thumb towards me.

Jack looks at me. "I said *kiss* her, man." He shakes his head.

"Oh, he did." Dalton laughs.

"Are you both finished?" I ask, growing more irritated. If Nora ever found out I blabbed about last night, she'd probably never want to see me again.

"Well, I've never slept with a sweet nurse before, man. I'm jealous." Jack admits.

"And you both can keep your mouths shut about it. I don't need Nora finding out you two know. Not that it's any of your business."

"Hey, for someone who just got laid, you're awfully uptight." Jack comments.

"Shut up." I whine. "I'm uptight because of you two losers."

Dalton serves the eggs on the plates and hands one to each of us, taking the last plate for himself. "Eat. You're hangry. All that sex made you work up an appetite." Dalton teases.

"Fuck off." I say, taking a bite. He's lucky he's a good cook and the eggs are delicious. I never swear except around my brothers. Especially these two. Colton's similar to me, but he tends to 'f' bomb around Dalton and Jack, too. They have that effect on us. Wade...he's a born potty mouth. We sit in silence, eating like it's our last meal ever. As I walk my dishes to the sink, I tell Jack to do the dishes, since it's my food and Dalton cooked it. "I've gotta finish getting dressed. I have a flight in a couple of hours."

As I drive to the airport, I start thinking about selling my dad's old place and getting a place of my own again. After what happened this morning, I think it's time to say goodbye to the old Ford mansion and get a house that's mine. All mine. With locks that don't match any of my brother's keys.

***

After receiving a lone text message from Nora, I was getting a little worried that maybe I had become a one-night-stand to her. International waters don't challenge cell phone barriers much anymore, so I knew it wasn't a cell phone reception issue, especially when I flew back onto US soil and there was still nothing on my phone from her. She hadn't broken the date we'd planned, so there was still some hope. Half expecting to be stood up, I wait outside the restaurant for her at the proposed time. This restaurant isn't fluffy at all, in fact, it serves the best burgers and fries in town.

When she finally appears, driving into the parking lot, I feel at ease. Walking to her car, I wait for her to exit, and kiss her chastely on the mouth. "Hi, you." I say.

"Hi, yourself." She says, kissing me back. I love it that she doesn't wait for me to make all the moves. Nora isn't afraid to take the next step. "Sorry I haven't been keeping in touch much in the last couple of days. You'd be surprised if you knew how much drama is in my life. Between Missy and her father, sometimes I don't know who's more of a child."

"Sorry to hear that." I kiss her on the head. "You look nice." She's wearing a pair of blue jeans and a red plaid blouse with red flat shoes to match. Her hair is half up, half down in a red barrette.

"Thanks. You look good enough to eat."

I bark out a laugh. She's a pistol. "Okay, then." I chuckle. I'm wearing black jeans and a golf shirt. "Thanks." I give her a lopsided smile. I'm not really used to compliments, especially blatant ones like that.

"Did I embarrass you?" she grins.

"No," I lie. "Are you hungry?"

"Starving." She says, taking my hand in hers.

The restaurant serves delicious food, and we eat while chatting about the last few days. My side of the conversation is kind of boring; flights and work, but hers is a little more interesting.

"So, tell me about your daughter's father." I start. "Is he in her life a lot?"

She puts her burger down on the plate and takes a sip of water. "Sort of. He's been in a lot of trouble with the law, so I keep him at a distance. He's only allowed supervised visits for now, which is hard on Missy."

"Oh, wow. That would be." I say, growing concerned.

"Yeah. He wasn't always like that. When we met in high school, he was a straight A student. That's part of the reason I fell for him. But he got in with the wrong crowd when I got pregnant, and the next thing I knew he was in juvenile hall for drugs. That's when it all started."

"So, it's been mostly a drug problem with him?"

She sighs. "Drugs, theft, and who knows what else. He's been in and out of jail so many times I've lost count. But the first person he contacts when he's out, is Missy. He loves her to death, and he tries, he really does try to be a better person for her, but it never sticks."

"How does Missy feel about him?"

"She loves him so much. In a lot of ways, he's her best friend. It's the drugs that get him. He's tried rehab but it doesn't work and half the time he busts out...and comes to see Missy." She pauses and lifts her hand, "I know what you're thinking...that you wouldn't dare let a person like that near your child, but I'm telling you, he's an old soul. He lectures her all the time about not doing drugs and not getting into trouble. He knows what he does is wrong, and he tells her all the time that this is what happens if you do 'x' or 'y'. It sounds twisted but that's the only reason, that and the fact that they love each other so much, why I let him stay in her life."

"And she would probably revolt if you were to forbid it." I add.

"Exactly."

"How old were you when you had her?"

She purses her lips together. "Sixteen. I got pregnant on my sixteenth birthday. It wasn't my first time, but it was close. David was my first love and I couldn't have an abortion; couldn't stomach the thought. He was so sweet and caring then and he begged me not to give the baby up to abortion or adoption. So, I had her, and my mom helped me raise her when David wasn't around."

"Did your mom like David?"

She gives me a look like I'd just asked if her mother was a whore. "No. She hated him. She tried to keep him from seeing Missy, but I threatened to move out and never let her see her only grandchild again. That was cruel, I know. But I had to intervene for Missy. Mom didn't understand the relationship that they had. I didn't expect her to. Mom was old-fashioned and it was bad enough that David couldn't stay out of prison long enough to marry me or clean his life up. I don't blame her for how she felt."

"Wow." Is all I can think of to say.

Nora changes the subject. "Tell me about your father."

"He was a man of few words. When he spoke, we listened, since it was so infrequent. He founded the airline and built it from the ground up. My grandfather was very much into aviation as well. When I was born, it came natural to me, and that was a strong bond that he and I had, that none of my brothers did. Colton, some, but Colton was a bit of a rebel in his teen years."

Nora chuckles. "I can relate."

"Yeah, Colton was such a rebel that dad sent him off to the military. He's still there."

"Really?"

"Yep. His mission is almost finished now, but once he's done it'll be just about ten years that he's served. My brothers and I all served, but Colton for the longest."

"When does he come home?"

"Not for a while yet. Couple of months." I take the last bite of my burger and she looks at me. I swallow and smile at her.

"I really like you." She says.

"I really like you, too." I take her hand in mine.

"I haven't been in a relationship since Missy was born. Missy means everything to me, and I can't ever change that. I need you to understand that when I'm distant, it's not because of you, because if it was, I would tell you straight away," she cuts the air with her hand for emphasis, "My life is up and down a lot and that's why I've never complicated it further with a relationship."

I digest that for a moment as I stroke the back of her hand with my thumb. "I would never ask you to place me in any priority over your daughter. And *my* life is up and down a lot, too...literally," that gets a chuckle out of her, breaking the tension slightly, "I'm not here to be a complication, Nora. I'm here to be a complement."

She grins and leans forward, kissing me full on the mouth. "How do you feel about meeting Missy?"

I tilt my head. "How do *you* feel about me meeting Missy?"

"Well, the thing is...I don't enjoy lying to her. I also don't want to introduce her to someone unless it's more than something casual. I guess that's what I'm asking. Are you looking for something casual, or are you looking for a solid relationship...because that's what makes the difference."

"She's thirteen, right?"

Nora nods.

"So, she's technically not a child." I prompt her,

seeing if she understands where I'm going.

"Alright, no. She's not a child. Good Lord, did they put something in the food? Is my mother watching?" she laughs with a trace of tension, covering her face.

"I get what you're saying, Nora. It's not a great idea to be traipsing in and out of the house with different men in your wake...not that I'm suggesting that's what you do..." I lift a hand in defence, "but I think a thirteen-year-old can handle meeting her mom's new friend."

She lifts a brow. "I thought you kissed me the other night to get *out* of the friend zone?"

"Fair enough. Her mom's new..." I prompt her to fill in the blank with whatever title she feels comfortable with.

"Boyfriend?"

"Sure. Boyfriend. But I'm sure she'll correct you and say partner." I grin, impressed with myself.

"You're going to get along well with her." She says, leaning in to kiss me again. Her kiss is open-mouthed and noisy. "Let's go back to your place." She says, shocking me.

"In light of the conversation we had, are you sure you don't want to go to your place?" I offer.

She kisses me again, dipping her tongue in slightly. "Garrett, what I have in mind to do isn't for Missy to witness."

I chuckle. "Lead the way."

***

When we get inside my place, I lock the door immediately, and the first thing on my mind is that one of my brothers could arrive any time, unannounced. I really need to sell this place, otherwise I'm never going to be able to move on. Nora removes her shoes and snakes her arms around my neck. "Alright, Garrett. You never did get to show me your place the other night."

"Well, that's because you fell asleep, and then you ravaged me." I joke.

"Fair enough. But you didn't seem to complain at all."

"No, ma'am, I didn't. What would you like to see first?"

She kisses me chastely and removes her arms from my neck. "Give me the grand tour."

My eyes are slits. "Vixen."

She laughs out loud and I hold out my hand for her to hold, giving her a tour of the kitchen, dining room, office and backyard. "So, you and all your family used to live here?"

"Yes, that's right."

"Are you going to stay here...I mean, this place is humongous just for one person."

"You read my mind. Yeah, I'm going to sell it. My dad left it for me, but I don't think he ever intended for me to live here...unless I had a big family as well. It's ridiculous to stay. I don't even use half of it, and I'm not really home often enough, anyway."

"That's what I would do. Unless you have too many memories here."

"Well, there are a lot of memories, yes. But they're up here," I point to my head, "and in here," I place my hand on my heart, "this house is just a shell now without all us Ford boys living in it."

She places her hand on her heart. "Wow, Garrett. I didn't take you for the sentimental type."

I smile and lead her to the second floor. I point out which bedrooms belonged to which brother. Most of the rooms are empty, except for Wade's. He comes to stay with me sometimes, so he's left a few things. When we get to my room, she smiles. "I knew right away this would be your room." She says, pointing to the large, framed photo of a fighter jet on my wall. "That's a dead giveaway."

"I suppose so." I chuckle. She walks to my window and looks outside.

"When I was a little girl, we lived in a house that had window boxes on the side of the house, just like this."

I walk over and stand behind her. "I think my mom had those installed. My dad kept the boxes filled all the time. I suppose I should continue the tradition." I comment, observing the empty boxes.

"Your dad must have loved your mom a lot."

"Yeah. He did. But she left and life goes on." I place my hands on her shoulders and give them a gentle massage. She rears her head back, taking in the contact.

"You're hired." She purrs.

I laugh softly, kissing her head, which is leaning against my chest. She turns to face me. I kiss her sweetly on the lips. She wraps her arms around my neck and embraces me. It feels so good to hold a woman close. I rub her back and she breathes in deeply. We stand there holding each other for a few minutes. When she pulls back, she looks at me and strokes the sides of my head by my ears. I close my eyes to her touch. As they're closed, she kisses my lips. I kiss her back, keeping the kisses chaste. I keep my eyes closed as she kisses me again, this time letting the contact linger. Pulling back, I gauge her next move. The look she gives me is intense. I recognize it from the other night.

"I know that look."

"You should get used to it." He voice is silk.

Her mouth opens as she tilts her head. I lift her so we're nose to nose and kiss her back, softly plunging my tongue into her mouth. Her hands snake around my neck and she lifts her lips from mine. "I haven't been able to stop thinking about you since the other night."

"Me neither."

"No man has ever made me feel like that before." I look at her lips, still holding her up, close to my body. The intensity of her kiss makes me instantly hard. I've never experienced this kind of passion before. Walking with her body against mine, I bring her over to the bed and lower her down. She gently sucks on my bottom lip and my cock twitches it's so hot.

"God, you do things to me." I breathe, she responds by kissing me deeper, as she is almost breathless. Reaching to the hem of her shirt, I lift it over her head and drink in her breasts. She's chosen to be bra less underneath. "Lord Jesus." I kiss her flesh, sucking her nipples, first one then the other. Writhing beneath me, she holds my head, as if begging me to stay there.

"This hardly seems fair." She groans.

I speak against her breasts without lifting me head. "What's that"

"Tit for tat." She chuckles

I get the hint, grabbing at the hem of my shirt and pulling it off in one fell swoop. Her hands are immediately on my chest, skating her fingers down my skin, giving me shivers. Her hands reach the waistband of my jeans and she opens the top button and unzips the zipper. Her hand slides inside, making me involuntarily groan. Caressing my cock, which has now become steel, she begins rubbing up and down, and it feels amazing.

"Take them off." She whispers, giving me a sultry look. I don't need to be told twice. As I remove my pants and underwear, I take a step towards the nightstand and open the drawer. I had the foresight to actually go buy condoms earlier. I toss the box on the bed and her eyes are on me.

"You're so freaking delicious I could die." She says, ogling me in such a sexy way. I'm fully hard, standing there naked.

"Like what you see." I say as more of a comment than a question.

She licks her lips seductively, making my cock twitch again. Nora removes her pants and underwear, not taking her eyes off me. I help her slide them off the bottom of her legs and take the opportunity to kiss her legs, trail kisses up her thighs, across her belly, and back to her breasts. Grasping my head, she cradles me with her hands as I make love to her breasts. Her breathing is in gasps as I suck and lick her breasts. "God, you're so good at that." She's mewling and I'm curious if she's as ready as she was the other night. Inching my hand down, I circle her clit with my finger, and she lets out a loud moan. Speeding up, I feel her hips bucking under my touch. "Oh...." She cries out before her breathing becomes very ragged and I know she's coming. It's sexy as hell as I hear her cry out my name, reacting so passionately to my touch.

When her muscles stop contracting, I inch my way up to her mouth and kiss her full, making an "Mmm...." Sound, indicating that I enjoyed pleasing her. She grasps my face in her hands and kisses me, plunging her tongue inside to meet mine, making me impossibly hard. I feel her part her legs further. "Easy, baby. I gotta get one of these on first." I say, reaching for the box of condoms.

She giggles and I begin understanding possibly how she got pregnant as a teen. Her eyes don't leave me as I rip the foil and roll the condom on. Her legs remain parted and I lean in and kiss her clit, giving it a teasing swirl with my tongue. As I meet her eyes, I kiss her full on the mouth, and let her guide me inside her with her foot on my rear. As I enter her, I'm thankful for the condom and its slight desensitizing properties. She's incredibly warm and soft and tight and I'd hate to come as quickly as I did the last time.

The bedroom door is open, and oddly I feel like I need to close it. It's freaky having sex in the house that I grew up in. It's entirely possible that one of my brothers could walk in at any moment. I really need to sell this place. Nora is meeting my slow thrusts, as if telling me to go faster, but I want to savor her this time. And I want her to come slowly, and discover what it's like to make love when it isn't rushed or forced. Caressing her face with both hands, I kiss her deeply, dipping my tongue inside gently as I move inside her.

Her kisses are just as strong and passionate as mine as we ride the waves of pleasure together. As I start picking up speed the bed begins to squeak slightly, and I'm suddenly gratcful that I live alone. Nora's muscles begin to clench, and I inch down to suck her breasts. She moans and I feel my cock twitch inside her. Her hands are snaked around my neck. She reaches down and smoothes her palms over my nipples. Aside from my dick that's the most sensitive spot on my body. I suck in air, feeling the pulse below the belt.

"Mmm... you like that." She purrs. Then she lifts slightly, forcing me away from her breasts, and she begins licking and sucking my nipples, making me groan. "You like *that* even better." She murmurs against my skin.

"Mmm..."

"Flip over." She whispers to me. I do as I'm told, and she climbs on top of me. Filling herself with me as soon as she's in position. Good God it feels fantastic. Her body starts to move, and I move with her as we get into a rhythm. I'm deep inside her and she's so sexy I don't take my eyes off her. Her lips are parted, and her breasts are bouncing with the movement; her nipples are beaded from desire. Her head is reared back as she takes it all in. My hands find her hips as I help lift her with my pelvis. As I do this, she cries out and I feel it in my cock.

"Oh, Nora," I moan, and then a hiss escapes my lips. The feeling is intense, and I know that she feels it too. Leaning down she begins sucking and licking my nipples, driving me crazy. "Oh, yesss...." My voice is a whisper. My pace picks up and she lifts her head, kissing me with deep tongue thrusts, and I match her with the same; dipping my tongue inside her mouth. We're breathless as we kiss voraciously, feeling deep mutual sensation. She lowers herself down to my nipples again and it feels so good I'm too close to the edge. I want her to come before I do, if not together, so I lean up to her, kissing and sucking her nipples, knowing it has an equal effect on her.

"Oh, God...Garrett..." she moans, and I can feel her

insides tighten, bringing me more pleasure. I slow, bringing her legs over so I can slide on top. As I bring my weight on her she rakes her hands through my hair and I kiss her deep yet slow, gently sliding my tongue inside. She reciprocates as I start to build speed. Pulling back I inch my way to her nipples, licking them as she lifts her chest off the mattress. Her breathing is ragged, almost a pant, matching mine.

I take her nipple in my mouth, right to the areola, and she lets out a cry as her hips buck up, meeting my thrusts. It feels so amazing I involuntarily moan, and then she tells me she's close. Those words out of her mouth bring me to the edge. I rear up, filling her completely, as I feel my seed reaching the tip. I try to hold out a second longer, but Nora's muscles are contracting, hugging my dick, begging for me to explode inside her. We're both a writhing, panting mess as we feel our release together. "Mmmmm...." I murmur against her chest as I come down from ecstasy, kissing the flesh between her breasts.

Catching my breath, I wrap my arms under her, kissing her shoulders. Her arms snake around my neck as her lips find mine. We give each other open-mouthed kisses as our breathing returns to normal. "Let me take care of this." I grunt as I get up and remove the condom, disposing it in the garbage pail next to the bed. I slide in bed beside her a moment later, still a little breathless.

"God, we're so good together." She comments, raking her fingers through my hair. I kiss her lips, letting the contact linger, telling her that I agree with what she said. "I have to go home soon." She says after a beat. "But I want you to come to dinner tomorrow night if you're able to. I want you to meet Missy."

"If there are no flight delays, I can certainly make it." I say honestly. "I'm flying domestically tomorrow."

She tosses a lock of her dirty-blonde hair over her shoulder and looks at me intently. "Missy's a sweet girl, but she's a teenager and has the attitude to prove it." Nora is matter-of-fact. "She doesn't have much of a filter, so what she says is at face value. Also, she tends to become obsessed with things, and she'll go on for what seems like forever sometimes, but if you cut her off, she gets really upset, so it's always best to just let her continue."

I smile. "Nora, it'll be fine. There's no need to be nervous. She's a person. I'm a person. I'll treat her with respect and hope that she reciprocates."

Nora lifts a brow.

"Kids tend to be nicer to people that they don't know well than they are to their parents." I say, responding to her look.

"I suppose that's true in a way." She surmises. "I just hope that she likes you. I haven't really thought about how to handle it if she doesn't."

I place a hand on her shoulder. "How about we cross that bridge when we come to it."

Other Books in this series

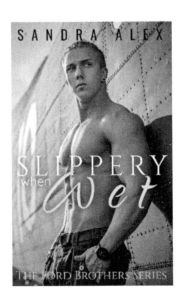

An underloved widower. Her younger, sexy, CEO neighbor. The move that changes more than her address...

Moving to a new neighborhood is never easy. But after Aaron's accident there wasn't a choice. He's a stubborn man, a hard-working man, and now he's a disabled man. Marriage is never easy, either, especially when we got married so young. We both traveled down different paths, and what we both wanted then isn't necessarily what we both want now. A new friend helps me see that, but he also helps me see that I deserve those things that I still want. It may be too late. Lots of things I think I've grown too old for suddenly come to light when Dalton shows me what I think I've missed out on. He also shows me that I haven't missed out, that my time is coming. He also comes to my rescue one night when both Aaron and I are helpless. Sometimes the kindness of strangers can be severely underrated.

***

Kathy, my girlfriend, there's something up with her. Amelia, my new neighbor, sees right through her, and helps me pick up the pieces. Her husband I'm not sure of. Never met him, but he watches me when I walk her home one night. There's something up with him, too. When I learn that our paths crossed once before, it makes Amelia see me in a whole new light. She's almost ten years older than me, but she acts as though it's more like a hundred. What she doesn't realize is that she's incredible, beautiful, intelligent as hell, and she is no more outdated than I am in so many ways. It takes a tragedy for her to see that, and it takes a miracle for her to believe it. And it takes a hard lesson from me for her to learn that everything happens for a reason, and it's more than just Aaron that brought her to me...it's fate.

HEA (Happily Ever After)

Second chance romance
Best friends to lovers romance
Medical romance
Military romance
Medium heat
Course language
Mild cliffhanger ending
Fourth book in a complete 5 book standalone series

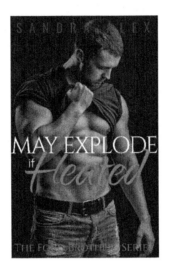

A tarnished Russian genius. A blinded CFO. A shocking interview that opens more than Jack's eyes...

No, really, I'm not afraid of anything. Born and raised in Russia, I've seen things. I've experienced things that I'll take to the grave. After our parents died, my sister and I began another life...in America. Seems men aren't much different in the land of opportunity. And when a once in a lifetime career choice pops up on my radar, I go for it, despite the fact that the CFO of the company looks like he wants more than just my list of references. When Jack Ford turns his back, I ready myself, but instead of taking a piece of what's being offered, for the first time in my life...a man surprises me.

***

Kristina's resume is unfounded. She looks great on paper, and she's even better in person. Her articulation is at a level of professionalism and passion that is unsurpassed, and she can demonstrate that ability easily when given a sample task. This first interview goes off without a hitch. And then I find her later in a place where I would never expect her to be. My brothers instantly veto me bringing her in for a second interview, but something draws me to her, despite that. But when the second interview ends in a shocking and unforgettable twist, I walk out of there shaking her hand, not realizing that I'm in the presence of a woman who will help me a hundred times more than I will ever help her.

HEA (Happily Ever After)
Second chance romance
Medical romance
Military romance
Office romance
Medium heat
Course language
Mild cliffhanger ending
Fifth book in a complete 5 book standalone series
Sneak peek into 'Crossing Boundaries'

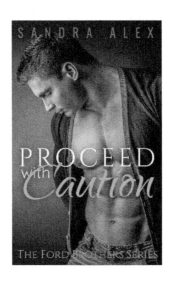

SANDRA ALEX

PROCEED
with Caution

THE FORD BROTHERS SERIES

He's a heartbroken heartthrob. She's a fugitive fiancé. Sparks fly when Julia flees...right into Colton.

He had me at hello. Months later, I'm fleeing the state with an engagement ring on my finger. John isn't the one. What looks good on paper is ugly behind closed doors. My sister Liz doesn't know about John, but she takes me in, with problems of her own. The night I help tend bar with Liz is when I meet Colton. Liz warns me about him. Says that he's a hardened man. And he looks it, too. With his smouldering eyes and square shoulders, he's a force to be reckoned with. But he notices me looking over my shoulder and teaches me a thing or two about men like John, and not in a way that I would expect.

***

Afghanistan changes a man in a way that nothing else can. Betrayal does the same. Mix the two and you get me. It's like I wear a badge, marking my military background, and then they find out that I'm a Ford boy and suddenly I'm a piece of meat with dollar signs. But they can all drop dead, because a woman is the last thing that I want. I bounce at a bar strictly to protect my little brother. He plays in a band in this seedy joint, and I'm here to keep his nose clean in more ways than one. But then Liz brings her little sister Julia in one night to cover, and I realize that I'm not the only one with a sibling looking over their shoulder.

A suspenseful, steamy romance, with loads of family drama, *Proceed with Caution* has feel-good elements with heart-stopping, page-turning twists and angst.

HEA (Happily Ever After)
Second chance romance

Military romance
Medium heat
Course language
Mild violence
Mild cliffhanger ending
First book in a complete 5 book standalone series

Did you enjoy this book? You can make a big difference.

Do you know what the difference between an author that sells a few copies of their book a month and a New York Times bestselling author is?

<u>The answer is clear and simple</u>:

REVIEWS

Don't believe me?

Take a look at any NYT bestselling author and a regular author (like me) and see the difference in the number of reviews.

The fact is clear: **reviews lead to sales. Sales lead to bestseller charts**.

One other simple fact is that *many advertisers won't look at a book unless it has a minimum of 50 book reviews.*

That's where you come in. <u>I need your help</u>.

Honest reviews of my books help bring them to the attention of other readers.

If you've enjoyed this book, I would be very grateful if you could <u>spend just five minutes leaving a review</u> (it can be as short as a like).

Thank you very much,

Sandra Alex

Author's Note

Thanks so much for reading *Enter at Your Own Risk*. I'm so excited about writing a new genre!

Want to know when I have a new release? Visit www.sandraalexbooks.com and hit subscribe for new release updates.

Thanks so much for your support!

~Sandra

Printed in Great Britain
by Amazon